TERROR IS APPROACHING . . .
AT BREA

Also by Paul Garrison

RED SKY AT MORNING
FIRE AND ICE

Available in hardcover

SEA HUNTER

PAUL GARRISON

BURIED AT SEA

HarperTorch
An Imprint of HarperCollinsPublishers

HARPERTORCH
An Imprint of HarperCollins*Publishers*
10 East 53rd Street
New York, New York 10022-5299

Copyright © 2002 by Paul Garrison
Excerpt from *Sea Hunter* copyright © 2003 by Paul Garrison
ISBN: 0-06-103103-8

First HarperTorch paperback printing: January 2003
First William Morrow hardcover printing: February 2002

HarperCollins®, HarperTorch™, and ❦™ are trademarks of Harper-Collins Publishers Inc.

Printed in the United States of America

Visit HarperTorch on the World Wide Web at www.harpercollins.com

10 9 8 7 6 5 4 3 2 1

For AE
(in b-flat)
". . . but look what I found"

BURIED AT SEA

BOOK I

Strongman's Land

1

NOTHING JIM SAW, nothing around him was familiar. Not the moving gray back of the sea, not the shifting sky, not the ropes that were called lines nor the lines named sheets nor the pulleys dubbed blocks. The navigation instruments were magic, the machine that made fresh drinking water a mystery.

He had not seen another vessel in two weeks.

On the chart that Shannon had found on the Internet when they decided he should take this crazy job, shipping lanes crisscrossed the North and South Atlantic like highways. But the ocean itself was empty as space and almost as barren. The only sign of civilization was the occasional silent glow of a satellite moving through the stars. The only living creatures were flying fish thumping into the hull and a barrel-thick shark that sometimes swam in their shadow. His only companion: his employer, Will Spark.

It had to be the strangest gig ever. Personal trainer for a rich old guy on a sailboat in the middle of the ocean. This evening Jim was leading a spinning class, pedaling sprints and hill climbs beneath a heavy, cloud-jumbled sky.

"Big hill. Increase resistance. On a scale of ten, call it a seven, and . . . *up* to second position."

Will, who was some kind of venture capitalist, had squeezed a pair of Schwinn Spinner Elites into his luxurious fifty-footer so they could work out just like they did back home in the health club, with Supertramp blasting and heart rates nudging threshold. All by themselves, closing in on the equator, somewhere between Africa and Brazil.

"Pick it up, Will!"

Jim jumped off while the pedals were still turning, a trick he'd done a million times ashore. The boat surprised him with a sudden tilt and a sharp pitch. Catapulted toward the water, he saved himself by grabbing the lifelines that fenced the deck. Then he slogged across the cockpit—it really was a pit, two big steps lower than the decks—to adjust Will's bike.

He loosened the resistance knob, which squeezed the fly-wheel to simulate a hill climb, and beat the tempo with his running shoe—*boom, boom, boom, boom*—until Will pedaled faster. "Good. Hold that count. If you can't maintain the RPMs, reduce your resistance."

He made his way back to his own bike, toweled his face, drank water. Will had even wired his headset receiver to the boat's loud-hailer, so that Jim's amplified order, "If you're thirsty, drink. If you're not thirsty, drink," echoed against the hard, smooth hollows that the trade wind forged in the sails.

"Resistance on a scale of one to ten, fairly heavy . . . seven . . . seven and a half—and *up* to third."

Will Spark rose from the saddle and extended his hands over the handlebars to third position. He was dripping; his white hair was pasted to his scalp and matted to his chest; perspiration soaked his faded Yale running shorts. The humid heat was like a steam room when the trade wind slowed at sunset. You could break a sweat just cranking one of the winches that controlled the sails. Will was sucking air through his mouth, and it suddenly struck Jim that he was utterly dependent on Will Spark to sail the boat to land.

What if Will had a heart attack?

The personal trainer's nightmare: You let an aggressive type A geezer push too deep into oxygen debt and suddenly you're cracking ribs with your best CPR and praying the ambulance comes ahead of the negligence lawyers. That was on land. What would happen out here if the trainer was a novice sailor in nautical culture shock and the old guy fell over dead?

Jim knew a little about how to steer the boat, next to nothing about the sails, even less about navigation. Most of the time he had been too seasick to take note of his surroundings, much less learn the mechanics of this strange new world.

"Back it off, spin 'em out."

Both men drank from their water bottles.

"How you doing, Will?"

"Better than you, sonny."

There was truth in that. Jim had been so seasick it had been two weeks before he could properly hydrate, much less stomach his regular protein drinks or the fruits, which had gone moldy in the tropical heat as Will had warned they would. His legs still felt as if some gigantic seagoing vampire bat had drained his veins. Hard as he pedaled, the highest his heart-rate monitor would read was 175.

Sicker longer, Will had bitched, than anyone he had ever seen. "I've had better company sailing with houseplants."

"Seated climb. Call it an easy six."

The boat topped a big wave just as Jim stood tall on the pedals. Glimpsing the suddenly longer view to the horizon, Jim was astonished to see a dark smudge that looked sharper than a cloud, smaller than a rain squall. A ship? Another vessel crawling into the uncertain space between the lead-gray sky and the sea's bare surface?

Be a luxury cruise ship, please. With an air-conditioned health club, Cybex machines, and hot showers. And while we're dreaming, make it headed for a port where a guy can catch a flight home. Except even if he could somehow magically beam aboard, he had signed on for the entire voyage with Will. And to Jim Leighton—who owned little but his skills, a pleasant manner, ripped abs, and his good name—a deal was a deal.

He probably should alert Will. The old man was kind of obsessed on the subject of ships. One night last week Jim thought he'd spotted a light. Will, catnapping in his hammock, had issued his usual strict orders to wake him if he saw anything; but in the seconds that took, the light had vanished. He said that Jim had probably seen a star sinking in the west. Still, he had stayed up in the cockpit for the rest of Jim's watch, sweeping the dark with his binoculars.

But this ship, if it was a ship, looked faraway. And they were only twenty minutes into the class. Unlike most of Jim's private clients, Will was more interested in keeping fit than paying for a friend to talk at; he wanted to be pushed. The ship, if it was a ship, could wait.

Probably a cloud, maybe a rain squall.

Will was starting to tire. Jim saw him cheating on the resistance, pretending to crank the knob tighter than he did.

"Listen to your body, Will." Jim's voice boomed off the sails again. "And if you can, add a little more resistance. Just a little."

He dealt with his own struggle by concentrating on form, pedaling a smooth circle, knees in, shoulders back, head down, chest out, feet and shoulders relaxed. His body was a mess. With weeks to go before he could get off in Rio de Janeiro, and his stomach still protesting every time a shift in the wind changed the nature of the boat's ceaseless motion, Jim was asking himself, What in hell am I doing here?

He had hoped this voyage would be like a big-adventure bachelor party. But sailing across the ocean—instead of the usual stripper, cigars, and home to your honey—had imploded into "go away and experience the world" when Shannon turned him down point-blank. So he was stuck out here searching his soul to be sure he really wanted to marry Shannon—which he thought he had made clear by proposing to the woman, for Christ's sake.

Will glanced over and saw that Jim was struggling on the bike. Gasping, he teased, "You can take the mall rat out of the suburb, but you can't take the suburb out of the mall rat."

The old man was forever on Jim's case for having been raised in the suburbs—like he'd had a choice—because Jim had made the mistake of asking where, among all the ingen-

BURIED AT SEA 7

iously stowed gear and machinery that made the sailboat self-sufficient, the dishwasher was hidden.

"Hands to second, and up! Accelerate a few pedal strokes if you can." Standing, pedaling as if he were running in place, Jim searched the checkered horizon.

There *was* a mini washing machine, big enough for shorts and shirts, which was all they wore in the heat; but the dishwasher request had branded him the personal representative of every suburban cliché Will knew, from antiseptic homogeneity to bland conformity to mindless consumerism. No TV reception, either. Will had laughed. No Gap. No McDonald's. No pizza. No surfing the Web.

They did have e-mail, but it was a slow joke. You could send high-priced flashmails by satellite phone, provided the boat wasn't rolling too hard to lock the signal. Or you could transmit half a page in two minutes for free, if atmospheric conditions suited the battery-straining, temperamental single-sideband (SSB) radio.

"What's up?" called Will when he saw Jim craning his neck.

"I thought I saw a ship."

"Where?"

2

WILL SPARK YANKED up on his resistance knob to stop the flywheel, jumped off the Schwinn, and snatched his binoculars from their rack beside the helm. "Where?"

Jim pointed. Will focused expertly. "Turn that damned music off."

In the sudden quiet the hull's bow wave sounded loud.

Will watched for a full minute, a muscle rippling beneath his weather-beaten cheek. Daylight was failing and Jim was no longer sure he had seen anything.

"Sons of bitches," Will muttered softly.

"What's wrong?"

"Take the helm! Head into the wind."

"Why?"

"Do it!"

Will was running forward to the mast, where he began yanking ropes from the rat's nest of halyards. "Into the wind," he yelled again, and Jim climbed down into the cockpit and took the big wooden steering wheel in an unfamiliar grip. Turning it automatically overrode the auto-helm. The boat heeled sharply and he would have fallen if he wasn't hanging on to the wheel.

"Other way!" yelled Will.

"Sorry." Jim turned the other way. Both sails, flapping wildly, swung in over the boat, the stiff fabric thundering as the wind streamed past. Will released a couple of ropes and down they came, burying the decks like snow crashing off a roof. The mainsail covered the cabin in heaps of cloth. The big sail in front, the genoa jib, spilled over the lifelines and fell into the sea.

"What's going on?" Ordinarily, Will moved about the boat with an easy deliberation, furling sails as precisely as a sky diver packing parachutes.

Will ran back to the cockpit, skidding on the slippery Dacron. "Get up to the bow," he yelled, then shouldered Jim away from the wheel and pushed him toward the foredeck. "Pull that sail out of the water! No, wait! The bikes are made of steel; we have to get the bikes below."

The spinners each weighed ninety pounds with their massive flywheels and solid steel frames. Will had winched them up from the cabin with a halyard. He released the jam cleats he had rigged to the car tracks and together they muscled them into the cockpit. "Lay them flat. Okay, get forward and pull that sail out of the water."

The diesel start alarm shrilled, and seconds later, as Jim was struggling forward on the suddenly rolling and pitching boat, the auxiliary engine rumbled to life.

"Dammit!" Will came running forward again, as frightened and bewildered as a lost dog in traffic. "If that sail falls in the prop we're dead." He leaned over the lifelines to help Jim pull the dripping sail onto the deck. "Okay, we're outta here."

"*What* is going on?"

"Grab some sail ties, secure it to the spinnaker pole." He pointed at the big aluminum spar cradled on the foredeck and ran back to the cockpit, where he put the engine in gear and accelerated. The propeller shoved the boat reluctantly into a clumsy, wallowing turn until at last her bow pointed into the wind and the smudge on the horizon fell directly astern.

Mystified, Jim found the sail ties and wrapped the loose sail to the spinnaker pole. Then he returned to the cockpit and demanded, for the fourth time, what was going on. Will engaged the auto-helm and turned around and scanned the sea behind with his binoculars.

"You got good eyes, kid. I wouldn't have seen 'em in time."

"Who?"

Will's jaw tightened. "Son of a bitch, they're coming after us." He looked around frantically. His gaze locked on the heart-rate monitor strapped to Jim's wrist.

"Where'd you get that?"

"It's my heart monitor. Like you should wear."

"That's not your regular one."

"My clients gave it to me."

"*Gave?* What do you mean, 'gave'?"

"A bon voyage gift." It was a top-of-the-line Polar Accurex, three hundred bucks with all the bells and whistles.

"Which client?"

"They got together and gave it to me."

"Which ones?"

"None you knew. From my new job at the Westport Club. After you left. Will, what's going on?"

Will had worked out regularly for months in Jim's spinning classes at the health club, then suddenly disappeared. A year later, out of the blue, came the telephone call from the Caribbean island of Barbados. Will had tracked Jim down at his new job to offer him a six-week stint as his personal trainer and novice deckhand on a sail to Rio de Janeiro.

Two hundred bucks a day for the experience of a lifetime: bed—a tilting bunk with a lee cloth to keep him from falling out when the boat rolled the other way; board—all the food he could keep down; and airfare—outta here when the experience of a lifetime was finally over.

"Let me see it."

Jim unstrapped the wristwatch receiver and passed it to Will. Will inspected it closely, shook it, held it to the sky. "And the sensor."

Jim unbuckled the chest strap that pressed the electrode to his chest. Will snatched it from his hand and examined it as he had the receiver. He shot another anxious glance behind the boat. Then he plunged down the companionway steps into the cabin. Jim peered down through the hatch and saw Will hunched over the navigation table. He wrote something in the log. Then he jumped up and turned into the galley, which was opposite the nav station, opened one of the big freezers, leaned in, and came out with his hands full.

"How about lamb for dinner?" he called in a tight voice.

"What?"

Will yanked a frozen leg of lamb from its Ziploc freezer bag and tossed it into the sink, where it landed with a *clang* that Jim heard over the roar of the engine. He slipped both parts of Jim's heart-rate monitor into the plastic bag, zipped it shut, and hurried up the steps into the cockpit. The bag was ballooned with trapped air.

"What are you— Hey!"

Will leaned over the back of the boat, and Jim heard a splash. When he lunged to the stern rail, he saw his heart monitor bobbing in the propeller wake. "That's mine!"

"They're tracking us with it."

"Tracking us?"

"They bugged your heart monitor. They put a homing device in it."

"They? Who? What are you talking about?"

"Their 'gift' beeps out a radio signal that shows them exactly where we are."

Jim Leighton stared at the older man. "Who are you talking about?"

A variation on the personal trainer's nightmare: You let a type A geezer push too hard and suddenly your client has a stroke and goes mental.

"Who, Will?" Jim repeated. He probed Will's eyes for some hopeful clue that a clot wasn't blocking a capillary or an aneurysm hadn't ruptured, leaking blood in his brain. His pupils were dilated. The sign of a stroke? Or was it simply due to the fear that was chewing up his mind? "Who's tracking us?" Jim asked again.

"The sons of bitches on that ship."

"What ship?"

"Look." He handed Jim the binoculars. Clumsily, Jim

tried to find the smudge. But the engine caused Will's boat to pound against the waves, and the horizon line lurched and jumped like something living no matter how hard Jim tried to steady the glasses. "I don't see anything."

"They're behind that squall. See that dark area? That's a rain squall. They're behind it. Lucky break for us."

"I'm not even sure I saw a ship. There might have been nothing there."

"They're there, all right. Pray by the time they find your 'gift' we'll be gone in the night."

Jim lowered the glasses and looked hard at Will. He was used to working with people to help them overcome doubt and fear to fix their bodies and get where they wanted to go. He could deal with the man's fear.

"Will, turn around. Go back and get my monitor."

"What are you, nuts?"

"No, I'm not nuts. It's mine. It cost three hundred bucks. I want it back."

"I'll give you the three hundred bucks. Soon as it's dark I'll go below and write you a check. Okay?"

"I don't want your check. It was a gift. It means something to me."

Jim was fully aware that he was arguing the wrong issue. This was not about the Accurex, it was about Will's mysterious "they." But if he could convince Will to turn the boat around, he might make him realize that he had temporarily lost his grip. Out of that realization would come reflection; out of reflection, some simple explanation.

"They will kill us, Jim. There is no way we're going back."

"Who will kill us?" Jim asked. "Who are 'they'?"

Will looked at him. He wasn't buying into realization, reflection, and simple explanation. "You think I'm making this up? You think I'm crazy?"

Jim felt the first stab of fear.

3

HOW DO WE know he's a competent sailor?" Shannon had asked Jim when Will first telephoned. She inhaled adventure books—the wetter, the colder, the higher, the better—and knew from her reading that offshore sailing demanded boat skills, sea skills, and navigation skills.

Will's answer, which they had both found completely reassuring, was that he had bought his latest boat (his third) in Hong Kong, personally supervised an extensive refit, and then sailed it halfway around the world to Barbados. Based on that feat, Jim had put his life in the older man's hands. And judging by the effortless way Will handled the boat, Jim had e-mailed Shannon, he couldn't have asked for a safer captain. Until now. What they should have demanded was a letter from his shrink.

"No," he said carefully. "I don't think you're nuts. But I am very confused. What's going on?"

"Long story, kid. Most of it I can't talk about."

"I want to hear it."

"Maybe later. For the moment, let's just say we're goddamned lucky you spotted them in time." Will looked back again and snorted a little laugh. "I'd love to see their faces when they find that homing device floating all by its lonesome."

"They?" Jim repeated, treading very carefully. In one of his recurring dreams, he is snatching three hundred pounds when the bar snaps, and the weights smash his feet. Shannon called it his "fear of trying" dream. But that's how he felt now, as he talked to Will. If he asked the wrong question, the old man would suddenly snap and fall to pieces before his eyes. Where would that leave him?

"Do 'they' know that we're sailing to Rio de Janeiro?"

"Good question." Will paused to reflect on what "they" knew. "Probably," he said. "Though maybe not—considering they planted that homing device on you—but I'm not taking the chance."

"What do you mean?" Jim asked.

"No way we're going to Brazil."

"What?"

"You heard me."

"Where are we going?"

"Africa."

"*Africa?* What are you talking about? We're going to Brazil. My flight home leaves from Brazil."

"I'll buy you a ticket from Lagos."

"Nigeria? Isn't there a civil war going on there?"

"No," said Will.

"The *Daily Show* said the UN was sending slave ships to rescue West African refugees."

"That is cruel, crude, sophomoric—"

"But they made it clear that it's dangerous."

"Not where we're going."

"How far from here? How long are we talking about?"

"Month or so. Depending on the wind."

"Or so? Five weeks?"

"Could be six or seven depending on conditions. We've got to get through the Doldrums, which can slow us down. We've got to sail the rest of the way across the Atlantic and pretty deep into the Gulf of Guinea."

"We had a deal, Will. We're going to Rio. Three more weeks, you said. Now you're talking six or seven."

Will Spark scanned the darkening water behind them. "It's your watch. I've set her due east. I'll go below and work out an exact course. You keep an eye astern. Call me if you see any lights."

"No, Will. We had a deal."

"Don't blame me: it's *you* who brought them after us with that goddamned monitor."

Jim started after him, then stopped and waited in the cockpit, trying to figure out a way to talk sense into Will. The trouble was when he took this job, he hadn't really known Will much better than any of the students who had taken his group spinning classes. He didn't know anything. In retrospect, Jim realized, he had been in a state of confusion since the night he'd landed in Barbados.

Instead of picking him up at the airport, as promised, Will had sent a taxi driver who had Jim's name scrawled on a piece of paper and spoke with an accent he couldn't begin to understand. The taxi drove through dark villages to a wind-whipped cove where a small fishing boat was banging against a rickety dock.

"Captain Spark" had left already, the fisherman explained in only slightly more intelligible pidgin English. He was trying to outdistance a weather front bearing down on the Caribbean island. The fishing boat headed to sea, pounding for hours through ink-black water, until Will's sailboat finally appeared in its searchlight.

The seas were rough: the two boats scissored up and down, and Jim had nearly fallen between them in the transfer. As the fishing boat's motor faded he found himself as thoroughly disoriented as a kidnap victim who'd been bound and gagged in a car trunk. Will had greeted him with a cup of coffee and a doughnut, and before Jim knew it he was seasick.

There was no way he was going to Africa.

He went below, down the four-step companionway into the luxurious main salon. By day the rich, dark woodwork made the cabin a serene retreat from the harsh sun and the dazzling sky; now, little lamps cast a soft, golden glow. It reminded him of the fancy libraries in the Gold Coast mansion museums his mother used to drag him to.

Will was in the galley, an elegant workspace of brushed stainless steel with a maple block countertop, a gimballed stove that swung level when the boat heeled, knives like razors, and spices Jim had never heard of. Will was braced against the sink as he peeled foil off the frozen leg of lamb.

Jim stood by the chart table opposite the galley and stared at the chart, rehearsing what he had to say. He noticed that Will had penciled in their global positioning system fix. The chart showed that the water here was shallow, relatively speaking, a mile deep instead of three. There was a kind of shelf midocean on which sat Saint Paul's Rocks.

"I probably saw these rocks."

Will shook his head. "Doubt that."

"I never really saw a ship. It could have been these rocks."

"Was it white?"

"What?"

"Was what you saw white?"

"No. Grayish."

"Saint Paul's are white as snow. Covered with bird crap."

"The sun was behind the clouds. It could have been white."

Will laid the lamb in the sink, crossed the narrow space between the galley and the nav station, and reached past Jim to lift a fat green volume from the bookshelf.

"Nathaniel Bowditch, *American Practical Navigator*."

He flipped pages to an article titled "Distance Off."

"Bowditch is the bible. And the bible says here that the distance you can see in miles is about one and one-seventh times the square root of your height. Figure when you're standing in the cockpit your eye is about nine feet above the water."

"I was on the bike, up on the deck."

"Okay," said Will. "So figure your eye was *eleven* feet above the water." If your eye is eleven feet high, the distance you can see to the horizon is about 3.8 miles. Now, the *Sailing Directions* say"—he pulled down the blue-jacketed *Sailing Directions for East Coast of South America* and showed

Jim an article titled "Off-Lying Islands and Rocks"—"that the tallest of Saint Paul's Rocks are twenty meters, or sixty-five feet, out of the sea. So you add to the distance you can see the square root of sixty-five times one and one-seventh, which equals . . ." He picked up the calculator, punched in a slew of numbers, and showed Jim the screen. "That increases the distance you could see Saint Paul's to 12.7 miles. But according to the GPS we are *fifty* miles from Saint Paul's Rocks. So, sorry, you didn't see rocks. You saw a ship hunting us."

"Maybe I saw a ship. But I didn't see a ship *hunting* us." He looked around the main cabin. Nothing he saw gave him hope. The polished teak aglow in the soft golden light of the brass lamps, the dark mahogany cabinets, the leather-bound books, the banks of expensive electronics were all vivid reminders that Will Spark was a very wealthy man who was accustomed to getting his own way. While Jim Leighton was a lopsided cross between employee and guest with less say in important matters than a house pet.

"Look, Will. A deal is a deal."

"I thought you were on watch." He went back to the sink and resumed pulling foil, and the plastic wrap under it, from the frozen lamb.

"You can't just change everything like this. I have a right to be dropped off where you promised."

"I told you. That is no longer possible."

"Will, I don't want to be hard-assed about this. Don't make me force you to turn the boat around."

"Force?" Will Spark looked up from the sink. He dropped the leg of lamb and moved quickly toward him.

Jim backed up, startled.

"You may be younger and stronger, sonny. But suburban college boys don't learn street fighting in health clubs."

Jim had wondered about the scar tissue on Will's fists and the boxer's white ridges over his brow, and the time-bleached U.S. Marine Corps *Semper fi* tattoo on his biceps, none of which fit the Yale-man image. What was new was the suddenly implacable expression on his face. Well, fuck him. Jim *was* younger. Lots younger. And much stronger. Health clubs taught kickboxing, and the places he worked in now featured the Brazilian martial art *capoeira*.

Will seemed to read his mind. He stepped closer and tapped his chest, hard. "You have muscles like a pocket Schwarzenegger. But you're really a little guy. You have lousy bones. You're built too light in your knees and your wrists and your ankles. It must have taken twice the work to bulk up like that. What kind of problem drove you to put on all that muscle?"

"It comes in handy. At times like this."

"Go ahead. Take your best shot."

"Come on, Will."

"Makes me wonder what a bright kid like you is avoiding to shift all that effort into bodybuilding."

"Turn the boat around."

"Or what?" Will shot back. "Even if you could take me, how will you sleep? You going to watch me twenty-four hours a day? What's to stop me from bashing your head in when you close your eyes?"

"Come on, Will," Jim said. But he couldn't help glancing at the pilot berth where he usually slept between watches. The weird thing was, he could almost see it in his mind: Will creeping down the companionway with one of the heavy chrome winch handles.

"You could always tie me to my bunk," Will mocked. "Except, how are you going to sail home alone?"

"All I'm saying is I want to go to Rio like you promised."

"And I'm saying I apologize for disappointing you, and I also apologize for dragging you into this mess. But the fact is, you're with me, so you're in it. I've got no choice but to run. So you've got no choice but to run with me. Remember, if they catch me, they've caught you too. Lotsa luck explaining that you're just along for the ride."

" 'They' are in your head, Will. There is no 'they.' I'll prove it to you. Let's look on the radar."

"We can't chance using the radar."

"Why not?"

"What if they have ECM?"

"Excuse me, what's ECM?"

"Electronic countermeasures. I can't take a chance they wouldn't lock onto my radar pulse."

"Just for a second. We'll just turn it on, look, and turn it off."

"They'd have our bearing and range in a microsecond."

Jim slipped into the leather bench built into the bulkhead beside the nav table. "One quick look."

"No."

The electric panel had a triple array of switches. Running lights, work lights, interior lights, stereo, TV, VCR, microwave, washing machine, three radios, sat phone, electronic autopilot, water pumps, bilge pumps, fire pump, fuel pump, electric windlass, freezer, global positioning system, computer, radar. As Jim groped for the right one, Will reached past him and flicked a toggle marked "Master Switch." The cabin went dark.

"You're out of your element, Jim."

"Will?"

"Trust me on this."

"Will!"

"What?"

"If the ship is hunting us—"

"If?"

"If it is hunting us," Jim asked, "why doesn't it see *us* on *its* radar?"

"It can't."

"Why not?"

"We're invisible," said Will, and again Jim felt fear. Not only was he trapped aboard a boat he couldn't sail, he was trapped with a crazy man who had already threatened to kill him in his sleep.

"Oh, Will. Come on."

Will Spark laughed and slapped Jim's shoulder. Jim recoiled. Will laughed again and turned the lights back on.

"Relax, kid. I'm not crazy. What I mean is, we are invisible to radar. Mostly. Because we present a very small signature. There's not much on the boat to return a strong echo. Her hull's fiberglass, her spars are carbon fiber, the wheel's wood. Soon as we lowered the bikes into the cockpit, about the only steel above the waterline was her winches.

"The only way those bastards can see us is to eyeball us—that's why I struck the sails. Our hull lies too low on the water to be seen from any distance, but the sails stand out like a bull's-eye. . . . Any more questions?"

Jim shook his head. He didn't believe Will, but even if Will had lost his mind, this was his scene, his turf, and he had an endless store of answers to fit every doubt Jim raised.

Another thing was clear: Will Spark wasn't so scared anymore. He wore the content expression of a man at peace with a big decision. Back in charge, the rich guy on his yacht. Unlike his clueless deckhand, caught like a bug swirling down a drain.

"Would you feel better," Will asked gently, "if you e-mailed Shannon? Tell her you'll be a little late, not to worry. Tell her we got shoved east by heavy weather and the boat's beat up, so we're heading into the Cape Verde Islands for repairs."

"She'll know it's a lie. She's following the weather on the Internet. Why don't I just tell her you freaked out when you saw a ship and you're acting crazy?"

"Tell her what you want, just don't mention Nigeria in case they're breaking into our e-mail."

Jim looked at him in disbelief.

"You never heard of a computer program called Carnivore?" Will asked.

"But the FBI uses Carnivore to scan e-mail. Not some—wait a minute, please don't tell me 'they' are the FBI."

"I'll tell you this, sonny: when these folks go head-to-head with the FBI, the FBI blinks."

Jim gave up. What could he say about demons with a longer reach than the FBI's?

Will said, "I'll flashmail it along with my stuff."

Will's ThinkPad was connected to a satellite transceiver antenna attached to the stern rail. If the boat wasn't rocking too hard to beam up, the communications satellite above the equator relayed their messages to ground teleports that were telephone-wired into the Internet.

But it wasn't private, because to send flashmail on Will's system, Jim had to log on as Will. For total privacy, he had to go on-line using the SSB radio, which didn't always work.

> Guess what? I'm going to be away a little longer than we thought. Will's changing course, but I'll get home as soon as I can. I'm really sorry. I miss you.
> He promises it won't take us much longer. I didn't get much say in this. Sorry.

Wait a minute, Jim thought. What the fuck am I doing? She doesn't care if I'm gone another month.

The boat rolled abysmally and the air was close belowdecks. He felt the seasickness coming back, licking tentatively at his throat. A cloying mix of diesel exhaust and fiberglass gel coat clogged his mouth and nose.

He punched Delete and wrote,

> I'm going to be away longer than I thought. Will's changing course. Looks like my big adventure's getting bigger.
> Love,
> Jim

then fled for fresh air in the cockpit.

When it was fully dark, they raised the sails, which steadied the boat considerably. The wind and the weight of the lead keel, Will explained, counteracted the wave action simultaneously from top and bottom. "As if you extended your arms on a balance bar."

He studied the horizon behind them with his night glasses. Then he went below to cook dinner. Jim continued his watch in the cockpit, which for him meant keeping his eyes open and calling Will if he was in doubt about anything.

Will kept the diesel running for the hot water, the freezer, and the electricity to thaw the lamb in the microwave, and he left it running until he had established contact with the Inmarsat satellite and flashmailed Jim's message to Shannon.

At their next watch change, midnight, Will noted their miles run with satisfaction, made some minor adjustments to the sails, and again swept the blackness astern with the night glasses. "We're doing pretty good."

He cast an eye skyward, where the stars shone weakly through the haze, then took the wheel, overriding the auto-helm. "I'll see if I can get some more miles under the keel. Just pray we don't lose the wind."

That didn't seem likely to Jim. The northeast trade wind had been blowing like a machine for two weeks straight since the storm off Barbados.

"Better catch some sleep, Jim. See you at oh-three-hundred."

They were standing watches: three hours on, three hours off. It was good manners, Will had explained, to arrive on deck five minutes before your time, ready to go. Jim set his wrist alarm for ten to three, then lay awake listening to the water rub past the hull a couple of inches from his face.

Suddenly, Will was shaking him awake. He handed Jim a mug of coffee. He'd slept through his alarm.

"Sorry," mumbled Jim. He struggled into his running shoes and followed Will up the companionway. Blearily, he repeated their compass course. The clouds had peeled back, revealing thousands of stars so bright that Jim could see the sea's rolling surface by their light.

Will suggested that he shut off the auto-helm and practice his steering. He showed him a star to steer by. "It's good for fifteen minutes, then find yourself another. When in doubt look over your shoulder. See those three? Orion's belt. It's settling toward the west; just keep it right behind you. But as soon as you get tired, put her back on the auto-helm; we don't want to lose any time. I'm going to get some shut-eye." He started to go below. "Oh, by the way, Shannon wrote back. I left it on the screen. You can read it after your watch."

"What did she say?"

"It doesn't sound to me like an extra month'll hurt. Quote: 'Adventures should not run on schedule. Have a ball.' End quote."

It sounded to Jim like she didn't care, and he felt, anew, the sting of rejection. Have a nice time; give me a ring when you get back?

"Shannon wanted me to do this trip," he blurted.

"Why?"

"She's done a lot of exciting things in her life. She used to be very adventurous. Much more than I am. I think she's trying to save me from feeling trapped or regretful about being tied down—in the future."

"Why do I get the impression that Shannon does the thinking for both of you?"

"No, I liked the idea. I just probably wouldn't have come if she hadn't pushed me. She found subs to cover my classes, reserved my plane ticket."

If he allowed himself to get really paranoid he would think she had seized on the voyage as an opportunity to start easing him out of her life even before he asked her to marry him. . . . No. . . . She had seemed genuinely surprised. By the time he proposed, he had already accepted Will's invitation and even had his plane ticket. . . . Funny thought: Had he proposed marriage partly out of fear of going away?

"She bought me that awesome Helly Hansen foul-weather gear."

Will put on his "me hearties" voice: "Aye, ya looked ready for Cape Horn, matey." Jim couldn't help but laugh.

"Her parents chipped in—hoping I'd just keep sailing around the world."

"Could it be the lass herself who paid you off, matey?"

"What is that supposed to mean?"

"Not her parents."

"She did not pay me to go away," Jim shot back. "Don't you get it? She's giving me an out."

"What kind of out?"

"Time to reflect on whether I really want to marry her." Or, he wondered silently, time to get over her.

"Why wouldn't you?"

"None of your damned business."

"Sorry. I'm a nosy old coot. It just seems there's a mystery about you two I don't understand." Will started down the companionway again, adding, darkly, "Remember what I told you: if you write her back, leave out our course and position."

"I'm not going to write her back."

The first two hours of the three-to-six watch were the longest of the night. Even the heavens seemed to wheel more slowly. The constellations lagged in their tracks and the Milky Way lay across the stars still as a frozen river. It was a time for the mind to swarm with doubts, confusion, and fear. A time to dwell on Will's crazy actions and his intrusive questions.

Shannon wanted him to have an adventure? Well, she'd succeeded in spades. His ticket home was freaking out and he was well and truly fucked until he figured a way out of this mess. Which allowed Jim even more time to think the unthinkable: Was this whole voyage truly his escape, his chance to opt out of a stunted life with someone he happened to love?

He had promised to think about what it would mean to be married to her. "Really think, Jim," were her parting words. "I don't want to be your job. And I don't want a man who thinks he doesn't deserve more than a wounded bird."

He had printed her last e-mail before erasing it from Will's files. He unfolded the paper and read it by the rose glow of the compass, though he knew it by heart.

Your mom drove your dad nuts. And your dad just took it. Sometimes kids from unhappy homes are obsessed to make a better family. I wonder if that's part of what's driving you to marry me. And I wonder if a boy who struggled to make his unhappy mom happy will go way too far trying to make every girl he meets happy. So I ask you again: You've worked very hard to make a beautiful body. Why shouldn't you demand the same from your wife?

*I can't walk.*Remember?*I am crippled.*

Love,

Shannon

She loved driving people nuts by insisting on the word *crippled. Handicapped* didn't do justice to how thoroughly you could shatter bones by skiing into solid steel at fifty miles an hour. After six operations and a year of therapy she could stand, briefly, with crutches. "Golfers," she said, "have handicaps; cripples have multiple compound fractures."

Crippled was a much better way to describe the young woman whose family had hired him to work up an exercise routine to get the rest of her body back into healthy shape. Holed up in her bedroom, hooked on painkillers and weeping with despair, she had rejected every physical therapist they engaged.

Jim knew that he couldn't take much credit for slipping under her radar. The fact was that they had just plain liked each other from the very first day. And to Jim, at least, that friendship seemed to have grown into a firm basis for a marriage.

A thin, pale line began to form where the eastern sky met the sea. The stars faded quickly.

Will came up, coffee mug in hand, eyes on the sails, at five minutes before six. He was humming a tune, which Jim took as a sign that the old man was over his fright and felt back on top. He hummed when he felt happy, and when he was really pumped, he sang out loud.

Jim went below to delete Shannon's e-mail. Up in the cockpit, Will broke into a blues song, rasping the verse with a high-pitched nasal twang:

> *"Standin' on the corner,*
> *I didn't mean no harm.*
> *Along came a po-lice,*
> *Took me by the arm"*

4

SOARING ON TWIN hulls like a gigantic manta ray, the fast ferry *Barcelona* raced through the thirteenth hour of her ever-expanding pattern search even as the sun rose on vast and empty waters.

The huge catamaran—built for high-speed blue water crossings—was manned by an Australian delivery crew, most of whom were shipyard mechanics tending the four brand-new Caterpillar turbo-charged diesels that hurled her along at eighty miles an hour. Trailing wings of mist and spray, she whipped back and forth across a hundred square miles of ocean.

The *Barcelona*'s glassed-in bridge sat high above the main passenger cabin, which spanned her widely separated hulls. Her pilot station resembled an airbus flight deck, with digital readouts and flat-screen monitors relaying information from the engines, trim monitors, and navigational instruments.

Big windows offered a bird's-eye view of the sea and there was ample room for the *Barcelona*'s Australian delivery captain, his first officer, and the helmsman, as well as the American who had chartered her and his bodyguards. Three big blokes—quiet as mountain shadows—two white, one black. Ex–U.S. Navy SEALs, the *Barcelona*'s captain guessed, judging by their swimmers' shoulders and barrel chests.

"Mr. Nickels," the captain said, "we're running out of time."

At well under six feet, Nickels was not as tall as his bodyguards, but as lean in the gut and big in the shoulders, and immensely powerful. The captain rated him Special Forces, what with the buzz cut, the high-top black Adidas, and the anvil build. His men looked the sort you might have a pint with, but there was a cold, bloodless emptiness in Nickels's eyes that warned he was one vicious piece of work.

It had been a long, long night and the captain, a hard-bitten, hard-drinking former salvage master, was fed up. What had looked like easy money back at the Panama Canal had turned into a royal pain in the butt.

"I said we're running out of time, Mr. Nickels."

The near silence on the bridge was broken only by the distant whine of the engines and the maddening on-again, off-again *ping* of the elusive homing signal. Finally, Andy Nickels looked up from the receiver and said to the Australian, "Shut your fucking mouth."

"You've no call to talk that way, mate. I delivered. I've been tracking that bloody bug for three days."

Nickels spoke to one of his shadows, who strode swiftly from the bridge. The captain watched the security cameras trace his route into the elevator, then down below to the main deck to the galley. Another camera picked him up as he flung open the door of the walk-in refrigerator and disappeared inside. Puzzled, the captain stole a glance at his first officer; Hoskins shot back a disgusted look that conveyed the message, Not my idea to accept an illicit off-the-books charter.

"You know as well as I do that your ruddy bug has gone down. We've been running circles all night. I'm due in Spain. I told you from the get go, you paid for two extra days. You've had three and a half—that's it."

Nickels said, "Stop the ship!"

The captain hesitated. Nickels's other shadows stepped forward like Rotweilers.

"Stop engines," he ordered. The helmsman gathered the throttle clutches—port in his left hand, starboard in his right—and hauled back. The big cat slowed rapidly as her hulls settled into the water.

Nickels stood up and tucked the pinging monitor under his arm.

"What do you say we catch some air, Captain?"

The bodyguards crowded in behind the captain, and he started reluctantly after Nickels, who moved as lightly as a swordfish dancing on its tail.

"Bring the mate," Nickels called over his shoulder. "Leave the helmsman."

Captain Moser nodded for Hoskins to come, too, and they followed Nickels through the main cabin, past rows and rows of reclining airline seats, then downstairs to the lobby on the embarkation deck and through an insulated door out to the fantail, an abbreviated stern deck fifteen feet above the water.

Greg, the man Nickels had sent to the galley, was waiting with a five-gallon bucket of hamburger meat. At a nod from Nickels, he dipped into the bucket and flung a bloody handful into the water.

The morning heat was in thick contrast to the air-conditioning. The cat was pitching a little as it drifted on the swell.

"Dump it all!" snapped Nickels.

Greg upended the bucket. He watched the meat splash red in the water and a moment later he said, "Sharks!"

A long, dark shape cruised beneath the waves. Rolling sideways, it revealed a flash of white underbelly. When it straightened up, its fin cut the surface. A second shot through the bloodied water like a sinuous torpedo, then a third, accelerating with effortless strokes of its scythe-shaped tail.

"Throw the mate," Nickels ordered.

Two men grabbed Hoskins. And while Greg blocked the catamaran's captain, they dragged the Australian to the rail.

The captain could not believe that they would actually throw the man to the sharks. But they were lifting him over the rail now. The captain yelled for them to stop. Hoskins's terror gave him the strength to fight back. Nickels's men were taller and broader, with slablike hands and arms as big as a woman's waist. But the mate broke loose and tried to run.

They surrounded him in a flash and buckled him over with body punches. He went down, gasping for air, then shrieked in pain as the bodyguards kicked him repeatedly.

"Stop them," the captain yelled. "I'll do what you want."

Nickels's face hardened. His expression changed from cold fury to even colder contempt as they lifted the whimpering mate and hoisted his helpless body over the railing.

The mate stared bug-eyed at the sharks roving beneath the stern. He was struggling to breathe, gasping. With no wind to scream, no strength to fight, he could only utter his terror in a rattling moan.

The sharks broke the surface, wheeling in tight circles. It seemed, the captain thought, as if they were inflamed by weakness. The biggest was as long as a car and nearly as thick around.

"I'll do anything you want," the captain yelled. He shoved past Greg. But Greg staggered him with a sharp blow to the head. He fell back, clasping his eye, reeling. Grunting with effort, Nickels's men lifted the mate shoulder high.

Suddenly, the homing receiver pinged rapidly—a high-pitched *ping-ping-ping-ping-ping* that brought Nickels's head up in a flash. He shoved past the struggling men, leaned far out over the railing, and stared at the sea. "What do you see?"

They scanned the sea, searching for a sail. Nothing. The sea was still empty, their ship alone. But the receiver was pinging away, as persistent as a car alarm. The rhythm grew faster. It sounded as if Will Spark's sailboat was less than a hundred feet away.

"There!"

Nickels pointed. The sun flashed on a shiny ball, which the wind was bouncing across the waves. "Captain!" he yelled. "Launch a boat. Get that! You"—he pointed at his bodyguards—"go with him! Keep your eye on that. Don't lose it."

They dropped the mate on the deck, grabbed the captain, who was still holding his eye, and marched him below. A pilot hatch opened in the back of the starboard hull and a rubber boat skidded down a ramp into the water. The sharks arrowed to it, the biggest passing so close it lifted the boat on its back.

"Go!" Nickels yelled. "Go now!"

One bodyguard shoved the captain into the boat. Greg took out a pistol and sprayed the water with automatic fire. But the sharks kept circling until the captain yanked the outboard starter. The motor roared. The boat sped from the catamaran, the captain looking back to steer by Nickels's hand signals. The wind had blown the ball hundreds of yards before they caught up and lifted it from the sea.

"What is it?" Nickels snapped into his two-way.

Greg directed the captain back to the catamaran before he radioed back, carefully, "I don't know, Andy. It's something in a bag."

When he saw the contents for himself, Nickels ripped open the plastic. He slammed the heart-rate monitor to the deck and ground it beneath his boot. The tracker receiver kept pinging and pinging and pinging. Andy Nickels stomped the chest sensor and the noise stopped.

"We wasted all fucking night!" he shouted. "All night on a wild-goose chase. We gave them all night to run—Captain!"

"Yes, sir." The captain was watching him warily.

"How far can he have gotten, Captain?"

Captain Moser rubbed his aching eye, concealing his glee at the American's misfortune. "Assume the yacht's making six-seven knots."

Nickels turned to Greg. "Is that right?"

"No. If he's sailing the boat we think, it's fast; but he's an old guy. And the kid is a novice. Besides, the wind was light all night. They made five knots if they were lucky, maybe six, depending on their heading."

Nickels nodded for the captain to continue.

"All right, make it six knots," said Captain Moser. "We know he must have spotted us before dark. After dark he wouldn't have seen us with no lights and we never picked up his radar. So at six knots he'd make seventy-two nautical miles in the past twelve hours. East, west, north, or south."

Again Nickels looked at Greg, who shook his head. "The wind veered east in the night. I doubt he beat to the east."

"Could have used his engine," the captain countered. "At any rate, he's somewhere in a circle 144 miles in diameter. That's 450 miles around. And *that's* an area of sixteen thousand square miles, mate—one big patch of ocean. And getting bigger every minute, assuming the bloke hasn't stopped, which don't seem likely with you lot after him."

"East!" said Nickels. "He would drop his sails to make a smaller target and motor east. Find him!"

"Now, hold on, Mr. Nickels."

Nickels turned beet red. "Hold on?" he roared. "Hold on? Greg! Take everybody up to the bridge."

"You okay here?"

"I'll be up in a minute."

The heavy door sighed shut behind them.

Andy Nickels stalked to the rail. The sharks had gone. But not far. When he reached down to pick up the shattered heart-rate monitor, the bloodied mate flinched. Nickels tossed it into the water and heaved the empty bucket after it. Instantly the gray shapes razored toward the splash.

To the *Barcelona*'s captain he said, "It's just you and me, babe, and for the rest of your miserable life, whatever I ask, you will always answer yes." He seized the cringing mate by his belt and shirt collar. Muscles and tendons leaping with the strain, he lifted the man clear off the deck and began to spin in a circle, gathering momentum like an athlete throwing the hammer.

"You can't do that," cried the captain.

"The hell I can't. We're in international waters—strongman's land."

He whirled, once, twice, three times, accelerating to maximum power, and threw the screaming mate.

Captain Moser had already closed his eyes. When

Hoskins's head crashed into his chest, he staggered and fell hard on his butt. Hoskins landed beside him, curled his arms and legs into a tight ball, and wept.

"Captain?" said Nickels, looming over them.

Captain Moser sat with his back pressed to the bulkhead, gasping for air, his eyes raised to the pearly sky. He patted Hoskins's shoulder. "Easy, mate. Easy."

"Captain?"

"Yes."

"Less mess this way. For you. Makes no difference to me. But when you get to Spain they're going to be asking, Where's the mate? You know what I'm saying, *mate?* It can still go the other way. So what do you say you order full speed east!"

The captain tugged his handheld off his belt, raised it in a trembling hand, and radioed the helmsman: "Come to zero-niner-zero—hook her up!"

The catamaran squatted on her stern when the helmsman pushed all four engines to full ahead. Then her hulls sprang from the water and she soared east on skirts of spray at eighty miles an hour.

"Get up to the bridge, both of you."

Andy Nickels took out his sat phone and punched Redial and Encrypt for a secure line to Lloyd McVay. He hoped Val would answer. Val McVay was no less a ball-buster than her father, but it was the senior McVay whom Nickels owed big-time and dreaded to disappoint. Val answered on the first ring, asking, "Do you have him?"

"No, ma'am, I—"

"Save it for my father."

Lloyd McVay picked up with a cold "What is it, Andy?" and Nickels knew he was in for a real reaming.

Usually Mr. McVay spoke in sentences that were long and round and full, smacking his lips over high-class words the way a fat man worked his mouth over a sausage. But today he sounded as cold and tight as the grunt of a silenced Glock.

"I'm very sorry, Mr. McVay, I don't have him yet. He pulled another fast one on us. . . . Yes, sir."

With his head down and one ear covered against the roar of the ship, Andy Nickels watched his Adidas pace an ever-tightening circle. He had no one but himself to blame. Val McVay had arranged the tracking signal. His job had been to follow it. "Yes, sir. . . . No, sir. . . . No, sir, I don't underestimate him . . . Oh, I'll get him. . . . Don't you worry, sir, I'll get him."

Suddenly, Lloyd McVay's tone softened. "Now, Andy . . ."

Andy Nickels braced for the bayonet in the ribs. How often had he himself delivered McVay's kiss-off: The foundation no longer needs your services.

"You may recall that I went to some length to emphasize the importance of the Sentinel project to the McVay Foundation."

"Yes, sir." Shit, he was going to drag it out.

"Sentinel will change medicine as the world knows it—an advance greater than X rays and antibiotics."

"Yes, sir."

"Your uncle—not a man given to hyperbole—said that Sentinel would, and I believe I quote him accurately, 'put the doctors on unemployment and the insurance companies into receivership.' "

McVay's sentences were getting longer, Andy realized with a glimmer of hope, and his voice was sliding back into the familiar flat, Ivy League, above-it-all drawl.

"Yes, sir. Uncle Andrew said Sentinel would change the world." Uncle Andrew, chief of security for the McVay Foundation for Humane Science until the day he died, had explained to Andy, during one of their "hitters' conferences," that Sentinel would make the McVays the Microsoft of medical technology.

Lloyd McVay said, "With the health and happiness of all humanity in the balance, I was counting on an A-plus performance from you." He was stringing out the words, as if he were tasting them on his tongue.

"Yes, sir." The breakthrough would not only make more money for the McVays on the Internet than Bill Gates ever earned, but also win them a Nobel Prize for service to humanity. With that much at stake, the rules of engagement were no rules. If caught, deny. The McVays would get you out of it in due course. Do anything to get Sentinel back.

"I would define an A-plus as securing Will Spark *immediately*!"

"Yes, sir."

"Your uncle Andrew worked for me for many, many years—so many that I confess I came to take him for granted. What Andrew Nickels promised, Andrew Nickels delivered."

"Yes, sir."

"Andrew Nickels was a first-class facilitator. He was by my side through two corporations and the creation of the foundation. No problem was too big, no detail too small, no challenge too great."

"Yes, sir."

"He had high hopes for his protégé—you, Andy. Now that he's gone, I'm left to hope that Andrew Nickels's sudden death hasn't torn too wide a breach in our lines."

"Yes, sir."

"You were, by all accounts, a fine soldier once. When your uncle asked me to intercede—what is it, now, four years ago—your commanding officer and right on up the Ranger chain of command all assured me you were an A-plus fighting man."

McVay interrupted himself with a dry chuckle. Nickels scuffed his boot at a bloodstain the mate had left on the deck, still not sure where this was going.

"Even the colonel praised you—in writing."

"Yes, sir." Uncle Andrew had come up with the scheme to break the colonel's jaw, thereby allowing the army to discharge him for striking an officer rather than send the wrong message to Congress by court-martialing him for selling cocaine that his unit had seized fair and square from Colombian narcoterrorists.

"Stesichorus may have convinced the Ancients not to bewail the dead, but I'm certain you agree that Washington Irving speaks to *our* hearts: 'The sorrow for the dead is the only sorrow from which we refuse to be divorced. Every other wound we seek to heal . . . ; but this wound we consider it a *duty* to keep open. . . . ' I have not forgotten how your uncle died."

"Neither have I, sir."

"Then get cracking on that A-plus."

5

JIM AWAKENED SWEATY and blurry-eyed after only an hour's sleep. It was stifling hot in the cabin. But it wasn't the heat that had jarred him into a murky awareness. Something was wrong. Something had changed. The familiar rush of water past the hull had ceased. In its absence he heard gear banging on deck; it sounded like somebody was clapping frying pans. He tried to stand. The boat rolled hard just as his feet hit the deck, and he flew across the cabin and smashed into the table.

He dragged himself by the ceiling handholds to the companionway and up the steps. The water looked glassy. But under its smooth surface, a heavy swell surged, rising and falling, slick as the back of a whale. Without a breath of wind in the sails to stop the swell from rolling the boat, the mast was whipping across the sky and the boom jerked sullenly at its sheets. Pulleys—blocks, sorry, Will—were banging, a winch was rattling, and ropes slapped the sails.

They had stopped dead. Becalmed.

"Goddamned lousy timing," Will yelled from the mast.

Jim turned around and saw Will at a halyard winch, cranking up the big, light air sail he called a blooper. The thin Dacron drooped from its halyard like panty hose hung from a shower rod.

"What happened?"

"We ran into the bloody Doldrums."

Will gazed despairingly at the useless sail. Then he turned his back on the sun and cast an anxious look west. The boat had drifted around so its stern was no longer facing the direction from which they had fled. "I hope to God they're not still following us."

"What about the motor?"

"There is no point wasting fuel," he answered slowly. "Not till we find out where the wind is. This calm could be ten miles wide or two hundred."

"Can we check the weather?"

"We'll see what comes in on the weather fax."

"Can't we go on-line?"

Will looked at his watch. "In a while," he said, still not moving.

Jim clung to the steps, bracing against the swell. It was too hot to sleep below. The slack sails shook in their frames, left, right, left, right, with every roll of the boat. He could feel a queasy wave of seasickness rising again.

Will walked heavily back to the cockpit, plodding like an old man, teetering on the moving deck. His face was as slack as the sails, more deeply lined than usual, and he looked as if he had put on twenty years since last night. He slumped into a cockpit seat and stared.

"I wish," he muttered. "I wish . . . Jim, do you ever ask yourself what you're doing with your life?"

"What?"

"Where it's going—what have you done?"

"Sure. When I'm trying to decide what to do next—how long do these Doldrums last?"

"Hours. Days. Weeks."

"Weeks?" Jim stared at the glassy water. Un-fucking-believable. And they had to get through this before they even got started to goddamned Africa. "Look, Will, if 'they' are following we should use the motor, right? Keep ahead of them."

"We'd run out of fuel."

"We should at least try the motor—do something to get away from them. . . ."

"Don't you ever look back? No, you're too young. What's to look back on? You've got your whole life ahead of you. Just you wait, it comes to all of us. You'll look back and say, Man, did I blow it. Look at the damage I caused. Why didn't I make something of myself, something real, instead of scrambling from scratch every morning I wake up?"

Jim couldn't help but laugh. "What are you talking about, Will? You're rich. You've got a beautiful boat. You don't have to go to work every day. Most people would kill to have your life."

"They're welcome to it. Body breaking down. Disks deteriorating. My neck hurts so much I can't sleep."

"I told you, look down when you're spinning. When you look ahead, you squeeze those disks."

"Yeah . . ." he trailed off, morosely.

Jim saw a little breeze riffle the water behind the boat. The sails filled, tentatively, and the boat began to move, but so slowly that she left no wake. Then a stronger gust fanned his face and she heeled a little, gathering way. On the road again, thought Jim. We're outta here. If the speed picked up a little more they would hear the water rushing again.

A loud *bang* shattered the silence.

Jim tried to look everywhere at once. It sounded like something had hit the boat or they'd run into something.

Then he saw the jib collapsing onto the foredeck. Will's voice cut through his confusion. "Let's get that sail in before we run it over." He scampered lightly forward. Jim followed and helped gather and tie the cloth.

"What happened?"

"We popped the head stay," Will said calmly, hurrying back to the wheel and overriding the auto-helm to put the boat into a broad turn.

"What does that mean?"

"It means there's not much holding the mast. Maybe our timing isn't so bad after all; if it parted in a real wind, we'd have serious problems."

"What do you mean, 'holding the mast'? It would fall overboard?"

"On the cockpit, actually." Will smiled. "Which would be hell on the mast and make a mess of the teak, not to mention those of us it landed on. You want to jump below and bring me the red tool kit?"

Jim scrambled down the companionway, pawed frantically through the tool locker, and ran back up with the red box.

Will had completed the turn and what little wind there was blowing was now behind the boat. "All right, that'll take the pressure off. We're going to jury-rig a temporary stay with a halyard. Take the wheel. Just keep the wind behind us."

The old man loped forward, released an idle halyard, and walked to the bow, where he threaded it through the bullnose hole in the center of the bow and clipped it onto a sturdy mooring cleat. Jim couldn't help but admire his ease: Will might be nuts, but when handling tools or cooking a meal or steering the sailboat through heavy seas he was always in the zone.

Returning to the mast, Will cranked a winch until the halyard ran taut from the top of the mast to the front of the boat.

"Okay, let's drop the main."

They furled the mainsail and the boat started rolling again. "The halyard will act as a stay to hold the mast up until we replace the head stay. You want to learn how to crimp wire cable?"

He opened the red box, which contained his rigging tools. "Flip a coin to see who goes up the mast."

Jim lost. Will winched him skyward in a safety harness. It was sort of like a climbing wall. But height multiplied the boat's motion, until the mast was whipping him around like a yo-yo.

Andy Nickels turned a slow, grim circle. I can smell that prick, he thought. I am so close.

The catamaran had covered eighty miles in an hour, a distance that would have taken Will Spark all night. He must have come this way. He had to lower his sails to not be seen, and the east wind would not stop him from motoring east.

But the equatorial ocean was closing in flat and empty everywhere Nickels looked, and shrinking smaller in the haze. The whitecaps had dissolved in the failing wind, so that the only change in the featureless glare was the relentless ascent of the sun. Had he guessed wrong? Should he have gone west? Or north? Or south?

"How much fuel would he carry?"

The captain answered. The fight was out of him. He would steer his ferry to Antarctica if Nickels told him to. "Hundred, hundred and fifty gallons."

"More like seventy-five," Greg interrupted. Nickels nodded. He had recruited his chief bodyguard from the navy, so he ought to know about boats. "Range?"

Greg said, "Modern fifty-foot sailboat, he's got a seventy-five-horse diesel. Burns a gallon an hour at eight knots. Depends on when he topped his tank up and how much he's burned for refrigeration, electricity, and hot water—four hundred and fifty to six hundred miles."

"So he can't keep on motoring."

"Two or three days he'll be running on empty. No electricity. No radar, no radio, no GPS. Blind, deaf, and lost."

"Captain, what do you make of the weather?"

"It looks like the Doldrums are spreading. If he's come this way he's lost his wind."

"No shit. What about this haze?"

"My guess, it'll get thicker."

Nickels stared at the radar. He picked up a two-way radio and spoke to the lookouts he'd posted atop the *Barcelona*'s wheelhouse. "Report."

"Nothing."

"Nothing."

"Captain! No way he got past here. Start another search pattern."

* * *

It took what seemed like hours to get the crimp right. When Jim was done, Will lowered him from the masthead, then went up himself to check it.

He came down, elated.

"I just saw cat's-paws about a mile off and the haze is lifting. We've got some wind. Let's get the sails up. Nice job on the crimp."

But moments after they got under way, the wind died again. Will's spirit, which had risen while he made the repair, plummeted deeper than before.

Jim brought his dumbbells up on deck and started doing reps. The spinning bikes were keeping his legs in shape, but he was losing definition in his arms and pecs.

"Sometimes," Will said out of nowhere, picking up the old lament, "I feel so tired. Like I've used up my strength, and I'll never restore my energy."

Jim pretended neutral sympathy while he curled the weights. For a personal trainer, listening to the road-not-taken lament went with the job. He could recite by heart the dirges of his middle-aged clients: the executive wished he had been a photographer; the lawyer wanted to make movies; the doctor should have served in an inner-city clinic; the Wall Street guy wished he had spent time with his children, or at least stayed in touch after the divorce.

The only thing unusual about Will's lament was that Jim had never heard it before from Will. That was one of things Jim had liked about him, and a chief reason he'd agreed to go sailing. Now Will, too, was turning maudlin with regrets.

"Don't waste it like I did."

"Waste what, Will?" For some reason, when older rich men got regretful, they always warned *him* not to waste *his* talents. As if every young person had talents to waste. But Will surprised him.

"Your good manners. Don't waste your good manners. I learned ease and polish to sell myself. My 'social skills' were like a sail catching whatever wind came along. I should have just enjoyed them."

Suddenly, Will stood up, braced himself against the vicious roll by gripping the traveler sheets, and stared west.

"What do you see?"

"I'm not sure." He scoped the horizon with his binoculars. Then he passed them to Jim. "Your eyes are better. White on white—moving—almost dead astern."

Jim swept the glasses clumsily over the horizon. The haze had lifted, but not by much. The rolling made it impossible to concentrate on a specific field; sky, horizon, and sea tumbled in the lenses.

"I don't see anything. Why don't you try your radar?"

"I told you. Our radar will give away our position."

Jim shook his head, silently. If you wanted an answer, ask a paranoid.

"Jim, I'm sorry I got you into this mess."

"Why don't we start the motor?"

"Not yet. We need our fuel for the freezers and emergencies."

"Maybe this is an emergency."

"You ever just wish you could start over again?"

Jim said, "I think we're ready for another spinning class. What do you say we hump the bikes up and do a hill climb?"

But Will just shook his head and stared at the sea. Then he closed his eyes and fell asleep. The wind died. The swells rolled the boat worse, even though the water surface was as still as glass. Jim felt like an ant trying to cross a bowl of Jell-O.

Ten minutes before Jim's watch ended, Will was awake, alert, ready to take over, and Jim was struck by his ability to operate so efficiently on little more sleep than catnaps in the cockpit. But his spirit was bleaker than before.

If I could only cheer him up, Jim thought, then maybe I could make him see sense. "I could use some exercise. Are you sure you don't want to spin?"

"Positive. You want exercise, use the rowing machine."

"What rowing machine?"

Silently, communicating with impatient gestures, Will showed Jim how to unpack the yacht's rubber dinghy, inflate it, and boom it over the side. It bounced on the water like a toy. "Be my guest."

Stepping off the yacht into a tiny rubber boat in the middle of the ocean seemed foolhardy. What if the wind suddenly sprang up and blew him away? What if night fell and he found himself all alone with a pair of oars in his hand and no food or water?

"Are you coming?"

"I'm on watch. I'll stay with the boat."

"Any advice?"

"It's just like a rowing machine."

"I've never seen a rowing machine jump around like that. Listen, I'm kind of new at this. I think I'd like a rope."

"What for?"

"To tie on. What if I drop an oar or something? How do I get back?"

A faint smile lit Will's face. "I'll give you a three-hundred-foot line—don't worry, you don't have to use the whole thing. Besides, we're not going anywhere anytime soon."

Suddenly *Barcelona*'s radar showed a target three miles north. "Go! Go!"

The ferry closed in minutes.

"Lookouts!"

"Nothing."

"Nothing."

". . . There!"

Nickels saw it at the same time as Greg, glinting gray, low in the water. It looked like they had lowered their mast to make a smaller target.

Captain Moser shouldered the helmsman aside, slowed the catamaran, and circled. But as they drew nearer, Andy Nickels saw that the boat had foundered or capsized. It was mostly underwater, just breaking the smooth surface as it rose and fell on the swells.

"Greg, send a diver. I want him alive!"

But before Greg could move, Captain Moser said, "It's not a boat. It's a container."

"What?"

"A cargo container that fell off a freighter. It's half sunken. You see 'em all the time."

Nickels studied the object through binoculars, bitterly disappointed, yet relieved that Will Spark hadn't drowned. The McVays needed him alive. He looked at the radar.

"You can see a submerged container, but you can't see an entire sailboat?"

Figuring that it was best not to rile the American by suggesting that for all they knew the sailboat was 150 miles in the opposite direction, the captain answered, "I've seen radar pick up a floating barrel. And I've seen it confuse a barge tow with a headland. It's not a perfect science."

Nickels signaled the captain to resume the search pattern and the catamaran regained speed. But they were skimming the murky sea in an ever-contracting dome of visibility.

And it would be night soon. A needle in a haystack. He was wasting time out here. There were better ways to track the bastard.

"Captain, where's the nearest land with an airport?"

"Cape Verde Islands."

"Do it!"

"Yes, sir!"

Captain Moser punched the Portuguese islands' coordinates into the GPS. *Barcelona* could cover the thousand miles in fifteen hours. "I'll have you in Praia tomorrow morning." To the helmsman he said, "Come to zero-four-zero," and the helmsman banked her hard left before Andy Nickels changed his mind.

Nickels left Greg in charge of the bridge and went down to the passenger cabin. Rage, he knew, was mangling his ability to think straight. So he began to walk in an endless circle. Round and round the bland, gray cabin he went, plodding angrily through the empty seats. He shouted out loud, cursed, and slammed his massive fists into the padded headrests. A Caterpillar mechanic sacked out on a row of seats crawled in terror to the nearest door. Nickels began to move faster, rising onto the balls of his feet, shadowboxing now, throwing quick jabs and startling combinations. Gradually, he formed a plan.

The way to catch Will Spark was to station patrols at his likely stops: ambush him east, west, north, and south. Deny him access to his lairs. Wear him down with disappointed hopes until the thief lost the strength to run.

Nickels took his sat phone to a quiet corner and commenced a long day and night of encrypted conversations with arms dealers, soldiers, smugglers, and cops in ports on both coasts of the North and South Atlantic. Ten years with the U.S. Army Rangers fighting narcoterrorists left him well connected in Central and South America and throughout the Caribbean. He was thinner on the ground in Africa, though not by much, having established contacts there among the oilmen drilling offshore. Wherever his uncle had taken him around, the local security guy was often someone he'd known in the service. Still, it would have been easier if Will Spark had gone west. Problem was, Nickels could still almost smell him; the thief was out here, somewhere, headed east.

6

Dear Shannon,
Just wanted to flashmail a quick hi.
I learned how to row. We were stuck in the Doldrums—no wind—so I went rowing in the rubber dinghy.

Dear Jim,
Rowing sounds great. Did you tie a rope to the boat in case the wind came up and blew you away?

Dear Shannon,
Yeah, I had a line tied on real tight. For the first couple of times, until I knew I could get back on my own.
And, hey, I climbed the mast to fix a broken stay! Will taught me how to crimp the wire and he said I did a good job.

Dear Jim,
Boy, I'll bet you were glad you worked out on the climbing wall. What was it like when you looked down? How high is the mast?

"Will, let's talk about 'they.'"
"What about 'em?"

"Who is chasing you? And why?"

It was a week since their abrupt change of course—five days since they had finally motored out of the Doldrums—monotonous days of pearly overcast skies, dark nights, and a slow if steady six knots on the knot meter. Jim began to entertain vague hopes of a storm—anything for a change. Will's retort was "Bite your tongue."

Lulled (dulled?) by the constant northeast trade wind, calmed (numbed?) by the orderly, moderate swell, the thick heat, and the regular watches on and off by the clock, Jim had submitted to the reality that Will had added weeks to their voyage. But if the "adventure" was longer, it wasn't any bigger and he still entertained the hope that if he could convince Will that "they" were a fantasy, his employer would change course and let him off early. The books in the nav station said that the Cape Verde Islands had an international airport. The Cape Verde Islands were a lot closer than Nigeria and sounded a lot safer.

"Who are 'they,' Will? Who's chasing you?"

Will shrugged. He looked away. "Sometimes in business you disappoint people."

"What do you mean?"

"Let's say you forgot to show up for a spinning class. Or you missed a personal trainer appointment, pissed off your clients."

"But they're not chasing me. Or, should I say, I'm not running from them."

"Well, sometimes you disappoint the wrong people. People who take disappointment personally. Hey, it's hot as hell. Feel like going swimming?"

"Here?"

Jim looked over the side. The water sliding past was several miles deep, an unappetizing gray color, with God-knows-what swimming under its impenetrable surface. "I'll pass. These people you disappointed? What kind of people are we talking about?"

"Angry people." Will winked and flashed his most engaging smile. Jim ignored the invitation to join the laugh, insisting instead, "I don't know a lot about business, but I gather from my lawyer clients that angry people usually sue when they're disappointed. Then, if you keep on disappointing them, the law chases you."

"There is no law out here, son."

"So . . . how do I put this? That ship—if it was a ship—contained angry, disappointed people who are, shall we say, outlaws?"

"Listen, smart mouth, there's no 'if.' It was a ship. The people on board that ship don't mess around with lawsuits. Okay? You got your answer?"

"You're being hunted by criminals?"

"If only that were true."

"Why?"

"If they were common criminals, I could call the cops. I'm going swimming. You want to come?"

"No."

"Up to you."

"If they're not criminals, and you can't call the cops, who the hell are they?"

Will opened a hatch and pulled out a neatly coiled length of line and a safety harness, which he buckled around his chest. Then he climbed out of the cockpit and ran the line through a block at the end of the boom. He tied one end to his harness and ran the other through a deck block and wrapped it around an idle winch.

"Let out the main."

Jim traced the mainsheet from the boom through its traveler and loosened the proper winch. The mainsail swung away.

"Cleat it off," Will ordered when the boom was hanging six feet over the water, rising and falling with the roll of the boat.

He handed Jim the end of his line, stepped over the safety lines, and jumped. Then, dangling in his harness, hanging from the end of the boom, he yelled, "Lower me into the water."

Jim eased on Will's line until Will was dragged along the side of the boat, pushing off the hull with his feet and being alternately submerged and raised as the boat rolled.

"Fantastic!" he whooped. "Oh man, this is beautiful."

Watching him frolic, Jim began to feel the oppressive heat more than ever. Will looked cool and clean, as happy as a baby in a backyard pool.

"You gotta try this. It's fantastic."

But the water was gray, the body of it invisible. It looked like it was eating Will, who disappeared every time the boat dunked him.

"Okay, haul me in."

Jim cranked the winch, which raised Will out of the water. Then he cranked the mainsheet and drew the boom into the boat.

Will scrambled over the safety lines, laughing. "Oh man, you gotta try it."

Jim was afraid. What if there were sharks?

"You know what you are?" Will teased. "You're the 'Climate-Control Kid.'"

"What is that supposed to mean?"

"If you're not in the air-conditioned mall with a roof over your head, you're scared."

"What are you talking about? I just don't feel like swimming."

"You're a suburban health club mall rat. You're afraid of the outdoors."

"Hey, screw you. I'm not afraid. I'll swim if it makes you happy."

"It'll make *you* happy." Will laughed. "You'll feel like you're flying."

Flying turned out to be the perfect word. The boat rolled and the boom swept him high. When it rolled the other way, the boom dropped him in the warm water. It was incredibly exhilarating, and the jolt of the water yanked a happy yell from deep in his gut.

"Shove off with your feet!"

Jim swung himself in the harness, aligned his feet with the hull, and pushed off. Then he was whipped into the sky again and dunked a moment later, the water rubbing him, sluicing him clean of sweat.

"This is fantastic." He hadn't felt so clean in his life. He should have done this days ago. He yelled again, pushed off, jumped high. As he rose from the water, he saw Will peering past him. Watching something. There was something alongside, something in the water. Jim could sense it moving beside him, keeping pace. His heart jumped, his stomach shriveled. "Will!"

Will leaned out. "Jesus, is that a dolphin?"

The rolling boat plunged Jim into the water again. He craned his neck and saw a thick gray body draw near. "It's a shark! It's a shark. Pull me in."

"That's not a shark—hell, maybe it is."

"Will, pull me up." Trapped in the sling, bouncing in and out of the water, Jim panicked. "Will, save me!"

"Easy, easy, easy. I got you." But to Jim's horror, Will seemed to be moving very, very slowly, reaching for the winch handle as if he had all the time in the world. The thing in the water came closer and Jim screamed.

The boom snapped him out of the water. But a second later it dropped him in again as if to feed him to whatever was waiting. "Will!"

"I got you. Don't blow a gasket," Will shouted from the winch. Slowly he cranked and slowly Jim rose higher in the water. Will called, "Hey, you're in great shape, which is always an advantage in surviving shark bites. Main thing is . . . don't go into shock when they bite you. Shock will kill you."

"Get me up!"

Will cranked harder. Then he hauled in the mainsheet, and Jim found himself clinging to the safety lines, desperately holding up his legs, imagining a shark sliding up the side of the boat and taking his foot in jagged rows of razor teeth.

Will helped him over the lines and he half fell into the cockpit, where he huddled as he tried to contain his panic by gulping deep breaths of air to dissipate the adrenaline rampaging through his system.

"Give you a tip," said Will. "If you want to swim with the sharks, you better swim with strong strokes; don't splash around like you're weak and dying, and bump them back when they bump you. Bump 'em back! Show 'em you're still alive—though I got to tell you, that looked to me like a friendly dolphin. In fact, there's some now. Aren't those dolphins?"

Jim looked at the gray water. Crescent shapes were cutting in and out of the sea, pacing the boat.

"Looks to me like you got spooked by Flipper."

Frightened, angry, and embarrassed by his weakness, Jim slowly caught his breath and took charge of his body and his spirit. Will was chuckling as if it were the funniest joke he'd ever heard.

"The CC Kid," he said. "I'm shipmates with the Climate-Control Kid."

Jim stood up. His knees were trembling. His hands were still shaking. But terror and the mind-dissolving panic were coiling into rage. He wanted to take Will by the throat and squeeze the laughter out of him. He stared fixedly behind the boat. "Here comes that ship again."

Will went dead white. He spun around, pawed his binoculars from their rack, and swept a barren and completely empty horizon. Slowly the color returned to his face.

" 'Bumped' me back." He smiled at last, "Very funny. So you're a counterpuncher. Didn't know you had it in you."

"If you ever do something like that to me again I'll tear your fucking head off."

"Or maybe it's just a hot temper," Will replied. Then he fell silent. A vague smile played on his lips, as if he knew something even funnier.

As the old man slid down into his private world, the truth struck Jim like lightning. Will Spark truly believed he was being hunted.

Dear Shannon,

Jim stared at the screen. He was more baffled than ever by Will's behavior. Even if the man was being hunted by his enemies, how did that relate to "Shark Attack"?

He started typing, watching the event unfold on the computer screen,

> ... And now I'm wondering—why? Was he just plain cruel? Or did he do it to control me, shut me up, make me his obedient shipmate?

Delete.

In the cool lines of computer print, he looked like a real jerk.

> Dear Shannon,
> Funny thing happened the other day: I mistook a dolphin for a shark, which ordinarily wouldn't have mattered a whole hell of a lot. But being in the water, swimming from the boom, it mattered a lot. To me, at least. In fact, you might even say I flipped out over Flipper.
> Fortunately, Will was not fooled. So he took a long, long, long time to pull me out. A *llloooooonggg* time. Huge laugh. But maybe you had to be here.

7

WILL'S YACHT WAS named *Hustle*.

Jim's first sight of the fifty-foot sloop had been a saber silhouette in the glare of the Barbados fishing boat's search-light: a spiry mast, two drum-tight sails, and a lean hull slashing the waves. What had looked from a distance like slicing the seas was altogether different on board—an end-less, erratic chain of heart-stopping crashes as *Hustle* pounded through waves and stomach-dropping lurches as she fell into their troughs.

Will had assured him that things would calm down once they sailed into deeper water. But by daylight, they were get-ting mauled by short, steep seas breaking over the deck. Jim, unable to eat, drink, sleep, or even move from the bunk Will finally dumped him into after he had emptied his guts in the airless toilet, would gladly have died.

Only many days later, after tentatively ingesting warm water and saltines, and prompted by Shannon's e-mail beg-ging him to describe everything he saw, could he begin to admire the drama of the boat's towering mast, the power of her thickset winches, and the rugged beauty of her broad wooden decks.

The sloop was, he came to realize, both a rich man's toy and a potent machine. Shannon's parents' health clubs were making money hand over fist, but none of the stuff they owned—house, ski house, SUVs, diamond jewelry—seemed as costly, as extravagant, or as purposeful as Will's yacht.

"Do you mind my asking what *Hustle* cost?" Jim asked one evening in the cockpit.

"I bought her cheap," Will answered casually, pausing for a sip from a tall gin and tonic. "Hong Kong's the best place in the world to get a bargain on a boat."

The old man had emerged from his paralyzing depression and seemed to have forgotten the fear that had driven him to change course. He was, this evening, in one of his talkative moods. So talk, Jim thought. You talk, and I'll ask questions till I nudge you around to "they."

"Why are boats cheap in Hong Kong?"

"That's how far couples sailing around the world to save their marriages get before they admit it was a lousy idea," Will said.

"Sailing or the marriage?"

Will grinned. "Both—don't get me started on marriage. I know you asked Shannon to marry you."

Jim regretted going into it, but Will had gotten him talking one night.

Will's grin broadened, exposing remarkably straight teeth. "I won't be the naysayer. You poor deluded fool. Fact is, Hong Kong was the only place I could *afford* to buy. These days, every time you turn around there're newer, richer new-rich parvenus crawling out of the woodwork, driving prices up. And I was broke."

Jim had worked for a number of well-off clients, but he was sure that Will was the richest man he had ever met. Will's kind of broke had nothing to do with how to pay next month's rent.

"My last divorce had really wiped me out. Ruinous— though worth every penny."

Jim looked away, irritated by the bluster. Aging macho man Will, with his faded Marine Corps tattoos and "manly" proclamations, was acting like an Ernest Hemingway retread.

"Am I offending you?" Will asked.

"Like you said, I was hoping to get married. I'm looking at the upside."

"Actually, I'm curious. Why'd she say no? Good-looking guy, sleepy eyes girls go for, and all them muscles . . . Did you tell me your parents were divorced?"

"No!"

Will gave him a quizzical look. "Something tells me—stop me if I'm wrong—they should have been. A long time ago."

"Why do you say that?"

"You're a nice kid. You're very polite. You have good manners. But you dislike older people. I'm guessing they put you through the wringer."

Jim stood up and climbed out of the cockpit. Crouching low and gripping the safety lines that fenced the decks, he headed forward.

"Hey, relax," Will called after him. "Forget I said that. Nobody knows about anybody else's marriage, especially their parents'. Inge had it right: *The Dark at the Top of the Stairs.*"

Jim kept going. Timing the roll of the boat—he was finally getting used to it—he swung through the narrow alley between the mast and the thick wire stays that guyed it—the shrouds, the side stays were called shrouds—and worked his way along the foredeck. At the bow he propped himself within the rails of the pulpit and gripped the forestay, which was thrumming with the press of the wind on the jib, and stared down at the water the hull was cleaving.

It wasn't that he hated older people. He didn't hate anybody. But he did carry baggage—Shannon's word—filled with his mother's frustrated longings and his father's inability to do anything about them. In reaction, he had learned from watching his mother not to want too much. While from his father, he feared, he had learned not to hope for too much and not to try too hard. So in a way, Will had guessed right.

He had always equated age with discouragement, disappointment, and deceit, and he had dreamed that when he left home the world would be a sunnier place.

For some reason, he had ended up commuting to college, not moving out until graduation. And after three longish relationships with gloomy, troubled women he had begun to question whether he deliberately sought out disappointment. Then he met Shannon. She was sunny enough for both of them, baggage and all. His and hers.

"You can't fix my legs," she had said when her father brought Jim into her bedroom.

Somehow—perhaps guessing that she had been a cheerful soul before the accident—he had known to answer, "I don't do legs. I'm here for the flabby arms."

She stared, stung, her gaze flicking to her sagging arms. "You'd be flabby, too, if you were stuck in bed for a year."

"This is what I would do if I were stuck in bed for a year."

Where he had gotten the nerve he would never know, but he had startled the heck out of her, himself, and her father by lying down on the bed beside her and curling ten reps of a five-pound dumbbell. They had held eye contact for the full ten reps of the right hand, and ten more of his left.

As they lay face-to-face on the sheets, six inches apart, her father gaping like a guy at a zoo, Jim had thought, God, what a pretty girl, and a smile had begun to light her blue eyes.

With their eyes still locked, Jim had rolled on his side, balanced on his hand, and started one-arm push-ups. The smile had traveled over her face and she said, still holding Jim's gaze, "Daddy, go away."

Where, Jim still wondered, had he gotten the nerve? How had he sensed that she was ready to emerge from despair? In any case, it had worked.

He could never make her walk normally. No one could. But he could help her get strong. Though that success had led them both to a new form of despair. "I don't want to be your job."

Suddenly the loud-hailer clacked on—Will was doing his "me hearties" voice. "Now hear this. All hands to the galley.

Them that helps bake apple pie gets a slice. Them that don't, starve."

Jim stayed on the bow long enough to preserve his dignity, then joined Will below, tempted less by food than by the prospect of any break in the routine. Will did his cooking at night, when the boat was the coolest.

"Hey, there you are," Will greeted him. "You start the crust. Sift two cups of flour into the big mixing bowl. Put the bowl in the sink. Remember what I told you: your only friend in a rolling galley is the sink."

Jim put the bowl on the counter instead and immediately regretted it. Will helped mop up the spilled flour. His crust, Will promised Jim, contained no unhealthy hydrogenized oil and only half a stick of butter for the whole pie. "We're here for apples, not butter." He showed Jim how to cut the butter into the flour with two knives. "Utensils only. Piecrust likes an icy touch." He put half the pastry aside in the cooler.

"Now I'm going to let you in on a secret. Never trust a woman, or a man, for that matter, who covers an apple pie with a top crust. A top crust *steams* the apples—ruins them. Now I know what you're going to say: your mom makes a little chimney in the middle of the crust, or she pricks it with a fork. Sorry, Mom, you can't vent the steam with pricks and chimneys."

"My mother bought pies at the Grand Union."

"And I suppose your old man never taught you how to change a tire."

"He called Triple A."

"You'd have been better off in a foster home. Your parents robbed you of a hands-on life. It's never too late to change—I told you, you did a good job crimping that head stay."

"It was like working on the bike."

"Just remember you're dealing with a thousand times the loads—all right, half the dough we'll roll out for our bottom crust. The other half, we'll put aside for our crumb topping."

A wine bottle served as Will's rolling pin. He flattened the dough between sheets of waxed paper. "Note, we're not handling it too much, not pummeling it over and over, so we don't make it tough. Find the apples in the freezer—right-hand side, halfway down. In and out quick as you can—save the cold—use the flashlight."

Jim pawed through the Ziploc bags of fresh chickens Will had washed and salted before he froze them, dry-aged strip steaks, pork chops, cooked veal and sausage stews, and legs of lamb. Halfway down on the right he found a plastic bag of sliced apples, brown sugar, quince, cloves, cinnamon, ginger, allspice, and nutmeg—one of a dozen Will had prepared before he set sail.

The weather fax machine in the nav station beeped. "Check it out," said Will. "See what's coming our way."

Jim picked up the paper flowing from the printer. Superimposed across the weather map for the eastern equatorial Atlantic were three lines of computer-generated block print.

NO MAN IS AN ISLAND, NOT EVEN A CLOD ON A YACHT. COM-MUNICATE, BEFORE WE CATCH A THIEF.

"What the heck is this?" He recognized the fractured John Donne from Ren Lit. But how had it gotten into a public broadcast of the weather report?

"Will, look at this."

Will scanned it. "Son of a bitch," he whispered under his breath. Then he read aloud, affecting nonchalance. " 'No man is an island, not even a clod on a yacht.' Oh, very clever."

"Who's it from?" asked Jim.

"A poet who didn't know it." Will crumpled the sheet and climbed halfway up the companionway to toss it to the wind.

Jim stared at him, wondering whether Will's explanation about why he couldn't call the cops was bullshit. Was Will the criminal? Were the mysterious "they" the law?

"Sticks and stones will break my bones, but faxes will never hurt me." He slid his hand under the waxed paper, placed the pan upside down over the rolled dough, and flipped it into the pan. Quickly he fluted the edges of the crust, shaping the dough between his thumbs and index fingers.

"But how did that message get into the weather fax?"

"I told you, they are powerful. If it can be done, they can do it. How? Either they hacked their way in or they bribed some underpaid technician to look the other way. Pie filling, please."

"What do they mean, 'communicate'? Could it be an offer to negotiate?"

"If we were to slip this pie in the oven for an hour, we could build an appetite with a spinning class."

"Communicate or else?"

"Empty threat," said Will. "This poet who doesn't know it is stuck behind a PC somewhere and we're safe in the middle of the ocean—as long as we keep our eyes peeled for ships. *Ships* are a threat. They've got their hooks into the big shipping companies, the Russian merchant fleets, the oil company tankers, offshore towing outfits, Taiwanese container ships, the Dutch, the—"

"Every ship in the world?"

"The fleets, where they know the owners. That's why we're keeping our eyes peeled. Spinners on deck, Herr Instructor. *Mach schnell!"*

They showered the sweat off under the fire hose—pumping warm, salty seawater over each other on the foredeck. The pie, with Breyer's vanilla ice cream from the freezer, tasted like no pie Jim had ever eaten: the apples seemed like an impossible combination of tart and sweet, and the crust was crisp and airy.

I'm like Shannon's cat, he thought. All good things come from Will. If Will opens the door and fills my food dish, I eat. If he freaks out and jumps overboard, I drift until I sink. I either starve or have to go hunting on my own. That's where the analogy breaks down. I don't know how to hunt.

"Where'd you learn your table manners?"

"What?"

"You know how to use a knife and fork. I don't meet many thirty-year-olds who do. Our 'gold rush' economy spawns frontier manners. You have . . . habits."

"My mother was a nut for properness. Drove me and my dad nuts with it. 'We may not have money, but we use a proper linen napkin.' That sort of thing."

"Sounds like an old-fashioned upbringing."

"They were older and I think my mother, at least, thought things had been better in the past."

"What did your father think?"

"He didn't say. . . . He thought it was bullshit, but he went along. . . . He was an old hippie. Love and peace at any cost."

"Sounds like Mom was a force to be reckoned with."

"Shannon says she was a control freak at home because she couldn't make it in the real world."

"What do you think?"

"I'm still too close to it. But I think Shannon's right. Underneath all her demandingness, my mother was very, very needy." He smiled, suddenly happy. "You won't be surprised to hear that she and Shannon can't stand each other—I'm going to check my e-mail."

"Why not? Maybe Shannon's changed her mind."

"Maybe 'they' have changed their minds."

Dear Jim,
Your shark-and-flipper experience sounds a little weird. Is Will a little weird?

Dear Shannon,
Weird, I don't know. Maybe Will was a little cold-blooded, but maybe cold-blooded is what makes him so cool and collected when something goes wrong with the boat.
I have to admit that if it happened again, I hope I'd keep my eyes open long enough to really see what's going on before I freak out.

Lloyd McVay, a tall, stooped man in a glen-plaid suit and florid bow tie, telephoned ports up and down the coasts that rimmed the Atlantic Ocean. His reach extended from Brazil to the island of Antigua in the Caribbean, to Miami on the

American mainland, to Dakar in Senegal on the great bulge of West Africa; in Freetown, Lagos, Gibraltar, the Azores, and Bermuda, bankers, importers, shipping agents, oilmen, diamond merchants, and diplomats took his calls, eager to please.

Val McVay, his daughter and chief grant officer of the McVay Foundation for Humane Science, worked across from him on the other side of their partners desk, e-mailing yacht clubs and marinas on those same coasts. She was a pale woman, dressed all in black; her face was as white as paper, her close-cropped hair was ash-blond, and her wide-open, wide-set eyes were dark. The goals list she kept on a pad beside her included polling a score of charter yacht captains she knew from her sailing days and a hundred scientists, engineers, and academics beholden to the foundation.

Raised a lone child among adults, she had learned early to read faces and eyes: their assistants—three recently minted MBAs in dark suits, white shirts, and bow ties deferentially imitative of her father's signature neckwear—were experiencing real terror; even her father was feeling pressed.

The disaster was writ large on the jumbo high-resolution flat-panel display that showed an electronic chart of the Atlantic Ocean. The red line that marked Will Spark's voyage from Barbados ran out abruptly midocean. The icon that had represented the fast ferry *Barcelona* was beached, as it were, in the Cape Verde Islands, where Andy Nickels had disembarked. Except for the useless red line and the ferry icon, nine million square miles of seawater depicted on the chart were empty. The enormous circle of blue that marked how far Spark could have sailed in the past week already encompassed an area larger than Europe.

A dozen smaller monitors displayed CNBC, CNN, C-SPAN, and a range of science and engineering websites. The only decoration in their large, windowless office was a vintage poster for the movie *Fantastic Voyage*—her father's idea. Their desk was littered with telephones and computer monitors. A printer sighed in a corner, attended by an MBA. A second MBA was whispering into a phone. The third was poised to retrieve paper files from a bank of cabinets.

Lloyd McVay said, "I should speak with someone in the oil business, in the event Spark heads for his old stomping grounds in West Africa."

"Richard Hood at Shell," suggested Val. "We gave his brother a lab grant."

"Dick's an accountant, for goodness' sake. Bob Hunt oversees security."

Val's grandfather had founded McVay Radio, building transceivers for the air force in World War II and microwave generators for the then-new radar. After a long stint with the CIA, her father had taken over, renaming the company Mc-Vay Microwaves in time for the Vietnam War and the NASA moon project, and developing transmitters and laser generators for the Defense Department, NASA, and private industry. He had made a second fortune by jumping down from elite technology into PCs for ordinary people. With the company catchphrase, "There are more of them than us," McVay Computers sold cheaper and cheaper computer chips by the billions.

After graduating first in her class at Stanford, Val had joined him in the race to design high-speed browsers for the Internet. But here they stumbled. Their technically brilliant effort was steamrollered by Microsoft at the cost of much money and most of the McVay prestige. Silicon Valley now knew the tall, stooped patrician Lloyd McVay as an older businessman who managed the benevolent-sounding, nonprofit, tax-exempt McVay Foundation for Humane Science, and his reclusive daughter as one of the legion of thirty-something women left in the cyber dust.

In fact, the McVays had regrouped in New Jersey horse country and, under the cloak of their foundation, set their sights on a third fortune that would dwarf the first two. It meant being first on-line when the fifty-year-old electronics mantra "smaller and faster" transformed the Internet by linking ultra-miniature microprocessors to the world's database.

Dispensing grants to an array of engineering projects, Val and her father had devoted the past six years to launching the next great Internet breakthrough. They had finally found it in Sentinel—one of hundreds of developments the foundation had financed. But first they had to find Will Spark, who had stolen it.

"Merchant ships should watch for them offshore. Can you call Vassily Nikolin?"

"The man authenticates with relentless enthusiasm the cliché of Russian dipsomania."

"Whom do you suggest?" she shot back. She hated playing catch-up. It went against her grain. She was willing to accept that plenty of people were smarter than she, but no one was better organized or worked harder.

"Admiral Boris Rugoff," her father replied. "And, obviously, I'm already in touch with the towing companies that service the oil fields."

"And fishing fleets?"

"You know perfectly well that we're thin on the ground there," her father snapped.

"I know that there are thirteen hundred European Union trawlers licensed around the world."

"Well, unless you've become intimate with some fishermen I've yet to meet—"

"What about the navy?"

"It goes without saying that I've already had a preliminary conversation with Fleet Ocean Intelligence."

Val checked her goals list. Yacht clubs, merchant ships, work boats, fishing fleets, and the possibility of enlisting the U.S. Navy had all been covered.

For her, the worst part of this catastrophe was that she had come aboard late. When it first hit—which was to say, when Will Spark first screwed them—they had decided that she would take care of day-to-day affairs, freeing her father to devote his full time to managing the crisis. It was he, after all, who had always handled the dark side of the business— assisted by old Andrew Nickels—when lobbying had to be augmented by the well-placed bribe, dirt had to be dug up to smear a persistent rival, a critic was to be silenced, a security breach plugged, or an enemy punished.

But when Spark suddenly disappeared and Andrew Nickels killed himself, Val, with her entire future at stake, had had to step in. She had discovered that her flair for conceiving and managing long-term projects was suited to fighting deceit with deceit. Coupled with her technical expertise, she had the powerful feeling that she could play the dark games even better than her father. Proof was her idea to trace Spark by bugging Jim Leighton's heart-rate monitor. An opportunity that Andy Nickels, her father's latest protégé, had squandered.

She watched an assistant slide an open folder onto Lloyd McVay's desk. Another handed him a wireless telephone. McVay ran his finger down the dossier and glanced at the nine-by-twelve glossy photograph of the oil company executive.

"Bob Hunt! It's been too long since we've heard from you. . . . How's that tennis game going? Elbow still giving you trouble?" His finger traced columns of print. "Estelle is well, I trust? Must be wrapping up that nanotech book by now. . . . Still at it? . . . No thanks are necessary; we prefer to support better causes than the Internal Revenue Service— though you might remind Estelle that we like to see our projects completed on time. . . . Now, Bob, we've gotten a hint of trouble in your patch . . . over the transom as it were. It's possible—not yet a certainty—that Greenpeace is targeting your offshore operations in the Niger Delta. . . . A two-lantern coming, if you get my meaning. . . . By sea. Under your radar on a sailboat. . . . I'll send a man around with a description of the boat and crew. . . . You're welcome—but there is one thing, Bob. We have first dibs on them. . . . That's *exactly* what I mean." McVay's voice was abruptly drained of good nature. "They severely injured the captain of one of our research vessels with their shenanigans and we intend to bring charges. We'll take them off your hands the instant you get them. . . . That's right, Bob. No skin off your nose."

A message from a receptionist crawled across Val's monitor: a geology team from Cambridge was still waiting to present their final report on earthquake predictors. She forwarded "I'll blow them off" to her father's screen.

Exiting their private office, she opened double-locked foyer doors with her thumbprint, then hurried out of the mansion she shared with her father, descended the granite front steps, and crossed the winter-bleak gardens on a path of crushed slate.

The McVay Foundation for Humane Science presented its public face in a former fifty-stall brood barn—a huge stone structure converted into numerous offices, conference rooms, and a great hall that could be used for presentations and formal dinners. The Cambridge scientists were waiting in the reception room, leafing through the foundation's four-color annual reports and making the rounds of the many framed photographs of her father, who was pictured shaking hands with presidents and grinning at disadvantaged children who had benefited from McVay generosity. They leapt to their feet when Val strode in.

"Ladies. Gentlemen. Mr. McVay is disappointed he will not be able to greet you in person. He looks forward to reading your report and we will get back to you in due course. The limousines will take you back to New York. Thank you for coming."

"But we brought slides," said a long-haired geologist.

"We'll look at them," said Val, and then, with a hazy realization that the scientists were not happy, she added, "Of course we'll look at them. We paid for them."

She hurried back to the house and her desk. A new file was being presented to her father along with a telephone.

Val, who vastly preferred the bluntness of e-mail to the chitchat required on the telephone, turned to her keypad to send blind copies to every yacht captain in her address file:

Have you seen the fifty-foot, one-off sloop *Hustle*? Center cockpit, high aspect rig, Hong Kong registry, new teak decks, distinctive wooden spoked wheel, white hull.

Val brought a file of research vessels up on her screen and began e-mailing McVay grant recipients aboard those currently at sea. Across the desk, her father was describing *Hustle* to the chairman of a Taiwanese container fleet.

Will Spark had contrived to lose himself on a big ocean. But for the owners of a foundation that underwrote research and development with grants and incubator money, disbursed first-class travel expenses to conferences and retreats, and lobbied congressmen and military officers with studied generosity, the big ocean was surrounded by a very small world.

8

SECOND-DAY PIE tastes better than first-day pie, because pie needs time to steep. So real wealth," said Will Spark, "would be the means to employ servants to eat your first-day pie."

He chewed slowly, savoring a forkful. "I mean *real* wealth."

"Who are 'they,' Will? Who's chasing you?"

"Question is, how the heck wealthy are *you* going to get as a personal trainer?"

"Not very. Who is chasing you?"

"Personal trainers serve money, they don't make money. You ever ask yourself where it's taking you?"

Jim looked out at the water. *Hustle* was slogging through low swells. The horizon pressed close today. The sky sagged low. The air was so thick that the shirts and shorts he had hung out to dry were still as wet as when he pulled them from the washing machine.

"I mean long-term," said Will.

His career future was not a happy subject. He was twenty-nine. Thirty loomed and cast a shadow of his limitations. "I used to think I'd hit the big bucks bike racing."

"Endorsements? You're talking top ten. That's like breaking into the NBA."

"And I was also hoping to get into the top ten of triathlon. My swimming was tops. I'm good on the bike. But I'm too slow a runner. I'd lose my points running. I don't even compete anymore."

"Well, what rank did you get to?"

"Nothing to write home about. . . . I wouldn't do the blood doping or any hormones, but like it or not, if you don't, you're not in the top twenty."

Will reached over and lightly punched his biceps. "Not even steroids?"

"No way, man!"

"I wondered. Lot of bulk. So what are you going to do? Live off your wife?"

"No!"

"Hey, I'm just kidding you. I know you wouldn't do that. But how are you going to live?"

"I live. I pay my rent. I can cover my bills, run my car, but . . . I don't know, maybe I'll go back to school."

Will's jowls and scars scrunched up in an expression that scorned professional students. "What did you study in college?"

"Lit and history."

"Good beginning. No reason why you couldn't turn that into an MBA. These days there's more and more respect for a liberal arts degree—the flexibility it teaches you—*if* you cap it with a business degree."

"I don't want to be a businessman."

"Why not? You got a problem with business?"

"I don't think I'm competitive enough."

Will looked at him, surprise on his face. "Good answer. That why you didn't win your bike races?"

"That and injuries."

"What injuries? That?" He pointed at a white scar on Jim's right knee.

"I got hurt a lot. Too many crashes. Too much overtraining. Shannon says I try to overcome my lack of competitiveness by beating up on my body."

"What does Shannon want?"

Jim, only vaguely aware that Will had once again turned their conversation on its ear and that he was answering more questions than he was asking, admitted, "That's complicated. She *says* she wants a simple life. She doesn't want the whole two-jobs, half-the-day-commuting lifestyle, nannies and housekeepers, all that fast-track-to-nowhere stuff. And no time for the kids."

"Not to mention each other," said Will.

"Shannon says young parents are like cellmates."

"I've said it before: she sounds like a sensible girl."

"Yeah, except that she doesn't have a clue about what it's like not to have money. Her father gives her anything she wants. She thinks it's normal to drive a new BMW."

"A boom-time baby."

Jim nodded. "If it wasn't for her mother nagging her to find a rich guy, she probably would have married one of their Westport neighbors."

"You were the rebellion?" Will asked with a smile.

"Not really. I mean, I was—as far as her mother is concerned."

"If I may be so blunt," said Will, "before she turned you down, did you ever ask yourself what you were doing with this girl?"

More often than Will could imagine, Jim reflected, for reasons he would never know. He answered, "We liked each other. In fact, we knew the second we met we were exactly what we wanted."

"I know the feeling well," Will said acidly. "Several of my marriages started on that basis."

"Yeah, well, it used to amaze me how I loved her more every day."

Will nodded gravely. "I underwrote some interesting research on a neuropeptide called oxytocin. Oxytocin influences pair bonding. And it seems that rubbing your sexual parts stimulates the brain to release oxytocin—which might explain your feelings. Scientists call it the 'cuddle hormone.' I'm still hoping to cash in."

Jim laughed. Then he said, "I still feel that way, even after she said no. I mean, I'm pissed, but Jesus, I miss her. And I gotta tell you, your long cut to Africa is killing me."

Will said, "Offshore, being a monk works best. Just shut it all down. You'd be amazed how you can crank it up again, when you get your arms around a warm woman. What did you say her father does?"

"He's got a chain of health clubs."

"Right. In Connecticut. How many?"

"Just took over his sixth. He's buying up the mom-and-pops and taking them big time. That's how we met. He bought one of the clubs I was working in. The one you came to in Bridgeport."

"And I'll bet that if Shannon ever changed her mind and married you, he and her mom would want you to manage one."

"If they couldn't strong-arm her into marrying a rich guy."

"But that's not money," Will scoffed. "*Money* is independence, not living off your father-in-law."

"Hey, I wouldn't be *living* off him. I'd be doing a job. A good job. I've got a lot of ideas for the clubs. Get people involved like it's their community. I'm thinking that the clubs could field bike-racing teams."

"Those fat-assed old ladies aren't paying to race bikes, Jim."

"You always came at the off-hours. There're plenty of young suits looking for a challenge. Business types and lawyers and all, who want to push themselves. It's not just fat ladies. . . . What am I saying? She doesn't want to marry me."

"If I wanted to run a gym, I'd do it in a big city. Give me a lean-and-hungry clientele."

"I wouldn't live in a city."

"Have you ever?"

"No."

"You really are a mall rat, aren't you?" Will chuckled. "Ever meet a black man?"

Jim did not answer. He didn't feel like he had to justify himself to Will. But the fact was, at work Jim always took pride in making eye contact with the towel boys and locker-room attendants, who were invariably black or Hispanic, and getting them to acknowledge his existence in return. It would often take months to bridge the divide of class and race, to make his face a recognizable island in a sea of white. But his reward, a friendly "Hey, buddy, how you doing?" made him feel he had made a place for himself in a world of blinding labels.

"Ever think of breaking out of the suburbs?"

"I got mugged in New York City."

Will laughed. "You're kidding. Nobody's been mugged there since Giuliani was mayor."

"Yeah, well, I was."

Will looked hard at him, suddenly serious. "What happened?"

"I was down there for the AIDS bike-a-thon. Guy flashed a knife: 'Gimme your dough.' I threw my bike at him."

"You're lucky he didn't have a gun."

"That's what Shannon said."

"A woman who continues to rise in my estimation."

"She was screaming at me. 'You could have been killed.' She was really freaking. 'What if he had a gun?'"

"That where you got that?" Will pointed at a thin white scar that formed a J down the front of Jim's thigh.

"Naw, that was a crash. I slugged him and he ran."

"Sounds like you have a temper, young friend."

"I was so pumped I didn't even think."

Will looked out over the sea. "Do you ever think of going for the big time?"

"What do you mean?" Jim asked warily. There were moments when he felt mired in failure. He liked his work, but fitness training was a prescription for low earnings, unless you turned it into a business.

"Everyone else has gotten rich these days—why shouldn't you?"

"Join the 'new rich'? How? Are you backing a company I should know about?"

"My boy, we are sailing to the African coast. Who knows what opportunities may come our way in the next few weeks."

Jim felt a sudden thrill. Was Will inviting him to share in

some deal? He never could quite figure out what venture capitalists did, except that they got rich at it. Clients sometimes gave him stock tips, but he never capitalized on them because he didn't have any money to invest.

"A guy told me about AOL back in 1996. I put my money into a four-year-old Honda instead. I could be worth three million now."

" 'If only,' " Will said, "makes the stock market go round."

"Are you going to give me stock tips in the middle of the ocean?"

"Why not? Trade on-line, and sail home to a fat bank account."

"What did you have in mind?" he asked.

"There's oil on the African coast, and where there's oil, there's money."

"Is that why you're going there?"

Will looked back at the wake and dashed his hopes of sudden wealth. "You know why I'm going there."

"No, Will, I don't. And I'd be goddamned grateful if you'd tell me."

Will sprang to his feet, took the helm, and overrode the autopilot. Like magic, *Hustle* felt suddenly livelier.

"I told you already: there are people who want my guts for garters. And I'll tell you something else, sonny: as long as there's water under this keel and wind in these sails, they're not going to get them."

Dear Shannon,
This is turning into a very strange trip.

Jim looked over his shoulder and glanced up the open hatch, where Will was standing watch in the cockpit. He would send this one in a quick Flash and Delete.

The real reason we changed course is that Will got spooked when he saw a ship and convinced himself that the people on it wanted to kill him. I know that sounds crazy. I think he is. A little.

He stopped typing. What was the point of scaring Shannon?

> But he's fine day to day. And sailing the boat beautifully. So what it comes down to is a longer trip for weird reasons. And a visit to Africa I'd never have experienced otherwise. In other words, a bigger adventure, but no big deal.

He checked his watch. The boat was one hour behind Greenwich Mean Time, four hours ahead of Connecticut. Shannon would be in her office, at her computer, when his message crawled across her screen.

He switched on the sat phone and flashmailed as Will.

When he checked ten minutes later, there was a letter from Shannon, titled "Learn!" and he wished right away he hadn't written.

> Jim, I'm so sorry I got you involved with a crazy man. Promise you'll learn immediately how to sail that boat by yourself. *Immediately!* What if he freaks out and jumps overboard?

Jim clicked Reply.

> Hey, don't worry, I didn't mean to upset you. I'm doing fine. I can take care of myself. I've already started to learn to sail. And please don't apologize. Encouraging me to do this was a wonderful gift.
>
> I'm having a ball. And I guarantee, Will is not the type to jump overboard.

After he flashmailed it, he was scanning the spines of the sailing manuals in Will's bookcase when he noticed the flashmail status window. E-mail had come in for Will entitled "Do not send. . . ."

> Do not imagine your sins can be washed away by the sea. No need to ask for whom the bell tolls, Will Spark, it tolls for the

thief. As the poet of the "sweet science" warns, "You can run but you cannot hide."

Jim printed it.

It was early afternoon. The sun was blazing high overhead and the sea would intensify it like a million moving mirrors. He donned a long-sleeve cotton shirt, rubbed sunblock on his hands and legs and face, put on sunglasses, and tugged a sailing visor low over his eyes.

Will, stripped to his shorts, was sweating in the shade of the canvas Bimini awning, which spanned the cockpit on a pipe frame. He had disassembled one of the water makers and spread its pieces out on the starboard bench.

"What's up?"

"Another letter from John Donne. And it's got your name on it."

Will read it in a glance and shook his head with a thin smile. "Frustrated English professor." He examined a gasket, picked through his green plumbing toolbox for a replacement, held them side by side to ensure they matched, and tossed the old one overboard.

"This guy knows you. He used your name. Is this the guy you disappointed? Is this the guy on the ship?"

"What if it is?"

"What do you mean, 'What if it is'? You're dragging me to Africa 'cause you think you saw a ship. Who's the poet? Come on, Will, you know the guy."

"I know the type. Beneath the veneer, he's a thug."

"You do know him! He calls you a thief, for Christ's sake. Did you rob him?"

"No!"

"Then why is he chasing you?"

Will sighed elaborately. "Okay, okay, I'll fill you in as best I can. . . . You know what perovskites are, right?"

"What?"

"Perovskites."

"No. What are you talking about?"

Will fit the various parts of the water maker together and

said, "Give me a hand putting this back and I'll explain perovskites."

Will spent an hour fiddling with the water maker in the
stifling heat belowdecks. When at last it was turning seawater fresh again, he said, "Let's reserve the first five gallons
for showers. I'll show you how to rig the sun bag to heat it."

"You were about to explain perovskites."

Will's answer started more circuitously than usual.

"Perovskites are a class of crystalline oxides that make
better computer chip insulators than conventional silicon
dioxides. You know about moletronics?"

"Little computers?"

"Molecular electronics. Chips as small as molecules.
How about quantum computing?"

"Tiny, powerful computers?"

Will laughed. "If that ThinkPad"—he pointed down the
companionway toward his laptop—"was represented as one
inch tall, IBM's new Blue Gene supercomputer would stand
twenty miles high. If they ever get it built. Do you know
about electron tunneling?"

Jim shook his head, thinking, I'm the young one, but he
knows a lot more about this crap than I do.

"Think of electrons as prisoners. When you shrink computer circuitry down from 'micro' to 'nano' you get a problem with electron tunneling; the insulators are so thin that
electrons bore right through the transistor. Say you were to
replace a penitentiary's stone walls with wallpaper—a lot of
prisoners will escape.

"Looking ahead a few years, microscopic semiconductor
circuitry technology is going to crash smack into its theoret-
ical limits: in other words, there won't be a prison built that
can hold those electrons.

"A related problem is that processor-to-memory delays
are a drag on high-speed computers. So even as we get faster
and faster processors it becomes crucial to move memory
close to the processor. Like on this boat, instead of climbing
out of the cockpit and running to the mast to raise a halyard,
you can run the halyards right next to you in the cockpit."

"Will, what do electron tunneling and processor-to-memory delays have to do with that letter?"

"Solving these 'small-and-fast' problems will completely reinvent computer design. Moletronics would throw out the current size and speed limits."

"How small?"

"As small as a single cell. You could pop a data chip into a hypodermic needle and inject it into your brain. Voilà! Now you speak French."

"How fast?"

"A billion times faster than anything on the shelf. I can see you're beginning to get the picture."

"How do you know all this stuff?"

"I am—or I was—what you could call a *proactive* investment banker. Part venture capitalist, part conceptualizer, part cheerleader. For the last big deal I was running, I rounded up a bunch of hotshot engineers who were out beyond the leading edge of code-morphing and perovskite chips. Indian software writers, Chinese engineers—real cowboys."

"I'm having a hard time picturing you bossing geeks in T-shirts."

"So you think computer geeks are some kind of rebels? Nonsense. Ninety-nine out of a hundred suffer the same herd mentality as the old-fashioned NASA ten-percenters who wore white shirts and ties. Herds of sheep. My guys are *wolves,* guys who couldn't get along. Ever hear about engineers starting labs in their garage? My guys lived in *caves*.

"I found them. I backed them. And I organized a breakthrough that paid off. Big time."

"Congratulations."

"I named it Sentinel. I've got Sentinel chips—right now—that outperform anything on the market by a thousand times. A hundred thousand times. Nothing stays new long, but a one-year lead in moletronics is like a century of the Industrial Revolution. Right now my cavemen are *two years* ahead of the biggest shops in Silicon Valley."

"Why are you sailing to Africa when you should be cheerleading your engineers?"

"Because you'll never buy Sentinel at Radio Shack. . . . Are you beginning to see the problem?"

"It doesn't sound like a problem. It sounds like you won."

"I'll put every billion-dollar chip factory in the world out of business overnight—you better believe there are people who don't want this to happen."

"I'll bet."

"That's who's chasing me."

"What do you mean?"

"They intend to stop me."

Suddenly, as if a plug had been pulled, the enthusiasm drained from his voice and the light dulled in his eyes.

"How?" Jim asked.

"They'll do to me whatever it takes."

Will's switch of emotions caught Jim completely off guard again. A moment ago the old man was relating his great victory in molecular electronics; now he was sinking into another depression, caught in the net of his paranoia.

"Sounds a bit Oliver Stone, Will."

"What do you mean?"

"A little heavy on the conspiracy theory, maybe? Sounds like you're saying that legitimate corporations would try to murder a competitor."

"Do you remember what happened in Barbados? Was I at the airport like I promised?"

"No. You sent some taxi driver who couldn't speak English. Next thing I knew I thought I was going to drown on a fishing boat."

"Don't you realize, now, why I had to leave before you?"

"Weather."

"No. Ordinarily I would have waited for the front to move on. But I got word they'd come to the island."

Back to "they," Jim despaired, as Will triggered another of his avalanches of words.

"I'm waltzing blithely around Bridgetown shopping for fresh vegetables to freeze for our trip. Fortunately, the market—damned good one, too, the best in the eastern Caribbean—is in a tough neighborhood and some boys I know warned me that a big Italian motor yacht had just dropped anchor in Deep Water Harbor." Will mimicked a Barbadian, " 'Say ol' mon, Mr. Spark, dere's folks askin' 'bout ya.' " He barked a rueful laugh. "What a way to go: a shiv in the ribs while haggling for imported parsnips."

As usual, a slew of details jacked up the likelihood of Will's story. But who was Will trying to convince, Jim wondered. Me or himself?

"On the other hand, what civilized man would roast a chicken without parsnips?"

"Will! . . . Who was on the Italian yacht?"

"Luckily, I was ready to split. I'd been shopping and cooking for days, stocking the freezers. The boat was fueled and at that moment they were just finishing watering her at the Careenage. I arranged for a taxi to meet your plane at Seawell and hired your fishing boat. Then I pretended to sail back to Deep Water Harbor. Instead, I just kept going. Wind was blowing up a gale and night fell dark as a bear's belly, so the Port Authority didn't notice me leave without clearance. I thought I was home free. Till you brought them down on us with that phony heart-rate monitor."

"Bullshit, Will."

"Thank God and your good eyes we spotted that ship."

"Bull*shit*."

"Oh, yeah? You want to explain this letter?" Will waved the bell-tolls printout in Jim's face. "Who sent this?"

"You just said it was an empty threat."

"I was trying to protect you from worrying."

"Are you saying you know the 'poet'?"

Will hesitated. "I know what he wants."

"What's that?"

"He wants me dead."

"I still find it hard to believe that legitimate corporations would—"

"Billions," Will cut him off angrily. "*Billions and billions* of dollars. There isn't a human being alive that somebody wouldn't kill for billions. Besides, the suits don't pull the trigger. They hire a professional."

"But even if they killed you, Will, what's to stop your

'caveman' engineers from implementing Sentinel without you?"

"Inventing new technology and manufacturing it are two very different things. I'm the only one who has the whole picture. They're still in their caves. Software and hardware don't even talk to each other. So if I'm killed, it's over. The big boys'll catch up in time and cash in. If I can hide out till they do, maybe killing me wouldn't be worth the trouble."

"Wait a minute. You knowingly put me in the line of fire?"

"No. No. No. That is not true. When I asked you to join me I thought I had pulled off a disappearing act. I vanished. I just wanted a strong crewman and the company to Rio. I'm too old to sail alone. She's a big boat. I can handle her alone if I have to, but it's brutal on a long passage. I had an Aussie kid crew from Hong Kong to Hawaii and picked up a little girl there, till Panama. When she jumped ship I found an Anguillan—best sailors in the Caribbean and they'll fix anything on the boat. He stayed till Barbados. And then I remembered you. I really thought I was home free."

"But not when you ran from Barbados."

"What do you mean?"

"You thought they were on to you and you let me come anyway."

Will Spark suddenly looked old. His cheeks caved in as he chewed the inside of his lips. "You're right. I should have left you."

"Why didn't you?"

"I just wasn't up to the long haul alone. Also, I figured, what if they were following you? If I got you aboard, you'd be safe. No one would know we were heading to Rio. How was I to know you'd let them put the bug on you? So, let's say I half apologize." He reread the printout of the e-mail threat. "The guy is such a phony," he snorted. "'. . . For whom the bell tolls . . .' So just because he can quote poetry means he's not a thug? You know what I say about guys like this? Big balls, little dick."

He shook his head in disgust.

"I'll get you out of this as soon as we hit Nigeria. Pal of

mine's an oilman on the Bonny River. I'll get him to send a helicopter. Chopper you out to Lagos. Put you on a London flight, first class, then straight to New York." He stuck out his hand and offered a smile. "Action beats an apology, right?"

Jim took his hand. It was uncharacteristically clammy, and he had to wonder whether Will's paranoia extended to fantasy friends with convenient helicopters and first-class airplane tickets.

"What's the matter?" asked Will.

"Nothing. Sounds great." But just in case it wasn't, he vowed that he would continue to learn to sail the boat.

"Are you sure?" Will pressed. "Something's on your mind."

"No. I was just trying to remember who said, 'You can run but you can't hide.' Mike Tyson?"

"Not likely," Will snorted.

"Muhammad Ali? Mick Jagger? The Eagles?"

"I believe it was Joe Louis."

"What are you going to do after you drop me?"

"Shove off. That's the beauty of owning a boat. . . . Here today, gone tomorrow."

Which made this boat owner, Jim thought, not the sort of person to stake his life on—and his boat no place for a passenger, much less a novice deckhand.

Val McVay read the county medical examiner's postmortem report on Andrew Nickels again. She retained a childhood image of the old man: an oversize reassuring presence slipping quietly into rooms, leaning over her father's shoulder to whisper in his ear, then her father's entire body relaxing.

She reread the second, private autopsy commissioned by the McVay Foundation.

She read for the fourth time the bulging report from the laboratory that had microsearched Andrew's brain and blood by magnetic resonance imaging and electron microscope, molecule by molecule, finding nothing. The old fixer's brain, she thought with a thin smile, proved as empty as his soul.

Where are you, Will Spark?

She had met him only once. She had liked his ideas and liked him.

She had *not* liked his penchant for secrecy, however. Science did not flourish in secret. That he had erected a Chinese wall between his various engineers made her suspicious. But, temporarily blinded by Sentinel's potential, she had allowed her father to overrule her.

She still couldn't believe she had slept with the man. That he was as old as her father hadn't mattered one whit during a long and memorable weekend. But conventional wisdom would deem it a stupid thing to do in the midst of negotiations.

She had analyzed her actions thoroughly and concluded that she was blameless. Good sex was a rarity. But it was also an intangible that a disciplined mind would always separate from substance.

She stepped out on a porch and watched a trainer *longe* a hunter. The animal resisted the leading rein, but the trainer, a patient Mexican, was implacable. The key to tracing Will Spark was still Jim Leighton.

She went back indoors and telephoned a private detective in Brooklyn. As always, he answered the phone like a starter pistol. "Vinnie Thomas!"

"Do you know who this is?" she asked.

"Not from my caller ID, which you're blocking."

Val watched her monitor as they spoke. "I see you're trying to get around it again. Stop it."

"Jesus, what kind of program are you running?"

"*My* program."

"Yeah, I know your voice."

"*Turn it off.*"

"Okay. I'm stopped."

"Both of them."

"Okay. Sorry, I forgot the second one was running."

When the monitor confirmed that the detective had

switched off all his tracers, Val McVay said, "We have another job for the woman you put into that spinning class."

"You are referring to the health club in Bridgeport, if I remember?"

"Mr. Thomas, how many spinning classes do you infiltrate?"

"You'd be surprised."

Her monitor flashed a warning. Vinnie Thomas was trying yet again to trace her telephone number. This time he was using a very sophisticated program some people had been pirating from the National Security Agency. She said, "Mr. Thomas, you *do* understand why I always block your caller ID. You don't learn more about me than you have to. My business remains my own. Your business is paid in cash. You do not invade my privacy. I do not file your earnings with the IRS. In other words, cutouts serve us both."

She had originally hired the Brooklyn detective years ago to investigate a man she was considering for an occasional no-strings afternoon in the privacy of her Manhattan town house. Thomas had done a thoroughly professional job of confirming that the bored husband and loving father her prospect claimed to be was not a pervert or a fortune hunter. Since then, he'd been occasionally useful in her ongoing battle to stay a jump ahead of her father and Andy Nickels.

"Cutouts are important," Thomas agreed.

"You must employ them, too. I'm sure that even your most trusted employees don't know your private home number, much less where you live."

"Yeah?"

"Write down this address, Mr. Thomas." She named a building in Red Hook.

"Hey! That's *my* loft. How'd you find—"

"Now can we get serious on the telephone? Or do you require a visit?"

9

IT SAYS HERE. . . . "—Jim climbed the companion-way, book in hand, and inspected the sails—"if you tighten that"—he pointed at the boom vang, which had slipped loose—"then we'll go faster."

Will, who was wearing a safety harness as he leaned over the back of the boat with a circuit tester, clipping wires to the portside wind generator in an attempt to trace an electrical short, returned an amused smile. "Be my guest. Try it."

Jim marked his place in Will's *Annapolis Book of Seamanship* with the dog-eared dust jacket, crawled onto the cabin roof, and pressed the vang sheet back into the jaws of its jam cleat. He hauled on the line; the jam cleat gripped it and the vang pulled the boom down. The result of the effort was to slightly flatten the mainsail.

Will peered over his shoulder at the knot meter on the steering pedestal. "Almost a tenth of a knot!" He laughed. "Really tramping."

"I'm not finished."

Jim studied the mainsail.

Since he had tightened the vang, there wasn't a ripple in the cloth. The taut triangular expanse pointed at the sky as trim as a spear. But when he looked forward, ahead of the mast, up at the jib, he saw that a small flutter—which hadn't been there before he tightened the vang—marred the trailing edge of the headsail.

Aware that Will had stopped working on the wind generator and was watching his every move, Jim took a chrome handle from its socket beside the companionway, inserted it in the top of the winch controlling the jib, braced his feet, and threw his weight into a half turn. The winch clicked; the jib sheet creaked with the strain. The fluttering stopped. The boat leaned a fraction and felt suddenly livelier.

"Half a knot!" Will called. "Good for you."

Grinning with satisfaction, Jim took the book back to the cockpit. He might not be a natural sailor, but he was beginning to get at least an inkling of how the boat worked. He reviewed the section he'd been reading, studied the illustrations, and looked up repeatedly at *Hustle*'s sails.

The boat was headed east and the trade wind was blowing from the northeast, which meant it was coming at them a bit left of straight ahead. A port tack. *Hustle* was cutting into the wind, and the flatter he had shaped her sails, the more like a knife, the closer she cut into the wind and the faster she sailed.

"May I?" he called to Will, placing his hand on the winch that controlled the mainsail.

"Be my guest."

He cranked it in. The boat leaned further over. It felt faster. The wind cut sharper and the hull thrust harder into the water. But the knot meter gave him a nasty surprise. The boat had actually dropped speed. He looked back at Will, who was removing the guts of the wind generator.

"Wha'd I do wrong?"

"She's heeling too far," Will said. "Leaning over at too sharp an angle. It's not a dynamic stance. You're spilling wind and her hull's fighting the water. Take the wheel a moment. . . . Do you feel how it's fighting you? Too much weather helm because she's overpowered. Ease off the main again and you'll see."

The rope that controlled the mainsail, the "sheet," was wrapped three times around the barrel of the winch. Easing off was a matter of letting the rope turns slip around the barrel, which was a tricky operation Jim had yet to master.

"Get your hand out of that line!" Will shouted. "It'll cut your fingers off. Mitts *outside* the line."

The straining sheet made a heavy grunting noise as Jim carefully let it slip.

"Good," said Will. "Good. . . . Feel her stand up?"

The boat straightened just a hair and, although it didn't give the impression of moving as fast, the knot meter showed a return to their previous speed.

That night, Jim wrote to Shannon.

He was getting the hang of the SSB radio, which allowed him to send her a private letter without worrying about Will's paranoid bitching—"Don't tell anybody we're sailing to Nigeria." The fact was, even if Will's "they" could intercept e-mail they'd have a hard time finding his and Shannon's: Shannon had secreted deep-cover private e-mail addresses into the busy RileySpa website to hide them from her extremely computer-literate, mega-nosy mother.

I'm beginning to realize that this whole sailing thing is about form. On the bike, when my knees start wobbling I lose speed; when I'm swimming and get tired I start twisting my legs, which wastes energy and creates drag that slows me down. On the boat, when a sail wobbles or flutters—"luffs" is the correct word—wind energy is wasted and she slows down. So, maybe I'm becoming a sailor in spite of myself. . . . And how are you? I must say, I've never felt so far away in my life. At the same time, I have to thank you for pushing me to try it. It's a hell of experience—a real "experience of a lifetime," just as you predicted. So, I miss you so far away and I owe you for sending me so far away. Best news is, Will thinks we'll hit the Nigerian coast in THREE WEEKS! I'm afraid they're going to feel like years—Omigod, time for my watch. I'm gooing to practice steering.

He corrected his typos, then fired it off—slowly on the SSB radio—and ran on deck with five minutes to spare.

That night, Will gave him a big vote of confidence. For

the first time, the old man slept in his luxurious cabin in the back of the boat, instead of in a hammock slung right beside the companionway.

Jim passed the first two hours practicing steering manually. Maintaining their compass course was much easier at night. By day, surrounded by the featureless horizon, the compass needle was a tedious guide—like a video game with a particularly lame joystick. By night, Will had taught him to steer by whatever distinctive stars or constellations lay ahead and only occasionally check the compass needle as the heavens wheeled. Easier, but not easy. Looking over his shoulder was a humbling experience: whereas the auto-helm, and Will, cut a trail as straight as a train track, his wake looped whimsically in the starlight, meandering like a country road.

Finally, tiring of trying to match the wheel to the movement of the water flowing across the rudder, the seas shouldering the hull, and the wind shoving the sails, Jim reengaged the auto-helm and experimented with sail trim again, which was a whole different proposition in the dark.

The night had started uncommonly bright, lit by a sky full of stars. But now, to his right, to the south, and ahead, to the east, the stars had begun to disappear one by one behind cloud, until half were dark. He could still see the telltales—the strips of black cloth that lay flat against the sails to indicate an efficient airflow but danced perpendicular when the wind was being wasted—but he couldn't see the edges of the sails themselves.

Even the telltales began to disappear as the dark spread across the sky. Blind now, he recalled that Shannon had written, "What do you hear when you're alone on night watch?" So he tried to listen for clues. At first it all sounded the same, a rush of sound like driving with the windows open. But when he strained he began to distinguish fluttering sailcloth from the hiss of waves breaking beside the boat, the smack of the hull cutting the water, and the rush of wind past his ears.

Suddenly, the boat heeled hard over. He couldn't figure out what had happened. Then he realized that the trade wind, which for days and days had cut across the bow at the same angle, blowing always from the same quarter, had abruptly changed direction.

He let out the mainsail. His instinct was good and the boat responded. He was moving toward the jib winch to do the same with the headsail when the wind shifted again, back where it had been. *Hustle* lost speed. Again his instincts served and he hauled in the main. But she kept slowing, so much so that the waves she'd been cutting through began batting her off course.

Baffled, Jim sat alone in the dark, trying to figure out what had changed so drastically. The wind. The northeast trade wind, that constant of every waking and sleeping hour on the boat, had stopped.

The sails went slack. The boat began rocking uncomfortably, pitching fore and aft, which caused the sails to slat and bang. When he looked up at them, he saw that the rest of the stars had vanished. Suddenly, the still air was stirred by a cold breeze.

Will ran up on deck. "What the—bloody hell, you should have waked me! It's going to hit us like a freight train."

Now Jim saw what he had missed. A quarter mile off to the right, so bright as to glow beneath the black sky, a heavy, bone white line was bearing down on them like a huge grin in a dark face.

"Furl the jib! I'll reef the main!" Will paused only to put Jim's hand on the proper line, reminding him that they were sailing with the roller-reefing jib instead of the enormous genoa he had dropped the day they spotted the ship.

Then he switched on the work lights—which shone down from the spreaders, illuminating the decks and a patch of sea around the boat—leapt out of the cockpit, and hastily lowered the mainsail halfway down the mast. This time, instead of letting the sailcloth tumble in an out-of-control avalanche, Will kept it in tight control as he made it smaller, tugging on the reefing lines and securing it firmly to the boom, even as he shot anxious looks at the swiftly advancing white line.

Jim, aware that he had screwed up big-time by not paying

attention to his surroundings, tried to furl in the jib. The line he was tugging turned a spool on the front of the boat that was supposed to crank the sail around its forestay like a vertical window shade. But it was balking: jamming, turning fitfully, and jamming again.

The next wind puff was warm and considerably stronger, and when it filled the sail there was no budging it.

"Furl it all the way. Hurry, hurry. Jesus, what were you thinking? When you see a squall coming at you, you have to act."

"I didn't see it."

A third puff struck the boat, icy cold and so strong that it whistled a low note in the rigging. It filled the reefed mainsail and ballooned the jib that Jim was struggling to furl.

"Will, I can't move it."

The wind had filled the headsail rock-hard, and though Jim put all his strength against the winch handle, it wouldn't budge. The next gust shoved the boat so violently that it overrode the auto-helm and turned downwind. Suddenly the sea was frothy white.

"Hang on!" yelled Will, lunging for the wheel.

Another gust from a new direction banged into the sails. The boom swung across the boat, slamming from left to right with a crash that shook the deck, and *Hustle* jibed about. Racing out of control, smashing sea to sea, she stampeded from the wind.

"Close that hatch!" Will roared from the helm. Jim slid the main hatch cover closed. A wave broke into the cockpit, surged around his legs, and poured down the companionway into the cabin.

"The washboards," Will yelled over the roar of the water. "Under the bench."

Kneeling on the floor of the cockpit, Jim opened the cockpit bench, found the wooden boards, and worked them clumsily into the vertical slots that flanked the companionway opening. When he was done and had the hatch closed tight, he realized that Will had somehow battled the boat around, back on course, and was forcing her to head into the wind so they could try again to furl the jib.

The wind was whining in the rigging and blowing cold spray. Neither man had had time to don a windbreaker. "Take the helm and try and hold her in the wind while I—"

The wind shifted again and knocked the boat half over. Jim was astonished to see the deck at so steep an angle it was nearly vertical. He fell down, toward the water, and smashed painfully into the lifelines that fenced the deck.

Will, braced at the helm, played the wheel until the boat began to level off. "We have to get that sail in. Here, you—"

An explosion cut off his words, a concussive *boom*. Where the jib had billowed full and stiff a second earlier, all that was left of the white sail was a black hole fringed by wildly flapping shreds of cloth.

Released from the overwhelming pressure on the sail, the boat snapped straight up and forged ahead, the reefed mainsail driving her hard. The seas were suddenly flattened by a roaring, hissing cascade of rain that blinded them. It turned into hail. Pellets of ice raked the deck, ricocheted, and piled ankle deep.

They grew larger, the size of marbles, then golf balls. Jim saw a baseball-size chunk explode on the gunnel and another clang against the steering pedestal. Then he was down, knocked off his feet, vaguely aware he was floundering on hands and knees, stunned by a huge hailstone that had smashed into his face. He clapped his hand over his nose and it came away blood red. Spray washed over him and salt stung in the wound. Shocked and confused, he tried to stand up just as a tremendous gust hit the boat full on her side. It bellied the mainsail and she tipped, tossing him toward the water again. He reached for the lifelines but fell smoothly between them—*swish* like a perfect basket—through the double wires and into the sea.

10

THE WATER WAS warmer than the frigid wind, as welcoming as a Jacuzzi. But it closed over his head with an awful silence as if the noise of wind and water were life and their absence death. The hull shouldered past him and Jim panicked. A triathlon swimmer might stay afloat for days, but the sailboat was plunging away from him into the storm and when he tired in the end, he would drown alone—a flailing speck under an enormous sky, his weaker and weaker struggles attracting scavengers. His heart hammered in his chest, his body went rigid, and he opened his mouth to scream for Will to stop the boat, turn it around, and pluck him from the sea.

All of which, Will had informed him repeatedly, shaking a safety harness under his nose for emphasis, was impossible. "No way anybody can save you." They should wear the harness whenever they left the cockpit, particularly at night. "You're gone in a flash. So don't fall overboard."

As Jim screamed for help, salt filled his mouth. And suddenly he was right back in the water with the sharks the day Will had dared him to swim. The sharks that had turned out to be dolphins. He closed his mouth, gagging brine from his airway, and tried to kick toward the surface.

Immediately, his foot struck something hard. And he realized that, in his panic, what had seemed like hours in the water had been a fraction of a second. He was still beside the boat; its smooth side was slipping past his shoulder. He lunged for it, reached out, and felt Will's hand close on his.

Then hail was stinging his face and drumming the water again. The squall was roaring in his ears and he was coughing and spitting, but he was sucking sweet air. His back was to the hull, his left arm twisted overhead. He felt the boat rise; it rolled violently and his hand began to slide from Will's. His hand felt flimsy and unsubstantial, his strength overwhelmed by floods of fear-spurred adrenaline.

"I can't pull you aboard," the old man gasped in his ear. "I cracked a rib."

Squinting up into the glare of the work lights, Jim saw Will sprawled half over the side of the boat, his chest crushed against the gunnel, his face contorted with pain as he stretched under the lifelines to hold Jim's hand.

Galvanized by Will's suffering, Jim called upon the discipline with which he had built his body. He had trained for years to override pain and hopelessness and expend his last reserves.

The boat rolled downward. A lifeline stanchion was for a brief instant almost in reach. He flutter-kicked and reared backward and seized it. "Let go. I've got it."

"You sure?" Will gasped.

"Let go."

Jim pivoted until he was facing the hull. He grabbed the lower safety wire with his other hand. The boat was rolling, jerking him up, driving him down. She was moving ahead, too, dragging him through the water. He stopped fighting it and let his legs and torso rise with that flow. When he was skimming the surface, he gathered arms and chest, pulled up, tucked his legs into a tight ball, and hooked a foot on the gunnel. The boat rolled up, nearly shaking him off. When it rolled down again, he used the force to stand, tumble over the safety wires onto the hail-slicked deck, and pull Will down into the cockpit.

"Are you okay?"

Will shook him off and scrambled to his knees. His eye leapt from the seas tumbling at *Hustle* to the double-reefed mainsail. Hunched over, favoring his right side, he hauled himself up by the steering pedestal and steadied the wheel. Jim sank to the cockpit sole and rested his head on the bench. He was trembling from head to toe and could barely raise his head when he heard Will barking orders at him.

"What?"

"Wake up, Jim. We're not out of this by a long shot."

All Jim could think about was how close he had come to dying. Will wouldn't shut up.

"Put on your harness." He shook Jim's shoulder and pointed at the bench hatch where the safety gear was stowed.

Jim crawled to it and fumbled the lid open. The boat rolled sharply and the lid banged shut, nearly crushing his fingers. "Put it on," Will yelled.

Jim pulled out a webbing harness, slowly untangled it, and buckled in.

"Clip onto the pedestal."

The snap shackle clicked onto a steel ring and he was now tethered to the boat by a six-foot length of braided nylon line.

"Help me into mine."

Will lifted one hand from the wheel, then the other, as Jim held the harness and clipped onto the pedestal.

"Now take the wheel," Will ordered. "Point her exactly where I tell you."

Steadying himself with his left hand, Will moved aside. Jim discovered that with the jib in tatters it was a lot harder to keep the boat on course. Breaking seas delivered unexpected blows from every direction. Crazy wind gusts banged the sail and rattled hailstones in his face.

"We've got too much sail up," Will yelled. "I'm going to take another reef in the main."

"Maybe I better do it," Jim offered. "Your ribs—"

"Hold her as close as you can into the wind—take the pressure off the sail." Will unclipped his harness line. "Ready?"

From the wheel, Jim watched in awe as Will, hunched way over, clutching his side, edged forward on the icy deck. His every motion was a model of economy as he clipped onto a ring in the cabin roof and tackled the sail, never wasting a move on unnecessary action. With clear arm gestures he showed Jim where to steer whenever the wind shifted direction. The crackling sail inched lower, the reefing line stretched taut, and the cloth shrank smaller between the mast and the boom. When Will finally reeled back to the cockpit, his face haggard with pain, a meager scrap of stiff Dacron the area of a diagonally folded bedsheet was all the boat offered the wind.

Will took the wheel with his good arm.

"Run below and get me two morphine from the medicine kit."

Desperate to atone for this catastrophe, Jim leapt toward the hatch. His safety harness brought him up short, and when he turned back to unclip from the steering pedestal, he saw in the work lights a weary grin on Will's face. The old man released the snap shackle and yelled, "Just take it easy. Calm down a little. And try and time the opening of the hatch so you don't let any waves in."

It was much quieter below deck.

There were three drawers of medicine and first-aid gear in a cabinet by the nav station. Bracing against the constant motion, he found the morphine. As he started to open the bottle, he had his first clear thought since the storm had struck, and he dried his hands before cupping two of the pain pills in his palm.

The coffee thermos was nearly full and he brought it to Will along with the pills and a windbreaker and received, for the still-warm coffee, a gratifying "Bless you, my son."

Sometime before dawn the wind began to slacken. The hail, which had intermittently raked the boat all night, turned to rain. A steely light began spreading, and as the rain diminished to a warm drizzle, what Jim saw was unlike anything he had yet seen from the boat. Despite the drop in the wind, the sea remained vividly alive and frightening. The word *jagged* took hold in his tired mind—the word he would use to describe the storm to Shannon. Jagged waves slashing at the sky, jagged cloud rocketing overhead, jagged tatters of sailcloth where the jib had blown out.

His face hurt where the hail had cut him, and his head throbbed. He was blind-tired. His skin burned where he had scraped it falling through the wire lifelines. And he blamed himself for the ruined headsail. But though he had fallen off the boat and nearly drowned, he was, instead, alive, and his spirit soared when Will put an end to his guilt with a generous, cheerful "Think you could raise the number three jib without falling overboard?"

It took an hour on the pitching foredeck to clear the ruined headsail and raise the spare, with Will calling instructions on the loud-hailer. The boat responded by settling down to a more comfortable ride.

Will welcomed him back to the cockpit with another question: "May I presume that a fitness instructor is qualified to tape cracked ribs?"

"Absolutely."

"Breakfast, first."

"I can get it."

"Not based on what I've seen of your cooking so far. But if you can drive, and keep your eyes open in case that squall has any cousins, I'll pop another morphine and rustle up something to eat."

As alarmed as she was that Spark would vanish forever, Val McVay had to admit that on some animal level she was enjoying the hunt. Do I have a talent for this sort of thing? she wondered. Could I excel at it?

Hurrying through the rambling mansion to her father's library, she found a book about commandos. She took it to the basement gymnasium and was reading it while pumping and pedaling a Schwinn Airdyne when a scrap of paper fell out and drifted to the polished oak floor. After her workout, she dried her hands, picked it up, and read it. It was a block-print note to her father, dated ten years ago.

Dear Mr. McVay,
I know how much you like books and thought you
might like this one. Some of my friends are in this book
and it may answer some questions as to what I do in
the army.
Sincerely,
Andy

It read, Val thought, like a child's letter dictated by an adult. She had no doubt that Andrew had put his nephew up to it, starting early to make a place for him in the firm. But she wondered, not for the first time, whether Andrew Nickels had gained too much influence over her father. It would have been in the fixer's nature to try; but there was no excuse for her father's allowing it to happen.

Later that afternoon, they broke for cocktails—a dry martini for Lloyd, a Gibson for Val.

"Tell me about Andy."

Her father answered with a brusqueness calculated to project total contempt for a pointless question. "Andrew Nickels's nephew."

"That much I know," she replied evenly.

"Dickensian childhood before Andrew stepped in," her father added. "Made Andy his ward. Took charge of his schooling until he joined the army. Andy flourished. Joined Special Forces—Rangers. Commando stuff down in South America."

"Drug interdiction?"

"Let's just say, not the sort of work where one presses for details. He joined us four years ago."

"Why did Andy quit the army? Specifically to 'join us'?"

"Why do you ask?"

"I found gaps in his Pentagon file."

Her father did not ask how she had cracked a Pentagon file. Nor did he quite answer the question, saying only, "To be frank, I suspect that Andrew realized he was losing his mind and brought Andy aboard while he still possessed sufficient faculties to train the boy to take over."

They finished their drinks, ate a light supper served by

liveried staff in the dining room next door, and went back to work.

Dear Shannon,

Almost home. Just two more weeks or so, with luck. We're making better time than Will thought. The wind's been good and the Guinea Current is with us—it's like an offshoot of the Equatorial Current—so we pick up another knot, sometimes two.

It seemed to Jim like months since they had escaped the Doldrums, though it was only three weeks. Even his memory of the squall had faded into an entry in the log—a waypoint in the two thousand miles they had sailed east since Will had changed course. Their course had veered gradually north of the equator to pick up a boost from the Guinea Current. It swept them under the bulge of West Africa parallel to the coasts of Liberia, Ivory Coast, Ghana, Togo, Benin but grew weak as they neared the Bight of Biafra.

But first, we're sailing into a sea of "buts." What's a sea of buts? For example, on the chart, the area we're entering off the oil coast of Nigeria is called the Bight of Biafra. But the locals, Will says, call it the Bight of Bonny. (A bight, in case you don't know, which I didn't, is an indentation in the shore that forms a big open bay.)

He says that the coast is rimmed for twenty or thirty miles by mangrove swamps and is virtually impenetrable except where the rivers of the Niger Delta, the Bonny among the biggest (where we're heading, I think), empty into the sea. *But,* says Will, sandbars block the mouth of each river and they're pounded by heavy surf.

Channels cut through some of the bars, marked with buoys. *But* the problem, Will says, is that when the channels shift, it sometimes takes a while for the Nigerians to realign the buoys. (Like the *Daily Show* said, there's a major corruption and chaos problem in the Niger Delta. Will says the *Daily Show* is tasteless. I say accurate.)

Anyway, before we even reach the sandbars, we'll have to

sail through a maze of offshore wellheads and drilling platforms. *But,* Will says, "Many are lighted, some aren't. Some are marked on the charts, others are not." If that weren't enough, he tells me that new wells are under construction. And abandoned old wells aren't lit. I couldn't resist telling him that it sounds more dangerous than the people chasing him. (He didn't laugh.) Will is kind of wired, but I don't think it's a tough piloting job that's worrying him. I think it's more about business. He keeps making sat calls and sending faxes, but no one's returning his calls. When he gets really jumpy I make him do a spinning class and that usually calms him down. Or at least exhausts him so he has to take a nap.

Then I do what I can with the free weights—my legs are in good shape from the bike, but I'm losing my pecs. Hope you'll still love me.

In the interest of not making Shannon crazy, Jim deleted "Hope you'll still love me." They were going to have to start at the beginning if they were going to work anything out. Fishing for "I'll still love you" wouldn't help.

He also decided to spare her the information that before they even got to the oil rigs, they would have to sail among scores of supertankers converging upon and steaming away from the Nigerian coast. Ships so big, Will noted cheerfully, that they could trample a sailboat like *Hustle* into the sea and never know they had done it.

11

SHANNON RILEY CHECKED her e-mail on the Palm V
beside her bed when she woke at five. When she checked
again from her chair at the front desk—during the brief
eight-thirty lull at the RileySpa and Health Club between
business types and the housewives and retirees—she
laughed out loud.

"What's so funny?" her father called from his office.

"Jim, trying to keep me from worrying."

Her father responded with his "Oh, Jim" grunt, which was a
lot easier to take than her mother's "That Jim" sigh. Although
both grunt and sigh conveyed pretty much the same message:
couldn't you have done better than one of the trainers?

"He's started writing wonderful letters."

"Really?"

"At first it was just like news reports, but now he's really
fun. Sometimes I feel like I'm there with him."

"That's nice," said her father.

Up yours, thought Shannon. She clicked Reply, then
typed like wildfire:

Jim!!! Look out for *supertankers.* They're a very dangerous
menace. They can't see yo uand they can't stop and if you think

about it they're all over the place around oil wells. Right? So look out. I could never forgive myself if you got hurt or killed out there because I pushed you there. Come home safe. Kisses.

She deleted "Kisses"—it wasn't fair to hint at promises she wasn't ready to keep—and replaced it with

I've been loving your letters. Thank you so much. I feel like I'm running around on the boat with you.

and flashed it off, typos and all.

But after her father brought her a fresh coffee, she took the last few minutes of quiet time to try to write Jim a longer e-mail.

I dreamed about you last night. It was so real, I could feel you inside me and

Delete.

What am I doing? Give him a break. Let's see . . .

Dear Jim,
The cat's been sleeping with me and—

High heels clicked across the marble lobby—her father had gone nuts with marble—and Shannon looked up from her computer. A tall and unbelievably beautiful woman, who was dressed like a *Vogue* model, came clicking toward the membership office with a worried smile.

"Hi, good morning." Shannon smiled back. "Can I help you?"

The woman had an accent, very European, very stylish-sounding. "My membership—I am trying to make new?"

"You want to renew. Sure, which club?" Had to be Greenwich.

"No, not new. It is . . . cold?"

"Cold?"

"No, no, no. How you say . . . ?" Her hands fluttered as if she were trying to pick a word out of the air. Large hands,

Shannon noticed. Tennis-player hands that didn't quite go with her Manolo Blahnik boots.

"I am back. . . . I was away."

"Frozen! Your membership was frozen. Right. You're back. You want to start up again."

"Ah. Of course. Frozen. I go away for two month and I lose all my new words."

"We say reactivate. Start up again. Do you have your card? If not, I'll just look your name up."

"I have it here, someplace." She opened a to-die-for Prada handbag and took out a little lizard case for her credit cards.

"I love your bag." Shannon was a Kate Spade girl when it came to bags, but the Prada was gorgeous and suited the woman to a T.

"Thank you. It is gift, from friend. Here, I have card."

Shannon swiped it through the reader and her screen brought up the woman's picture and the information that she had signed up several months ago at the Westport club, then froze her membership. Reason: travel. "Dina. Hi, Dina. I'm Shannon. How do you pronounce your last name, *U*-samov?"

"U-*sa*-mov," Dina replied, emphasizing the middle syllable.

"U-*sa*-mov. Dina U-*sa*-mov." Shannon quickly typed in a note for pronunciation. "What a great name. Welcome back, Dina." She reached up to shake hands and repeated, "I'm Shannon."

"Shannon, hello. It is very nice meeting you . . . So now, what am I to do?"

"It's done. You're back. We'll resume billing your credit card monthly. And next time, you don't have to bother coming to the central office. They can do it at your regular club."

"That is it? That is all? Thank you, thank you. I am very happy to be back. Oh, tell me, is my favorite spinning instructor back too?"

"Which one?"

"The boy named Jim."

"No, not yet. Soon, I hope."

"He went sailing, you know."

"I know. We're friends."

"Oh, he is the best boy." Dina gave her a little smile. "Good friends?"

"Are you one of the clients who gave him the heart-rate monitor?"

Dina's face fell. "No, I'm so sorry. I was with no money—broke—you say broke? I was broke."

Shannon kicked herself for embarrassing her. Dina was so cool-looking it never occurred to Shannon that she was a working girl struggling to make ends meet.

"I was wondering, though, is working no problem? I fear that salt water is very, very corrective—corrosive."

What if Dina told someone else in the class that Jim's crazy shipmate had thrown the gift overboard? "He told me that he really loves it."

"Do you know how he is doing? Does he telephone?"

"He e-mails me. It's great. Sometimes I feel like he's next door. Then I realize he is so far away it's unbelievable."

"Please to e-mail him my best regards and I hope he comes home soon."

"Two weeks, I hope."

"Where is he now?"

"Almost to Africa. Can you believe that? I mean, he was sailing to Rio de Janeiro, in Brazil. And now he's going to Africa."

"Where in Africa?"

"Shannon! Sweetie." Her father came barreling out of his office, as round and soft as a poster child for a join-a-health-club-to-get-some-exercise-before-you-die campaign with his belly straining his shirt and his chipmunk cheeks bulging around a Danish. "Where in hell did you put the workmen's comp check? They'll fine the hell out of us if it's late."

"It went out yesterday, registered mail, return receipt."

"I didn't sign it!"

"*I* did."

"You did? Oh. Thanks, sweetie. Hey, is my best girl going to have lunch with me today?"

"It's a little busy."

"I don't care. Name your favorite restaurant. I want to go out with the prettiest girl in town."

"The Fish House." She was not going to sit and watch him shovel steak into his mouth.

"We're on. Oh, sorry." As dense as a lawn jockey when it came to women, he had finally noticed Dina, who was truly the prettiest girl in any town she went to. "Sorry—did I interrupt? Hi, there. I'm the boss. Any problems, see my beautiful daughter."

Shannon was rolling her eyes at Dina when her telephone rang. At the same time a gang of stay-at-home moms came through the front door, and several beelined her way with problems on their faces. The second line rang. The lull was over.

"Nice to meet you, Dina. Welcome back. Hello, thanks for calling RileySpa. Please hold. Hello, thanks for calling RileySpa. Please hold. Dina," she called across the lobby, "e-mail him! He'd love to hear from a client. Here, I'll write it down for you: JLEIGHTON@RILEYSPA.COM."

Dina got into her rented car and called her boss. She told him everything she had seen and heard. Vinnie was pleased. "Now that's the kind of details that get you more jobs."

"Happy that would be making me." Dressing up and practicing accents while playing assistant detective beat bartending between casting calls.

"Talk normal, for Christ's sake."

"I'm staying in character."

"Character being the operative word." Vinnie told her to drive over to Bridgeport and check out Shannon Riley's rented condo.

"She's going to lunch with her father. Do you want me to follow them?"

"No! You gather information. I write a report. We don't do following for this client. They do their own—hang on a sec, I gotta put you on hold."

As Dina pulled out of the RileySpa parking lot, she saw the bright red BMW 740i with SHANNON vanity plates parked in a handicapped slot where no one would dare ticket the boss's daughter.

An eighty-thousand-dollar car for a ditz of a receptionist dating a spinning instructor? Had to be a gift from Daddy. No wonder she was so goddamned cheerful. Who wouldn't be, taking for granted living every day with your bills paid?

"I'm back," said Vinnie.

As she passed behind the 740 Dina saw the wheelchair emblem on the license plate. "Jesus H.!"

"What?" said Vinnie.

"Oh my God."

"*What?*"

"The poor kid can't walk. She's disabled."

"You been talking to her half an hour and you just figured that out?"

"She looked so normal sitting in a regular chair."

"There are signs on the highway for Bridgeport. It's spelled with a B."

"Let's take my car," said Shannon. She had mastered the motorcycle-like twist-grip accelerator and brake-lever hand controls on her 740, and when she was driving it was almost as if the accident had never happened. Compared to dragging around on sticks and her wheelchair it was like flying. Light as a bird. Fast as the wind.

As they pulled out of the lot, her father said, "I hope you don't mind, we're not going to the Fish House, we're going to Emil's."

"Why?"

"Uh . . . Fred had fish for dinner last night and he didn't feel like fish. Again."

"Fred?"

"Fred Bernstein. You know—"

"I *know* Fred. Why is he having lunch with us?"

"I was talking to him on the phone—just asked him last

minute. Give the two of you a chance to get to know each other a little better. Hon, you're driving awful fast."

"Did Mom set this up?"

Her father squirmed. Caught between her and her mother, he was like a toad trying to escape from two angry cats.

"Remember, Fred sold the company."

"You and Mom say 'sold the company' like he saved the world or something. He sold his company for a bunch of money; now what's he going to do with himself?"

"It made Fred a very wealthy man. And how many men would . . ." His voice trailed off as he saw the black hole he was stepping into.

"How many men would go out with a cripple?"

"Hon, don't say cripple."

"How many men would date a woman who is ambulatorily challenged?"

"You know what I mean."

It was hard to separate her life from an injury that affected her every waking hour. But she was also still what she had been before the accident: the daughter of a driven, competitive couple obsessed with getting rich. Her father had flourished in government work because he had a taste for power, and when that ran out, he had switched his ambition to money. Her childhood had been a daily battle to escape from their single-minded pursuit of success.

She knew plenty of kids like her, who were growing up in the strivers' towns her parents were drawn to. If they didn't become success-crazed like their parents—consumed with 800 board scores and Ivy League admissions—they found ways to escape: doing drugs, or zoning out in front of a screen, or hanging with a white-bread gang, or, as Shannon had done, skateboarding. One extreme had led to another, surfing, snowboarding, skiing, and rock climbing—all had taken her further and further from her parents' obsessions. Until her luck ran out one dark night and left her their prisoner.

She said, "I know two men who would date such a woman."

"Who?"

"Your Fred and my Jim."

"But Fred *sold the company.*"

Shannon gave the accelerator a vicious twist and the big car jumped like a lion.

"The man is loaded," her father said. "He's young. Rich. He doesn't just want to date you. He wants to marry you—hon, you're driving extremely fast."

"You know why Fred wants to marry me? Because he thinks a crippled woman would be easier to control. I mean, think about it, Daddy, *I can't run away.* Pretty good deal for a guy who's built like a pear with dandruff."

"He *sold* the company—dammit. I won't be around to take care of you forever."

"But Jim will. If I let him."

"Jim can't afford you."

"But he doesn't want to control me. He likes me the way I am."

"He's only a trainer. He's a goddamned fitness instructor, for Christ's sake. I've got forty of 'em working for me and a hundred on the wait list."

"Jim is not just a fitness instructor."

"Oh yeah?"

"He's *my* fitness instructor."

"If he loves you so much why'd he run off sailing?"

"I *made* him go sailing. He wouldn't have gone if I hadn't pushed him. I want him to have a chance to test himself. To grow up so he realizes he can do better than a cripple."

Ahead, an official-use-only cut crossed over the median. Shannon squeezed the brakes hard and took the crossover in a cloud of burning rubber.

"*Jesus Christ!* Hey, where are you going?"

"Back to the club. I'm not hungry."

"But Fred is waiting for us."

"Fuck Fred."

"Hon? Why are you crying?"

"I'm crying because Jim loves me and I don't want to wreck his life. . . . If I were really a good person . . . and a lot braver than I am . . . I would write Jim never to come home because I'm marrying your goddamned Fred."

"I was just trying to help."

"I'll bet it never occurred to you that I have to wonder what's wrong with Jim that he needs a crippled girl?"

That silenced her father. He slunk down in his seat, until he heard the siren. "Brilliant. There's a cop chasing us."

"I know." She signaled and pulled over onto the shoulder. "Jim is a good person," she said. "He may not be that ambitious. He may not have enough self-esteem. And he'll never have a company to sell. But what's so terrible about just wanting to do a good job?"

She extended her license and registration as the cop stormed up. He was a Connecticut state trooper and he looked angry and wary, his hand hovering near his weapon.

"Step out of the car, miss."

"Would you hand me my crutches, please? They're on the backseat." She pointed to the brake lever and a twist-grip accelerator on the steering wheel. "I'm crippled. I can't walk very far."

The trooper swallowed. Then he registered the tears streaking her makeup. "Are you all right, miss?"

"I'm okay."

"Who are you?" he asked her father.

"I'm her father. I'm attempting to explain to my daughter that her mother and I love her very much and only want what's best for her."

The trooper shook his head. "Yeah, well, you could start by telling her she's going to get killed driving like that. Miss, I'm going to issue you a verbal warning. These median crossers are reserved for police use. It's dangerous to turn in them because there's no deceleration lane."

"I'm sorry," said Shannon. She wiped her eyes and smiled.

"Yeah, well, take it easy; you'll live longer."

The cop started to walk away. Then he turned back and spoke in a low voice only Shannon could hear. "Between me and you, miss? I have never seen anyone, patrol officer or civilian, handicapped or whatever, handle a vehicle better. That was one cool turn."

"I used to ski. I was into speed."

Jim prepped for their approach to the African coast by reading the *Sailing Directions* and poring over the charts. Workboats, tugs, and various support craft churned the waters, the U.S. Defense Mapping Agency publication warned, serving the offshore rigs. Heavy seas displaced marker buoys.

Worse.

"It says they have pirates," he told Will (another fact that Shannon was going to have to discover on her own).

"Not like they used to."

"What happens if they attack us?"

"Pray we can pay them off with my stereo and your blue jeans. Don't worry about it. I'll ring up my old pal Steve Kenyon—he's the head American oilman in these parts, which makes him the big chief."

"How's an oil executive going to protect us two hundred miles from the coast?"

"I know for a fact that Steve had one of his helicopters fitted out as a private gunship. And so do the pirates."

While still a full week's sailing from the Niger Delta, they began to see the long, thick silhouettes of oil tankers on every watch. In the final days, they often had one steaming into view while another was prowling the horizon—until the dry Harmattan wind swirled dust off the African continent and blanketed the sea with haze.

With visibility unreliable, Will ran the radar day and night and set the collision alarm to sound whenever a ship came within three miles. At the same time, he moved back into his hammock for his off-watch catnaps. "Not that I doubt you, CC Kid. But two sets of eyes are better than one."

"I'd really prefer you call me Jim."

"In spinning class I'd have preferred you call me Will. Everybody had a name but me. You called me sir."

"You were older."

"It was so good of you to remind me."

"Sorry. How long am I going to remain the CC Kid?"

Will laughed. "Till you tell me why you're afraid of the outdoors."

"Hey, I'm pulling my own weight—starting to."

"Given the choice, you'll still stay indoors. When you're outdoors, I've never seen more sunblock and long sleeves—I know, I know. Skin cancer. I should cover up, too."

Jim picked up the binoculars and scanned the haze, dividing the circle of the horizon into small increments as Will had taught him. At that moment, a battered tanker flying the Panamanian flag was drawing close. A boat-show-bright Exxon tanker was passing outbound. And a freighter heaped with oil derricks was crossing their wake. "Sorry, Will. This is not indoors."

"What flag is that freighter?"

"I can't see his flag."

"What color is his funnel?"

The ship's smokestack was a stubby appendage to a murky-hued deckhouse. Seen through the haze it could be any light color. He blinked, refocused. "I can't tell. White, maybe, with a couple of thin blue stripes."

"Any red on the white?"

"It could be rust. It could be red."

"*Russian*. Douse the sails!"

"What for?"

"I told you, they have their hooks in shipping. Douse 'em!"

Shannon Riley was reading herself to sleep on Jim's side of the bed, when she was suddenly jolted awake by a creepy sense of menace.

Something had been troubling her since shortly after Jim left. Something he had written in an e-mail, early on, before the course change—even before the Flipper thing—long before she began to regret sending him with Will. She couldn't put her finger on it and found herself rereading the sailing magazines with a vague idea that the mystery—maybe a word she was trying to remember—was in one of them. And suddenly there it was, the word she remembered.

Time bomb.

An article about seasickness cautioned what not to eat when you set sail. Doughnuts. The author called doughnuts "time bombs": when the boat started rocking, a greasy doughnut was the last thing you wanted sloshing around in your stomach. Coffee was another.

Jim had written her that when the fishing boat caught up with Will's sailboat that first night in the gale off Barbados, Will Spark had fed him a snack of doughnuts and coffee.

Oh Jim, you should have known better—you'd never pop a doughnut before a bike race. She could just hear him saying, Thanks for being nice to me. Sure, I'll have a greasy doughnut.

And Will Spark, what were you up to? An experienced sailor had to know that poor Jim would end up puking his guts up. Why deliberately do that to him? Was it out-and-out cruelty like the big shark laugh, or was it a means to control Jim? But why would such a rich guy bother? Unless he wasn't as rich and successful as he claimed. Or was it merely some sort of twisted passive-aggressive act—heavy on aggressive. Should she e-mail Jim? But what good would that do? Thank God the trip was almost over.

BOOK II

Africa

12

A HUNDRED MILES from the Bonny River they turned north. The wind wheeled with them—a southwest monsoon that displaced the Harmattan and built an enormous swell. That night as they surfed the mountainous waves speeding toward the coast, the sky began to glow red.

"Gas flares," Will explained. "Burning off waste gas from the oil wellheads. We're almost there. What do you say we celebrate our last night at sea?"

Their previous "celebrations"—of their eventual escape from the Doldrums, surviving the squall, repairing the damage from Jim's first attempt to raise the spinnaker—had meant downing a magnum of French champagne iced in one of the freezers. But tonight, Jim thought, a clear head seemed a prerequisite for sailing among the supertankers converging on the Niger Delta. They had seen several of the lumbering behemoths before dark and one or two after nightfall, their red and green and white lights rendered beguilingly soft and buttery by the humid haze.

"Why don't we celebrate with one last spinning class?"

Will cast a longing glance down the companionway. Then he turned his face to the wind. "Harmattan will be back pretty soon," he mused. "Maybe you're right."

Jim winched the bikes up. Will patched the collision alarm into the loud-hailer just in case a ship bore down on them while they were concentrating on uphill sprints. But the old man was still in a playful mood and he rigged a strobe rescue light to flicker their shadows on the sails.

"Disco spin!"

"Resistance, not too heavy, not too light. It should feel like work, but we're still warming up. Let's say four on a scale of ten. . . ."

By the oscillating light, he could see a jerkily slow-motion Will pretend to turn up his resistance. But Jim gave his all, anticipating several travel days of enforced inactivity, trapped in airless airplanes and departure lounges. Soon he broke a sweat and minutes later was dripping.

Hustle plowed along, rising and falling on the following swell, her sails spread wide, pushed shoreward by the slackening monsoon.

"Okay, Will, back it off, spin 'em out. . . ." He gave him a sixty-second respite. "If you're thirsty, take a drink. If you're not thirsty, take a drink. And when I'm gone you're going to remember to hydrate. Right?"

"Right, boss. 'Hydrate or die.' "

"Resistance increases, RPMs drop. We'll turn it up to eight. . . . And in a minute we'll go up to third position. . . . Remembering to increase resistance . . . we go *up* to third."

He was feeling some regret that the voyage was ending. The boat routines had become a comfortable habit and he had been learning so much that he hadn't had time to get bored. He looked over at Will, who was pumping his heart out. He would miss the old guy a little; he wouldn't miss Will's crazy demons, real or imagined. But what a trip!

He checked his heart-rate monitor. His pulse was getting up there, with a full twenty minutes to go. He wondered where his new monitor, his clients' gift, had got to: still floating like a message in a bottle? Or sunk to the bottom of ocean? Or monitoring the belly of a shark?

He glanced over at Will again—crazy lunatic—jumped

off his bike, crossed over, and reduced Will's resistance. "Pick it up, Will. Pick it up." *Boom, boom, boom,* with his foot. "Yes! Beautiful! Now you're flying."

"Flying, hell," Will gasped a laugh. "I'm dying. You're killing me."

"You'll miss me when I'm gone."

He vaulted back on his own bike and pedaled as if he were climbing Mont Blanc and super-biker Lance Armstrong was the only racer still ahead of him. Flying. Eating the hill. Form: knees in line, chest up, shoulders down, hands relaxed. Shannon was right. The once-in-a-lifetime voyage had changed his life. He was stronger, surer. First thing he was going to do when he got home—second thing—was start swimming outdoors. To hell with the pool: he would swim every day in triathlon conditions. His heart was pounding, he was maxing out now, but his form was true, his body efficient, his effort sublime.

He felt the crazy tug of an endorphin high seeping into his brain. The music sounded unbearably beautiful. The strobe on the sails showed off the boat as the splendid creature she was. God, she'd been good to them. The endorphins were surging now, a tidal flow of joy juice. The sea glowed. He looked over at Will. The long voyage and all its hassles had been a crucible of friendship. Like team racing, or going to war together.

He could hear a loud thudding—his heart—a powerful *whomp, whomp, whomp.* A smile grabbed his face, a sob tugged at the corner of his mouth, involuntary tears warmed his eyes, and he felt a potent mingling of sensations, like laughter, weeping, and orgasm, all at once.

The thudding grew louder, thundering, and quite suddenly, something was very wrong.

A blinding light from above seared his eyes. He heard Will yell. The thundering shook the bike and the decks, and a hard gust smacked the sails.

A ship, Jim thought. We're being run down by a ship. Where was the collision alarm?

An amplified voice roared like the voice of God: "What

are you all doin' down there?" Jim realized that a helicopter was hovering close overhead, beaming a light down on the sailboat.

"Douse that goddamned light!" Will yelled back through the loud-hailer. "You're blinding us."

The helicopter drew back fifty feet. In a thick American Gulf Coast drawl, the pilot demanded, "What the hell is wrong with you, blinking your 'mergency strobe when there ain't no 'mergency?"

"What the hell are you doing so far offshore?" Will bellowed back.

"You all need rescuin' or not?"

The helicopter's searchlight probed the decks and lingered on the bikes. Will shouted to Jim, "Oil company rig tender. Way off base out here."

The searchlight locked onto Jim and Will dripping in their workout shorts.

"You all pansies?"

"Hey, pal," Will shot back. "You want to come down here and say that to my face? No? Then be a good ol' boy and patch me through to Mr. Kenyon."

"Who?"

"Steve Kenyon. Your boss."

"Kenyon? Kenyon's not with the company no mo'."

"What? Where'd he go?"

"Home, I guess. Hell, Kenyon hasn't been here fo' two, three years."

"Okay, get me Rick Hite!"

"Never heard of 'im."

The helicopter veered away and thundered toward the invisible coast leaving them in utter darkness.

"Bloody hell," muttered Will. "Bloody, bloody hell."

As his eyes recovered from the glare of the searchlight, Jim looked over at Will. The old man was staring north at the red glow.

"I thought Kenyon was your buddy."

"Biggest honcho in the oil patch."

"But he's been gone three years."

"We haven't kept in touch. . . . Damn, damn, damn."

"Will, when were you out here last?"

" 'Ninety-six."

"That's a long time ago."

Will plucked a spotlight from its charger and inspected the sails. Then he motioned to Jim to take the helm. "Keep out of eyeball range of the platforms. I want to check the charts."

When word came in on the sat phone that Will Spark had been spotted sixty miles off the Bonny River in the Niger Delta, Andy Nickels was airborne in the wrong direction. He immediately ordered a one-eighty and instructed the McVay Foundation pilots to plot fuel and relief-crew stops for the long haul to Nigeria.

Then he woke an American operations superintendent in Port Harcourt whose responsibilities—and primary headaches—entailed security for offshore oil rigs, terminals, pumping stations, submarine pipelines, storage tankers, and wellheads. Nickels offered no apologies for the late-night call. From the point of view of the operations superintendent this would sound like the McVay Foundation was doing him one big favor.

He confirmed Lloyd McVay's earlier warning to the superintendent's boss that Greenpeace fanatics were headed for the Bonny River in a sailboat and added that the Greenpeacers intended to hook up with local dissidents to shut down oil production.

"You've been told we'll take custody."

"You're welcome to 'em."

The oilman alerted Bonny River Joint Security, which maintained a fleet of high-speed patrol boats funded by several oil corporations working the Niger to protect their ships and terminals from pirates, protesters, insurgents, and renegade government soldiers. Dealing with the locals, whom you could usually buy off, was pain in the tail enough. But no one bribed Greenpeace. You had to stop them before their

PR machine got cranking. Thank the good Lord for small favors: this bunch on the sailboat had made the mistake of coming in the dark—which meant they'd be leaving in the dark.

13

JIM STAYED IN *Hustle*'s cockpit, where he watched for ships and workboats and steered around oil platforms and the bright patches lit by burning gas glares. He was excited. The boat was moving quickly, carried shoreward by the wind and the heavy swell. Each of the rolling waves was shoving him closer to an airport and home.

The closer they got, the more lights speckled the night, red and green and white, and the brighter burned the flares that lit the sky. In the middle of the night in the middle of nowhere, it looked like thousands of people were working the oil wells.

Not true, Will told him when he brought him tea—at least, not one person for every light. It wasn't a city. It was more like a highly automated factory. "It's good for us. They're too busy to notice us."

"Did you work here?"

"No, I sold them equipment, a seismograph I had some people develop for siting wells. We ought to see the fairway pretty soon—look for a couple of sea buoys. Four-second red blinker and a four-second green. How are you holding up?"

"I'm getting a little tired."

"Coming in is always tough. Bobbing around by yourself for months, you're just not used to close-quarters intensity."

"I'm surprised you trust me alone for so long in these conditions."

"I've been watching on the radar."

Five thousand miles to the west, Andy Nickels's plane rocketed out of Miami Airport, refueled and freshly crewed.

Greg had reported in. He and his boys were heading into Lagos from Freetown. They'd land in an hour and Greg was already dickering on the radio for a Nigerian army helicopter to make the pickup.

Nickels sat-phoned the captain of a McVay-funded geological research vessel drilling off Isla de Bioko and asked him to steam out of Guinea's territorial waters and clear his helipad for a dawn landing. The captain protested that he had a thousand meters of cable over the side.

"Would you like Mr. McVay to confirm your orders?"

Nickels knew he should catch some sleep. He'd been running flat out thirty hours, the last ten on enough coke to choke a horse. It was either sleep or drop some big E. He decided, with a grim smile, to do the mature thing and just close his eyes—arrive refreshed for the interrogation.

Joint Security's private navy was fanning out across the Bonny estuary. Their maneuverable semirigid shallow-draft boats crisscrossed at will the flats and creeks that led from the sea. Gunners and radar/infrared operators scoped the channels.

"What the hell is that? Hey, bright eyes, see there? What do you see?"

Jim looked where Will was focusing his night glasses. "I see white. . . ." It looked like a feather blowing along the orange horizon. "I think it's moving."

"It's a small boat throwing spray . . . going like a bat out of hell."

"A rig tender?"

"Too small . . . lost him. . . . You know what worries me? Who told that cracker we were coming?"

"What cracker?"

"The helicopter pilot."

"What are you talking about? He saw our flasher beacon. He thought we needed help."

"Forty miles from the nearest oil rig?"

"Will, I see three white lights on top of each other."

"That's a tug towing barges—look way back behind it. See that red light? That's the barge. Don't get between them. The tow wire will cut you in half. And the barge will run over what's left."

"I see a green flasher." Jim counted, "One . . . two . . . three . . . four-second green flasher! It's the sea buoy."

"Find me the red. It should appear a hair to the left of the green."

"I lost the green."

"There's a barge blocking it. . . . There!"

"I got the red."

"Good—what the hell is *that*?"

Jim saw another tiny splash of white whipping across their path. "Is that the same boat?"

"No, too far away. Jesus, there's another." Will leaped through the hatch. Jim picked up the binoculars and focused on the movement. He saw a spidery shape skitter through a light patch.

When he looked down the hatch, he saw Will hunched over the radar screen. A second later he came boiling up the companionway, shouting, "Head up! Douse the sails! They're all over the place!"

"Who?"

"Whole slew of patrol boats. Douse the sails."

Will cranked in the main. Jim furled the jib. Will started the engine and engaged the propeller.

"Told you that goddamned cracker was looking for us."

"He saw our flasher."

"Why was a chopper cruising so far from shore? I'll tell you why. Somebody paid him to keep an eye peeled. And now they know we're coming."

Jim couldn't believe this was starting all over again. They were so close. "Will, even if there is somebody chasing you—okay, okay, the poet is chasing you—there's no way he's going to know you're on the Bonny River. *What is that?*"

Something tall and dark loomed nearby, a sight blocked earlier by the sails. Will grabbed the binoculars. Then he tossed them to Jim, spun the helm, and steered toward it. "Good eyes, Jim. Good eyes. Get the mooring lines from the forepeak."

"What for?"

"Do it!"

When Jim returned with the lines, they were close enough to see what looked like the girders of a half-built office tower. "What is it, an oil well?"

"Abandoned rig."

"Where you going?"

"Right inside. Any luck, the patrols won't distinguish us from the rig."

They looked back. The lights of the patrol boats were still speeding in the orange dark.

As the sailboat motored closer and closer to the looming structure, Jim asked, "You said you were in the oil business?"

"Periphery," Will grunted.

"So you have a clear idea of what's under these things."

"Somewhat."

Jim held his breath. The heavy swell was surging between the thick round legs. High overhead, he could see the upper reaches against the orange-lit sky. The three legs of the structure looked twenty stories high, braced by cross girders.

"The mast is going to hit!"

"Optical illusion," Will said coolly. "Listen up. Take a mooring line up to the bow. See that leg with the ladder?" There was enough light from the flaming sky to see the swell sluicing through the steel understructure and a floating dock for the service boats. "I'll get you in close, you loop onto a mooring cleat—loop, not tie, in case we have to get off quick—and let her fall back on the current."

Hustle's engine echoed against steel as Will nosed the boat carefully between the stiltlike legs. "There you go—secure the line to the boat first!"

Jim ran forward, knelt on the foredeck to fasten the line, leaned out of the pulpit, and took a turn around a mooring cleat heavy enough to hold a tugboat. The current swung the stern around and the boat drifted back on her mooring line, hidden under the tower.

"Keep your eyes open," said Will and went below.

Ten minutes later Will called him down to the chart table. He was tense but collected, the way he got when he had settled on a decision.

"Okay, listen up. What we're going to do is head east for the Calabar River."

"What's there?"

"Friends they won't know about."

The chart showed the narrow Calabar River many miles to the east in the mangrove swamps. So far east that it formed the border between Nigeria and Cameroon. Will had underlined it in the *Sailing Directions*. They made the town of Calabar itself, forty miles inland, sound like the capital of nowhere.

"How do I get to the airport?"

"My pals will get you to Lagos."

"Why don't we land at the Bonny River, like we were going to? Just long enough to drop me on the dock." Port Harcourt was thirty miles upriver. So what if Will didn't have a "pal" with a helicopter. Port Harcourt looked like a fair-sized city. From there he could catch a train to Lagos, or maybe a ferry through the creeks that connected the rivers of the Delta.

Will answered slowly, as if he were attempting to talk sense to a drunk. "You see the patrols hunting us."

"No. I see patrols. But I don't see them hunting us."

"The chopper pilot told them he saw us. They've probably got a dossier on me as long as your arm, so they'll know

I was connected on the Bonny River. First place they'll look."

Jim molded his reasoning to fit Will's fears. "If it's me you're worried about, don't. 'They' won't bother me if I'm not with you."

"Unless they torture you to death to find out where I am."

Jim vaulted past that picture by reminding himself that Will had a gruesome way of drawing him into the circle of his fantasy. The only way around it was to answer Will in his own terms. "They'll know that you dropped me and sailed away. How would I know where you went?"

"I can't take the chance they won't be waiting at the dock."

"All you've got to do is drop me, you can keep going."

"No way. The boat would be in clear view from the time we cross the bar. Look here." Will touched a finger to the chart and traced the channel through shallow banks and breaking seas. "Eight miles from the bar to Peter Point. Nine, nearly ten, to the oil terminal. Two hours to prepare a 'welcome.'"

"Let's go in now, in the dark."

"At night? Are you serious? God almighty couldn't cross that bar in the dark. No, we'll head for the Calabar River."

"How am I going to get out of there?" Jim asked.

"I told you, my pals will get you to Lagos."

"Pals you haven't kept in touch with?"

"They'll be there."

"Well, if 'they' have a dossier on you as long as your arm, 'they' will look on the Calabar, too. Right?"

"Wrong. They won't connect me to the Calabar."

While they were arguing, the wind swung around and the Harmattan was back, blowing hard out of the northeast and throwing a gritty haze across the watery oil fields, blotting out terminal platforms and wellheads and derricks.

Will was delighted. "Thank you, Lord." And to Jim, he said, "It could last a week. We'll beat east along the ten-meter line. They can't see us from shore and they can't see us from offshore. The current is with us. With any luck we'll make the Calabar before tomorrow night."

Will led Jim up on deck. The "patrols"—if they were patrols—had vanished in the haze. Will started the engine. "Cast off. We're outta here."

The boat slipped from between the rig's legs. Shooting glances over his shoulder, Will set his course east. They maintained that course for hours, tracing the ten-meter line with the aid of the sonar depth finder and angling away from the coast until the soaring orange gas flares were miles behind.

"Take the helm. Steady as she goes."

As his McVay Foundation Hawker Horizon flew high above the dark Atlantic, Andy Nickels awoke with a start, lunged for the satellite phone, and dialed Greg in Lagos. Over the pilots' shoulders, he could see dawn faintly silvering the horizon far ahead. Last night, coked to the eyeballs, he had made a terrible mistake.

Greg reported that he had wrapped up the helicopter, but that the Joint Security patrol boats had found no sailboat anywhere near the Bonny estuary. He and his men were canvassing Will Spark's known haunts in case they had abandoned the boat and somehow come ashore in a dinghy.

Nickels cut him off. "Listen up, pal. We're getting indications that Spark operated under another name out there."

14

AS *HUSTLE* ZIGZAGGED to stay out of eyeball range, dodged obstructions, and rolled on the swell, the voyage to the Calabar River took much longer than Will had predicted.

"Oil wells have grown oil wells since I was here last. The joint is jumpin'."

Petroleum structures were strewn along the coast. Jim saw drilling rigs and huge production platforms and immense storage tankers tethered permanently to single buoy moorings. And scattered everywhere was the dangerous debris of failed enterprises, wreckage, and calamity. Just before dawn, startled to hear the swells crash where the water was supposed to be deep, they cast their searchlight on a sunken rig. A leg rose seventy feet out of the sea at a crazy angle. The swells were smashing against the upturned remains of a helicopter landing pad.

They ran all day and the dark was closing in again before they reached the Calabar. They dropped anchor outside the bar in ten meters of water. Will fixed their position precisely with the GPS.

A hideous night followed, with *Hustle* rolling violently. She swung with the east-setting current from her anchor chain, which put her hull broadside to the southerly swell.

Huge waves rolled her to the right as they approached, then heaved her left as they passed under. Fetching in from the Atlantic, they came like clockwork, a big roller every forty seconds. No sooner had one crashed, foaming on the bar, than the next shouldered the boat onto her side, flipped her the other way, and rolled on. Jim felt on the verge of throwing up all night. Will slept peacefully in his hammock, waking every twenty minutes to check their position with the GPS to confirm that they weren't dragging the anchor.

At daybreak they saw white breakers foaming on a reef that marked the west side of the river. Will started the engine and piloted through the haze, fighting currents, skirting shallows, and repeatedly stopping to check on the GPS the positions of buoys marking channels.

"Hey, young eyes. Do you see any fishing stakes? Sticks poking out of the water?"

Jim tried to pierce the haze. "No. Not yet."

"Good. If you did we'd be in trouble. No stakes means that's Tom Shot Bank. See why we didn't come in at night?"

And then, gradually, as if noticing a friend emerging from a crowd, Jim began to realize that he was looking at land. A low, flat coast lay gray-green in the haze. "Land. I see land!"

"Welcome to Africa."

The main channel was marked by a ghostly parade of ships, their shapes and colors blurred by the haze—bulk carriers, container vessels, and rusty old general cargo freighters heading upriver to Calabar.

Will aimed for a secondary channel, east of the main fairway, and the numbers on the sonar began jumping erratically as the water shallowed, deepened, shallowed again. At five meters, Jim checked the *Sailing Directions* spread on his lap and asked, "How much depth do we need?"

"She draws three meters—get the slickers!"

A sudden squall swept heavy rain across the estuary. It fell so hard they couldn't see the bow. Thunder cracked nearby. Lightning blazed. The squall passed, racing out to sea.

The wind slackened as the river narrowed. "Run below and get the Deep Woods Off! from the medicine locker."

Jim returned with the insect repellent just in time. Mosquitoes swarmed the cockpit, whining in their ears. "Slather it on," said Will. "Hair, ears, hat."

Suddenly Will spun the wheel and *Hustle* leaned clumsily into a sharp turn. "Missed!"

Will pointed and Jim saw floating just beneath the surface a submerged tree trunk twice as thick as a telephone pole.

"Ship behind us."

A Russian-flagged freighter steamed out of the murk. Will swung the wheel again and steered directly for the shore and into a clump of mangrove trees whose roots reached like spider legs into the water. *Hustle* came to a soft stop in the mud. The ship drew close, so close that Jim could read the name: *WorldSpan President.*

Hustle was deep in shadow and the freighter steamed past. So deep, in fact, that it took them an hour to kedge her out of the mud, which necessitated inflating the dinghy, rowing an anchor out to deep water, and pulling the anchor line with a winch while the motor ran in full reverse.

Towing the dinghy on a short line, Will headed upriver again, checking the GPS and the depth finder. "We're looking for a creek."

Jim shielded his eyes from the hazy sun glare and scanned the low, green, featureless shore, where the trees grew right into the water. Again, Will said, "You see why we don't go in at night?"

"Is the creek buoyed?"

"There'll be a stake or two, if we're lucky—there!"

Will spun the wheel and the bow swept west toward some sticks standing in the water. As they motored closer, Jim saw a dark hole in the trees. Will slowed the engine. A creek overhung with branches indented the muddy river and tunneled into a swamp.

Hustle nosed into semidarkness. Giant trees walled the sides. Their crowns met high overhead. There was no wind. The air felt thick and hot and was hard to breathe.

Will steered cautiously down the middle, his eyes moving between the sonar depth finder and the masthead. He veered left to avoid tangling the wind vane, anemometer cups, and radio antennae in the overhanging vegetation. He swung right to motor around the prong of a sunken tree trunk, which the sonar showed taking up half the channel four feet beneath the surface.

Will throttled back to dead slow and the boat moved in near silence. After weeks and weeks on the open sea, Jim felt the close-dwelling walls of trees loom oppressively. He had never suffered from claustrophobia, but at this moment, as they moved deeper and deeper into the dark slot, he longed to be out in the open.

"A little creepy, isn't it?" said Will.

"More than a little. How long is this creek?"

"Better to ask how deep," Will replied, peering intently at the depth finder and suddenly altering course to shave one side.

Ahead, at last, the trees thinned. Jim caught glimpses of the dull sky and finally the creek emptied into a broad lagoon. Deep in a mangrove swamp, the circular body of water was positioned like the hub of the spokes of a half-dozen creeks and streams.

A village of stilt houses simmered in the afternoon heat, lifeless, except for the smoke that drifted over tin roofs. They dropped anchor a quarter mile across the water from it. No one seemed to notice their arrival.

"Where is everybody?"

"The men are fishing. The women are indoors. Nobody but a damned fool goes out in the sun."

Jim thought that at least they'd stick their heads out the door. The place looked deserted. Canoes and skiffs littered a mud beach beside the dock. That narrow break below the smoky village was the only place where the mangroves didn't block access to the water.

"I see boats pulled up on the beach. They're not fishing."

"Maybe they're at a party."

"It doesn't look like they have much to party about. Shall we?"

"I'm going to clean up first. Run ahead if you like. I'll blow the airhorn when I want you to pick me up."

"It's a long way to row and hot as hell," said Jim. "Can't I take the motor?"

"They'll steal it," said Will.

Some children gathered on the dock. Jim inspected them in the binoculars. Stick children, skin and bones, the smallest naked, the older ones in scraps of cloth, all barefoot. Suddenly they scattered. An outboard-powered canoe nosed out of a narrow tributary and headed for the dock.

A shapely young woman in a tight white dress ran down to the water, shielding her eyes with one hand and waving toward *Hustle* with the other.

"Well, I'll be damned," said Will. "Give me the glasses."

"You know her?"

"Looks like I'm forgiven."

"For what?"

"Leaving . . ." Will answered and softly sung a new verse of the song he occasionally sang about "po-lice" taking him by the arm:

"My good gal loves me,
  Everybody knows.
  'Cause she paid a hundred cash dollars.
  Just to buy my suit of clothes."

Will passed Jim the binoculars. Jim adjusted the spread to his eyes as the woman hitched her skirt over her thighs and climbed down into the canoe. "She's eating a lot better than those skinny kids. Who is she?"

"Old friend."

She stood in the canoe, steadying herself on the shoulder of one of the men. The straps of her silver backpack tugged at her breasts. "She doesn't look old enough to be that old a friend. Jesus, Will, what was she, twelve, when you saw her last?"

"You might want to check out her little sister. Probably grown up by now. Condoms are in the medicine locker. . . ." Will took back the glasses and studied the village carefully.

"She's a chief's daughter—if you can believe her father's business card. These days, everybody's a chief. Damned few Indians left in Africa." Will began shaking his head in the same way Jim had seen him do at sea when rocketing thunderheads darkened the sky. "Strange."

"What's strange?" Everything about the broad lagoon looked strange to Jim's eyes—the deserted wooden shacks, the listing dock, the dark mass of the mangroves, the green, oil-streaked water.

"Strange that she's still hanging around here. I thought she lit out for Lagos. Maybe she's just home on a visit. She sure didn't buy that dress here."

"Or that disco pack."

". . . Wonder where Daddy is."

"Will, I'm going to run ashore. Check out the flights."

"Flights? From what airport?"

"You said you'd help me connect."

"Hang around. Maybe later you can catch a ferry heading upriver to Calabar."

Will made "catch a ferry" sound like "hop a Metro North commuter train." From a village with one rickety dock and an abandoned pier on a deserted lagoon?

"It's late. I don't want to get stuck in the dark. The sooner I get going, the better."

"Okay, if you think you can handle it. Got any cash?"

Jim nodded, eyeing the spider leg roots of the mangroves that barred the shoreline. He pulled out the wallet he'd stuffed into the pocket of his jeans.

"Don't flash your roll. Take fives—only fives. No twenties. And whatever you do, don't drink the water. They've got fleas swimming in it that'll give you river blindness."

Jim ran below, left his wallet in his bag—after rolling some five-dollar bills around his Visa card—and grabbed a bottle of Poland Spring water.

Back up on deck, Will handed him a can of Deep Woods Off! "Better spray more on. Mosquitoes carry malaria—you got your malaria shot?"

Even Shannon had laughed at all the shots Jim had gotten before he left. But he was glad of it now; this poison

green swamp looked like a giant stewpot for every Third
World disease and infection known to medical science. Will
Spark was playing on his fear of it, playing him like a vio-
lin. Fuck him.

"And don't get in any vehicle with a stranger."

"That won't be a problem. I don't see any vehicles. And
they're all strangers."

"You'll be okay. They'll know you're with me." Will
helped him over the side into the rubber boat and snubbed it
close with the painter while Jim fitted the oars. When he
started to shove off, Will held the rope. "A word of advice
about our Nigerian hosts."

"What?" Jim asked impatiently. Uninviting as the village
looked, he was anxious to get to it so he could arrange a way
out of here.

"They are convinced they're the smartest, most deserving
people on the continent. Ask any other African and they'll
tell you that Nigerians are the loudest, pushiest, most demanding people in Africa. A Nigerian would rather shout
than whisper. Here, what sounds like a bar brawl at home is
just two pals saying hello."

"Like guys yelling in the locker room."

"Exactly." Will beamed like a priest offering Communion
to his favorite acolyte. "Staking out turf with noise."

"Billy!" the girl called from the canoe. "Billy C."

"Who's Billy C.?"

"Nickname." Will glanced at the approaching canoe and
sobered rapidly. "Main thing is, never show fear—hang on a
minute. You might as well say hello to Margaret."

Margaret scrambled aboard, giggling and greeting Will
with lipstick kisses on his cheeks. "Billy. Billy. Billy."

Jim hardly registered that the silent men in her boat immediately pushed off and motored away. Margaret was practically falling out of her dress. Her skin was very black—as
black as the absence of light—and framed a friendly smile
that gleamed like ice.

Will introduced Jim as "my shipmate."

"Hello, muscle man."

Margaret leaned down toward Jim in the dinghy and extended a plump hand. A warm electric jolt of skin and her generous décolletage were acute reminders that it had been six long weeks since he had even seen a woman.

"Must you go?" she asked in an English accent.

He was vaguely aware that her eyes had the elsewhere glow of a woman seriously stoned. She wouldn't let go of his hand and was actually pulling him and the rubber boat closer. He smelled perfume, marijuana, and woman. She cocked her head, teasing him, daring him. Promising? Mocking? Who knew? She was older than he had guessed from her bouncy body, more woman than girl, closer to his own age—high and happy and out for a good time.

He glanced at Will. Will returned a shrug, vastly amused and apparently at ease with whatever decision Jim made.

He didn't suppose that Margaret fit Shannon's idea of an adventure when she'd sent him sailing. Squalls and breaking seas were more like it, and their unspoken thought, he assumed, was that they would fess up first, if either wanted to mess around. No blindsiding. No fait accompli–ing.

Trouble was, at this very moment in this very place, Margaret would fit any man's idea of adventure to a T. And it wasn't as if Shannon were waiting with a great big yes. It would serve her right for saying no. And it might be good for him to step out a little.

But if he wanted to try to pick up as close as possible to where they had left off, wouldn't it be better to go home still exclusive? Was he nuts? For all he knew at this very moment Shannon was—well, probably not. She would be up-front about it.

"Nice to meet you, Margaret. I have to go. See you later, Will."

She squeezed his hand with a wistful "Later."

Jim sat down in the dinghy, pushed off from *Hustle*'s high side, dipped the oars in the water, and rowed clumsily toward the distant dock. Margaret chirped a question he couldn't hear and Will laughed.

It was a hot pull over the still lagoon—long enough for a variety of erotic what-if scenarios to gallop through his mind. Maybe later, after he arranged a ride, grabbed a beer somewhere, and headed back to the boat. Will's remark about Margaret's sister was clanging in his skull, too. Maybe she'd be waiting at the dock. Or he'd bump into her on the street. Hi, there. Jim Leighton. Just dropped anchor in the lagoon. So what do you do for fun around here?

He looked over his shoulder to make sure he was on course. The smoke-shrouded village was still deserted. But at the dock, as he looped the dinghy's bow line around a weathered piling, the rickety structure began to shake.

He looked up to see four tall, gaunt teenagers drift out to greet him. Machetes dangled from their waists. Their feet were bare, the skin of their toes and heels cracked. Their plaid shirts were patched, the cuffs of their long pants in tatters. The handles of their machetes were wrapped in dirty cord and frayed electrical tape, and the blades were pitted. But where the edges showed through their makeshift scabbards, they gleamed as silvery as the sharpest knife in Will Spark's orderly tool chests.

He looked up into the nearest face and, before the kid's eyes slid away, said, "Hey, how you doing?"

"Five dollar."

"What?"

"You hear. Five dollar."

The *Sailing Directions* said that English was the official language, but that in the Delta there were many tribal dialects. He spoke slowly and loudly. "I don't follow what you're saying. Where is everybody?"

The answers came back fast and loud. Through the accents, he realized that they were speaking the pidgin English that Will had told him was the lingua franca. He heard a word that sounded like "money." And another that sounded like "chop."

"We take arm and chop!"

Any comparisons he might have entertained to making buddies with locker-room attendants were instantly dispelled and Jim fumbled the painter loose to get the hell out of there. Before he could, he got the phrase they were repeating over and over.

"*Landing* fee?"

"Are you stupid?" shouted one. "Money." Then Jim realized that what had sounded like "We take arm and chop," actually meant "Pay us money so we can go shop."

"Pay," yelled another, sticking out his free hand, and his friends started chanting, "Pay. Pay. Pay."

Jim shot a glance across the lagoon, where *Hustle* laid her upside-down reflection on the oily green water. Will, who was following Margaret down the companionway, waved as he disappeared below. The canoe that had delivered her was headed down the creek in the direction of the main channel, trailing thin Vs of ripples.

"Pay. Pay. Pay."

I'm getting mugged, Jim thought, his temper rising. All I want is a ride out of here and I'm getting mugged. He jumped without warning, using his arms to pull himself up and bound onto the dock in a single swift motion. The two in front backed up, bumping into those behind them and nervously fingering their weapons. They were taller than he but emaciated, their skeletal chests barely as broad as his arms, and he saw fear in their eyes as he prepared to kick the head off the first one who pulled his machete.

Then he stumbled. The dock felt as if it were rolling under his feet. He struggled to catch himself. But after six weeks on the moving boat, his slow-to-adjust inner ear, which had made him prey to seasickness, was betraying his sense of balance on land. It felt like an earthquake and he stood reeling visibly, which cost him the initiative as quickly as he had gained it.

They moved closer. "Landing fee. Pay."

He'd have a better chance duking it out drunk. The one who had yet to speak gave him a hard stoned-on-something grin and demanded in a loud British accent, "You pay for landing your boat a five-dollar landing fee. It is the custom."

"Five dollar."

Four against one. They had machetes. Don't get killed for nothing. Besides, they were dressed in rags. What the hell was five dollars? He kept his roll in his pocket as he peeled off one of the bills.

Out shot another hand. "Five dollar."

"I just paid you."

"Five dollar." Louder.

"I paid you. Get out of my way."

They drew their machetes and pointed them at the rubber dinghy.

Jim stared hard at the stoned kid, who explained with the dull, uncaring, but certain logic of a clerk in a bank, "You pay five dollar. We protect your boat."

He produced another five. Then he walked through them, toward the village.

The entire place seemed to be nothing more than twenty shacks on stilts. But he noticed two exceptions. One was a concrete structure with unglazed windows and the faded sign COMMUNITY CLINIC over the gaping door; goats had moved in and it stank of their dung. The other structure that stood out was a larger house made of three attached huts. The chief's? Jim wondered. It too was empty.

Maybe the main village was farther inland. There was a dirt road of sorts, twin tracks beaten in the sand and mud that indicated some vehicles had been through here at some point. The land was still rolling under him, and his feet kept slipping as the road seemed to fall away. At the next step they would scuff the dirt as it seemed to rise like a wave. He was still wobbly when the road forked. He followed it right. It narrowed, wandered into the mangroves, and petered out at the edge of another swampy creek.

Mangrove trees towered from the water up to a gloomy canopy. The treetops blocked the sun and it dawned on him that he had already walked through the village thinking that the wooden huts with tin roofs were the outskirts.

He walked slowly back. The left fork looked no more promising than the right, and he almost passed it by. Then he thought he heard music. A far-off pulse in the thick, hot atmosphere. So he took the left fork and followed it into the mangroves, still groping for balance, pausing occasionally to cock his ear to the music.

He walked for fifteen minutes, slapping at the bugs that hovered just beyond the aura of his insect repellent. The land began to rise. The stagnant pools disappeared, replaced by thick bushes, and the mangroves gave way to more ordinary-looking trees without the spidery roots. When he stopped again to hear the music, he heard people calling out and laughing. The main village: a bigger one on a main road.

Now he smelled food cooking in the still air. Climbing a steep rise, he found himself on a ridge. But instead of a bigger village, all he saw below was a shallow ravine where scores of people were digging with picks and shovels. The cooking smells came from an open fire above the excavation, where three women dressed in bright red blouses and long skirts were roasting sweet potatoes on sticks. There was no village in sight, no huts or buildings of any sort, just a raw earth gouge in the land, which looked like it had been dug that morning.

They had exposed a buried pipe. A long, narrow break in the trees, overgrown with bushes, marked the pipe's track. More people were streaming down the slopes carrying buckets, jerricans, and plastic pails.

Jim was still trying to figure out what they were doing when suddenly a cheer went up. People started pushing and shoving to get to the center, waving their buckets and pails. More people came streaming out of the woods and a sharp smell, much stronger than the roasted sweet potatoes, rose from the crowded pit the nostril pricking stink of gasoline.

A man in a ragged shirt burst from the crowd carrying a brimming bucket in each hand. He climbed the slope nearby, his face beaming. Jim backed away quickly and bumped into someone. An old man had come up behind him.

"Excuse me, sir."

"Sorry," said Jim. "My fault. You speak English?"

"Yes, of course." He had an accent like Will's friend Margaret's.

His hair was white. He wore a rope for a belt and a Shell Oil cap with a missing bill. His running shoes had been resewn by hand and his red plaid shirt was patched with green cloth.

"What are they doing?"

"Scooping," said the old man. "The white man's pipe

runs under the land. They've made a little puncture to scoop some petrol."

"Petrol? That's a *gasoline* pipeline? They'll get killed if it blows up."

"They know the danger of explosion. But they're poor. People have to survive."

"What do they use it for? I haven't seen any cars."

"There are no cars, sir. They mix it with oil to run a generator, or sell it to someone who owns an outboard motor."

That explained where everyone had gone. The adventure seemed to have emptied every village for miles around.

"Is there a way I could get to an airport?"

"There is no airport."

"A boat, maybe? To Lagos or Port Harcourt."

"Far away."

"How about Calabar?"

"You might find someone with a motor canoe. Go to the lagoon."

"I just came from there. No one's there."

"When this is done, they'll come back. I wonder, sir, if you would have a dollar?"

Jim was reaching into his pocket when suddenly the eager shouts and laughter turned to cries of alarm. The mob scattered. People clawed their way up the slopes, trampling one another. Jim saw fire jump skyward. Bright flame leapt from a puddle of gasoline onto a man's shirt and he ran, screaming, while the fiery puddle spilled toward the pipe.

The burning man slipped and fell facedown in the mud. Men pounced on him, pummeling at the flames, beating them out with bare hands.

Others kicked mud and dirt on the flames. There was a moment of utter silence, then nervous laughter rippled through the crowd. Shouting, laughing, people pounded one another on the back, shook hands, pulled the fallen man to his feet, and began picking up their buckets.

A big cheer greeted a pair of fat middle-aged women who marched out of the woods with cases of beer balanced on their heads.

"We live," the old man said, "by the mercy of God."

Jim turned away. Anyone who would risk burning to death to steal gasoline was stuck in the Niger Delta worse than he was. The old man was still glued to his side. Jim pressed one of his five-dollar bills into his hand.

"God bless you, sir. God bless you and yours."

Jim hurried back toward the dock, sweating in the heat, slapping at the bugs that grew bolder as his perspiration washed away the repellent. One of the machete gang had climbed into the dinghy.

The kid with the best English said, "What do you want?"

"I need a ride upriver to Calabar."

"How much you pay?"

Will had told him that the daily income in the Delta averaged thirty cents. Based on the ten-dollar bribe to come ashore with a promise of finding his boat on his return, and the blessings from the old man for five, Jim guessed a ferry price of twenty dollars.

The kid hooted. "You crazy, man. Twenty dollar. No way. Never happen. What's twenty dollars to a big man like you? Your family rich."

"No."

"They live in a big house?"

"I live in a little apartment."

"They drive big cars. SUV oarn."

"I drive a goddamned Honda," said Jim.

All three started shouting at once.

"You burn our oil."

"You take our oil. You pay us with pollution."

"You kill our fish."

What in hell had Will gotten him into here, a dead-end village with no way out? There was an American embassy in Lagos. But it might as well be on Mars for all the good it would do him on the Calabar River.

"Wait a minute. I'm not the oil company. I'm just trying to go home."

"Does your family miss you?"

The innocuous-sounding question seemed a welcome shift from blaming him for wrecking the environment; but they were suddenly extra-alert, all four intent on his answer.

Was he paranoid? Or did they sound like kidnappers assessing his ransom value? He glanced again at *Hustle*—perched upon her upside-down reflection as white as an egret—and realized with a sinking heart that driving a cheap car didn't make him any less of a jackpot to kids in bare feet. The rich white man's yacht had delivered a miracle: their winning lottery ticket dressed in a Gap shirt, Levi's, and New Balance 1220 running shoes whose cost could put food on their tables for a year.

A horn blast whipped their heads around. Jim tried to look in every direction at once. Some ways down the shoreline something large was emerging from a creek mouth overhung by mangrove trees. Salvation, he thought. Salvation in the form of an ungainly workboat like the offshore rig tenders he and Will had dodged as they motored through the oil fields.

The teens watched intently as the big boxy vessel lumbered into the lagoon. But when it swung toward the village, three of them backed hurriedly off the dock, calling to the fourth, who climbed out of Jim's dinghy but stayed defiantly on the dock. On the workboat's square bow stood a soldier in uniform cradling a rifle.

When it was a hundred yards away, a loud-hailer boomed, "Hey, bud, you wanna move your dinghy 'fore we squash it?"

Jim jumped down, fumbled his painter from the piling, and inched into the shallows. The workboat, with *Nellie H* on her smoke-stained stern, rotated on her twin screws. Engines thundering, she frothed the water into muddy soup and backed into the dock, which leaned and trembled from the strain.

Jim scanned *Nellie H* for a friendly face.

But no one appeared on deck, as if waiting for the Nigerian soldier to swagger back from the bow and take up station on the stern. The kid who had stayed on the dock—the most stoned one—jumped aboard and demanded, "Landing fee."

The soldier motioned him off with his rifle. The kid stood his ground. The gun butt whipped up and caught the kid full in the face, with an audible crunch. He fell backward into the water, splashed feebly toward the shore, and dragged himself onto the muddy beach.

A handful of black men trooped off the boat, looked around as if surprised to find the village empty, and wandered toward the huts. A heavily bulked-up white guy slid down the ladder from the wheelhouse and called after them, "Okay, boys, we'll be back for you in three days. Don't do anything I wouldn't."

"Three days," shouted one, without breaking stride. "Don't be late," yelled another, plodding toward the village.

"Hey, what's happening?" said Jim.

"What the hell are you doing here?"

"Came in on that sailboat," said Jim, extending his hand. "Jim Leighton."

"Frank Perry." He looked Jim over. "You a lifter, Jim?"

"A little," said Jim. "Not like you."

"Shit, man, I'm a mess. Haven't worked out in three months."

"Same thing on the boat. I've got a spinning bike and some free weights, but it's no gym."

"When I get home, it's going to take me six months to shape up for a pageant."

Jim nodded in sympathy. Competing in a body builders' pageant required the classic Mr. Olympia dimensions, which meant that Frank had to burn forty pounds of fat into ten pounds of muscle to match his arms and calves to his twenty-inch neck.

"*Cast off!*" boomed the loud-hailer.

"Gotta go. You take care, dude."

"Where are you heading?"

"Port Harcourt."

"Could I catch a ride?"

"Up to the old man," the roustabout said dubiously.

"I'm trying to get home. I'd be really grateful for a ride. Who's the old man? The captain?"

"I gotta warn you, he is one pissed-off skipper. Come on, I'll take you up to him." Jim jumped onto the boat and hurried forward with Frank Perry.

"Why's he pissed off?"

"We blew two cylinder heads 'cause the chief got drunk and the company said we had to drop these boys in the middle of their fucking-nowhere home village for community service and the tide's going out and there's a tornado coming in—not our kind of tornado, but a hell of a squall, buckets of rain, sixty-knot wind."

"Let me talk to him."

The "old man" was about Jim's age. He was slumped at the steering wheel, staring at the southern sky where huge cumulonimbus clouds looked ready to develop the solid tops Will had warned him to watch out for. Bloodshot eyes and a veiny red nose suggested that the "chief" had not been drinking alone.

"No rides. Company policy."

"I'll pay."

"You can't pay me enough to get fired."

"I'm really stuck, Captain."

"This ain't a goddamned ferry, just 'cause I gotta give the goddamned natives rides."

"Hey, Cap," said Perry. "Give the man a break. How'd you like to be a 'merican stuck in this shit hole?"

"Perry, get out of my face. You come in on that fancy sailboat?"

"Yes, sir."

"Where from?"

"We sailed from Barbados."

"So now you're bored and you want to go home?"

"No, sir. I was supposed to crew to Rio, but the owner changed his mind."

"Rio in Brazil? I'll say he's changed his mind. What do you mean, 'crew'? You work for him?"

Jim decided that the workboat captain would not regard a personal trainer as a fellow working stiff. "It's a job."

"What's he paying you?"

Jim lied. "Fifty bucks a day and a ticket home. From Brazil."

"Jeeez-sus . . . Okay. Okay. Give Perry a hand casting off."

"Thank you, Captain. Thanks a lot—can I get my stuff?"

"What?"

"His gear, Cap," Perry interjected. "His clothes and stuff."

"It'll just take a minute."

"We're outta here in ten minutes. No way I'm crossing that bar at low tide."

"I'll be right back."

"Ten minutes."

Jim scrambled down the wheelhouse ladder, off the workboat, jumped into the rubber dinghy, and rowed as fast as he could across the lagoon. Streaming sweat, his heart pounding, his head swimming from the heat, he pulled himself onto *Hustle,* hurriedly tied on the dinghy, and leaped down the companionway.

Margaret lay on the cabin floor.

Jim was stunned again by her raw beauty. Her dress had hitched up her thighs. For a crazy instant he wondered if she had changed her clothes. Changed from the tight white dress into a combination white skirt and red blouse. But he was dreaming. Wishing. The red was her blood. So much blood that she had to be dead.

15

WILL?"

The only sound he could hear was the distant rumble of the *Nellie H*'s engines. Her captain was revving them, chafing to get under way.

The woman's mouth was wide open as if to scream and yell or shriek with surprise. Her front teeth were as straight and white as a model's. But she was missing several deeper in her mouth.

"Will?"

What had the old man done?

"Will!"

"In here, kid" came the answer from Will's stateroom in the back of the boat.

Jim backed fearfully from the dead girl, past the nav station and the galley, where he noticed belatedly that the teakettle was whistling, and down the narrow corridor to Will's door. He glanced in and quickly stepped back.

Will was lying on his bunk, pointing a short-barreled gun at the door. Where, Jim wondered, had Will gotten the weapon? A sawed-off shotgun, he realized, as a crazy thought careened through his mind: Who would murder a beautiful young girl with a shotgun?

"Can you give me a hand, Jim?"

"Put down the gun."

"Can't. My fingers are locked. Help me off of here. Get me loose."

"I'm not walking in front of that gun," Jim said, even as his mind fastened on the absurdity. Will's shotgun would shred the thin teak bulkhead as it had shredded the African girl's chest.

"Oh Jesus, Jim, are you nuts? I won't hurt you. Pull the knife out."

Will was nearly sobbing. Jim looked into the cabin again and this time saw the long knife sticking out of Will's chest.

"What?" He lunged through the door and bent over the old man. Will was dead white from shock or blood loss. His pupils were dilated and he was gasping for air.

"I can't believe I fell for the oldest trick in the book."

"I'll get a doctor."

"Pull the knife out."

"I'll get a doctor."

"There's no time."

"I can't just pull it out. What if I cut an artery?" The blade had pierced him where his breast met his shoulder.

Will bit his lips. "I'll take the chance, for Christ's sake. Pull it out. Pull it out. It's killing me. I can't breathe."

Left side. An inch from his heart? A quarter inch? "I can't—there's an oil rig tender in the lagoon. Americans. They can radio in a helicopter. Fly you to a hospital."

"*No!* They'll find me in the hospital. They'll kill me."

The *Nellie H* blew her horn, the blast racing across the lagoon and reverberating off the walls of mangroves.

Jim whirled from Will's bunk, pushed out of his cabin, and scrambled up the companionway. He could hear the engines start to thunder and he thrust his head out of the hatch just as the rig tender began to depart from the dock. Perry waved frantically from the wheelhouse.

"Jim," Will called.

There was just time to jump into the dinghy. The hell with his stuff. Leave it and get out of here. The hell with crazy Will. When they saw him rowing, the rig tender would pick him up.

"Jim," Will called again. His voice sounded as if it were clawing the hot, still air, as if he had channeled every last remnant of his strength into one final, desperate bid to be heard. Jim prayed to Shannon, prayed for her advice. She had a clearer eye than he did behind her ready smile: a survivor's eye.

"Jim!"

They said you saw your past flash by when you died; what Jim Leighton saw was his life plowing across the lagoon, trailing a heavy wake, and vanishing into the narrow creek that led to the Calabar River and the Atlantic beyond if he didn't run now.

"Run for it, Jim," Will yelled. "I'm a goner."

Jim slumped halfway out of the hatch and whispered, "Oh my God."

He clung to the cockpit sill, watching the ponderous curl of the *Nellie H*'s big wake roll toward the anchored sailboat. It wasn't guilt that held him, nor fear that he would hate himself later. But the much more powerful and insidious grip of need—need that he had to serve.

Then he saw the deadly threat of the rig tender's wake.

He plunged down the companionway ladder, picturing the effect on the knife when the track of the passing vessel seized *Hustle* and threw her violently from side to side.

The sloop was already leaning into the cavity of the wake when he burst into the cabin. The old man was still conscious, eyes murky. He flinched at Jim's approach, pawed at the sheets, and struggled to lift the shotgun.

"It's Jim. Hang on."

He knelt beside the bunk and cradled Will in his arms, hoping to cushion him from the rocking. No good. As the boat leaned further, Will's body shifted hard and it was clear to Jim that nothing he did could prevent the man from rasping against the sharp steel in his shoulder.

He reached for the knife, closed his hand gingerly around the handle, which was wrapped in dirty cord, and forced himself to tighten his grip when all he wanted to do was let it go. Still kneeling, he braced every muscle in his body, counted to three, and yanked up.

Steel ground on bone. Will screamed.

The blade slid free. Jim flew backward and crashed into the bulkhead with the knife held high, dripping blood on his face. Before he could untangle his arms and legs, the rolling water tipped *Hustle* in the opposite direction and he fell facedown on Will's bunk.

Fearfully, he pulled the sheet away and watched the blood flow from Will's chest. The skin around the one-inch wound puckered out where the knife had exited, oozing red like a lipstick kiss. Jim noticed with faint hope that the blood was not spewing in the rhythmic pumping from a sliced artery. The boat was still rocking violently. As gently as he could, he lifted Will to inspect his back.

His skin was unblemished. The knife hadn't gone through him. But God knew what was going on inside the man.

"Jim," Will groaned. "Douse me with alcohol."

"What?"

"Goddamned Africa, every germ in the world. Douse me good before they get inside me. There's a bottle in the big medical kit."

He screamed when Jim dribbled the antiseptic onto his chest and struggled to break away. Appalled, Jim let go. The pain had turned Will into a frightened animal. But he moaned, "Sweet Jesus, get it over with. Do it! They probably cleaned fish with that goddamned thing. *Do it!*"

With a prayer that the old man would faint, Jim poured the alcohol into the wound. Will's scream pitched to a shriek. His whole body convulsed and he flipped onto his back and flailed out, pummeling Jim with his fists.

Jim took the weak blows, and as they subsided, he laid Will down again, wondering how to bandage the wound. Will lay still for a moment, his breath whistling through his teeth. "I'm bleeding," he said. "You have to pack the wound. Go to the medical locker. Get Iodoform gauze."

Jim pawed frantically through the locker. "I got it!"

"Stuff it in—Oh, Christ! . . . Good. Good. Well done. Well done. . . . Okay, we have to get out of here. Before her people come back."

"We have to find a doctor."

Will closed his eyes. "A doctor won't do us any good in a Nigerian jail."

The words *we* and *us* forced Jim's thoughts along a predictable series of events: the dead woman's friends return; they call the police; the police—or, more likely, a squad of thug soldiers like the one on the rig tender—arrest both him and an unconscious or dying Will Spark; Jim claims he wasn't even on the boat; ask the boys at the dock. What boys? Four stoned teenagers with machetes who tried to rob me?

Will whispered, "Do you really want to defend yourself against murder charges in a lawless state?"

"Me? What about you?"

"I'll have worse problems. They will kidnap me out of a hospital in twenty-four hours—listen to me. It was self-defense. They sent her to kidnap me—now help me up on deck. We've got to get out of here."

He raised his head and moved as if to swing his legs off his bunk, but fell back, sucking air. "I can't move, Jim. It's up to you."

16

THE TEENS WITH the machetes had returned to the dock. There was no time to waste booming the dinghy aboard. Jim tied it to a cleat on the stern, then hurried forward to the bow to figure out how to raise the anchor. Will had lowered it by stepping on a switch under a rubber jacket that controlled the electric windlass. But all that did was let the chain further out. A closer inspection revealed an up-down toggle that reversed the windlass. The chain began clanking aboard, dragging a stinking coat of mud and slime across the deck and into its locker below.

When the anchor itself finally emerged from the lagoon, stock and flukes trailing oily grass, it took Jim two tries to lock it into place and he still wasn't sure he had seated it correctly. But by then the boat was drifting toward the dock and he realized too late that he should have started the engine first.

When he tried the starter, it ground over but wouldn't fire. Again he pushed the starter button. Nothing. He glanced back: there were more people on the dock.

When Will started the engine, an alarm sounded first. The fuel alarm. He was so rattled, he had forgotten to flip the fuel switch. He cranked the starter again, and the diesel rumbled to life.

He steered for the narrow opening through which they had entered the lagoon. He had gotten comfortable steering under sail, but under power, in these close quarters, the boat seemed extraordinarily long—the bow far, far away. She was slow to respond to the steering wheel and the creek mouth was coming up fast.

Then the boat was in the creek, the trees hanging close and darkening the sky. *Hustle*'s exhaust echoed in the tunnel-like space.

Standing on tiptoe to see over the cabin, he was distracted by motion down the companionway. The dead woman seemed to be moving. He locked the wheel, started fearfully down the companionway, and stopped abruptly when he saw what was moving. Her bloodied chest was carpeted with flies.

How long would they have to carry her body? A cold voice from deep inside his head spoke firmly to that topic. He couldn't throw her overboard so close to the village. They'd have to wait until they were far out at sea. How far out would the flies—and the Nigerian police—follow?

Suddenly, directly ahead, something large hung suspended inches below the water's surface. The ominous dark cylinder of a huge waterlogged tree trunk. Jim spun the wheel, but it was too late. A loud *thunk* slammed through the decks and echoed from the cabin. *Hustle* staggered. The impact threw him against the spokes and the boat veered toward the forested creek bank, bumping along the heavy log.

What had he done? Had he damaged the hull? Terrified of sinking, he ran down the companionway, edged past the dead woman, and raced forward to the forepeak, where the extra sails were stowed.

He grabbed a flashlight from its charger and, wrestling with the heavy sailbags, probed the cramped space praying all the while that the beam wouldn't reflect the gleam of water. Nothing. He cocked his ear, listening. Nothing. No gushing water; no dents or cracks. He couldn't believe that the hull would survive such a hit unscathed. He backed out of the forepeak, pulled up the floorboards, and shined the light in the bilge. There was water, dark and oily, but no more than he had last seen under the floorboards while helping Will rewire the depth finder.

Lucky, lucky, lucky.

Then he heard a distant muttering. A chain saw? No. The noise was an engine approaching—like the high-pitched whine of the outboard canoe he'd last seen heading out of the creek.

Jim ran back through the main salon, jumped over the dead woman, climbed the companionway, and looked out. The sound was loud, close, coming from ahead. Just ahead to the left he saw an indent in the bank. He engaged the prop and swung cautiously into the opening, which led a hundred feet into the mangroves and then stopped at a wall of trees. High overhead, one of the spreaders jutting out from the mast caught on a hanging branch and the boat slewed to the side. An instant later, he felt the keel plow into the mud and then the sailboat was standing stock-still in the near darkness cast by the forest canopy.

Jim shut the engine. How stupid could he be? In his panic he had trapped himself in a dead-end canal.

As the outboard pulled abreast of *Hustle,* a glance in the creek mouth would reveal her white stern reflected on the water, or her mast rearing straighter than the trees. He looked up. Would the vines obscure it? Could he pull them over the boat? No time? He saw a flicker of motion through the mangrove forest; the canoe sped on the main creek, bearing down on the inlet.

What had he told Will when Will razzed him about bulking up? Muscle came in handy. Do it! He scrambled up the backstay, climbing the steeply inclined wire cable hand over hand. Fifteen feet above the deck, he let go with his right hand, gripped the wire with his left, and lunged for a thick, leafy vine.

The vine and several attached to it swung closer to the mast. Giddy with fear and flying on adrenaline, he almost laughed at the sight he cut, suspended between the backstay and the vine like a crucified monkey. Then a huge ant crawled off the vine onto the back of his hand and started down his arm. And Jim saw to his horror that the rough bark he clung to was filled with them.

The canoe pulled abreast of the inlet. Jim watched through the leafy scrim. There were three men in the boat: one standing in the bow, one driving, and one seated between them dragging on a blunt that was as fat as a cigar. The driver glanced down the inlet. The man in the middle reached back and passed him the smoke. The canoe flashed past and was gone.

When the noise of the motor had faded to a quiet buzz, Jim let go of the vine, frantically shook the ants off his arm, and slid down the backstay, burning his hands. Something was crawling inside his shirt. He stripped it off and slapped more ants from his back and chest. The canoe had left in its wake the stink of gasoline and oil, which lingered in the thick air, sweetened by a whiff of marijuana.

Jim started *Hustle*'s engine and engaged reverse. The propeller churned. Mud roiled and darkened the water. But the boat wouldn't move. Jim increased the power. She shuddered, decks vibrating, and threw mud. Then with a heart-stopping series of hesitations she began to move. Shoving the dinghy, bumping bottom with her keel, and dragging her spreaders through the branches, she backed out of the inlet. As soon as she reached the main channel, Jim shoved the throttle forward and drove her as fast as she would go toward the Calabar River.

The equatorial night was closing in quite suddenly, even more abruptly than it had at sea, abetted by the Harmattan haze and the storm clouds. It was dark among the trees, but the slot of sky he could see above the creek began to glow from the distant offshore oil well flares. And it was by that fiery orange and red light that he finally saw the creek open into the Calabar River. Breaking out of the trees, he steered for a string of lighted buoys, which marked the channel through the flat expanse of the estuary that led to the Atlantic. An expanse, he knew from their morning passage in, that was an illusion. The water was shallow, the channels treacherous.

17

THE FAIRWAY BUOYS appeared sporadically, and many were unlit. But ship lights moving downstream gave him a clue to the deepest water. He could follow a ship out to the main channel. Except that the *Sailing Directions* said that local pilots were mandatory for ships traveling on the river. What if the river pilots saw the sailboat? As soon as they knew a police manhunt was on, they'd radio his position.

He was getting ahead of himself. No one had seen the dead girl yet. Even if her friends realized she was missing, nothing he had seen ashore suggested it was the sort of place you dialed 911.

I'm overthinking this. Just sail away. No one would know until he was a hundred miles at sea. Unless, of course, Will's mysterious "they" really *had* sent the girl to kill him or distract him until they caught up. "They"—who, if Will were to be believed, could sic the cops on them, or the Nigerian army, or the oil company helicopters, or all three. Now I'm going mental as Will. Jim was so scared he couldn't think straight.

If only the night were truly night. But with the gas flares reflecting enough light from the low clouds to read by, night offered no cloak. To his right along the broad estuary he could see the low shore rise abruptly to the bluffs of Tom Shot Point, and anyone there could see him. To his left, a tall container ship and a low-slung tanker were passing on a main channel of the Calabar.

A dozen miles beyond the ships—invisible in the fine, gritty dust of the Harmattan—Cameroon lay on the far shore. Another country, but surely as strange. Will was right. Only the open ocean guaranteed sanctuary.

Jim ran below for the *Sailing Directions* and brought the book up to the cockpit. The channel that Will had used to enter the Calabar was described as a minor channel. Local knowledge was strongly recommended. Even Will had run aground. There was no way Jim could pilot it at night. But the main channel was too busy.

A secondary channel crossed the wide flats where the river met the sea. It ran between the shoals formed by Tom Shot Bank and Bakasi Bank to the east, and was too shallow for large ships: vessels drawing more than three meters, ten feet, were warned off. Will had steered it on the way in, before he cut across Tom Shot Bank. Jim switched on the depth finder—he kicked himself for not doing it earlier—and steered a new course that would bring him across the main channel to a less populated route through the flats.

He crossed behind the two ships. Suddenly, lightning flashed and turned the red-orange sky bright white. Everything stood in stark clarity and Jim saw a third vessel between the tanker and the freighter. It was smaller, low-slung, and moving fast. Patrol boat? He studied it with the binoculars.

A gun was mounted on the bow. Army? Or an armed oil company boat? Neither was a friend.

They hadn't seen him yet, because the sailboat was so low to the water. Surely they were tracking with radar. Will had claimed that *Hustle* was "invisible." She better be.

He ran the motor at top speed, spotted a buoy marking the secondary channel, and turned south, toward the sea. He held that course for more than an hour. Once he glimpsed the patrol boat's silhouette, tearing north at high speed, vaporizing in the fire-lit haze.

Then things quieted down and the sailboat was alone except for the distant ships plodding seaward in the parallel channel. They, too, faded in the strange light as the channels veered apart. Ahead, he saw a lighted oil well to the left of his channel. To the right he saw an angry white line on the water.

His stomach clenched with the memory of the line storm that had almost destroyed them in the Atlantic. As the sea began to roll the waters of the estuary and the line got closer, it grew thicker. A foamy white line bordered the channel. He checked the *Sailing Directions* and stopped the engine to listen.

Muted thunder confirmed that he was seeing surf—huge Atlantic waves fetching a thousand miles from Cape Town were breaking on Outer Reef. He was almost out. Now all he had to do was get past Outer Reef, skirt the oil fields, whose flares he could see dancing against the horizon, and break for the open sea.

He locked the wheel and went below to check on Will. Ignoring the body on the floor, he went into Will's cabin and played a flashlight over his face. The old man was sleeping. His lips looked parched, so he dribbled a little water on them and then more as Will licked hungrily at the bottle.

"What's happening?"

"We're passing Outer Reef."

"Well done, kid! . . . Which side?"

"We're east of it, in the second channel."

"Steer clear of the oil rigs on the left. Have you seen any patrols?"

"One."

"Call me if they get close."

"You bet," said Jim. That's all they needed: Will hemorrhaging all over the cockpit.

He took a fresh water bottle up to the helm and looked around. Far behind he could see the two ships, stopped. He recalled something in the *Sailing Directions* about night transits not allowed in the fairway.

A couple of miles to his left the oil field Will had mentioned sparkled with hundreds of electric lights. To his right, heavy seas pummeled Outer Reef. He steered a little closer—the *Sailing Directions* showed deep water on this side—to give the oil field a wider berth. He passed the reef, and when next he looked, several miles of orange- and red-smeared water lay between him and the foaming breakers.

His heart jumped. A helicopter—a cascade of blinking red and white running lights—was racing out from the now invisible shore. Helplessly, he watched it home in on *Hustle* as if they were attached by a wire. But in the final miles it stopped, midair, and hovered over Outer Reef, its lights rotating slowly as it turned three-sixties, watching the channels.

Jim stopped the engine. The boat lost way and began rolling on the swell. He went back down to the after cabin.

"Will!"

The old man had fallen back to sleep. But the boat's clumsy roll woke him. Groggy and confused, he asked, "What's up?"

"Helicopter. What do I do?"

"Jesus . . . Hide."

"Where?"

"Where . . . where are we?"

"Three miles past Outer Reef."

"Right . . . right. . . . Listen to me. You have to fox their radar."

"Radar? You said radar can't see us."

"Airborne radar can. Looking straight down, they can pick up the steel in the engine. Listen . . ."

"I'm listening. I'm right here."

"Remember the wreck I showed you on the way in?"

"The masts."

"Right. The masts. Get inside the masts."

"What do you mean?"

"Drive the boat among the masts. Use your depth finder. Get a bowline ready. Make your approach from downwind, real slow. Tie onto something solid and let her drift back a few yards. Keep watching your depth finder."

"There's a heavy swell, Will. Huge waves."

"I am goddamned well aware of that. Be careful so it doesn't pick you up and slam you down on solid steel."

Jim ran back to the cockpit and steered a dubious course outside the eight meters of dredged channel. Immediately, the depth finder showed a rolling bottom beneath the keel, five meters deep, then four meters of water, then five, six, four—and suddenly, some distance ahead, a wall. It had to be the sunken wreck, but he couldn't see it and he didn't dare turn on a spotlight, which would give away his position to the helicopter and anyone else watching.

The wind had turned southerly and brisk—the cause, he realized belatedly, of the suddenly greater visibility—and he smelled the wreck before he saw the masts, a coarse, lively odor of seaweed and barnacles exposed by the tide receding down the rusty flanks of the sunken ship. The masts jutted from the water in a dark and menacing cluster. When he slowed the engine to maneuver, he heard the sea sluicing furiously in and out of the steel pillars.

How in hell was he going to get close enough to attach a rope without smashing into the main body of the wreck? He slowed and circled, studying the depth finder, trying to form a picture in his mind of the shape beneath the surface. Will was confused. This was not possible. The boat was lurching around on the swell; it was almost uncontrollable. Of course Will was confused, half out of his mind with pain, shocked by trauma, and terrified of dying.

Something shook the air, a heavy vibration that whipped Jim's head up in alarm. The helicopter was moving again, its rotors beating the sky with a sharp *thump thump thump* as it swept a broad circle over the water.

He shot a desperate look at the companionway, half fantasizing, half praying to see a rejuvenated Will Spark hurry up the steps to take charge. Fat chance. Somehow he had to point the boat and throw a line at the same time. Then it struck him that Will himself would never tie the boat to the mast. Will would have run in close circles. But he didn't trust Jim, a novice helmsman, to maneuver close enough to blend the radar signature of *Hustle*'s engine with the steel wreck without smacking into it.

Jim decided he liked those odds much better. Besides, was he supposed to sit tied up until daylight? Hell, no. The second the helicopter went the other way, he was out of here.

Picturing the submerged wreck in his mind, he concluded that the bulk of the sunken vessel lay inshore of the masts. Maybe, like the oil tenders he'd seen racing around the oil fields, it had a cabin on the front, on top of which stood the mast. In that case, the safer depths were in front of it, which the sonar confirmed.

He looked up at the helicopter thumping around the horizon and tried to place himself inside it. Will had devised a good hiding trick. A local helicopter pilot would be familiar with the wreck and recognize its radar position. He just had to keep the sailboat in its sphere until the helicopter gave up and went home.

But the swell was rising and falling sharply, which made controlling the boat extremely difficult. It was like dancing drunk at the junior prom: the rusty masts were his high school principal, guidance counselor, and favorite teacher clustered worriedly next to the dance floor; *Hustle,* the poor girl he had his arms around, holding on to her for dear life; the helicopter, his mother, who had volunteered to monitor.

No, it was really more like sailing with Will Spark—an illusion of control while everything was really going to crash. Shannon, I am so sorry I didn't run when I had the chance. I tried to save Will and lost myself.

Hustle was caught suddenly off balance. The helm went dead in his hands and she made a nightmarish lurch at the wreck. Jim felt something crunch underneath—the keel was scraping the wreck. He held his breath. If *Hustle*'s keel hung up—or worse, her rudder—the next swell would throw the boat into the masts and pin her in them until the swell pounded her to pieces. But she rose on the next sea. The propeller bit and drove her to temporary safety.

Jim battled the swell for an hour that felt like a long, long night, repeating over and over the nerve-racking, exhausting maneuvers to hold the boat within the target range of the masts, while praying that the helicopter would give up and go home.

It kept swooping in wider and wider many-mile circles. Then it put down on a platform in the Kita pumping station. Jim steered away from the masts and tried to find the helicopter in Will's night binoculars. As he was scanning the myriad lights of the Kita field, the aircraft suddenly shot into the sky again. Jim raced back to the masts, his heart sinking as he saw the aircraft resume sweeping the Tom Shot Bank and realized that the helicopter had descended to refuel.

Suddenly, it dropped to the water. A pinprick of light below it revealed the familiar shape of the patrol boat. Not only weren't the crews stopping, they were coordinating to expand the search. Jim ran below.

"What's happening?" Will asked as Jim burst into the cabin. He had hauled himself into a sitting position so he could see out of the small oval porthole.

"The patrol boat just joined the helicopter."

"Bloody hell."

"They're not giving up."

"Get back to the wheel. Let me think."

Jim ran back to the cockpit and circled closer to the masts. He saw the lights of the helicopter and the patrol boat diverge, the helicopter swinging west toward the main channel, the patrol boat's white masthead light lined up between her red and green side lights. Will had taught him what that configuration meant: the vessel had turned toward him. It was heading south, outbound in the secondary channel, on a course that would take it within eyeball range of the wreck.

A red flash lit the sky behind the patrol boat.

They're shooting, thought Jim. They've seen us.

A second flash seared the clouds. A third turned the orange flare-lit sky vermilion red. The high bluff of Tom Shot Point was suddenly etched black against the brilliant sky. The water flats of Tom Shot Bank and Bakasi Bank turned red as deserts. The red light stretched to the Bakasi Peninsula, rimming the breakers with color.

An immense din rumbled across the water, three massive explosions spaced like the flashes. A pillar of fire rose behind Tom Shot Point.

"Jim!" yelled Will. "What happened?"

The helicopter and the patrol boat wheeled toward land. Jim immediately steered away from the masts, regained the channel, and headed south at full speed.

"What happened?" Will yelled again. Somehow he had managed to reach up and unlock one of the ports that opened into the side of the cockpit. His voice came at Jim's feet.

"Hang on, Will." The water had deepened, and Jim was concentrating on trying to line up a course between the lights of two distant oil fields. When he got it, he set the autopilot and went down to Will's cabin.

"What happened?"

"Something blew up."

"Oil rig?"

"No. I think it's back behind the village. They were scooping—stealing gas from a pipeline. It could have been them."

"Happens all the time, poor bastards. Where's the patrols?"

"It looks like they went to help."

"God bless 'em," said Will.

"It was like a big party. Everybody laughing and dancing and running around with buckets of gas."

"Probably smoking dope, too . . . Jim?"

"What?"

"I'm afraid I have to ask you to dump our friend."

"What do you mean?"

"You know what I mean. I can't move. You have to throw Margaret's body overboard."

Which meant picking it up. "I can't do that."

"This is no time to be squeamish."

"I won't do it," said Jim.

"You won't and I can't," Will replied slowly. "But may I suggest it will be easier before she rots?"

"I didn't kill her. You did."

Will sank back and closed his eyes. "That is true but useless information."

Jim looked forward up the corridor that led to the main salon, which was bathed in red-tinged darkness. What remained white of her dress glowed like an angry glance. Will started in on him again.

"You've done yourself proud tonight, Jim. I don't know anybody who could have gotten us out of that mess like you did. But you have to finish the job. There is no way we can sail all the way to South America with a rotting corpse."

Jim pushed back on the door frame. "We're sailing to *North* America," he said firmly, and went to finish the job.

"Give yourself a break," Will called after him. "Wrap her in one of the big garbage bags."

"I already thought of that."

"But don't seal it. You don't want her to float."

He hadn't thought of that.

Will had warned him repeatedly about not wasting fuel, and there came a point when Jim realized he had to, whether he wanted to or not, stop depending on the engine.

When the wind swung, dragging the African dust with it, Jim raised the main and unfurled the jib and set a course south. Once the sails were pulling reasonably well, he shut the fuel valve, and in the deep silence that ensued, he felt the boat come alive again. He sat in the cockpit all night, dozing by the wheel, afraid to go below with the big ships converging on the oil fields.

At dawn the GPS indicated they were crossing latitude 3°30' north—sixty miles from the coast. The depth finder showed no bottom, which the chart promised lay twelve hundred meters under *Hustle*'s keel. The air had cleared in the night and Jim was stunned to see looming on his left two mountains, shockingly steep compared with the flat, green swampy Niger coast he had fled in the night.

The taller was a precipitous volcanic cone that trickled a menacing twist of smoke. Jim located a drawing of their silhouettes in the *Sailing Directions* that identified the two peaks as capping Isla de Bioko. The island belonged to Equatorial Guinea, whose territorial waters the *Sailing Directions* advised avoiding.

Quickly, he turned the boat away from the island and headed west, checking his position repeatedly on the GPS. When Isla de Bioko was a safe twenty miles behind, he altered course again, turning to the southwest, aiming for the point nine hundred miles ahead where Africa jutted into the Atlantic. Will woke and called his name.

Jim brought him water and a glass of long-life ultrapasteurized orange juice. The old man looked awful.

"How are you?"

"Hurt like hell. Can't catch my breath. . . . She did something to my lung. . . . You have to douse my shoulder again. Infection will kill me."

"Let me see if the bleeding has stopped."

"It has," Will snapped, drawing the bloodstained sheet tighter to his chest.

"Hey, I have to see it when I douse it, right? Let me see."

Will lay back reluctantly. Jim stared at the wound, astonished. Somehow, sometime in the night, while he was in the cockpit, Will had gotten up, walked to the first-aid kit in the main salon, and repacked the wound. The pain must have been torture.

"You're like a wounded elephant that goes off to nurse itself."

"Elephants hang with the herd. I'm a warthog."

"Well, I'm impressed. And you're right, it's not bleeding."

"Thing is, what's going on inside? Douse me again. Give me some morphine and some penicillin. Let me sleep it off."

"First you're going to help me work out a course straight across the Atlantic Ocean to Florida."

Will said, "Listen, Jim. You have to hydrate me. There's a ton of saline and glucose bags in the medicine locker. Do you know how to hook up an IV?"

"I've had plenty stuck in my arm. I'll figure it out."

"I'd do it myself, except I'm so shaky. It's easy. I have good veins."

Jim hung the plastic bag from the clamp that held Will's ceiling compass. Then he wrapped a short length of elastic shock cord around Will's arm like a tourniquet. A fat vein popped up inside Will's elbow. He swabbed the skin with alcohol and attacked the vein with the sterile needle.

"You just have to line it up with the vein."

The boat's constant motion was the real problem. A sudden lurch took him by surprise and he accidentally pushed too deeply, through the vein and out the other side into the muscle.

"Margaret was gentler than you are, for Christ's sake."

"I'm not laughing, Will."

He tried again and missed.

"Collect your spirit," whispered Will. "Just calm down. You can do it."

He got it, finally, taped the catheter to Will's forearm, and hurried to attach the clear tubing.

"Try not to send any air bubbles into my heart. I'm in no mood for an embolism."

Jim checked again to make sure the IV tube had no bubbles. The solution began to flow. Will sagged back on the sheets. "Now, what's this about Florida?"

"Safe American territory."

"They will kill us in Florida," Will said flatly. "And they won't bungle it like the Nigerians. They'll send professionals."

Jim sat on the edge of the bed. "Is it possible," he asked gently, "that Margaret stabbed you for her own personal reasons?"

Will's laugh came out half snort, half painful gasp. "Crime of passion? Are you kidding?"

"You said you left her."

"Margaret lived in a country where men who can afford them keep a minimum of two wives, plus a cutie on the side. We're not talking about Latin passion in Nigeria. Nor are we talking about any kind of equality of the sexes. Besides, I didn't do anything terrible to the poor girl. We had a few laughs and then I left. She'd been with a Texas petroleum engineer before me. And after I left, she told me yesterday, she hooked up with the captain of an anchor handler. Jim, how the hell old are you? Where've you been? This is life. These are poor people. Poor people do what they have to do. They offered her enough money to do it."

"If 'they' are real."

"As real as death," muttered Will. His eyes were glazing over. "I need another morphine."

Jim gave him two. "Sleep tight."

It had taken a week to sail nine hundred miles into the Gulf of Guinea. So if the wind held, maybe another week to sail out. A week before he had to commit to a course for Florida. A week to read Will's books on navigation. A week to get some rest for the long, long haul back across the Atlantic Ocean.

BOOK III

Unshored, Harborless Immensities

18

ADMIRAL RUGOFF! SO pleasing on the ear—as Homer sings—to hear your voice again. . . . Your daughter is better? . . . Excellent. Excellent . . . Yes, yes. Young people have to find themselves, but no permanent damage done. . . . No thanks are necessary, we were delighted to intercede. Now, Admiral . . ."

Lloyd McVay described Will Spark's sloop, Will himself, and Jim Leighton, then gave Boris Rugoff Andy Nickels's guesstimate of their position in the Gulf of Guinea.

Rugoff—formerly admiral of the Soviet navy's auxiliary merchant fleet and now president of WorldSpan, Russia's largest privately held shipping conglomerate—said, "I have four tankers passing through that area this week, several freighters bound for Cape Town, and three for the Med. But it is a very big ocean, my friend."

"Well, with the shores of darkest Africa to the north and east, we're reasonably sure they can go only west or south."

"Perhaps with luck, my ships will get lucky. What do you want done with the yacht?"

"Can you trust your captains?" McVay asked.

Rugoff laughed. "They enjoy a little, shall we say, 'free trade' on the side. It makes them loyal."

"I want the yacht intact and Will Spark alive."

"The young man?"

"Of no consequence."

"And if my people happen to spot them in port?"

"Watch them until my people get there."

"How valuable are they?" the Russian asked.

Like any ex-Soviet official, Rugoff was used to carving portions from the living beast. So McVay was confident that the admiral's greed would be tempered by good sense. He gave the newly minted shipping magnate what he wanted to hear. "Your captains' requirements, of course, are best assessed by you. But between you and me, Admiral, you can name your price."

He punched End and looked quizzically at Val. "Your ears pricked up like a fawn's."

"What or who was 'of no consequence'?"

"Spark's crew."

"Not to put too fine a point on it, Dad, but he's just a kid along for the ride."

"He might have started out innocent, but who knows what ideas Spark's put in his head."

"All the more reason to keep him in the circle."

Lloyd McVay shot an angry look at his daughter.

Val McVay returned a self-absorbed, self-contained stare, defying him or anyone alive to challenge her on the facts. "If you had read his files as I have—with a view of asking 'What is this data telling me?'—you would conclude that Will Spark always teams up with some malleable young person whom he can control. Therefore, it doesn't take a genius to imagine that if Will Spark happened to fall overboard, then young Jim Leighton might know plenty about Sentinel—such as where Will put it."

McVay snapped his fingers for a phone. "Get me Admiral Rugoff again. . . . Admiral, I'm sure it doesn't matter, but the nervous Nellies on my staff want the young man, too."

Val was shaking her head at her computer.

"Now what?" McVay asked when he was done with the Russian.

Val said, "Those two are not e-mailing each other."

"Jim and Shannon?"

"We've been monitoring RileySpa.com since I got Jim's address. Nothing."

"Wrong address?"

"No. I think I obtained his 'public' address. That his clients would use. They probably use different names to write to each other."

"That goes without saying. RileySpa is owned by Shannon's parents. Young lovers might well maintain separate e-mail accounts for privacy. May I presume that you are also searching for those accounts?"

"I am, but it takes time. They've installed a respectable RSA hierarchical certificate security system and there are *two thousand five hundred and forty-eight* separate addresses registered to the RileySpa website. Apparently they offer their employees free e-mail as an inducement to stay. And every damned one of them uses seven screen names."

"Surely you're not surprised, Val. *I* would be surprised to discover in the entire country a single acquaintance of any of *our* employees who hasn't 'pickabacked' onto the foundation's gratis e-mail. 'Free gifts we scorn, and love what costs us pains.' "

Shannon's first reaction when she got Jim's e-mail was to dial 911. She had to tell someone who could help that Jim was in trouble. But who could help him hundreds of miles from shore in international waters?

"Daddy?"

"What's the matter, angel? You look like you're ready to cry."

She showed her father Jim's e-mail. He blinked at it a moment. Then he asked a question that had nothing to do with anything. "What's this e-mail address?"

"Jim and I keep private mailboxes for our personal stuff. JLEIGHTON@RILEYSPA.COM and SRILEY@ RILEYSPA.COM are for the customers."

"Why?"

"These are for us, and if you tell Mom I'll change them."

"Oh."

"Daddy, is there some way you could get the navy to help him?"

"Never happen. For one thing, the U.S. Navy doesn't dispatch ships for private citizens unless they are very rich and famous. For another, even if an American citizen could call up the U.S. Navy to send a ship, what would you tell the U.S. Navy? The reason this guy I know—"

"Let's call him my friend."

"—needs rescuing is that he's sailing with a man who shot a Nigerian woman? Sorry, hon. He's got a problem and you can't help him. But, hey, this reads like he's home free. He's coming home."

"If he can sail the boat all by himself."

"I can't believe they shot somebody. Must have been—"

"Jim didn't shoot anybody."

"Your mother will freak when she hears this."

"Don't tell her."

"Not in a million years."

Shannon figured that two days was more like it—an assessment of her father's ability to keep anything from her mother that he confirmed with an anxious, "But, honey, you've really got to wonder what Jim's mixed up in."

Worried sick, she felt helpless, useless, clueless, and very much to blame. And very much shut out by Jim's terse description of what had to have been momentous events.

Will Spark's 1987 edition of *Ocean Passages for the World* looked like it had endured most of them. The navy blue cover was rubbed smooth, with threads showing dirty white through the cloth. The pages were thumbed, water-rippled, and coffee-stained. On the title page, Will had printed the names of three yachts that had carried the guide: *Cordelia, Runner,* and *Hustle.*

Chapter 1 began matter-of-factly: "*Ocean Passages for the World* is written for use in planning deep-sea voyages." It made the challenge sound doable, or at least possible, an enterprise that could be undertaken with confidence if one went about it in a businesslike manner.

To exit the Bight of Biafra and the larger Gulf of Guinea—the great curve of the Atlantic Ocean that lay in the crook of Central Africa's south- and west-facing coasts—he had to reverse their inbound route from Cape Palmas on the southwest tip of the bulge of Africa. Back at Cape Palmas, he would hang a shallow right and sail northwest to the Cape Verde Islands. From there, it was 2,980 miles to New York.

Except it was winter. And a foldout chart in *Ocean Passages* showed in vivid yellow that in winter the New York route was beset by gale winds, heavy seas, and bitter cold. Will had talked about the North Atlantic in winter as a very dangerous ocean and Jim knew he had no business anywhere near it.

He found a southern route to Florida that looked promising. Florida was actually farther than New York—reached through the Bahamas via something called the North-East Providence Channel. The southern route looked warm and peaceful by contrast—a sun-drenched novice's voyage he would find all the easier because the trade wind and the North Equatorial Current were both going his way.

Ocean Passages gave him the courses to sail to each waypoint. And after a session with the GPS manual, which proved easier than programming his VCR, he learned to punch them into both the mast mounted Global Positioning System and Will's handhelds, which meant he could set the auto-helm to the proper compass course and constantly check his accuracy with the electronics.

So he had a sense of hope and even high optimism when he next e-mailed Shannon.

Things have settled a little. Will's still out of it. But I'm fine. Other than tired as hell. And I'm running the boat and I'm coming home! I know I can do it. I can navigate by the book. By the charts. And by the electronics, which make it simple.

The boat, he didn't have to tell her, was a much more complicated matter. It was big and the forces that the sails

generated were potent. He was violently reminded of that
when the second morning after escaping Nigeria a jib
sheet—a line that controlled the foresail—broke loose. As
he rushed forward to secure the huge sail, the flapping cloth
hit him so hard it knocked him to the deck. Ears ringing,
head spinning, he remembered too late that he should have
turned the boat into the wind to reduce the pressure on the
sail before he tried to wrestle with it.

> I can handle the sails, as long as I keep it simple. No fancy
> sail changes. I'll just stick to the roll-out jib and the easily
> reefed main. I've been practicing reefing them. But maybe
> when I get out in the middle of the Atlantic on a calm day I
> might try flying the other jibs. Hell, why not fly the spin-
> naker—just kidding, though I might try the big light-air
> blooper.
> The one thing I've gotten pretty good at is steering....

Often, he took over from the auto-helm to practice—particularly when the stars shone at night. On this westward
track, paralleling the distant shores of Nigeria, Ghana, Togo,
and Liberia, his guide was the row of three bright stars, the
belt of the constellation Orion, which rose directly behind
him after sunset, peaked above the mast, and sank into the
ocean ahead of the bow.

He could see at a glance whether he was on course.
Granted, clouds often blocked the sky in the Gulf of Guinea,
but whenever that happened, he could steer by the compass
and confirm his position with the GPS. Half the time the sky
was cloudy; on the other hand, he told Shannon, the Harmattan haze grew thinner with each mile he sailed west.

> Fact is, if worst comes to worst and Will doesn't make it, I
> can probably do it all alone.

He deleted "probably."

> Hopefully, nothing important will break—it shouldn't. Will
> keeps her in great shape—and the weather won't throw any

nasty surprises my way. It's a little scary, of course, but very, very exciting. I don't want to tempt fate by being overconfident. But Christopher Columbus crossed the ocean by this same route in a leaky old wooden boat and he had no idea what was on the other side. While I'm sailing a high-tech, million-dollar dream boat and have some idea of who, at least, is on the other side.

He took to sleeping in catnaps in the hammock right below the companionway. He felt safer three short steps from the helm and better in touch with the sea and the wind than in the pilot berth deeper in the cabin.

Shannon Riley began to investigate Will Spark—something, she realized, that they should have done before Jim went sailing with the man. She had been so caught up in the idea of the adventure, and Will was so clearly a competent bluewater sailor. Jim would still be safe at home if *she* hadn't pushed him.

She pulled Will Spark's membership file from the RileySpa computer, which stored the addresses of inactive members whom they routinely peppered with "come back" mailings. Will had left his club before RileySpa had bought it. But the transfer of Will's information had succeeded. It had even transferred his membership card photograph, which showed an older, white-haired man in glasses looking down and away from the camera. He had given his address as the Larchmont Yacht Club, which immediately made her wonder why he had joined a Bridgeport health club that was thirty miles away in a lower-rent area. Probably he'd had an office nearby.

Most members paid their monthly dues by credit card. Will Spark had paid cash.

He had left the space for his business address blank.

None of this really meant anything. He paid cash. His address was a fancy yacht club. He had left the notify-in-case-of-emergency line blank. So what did that mean? He was alone in the world.

Shannon telephoned the Larchmont Yacht Club and

asked for Will Spark's business address. The yacht club did not give out such information, she was told frostily.

"Is he still a member?" Shannon asked. The yacht club did not give out membership information, period. The person hung up on her.

The hot, dry Harmattan kicked in hard from the northeast and filled the sails. *Hustle* boomed along on a broad starboard reach, a fast yet comfortable point of sail with an easy rhythm that allowed Will to sleep in peace.

The speed was exhilarating and boosted Jim's confidence. Still, he kept her many, many miles from the coast— a separation that increased sharply as they passed the Bight of Benin. Its shore was so low that it offered no landmarks, while its surf-pounded beaches were further obscured by haze, "The Smokes" Will had called it on their way in. Jim wanted no part of it. He kept going straight west, paralleling the equator, some 150 miles to the south, while the Nigerian shore hooked away north to form the bight.

Soon he was over a hundred miles at sea. The air cleared a little as their western course took them farther and farther from the windblown sands of the African deserts. Ship traffic thinned—although oil tankers still raised the occasional ominous ridge on the horizon and solemn lights at night— and Jim drove the boat with a growing sense of relief that they had escaped the constraints and dangers of the land.

Dear Shannon,
Right now a huge shark is following the boat. He's got a big fin, like in the movie. And every now and then I can see his tail break the surface. Which reminds me, since I'm alone on deck all the time now, I'm going to start wearing my safety harness. Don't worry. I'm clipping it on right now. Things are going pretty good. Will is still pretty out of it, but sleep can't hurt at this point. He's got a lot of healing to do.

In the morning Will's dark, rich mix of French and Italian roast, ground powder-fine, suddenly appealed more than his regular tea and he brewed a cup in Will's "camp coffee" fashion—drenching it with boiling water and waiting for the grounds to settle. He was changing Will's IV solution bag— and wondering whether he should try to wake him to get him to eat or let him sleep—when the wind began to back, which usually meant trouble.

Sure enough, as the wind swung north and west in front of the boat, slowing it, the seas grew confused. The sails began to slat and the rigging bang. The heat thickened, thunder muttered, and lightning flickered on the clouds.

In another hour the wind died completely. The clouds closed in and rain showers fell straight from the sky, nudging the horizons, drifting over the boat, and wandering away. In the absence of the wind, the sea's surface flattened.

But big swells still marched below. The boat began to roll so violently that Jim had to raise the leeboards on Will's bed to keep the unconscious man from being thrown to the deck.

Hustle rolled on the oily swell in the peculiar way she had when they were becalmed in the Doldrums, and to Jim's amazement he felt himself getting seasick again. He could feel it rising in the back of his throat—nausea combined with a gloomy depression—a grim reminder that his fragile inner ear doomed him to repeat performances whenever sea conditions changed.

He was catnapping in the cockpit—despite the deepening impulse to vomit and occasional spatters of warm rain— waking regularly to check for tankers, when around noon his attention was drawn to a strange narrow column of rain a quarter mile from the boat. He thought it was another shower, but it was spinning, whirling as it descended from a black cloud.

A second whirling column of water rose from the sea. The two columns joined and grew large. It tripled in height and thickness and began to dart on the sea's glassy surface like a hungry tongue.

Jim started the engine.

The waterspout—for it was surely that now, a seaborne tornado—suddenly came straight at the sailboat. Jim tried to steer away from it. It parted in the middle—halfway to the sky. The top half rose to the clouds, the bottom splattered on the sea like a gigantic water balloon.

He thought he was home free. But just as quickly, top and bottom rejoined. Lunging suddenly, it tore through the place where Jim had started the engine, leaving wild white water in its wake, and raced off toward the horizon. It had almost disappeared, when it split vertically into two spouts that ran back at him like a pair of giant legs.

They flanked the boat. Water cascaded onto the decks. Jim tried to steer between the legs. They were moving in unison, closing, beginning to join. He shoved the throttle, but the engine was already running wide open.

The legs merged a hundred yards ahead of the boat and formed a single column again. As he turned away, it suddenly collapsed—half its water tumbling back into the ocean, half vanishing in cloud.

> Dear Shannon,
> I just saw a waterspout. Awesome. I was really scared—in fact so scared that the fear knocked some seasickness right out of me. I had always assumed waterspouts were mythic phenomena like mermaids. When it split into two legs and came at me from both sides, I looked up half expecting to see a giant groin. But way up in the sky was a patch of robin's-egg blue sky.
> I think I'm getting very lonely. Maybe because I don't get sleep running the boat. I feel like some homeless guy who keeps getting woken up by the cops. Move along, pal! Trim the jib, reef the main, look out for that supertanker.

The wind sprang up. It continued backing and gradually the warm, damp southwest monsoon displaced the Harmattan. The change in direction—the swing from the bow's right to left—caused the sails to jibe about. Jim saw the shift coming in time to haul in the sheets so they didn't crash around and was rewarded with a gentle, almost subtle, shift of boom and jib. Once he had established her onto a port tack, she sailed slowly west again, on a weak southwest breeze blowing over the port bow.

The air cleared some more and when he could see a five- or six-mile circle around the boat—a fifteen-minute safety factor of ship-steaming time—he went below to hydrate Will with another saline bag. The old man never woke.

Jim checked the horizon and put a veal stew he had thawed into a pot on the stove. Then he took the laptop up to the cockpit and wrote to Shannon again. To read the screen in the glare, he put on a navy T-shirt, which reflected dark on the screen:

> Hi. I'm on course and feeling better. Can't wait to get home. I don't let myself think about how long it will be. I just tell myself it will be soon. I mean, what's four thousand miles?
> I can't get those poor Nigerians out of my head. I have this picture of them all running from a burning wave. I can see the wave breaking right over the old guy with his stick and the fat ladies selling beer. You read about this stuff in the newspapers, but it's not the same. I guess the reporters have to stay above the fray, so they can't let their emotions really go. Have to have a blind or cold eye. Well, first time you see people living that bedraggled, there's no way you can have a cold eye, no way you can't wonder why. Are they supposed to always be poor because it's Africa? Or is the oil somehow keeping them poor? Listen to me. I sound like my dad.

He sent it and found an e-mail from Shannon waiting for him, titled "Who is Will?!?"

> Dear Jim,
> I'm very worried. Don't tell Will, but I've been looking into his background and I'm afraid that I sent you sailing with somebody pretty mysterious, like he's a criminal or a spy or something. Maybe this wouldn't mean much, if he hadn't killed that girl. But that makes me wonder even more who is he really and what is he up to. Please write as soon as you get this.

Jim quickly wrote back. He didn't want Shannon to worry needlessly. Will might be a little crazy, thoroughly paranoid, and maybe he knew some odd types, but by now, despite all Jim's unanswered questions, they had been through a lot together. He had to set Shannon straight about Will.

> Dear Shannon,
> He killed the girl in self-defense. That doesn't make him dangerous. I know him better than you do, having sailed with him for the past two months now. So don't worry. I think of him as my friend.

He radioed it off, went up to the deck to check the sails, and stayed at the helm until a freighter some miles off finally vanished over the horizon. When he radioed again to check his mail, he found Shannon's reply.

> He KILLED her—for whatever reason—

He wrote back immediately, realizing how helpless she must feel so far away.

> Dear Shannon,
> Relax. I know I don't know much about him. Though since he got stabbed I'm a little more inclined to believe his story about being chased—not completely. (For all I know she was pissed off; I do know she was stoned out of her gourd.) Fact is, he is one tough old bird and smart as hell, and I've grown to like him very much. And don't forget he saved my life when I went overboard. But none of that matters, because as far as my safety is concerned, I'm in charge now.
> Even if Will is somehow "bent" or a thief or whatever, he's flat on his back. I'm driving the boat. He can't do anything to me. And frankly, he wouldn't even if he could. To that extent I trust him. We've become shipmates—there's a bond, and he wouldn't break it. And that's all that matters. So relax. I can handle this and I can handle Will.
> Love,
> Jim

He radioed it and checked a few minutes later for Shannon's reply.

Dear Jim,
I would really appreciate it if you would just think about what I've said. Your "shipmate" is possibly a very dangerous man. You knew—or suspected—that before, when he first got paranoid. Now you've seen him kill somebody. And I can't find his name anywhere. So I just wish you would keep your eyes open and stay alert just in case you're in danger.

Jim fired back.

Wait a minute. First, if you don't like the word *shipmate* try *friend*. Second, I didn't see him kill anybody. I didn't see what happened. But I did see the knife in his chest, which I'm taking as a damn clear sign he was attacked. So I would really appreciate it if you would please not make him into something he isn't. I repeat, the main point is, I'm driving the boat to safe American territory in Florida, where I'm going to jump off and get on a plane home.

That evening he found another e-mail waiting for him.

A DAMN CLEAR SIGN HE WAS ATTACKED? The trouble with you, Jim, is you almost never get mad—and never at me—and then when you finally do, you get sarcastic. Which is really a sign that you get angry more often than you show—because you're afraid to show it. I don't like thinking of you as a coward. But sometimes I think that as strong as your workouts have made your body, the one part you haven't developed is your backbone.

Dear Shannon,
I would like to end this conversation now. If you've got a problem with my backbone, tell me to my face, not in a goddamned letter.

Dear Jim,
And I don't like you treating me like a hysterical idiot.

* * *

Shannon knew she had to find some way of putting Jim on guard against Will, some proof that the man he was stuck with alone on a boat was not to be trusted.

She went onto the Internet to PeopleFind. They needed full date of birth or an address. Will had filled in only the year on his application. She tried Larchmont Yacht Club as his address. No luck. For a criminal records search PeopleFind required a Social Security number in addition to a date of birth, and even if she had that, which she didn't, criminal records searches were restricted to a single county, of which there were over three thousand in the United States.

She went to a Web search engine and typed the search words: "William Spark." Ignoring a banner ad that asked "Striving for a washboard stomach?" she found matching sites for a literary webzine, a fan page for someone named William, a romance author, criticism and fiction of William Dean Howells—a name she recognized from one of Jim's college books—William Butler Yeats, William Tell, the Burlington Police Department, and something about "nakedness and naturalness." There were 674 sites for the name William Spark and not one related to the man Jim had gone sailing with.

She tried other search engines: Google, Hotbot/Lycos, AllTheWeb, and Savvy all yielded nothing. She signed onto the *New York Times* archives. Will's name produced no news stories.

She drove to the Westport Library and logged onto the DIALOG and DataTimes news services and found nothing under Will Spark. An interlibrary Lexis/Nexis subscription yielded nothing either. She tried variations on Will Spark's name—William Spark, Spark Corporation, Spark Enterprises—no Will.

Maybe she was expecting too much of the news services. But when she tested them by typing in her father's name, she got all sorts of news stories and press releases detailing his government career with the Agency for International Development, from his first assignment in a green revolution farm program in Zimbabwe right through his early retirement and subsequent foray into the health club business.

Jim had mentioned that Will Spark had gone to Yale. She tried various Yale University websites. Nothing. She practiced on Jim. She found his old bike-racing record, his final triathlon entries, a gory article in *Fitness* magazine about his worst crash, his résumé on the International Personal Trainers Association home page, and, of course, the bio she had written for the RileySpa's website.

Jim,
There's nothing on the entire Internet about him. Like he made up his name or something. Like I sent you sailing with someone who doesn't exist.

19

JIM LEANED ON Will's doorway, balanced against the ceaseless motion of the boat, and watched him sleep. His sunken cheeks, grizzled with stubble, quivered as he slowly drew in and expelled air.

Was he surprised? He hoped that Shannon was wrong. But how could he be surprised after all the stories, the half-truths, and sudden turnabouts? My pals in Lagos. My pals in Calabar. Old friends. Helicopter to the airport. My good gal loves me. . . .

Access codes blocked the files in Will's laptop. And his teak desk, which was built into the forward bulkhead of the main cabin, was always locked. But there was a brass key on the lanyard that secured his bosun's knife to his shorts.

Jim took the shorts, knife and all, to the main cabin and worked the key into the lock. The face hinged down, forming a writing surface. Inside, the desk was much deeper than it appeared from the front and riddled with cubbies, slots, and shelves.

Puzzled, Jim stepped forward into the tiny cabin where he had stowed his bags, tapped its aft bulkhead, and suddenly realized that the cabin was so small because the back of Will's desk had been extended into its space.

The cubbies and slots and shelves contained a row of identical green cloth-bound books, scraps of notepaper, magazine and newspaper clippings, micro floppy disks marked as e-mail copies, some exquisitely fine seashells, a red cloth sack of Krugerrand gold coins, a gold penknife, an antique pocket watch, and a silver derringer.

The breech of the derringer—a double-barreled affair, which Will had left hinged open in its safety position—revealed a bullet in each barrel. Jim picked it up. Loaded for a bear. A very small bear. If only Will had used it on Margaret instead of that damned shotgun.

The "books," as Jim discovered when he pulled one out, were actually hard-bound accordion files in which Will had stowed letters and invoices. Jim riffled through them: paperwork and more paperwork—bills, invoices, faxes—for the endless expenses required to keep *Hustle* afloat and habitable. Jib-furler replacement in Hawaii; freezer repairs in Panama City; a new wind generator in Barbados; a letter to Hild Sails of City Island requesting that a replacement jib be shipped to Hawaii, a diesel heater installed in Hong Kong, Gill sea boots from Team One; foul-weather gear; and shackles, blocks, line, oil filters, batteries.

Jim was about to turn his attention to the floppy disks when he noticed that the tropical damp had curled the covers of some of the files. A well-thumbed cover had peeled apart, the cloth separating from the cardboard. It smelled of an odd mix of mildew and perfume. The file was empty. But when Jim picked it up, a folded blue paper hidden between the cloth and the cardboard fell out.

Wondering if he had finally found something personal about Will Spark, Jim unfolded the paper. It was a letter, several pages long, handwritten in green ink. The opening lines told him that it was deeply personal and the fact that Will had hidden it meant it was heartfelt. He didn't want to read it—nor did he have to. The greeting read, "My dearest Billy." That was what Margaret had called him, too. Billy. It was signed, "Yours always, Cordelia." That seemed odd, because her opening lines had sounded like a good-bye.

Big deal. So he'd had a girlfriend named Cordelia—

which anyone could have guessed since he'd named a boat after her—and Cordelia called him Billy. Plenty of guys named William were called Billy. But how many Wills were also called Billy? There was a gulf of personality between those two names: Billy, warm and cuddly; Will, patrician and remote.

Jim thought for a moment, listening to *Hustle*'s hull plow its endless furrow. If he were going to put Shannon at ease, he had to read the damn letter, personal or not.

He had guessed right. It was a long, sad good-bye, with a lot of unhappy talk of perfect memories tempered by a firm belief in the right decision made. Cordelia forgave him, she said, for running out on her, and had taken him back more than once, she pointed out. But she could not forgive his business—"a dirty business," she called it—and so she was saying good-bye. "At the end of the day," she wrote, "were I to stay with you, I would be condoning behavior that falls far, far below the marginal standards I attempt to maintain for myself. Surely, I do not set myself up as an angel, but I cannot knowingly entwine my life with a thief, which is what you are, my dear, even though I know that I will miss you far, far more than the thief will ever miss 'his Cordi.'"

Though Cordelia might be wrong, Jim reflected. Will—Billy—had kept her letter and named a boat after her. But what kind of thief? he wondered. Hadn't the poet called Will a thief, too? Was the poet justified?

He went up on deck, looked around at an empty ocean, checked the sails, retrieved a sheet that had fallen over and was trailing the boat like a heavy fishing line, and made sure that the auto-helm was steering their course. Purely from the standpoint of personal safety, Shannon would have to agree, a shipmate who was a thief was better than a shipmate who was a murderer. If a thief was all Will was.

Jim went below and turned on Will's laptop. When prompted for a password, he typed "Cordelia."

Invalid.

Was a silver derringer the kind of knickknack a rich guy kept in his desk? Loaded? Like a gold penknife and an antique watch? The password prompt was blinking. He typed "Cordi."

"In like—" He shot a look over his shoulder, got up, and stepped back to Will's cabin. Out like a light—in like Flynn. Excited, he sat back down at Will's computer and opened his e-mail files, which went back six years.

He skimmed at first for the gist of the letters Will had received. With the exception of the occasional boat business, they were mostly reports from Kin Yiu Lam, Choy Yee, and Pathar Singh. Heavy on computer lingo. Lam, Yee, and Singh sounded like his moletronics genius "cavemen." Lam and Yee addressed Will as "Mr. Spark"; however, Singh, the software engineer, called him "my very good friend."

Interspersed among the engineering reports were letters from the Computing College of West Virginia thanking Will for generous gifts to their laboratory fund. Then came a request for Will to serve on the college's endowment committee. Will accepted and soon after funded a not-for-profit moletronics research laboratory. From then on, his letters were written under the heading "CompColl WV."

The most recent e-mail entry leaped off the screen. "Do not send . . ."

The repeat of the bell-tolls threats had arrived just before they landed in Nigeria. But Will hadn't mentioned it.

Jim went back to the desk and checked the news clippings. A marked-up *Economist* article about moletronics caught his eye. Some of the underlined phrases sounded very familiar. When he found science and technology articles from the *New York Times,* Jim glanced back at Will's ThinkPad lying open on the nav station. What had Will said when he was talking about Sentinel? "If that ThinkPad was represented as one inch tall, I.B.M.'s new Blue Gene supercomputer would stand twenty miles high." Here it was in a *New York Times* Tuesday science section damn near word for word.

". . . Processor-to-memory delays are a drag on high-speed computers. . . . A one-year lead in moletronics is like a century of the Industrial Revolution."

Like a rehearsal. For a show. A show for a sucker.

Jim went up on deck and checked the sails and the horizon. The long, low silhouette of an oil tanker he had noted earlier in the south had gone; a heavier one plowed eastbound in the north.

He returned to the e-mail files.

Lam, Yee, and Singh all referred to the microprocessor they were developing as "the project." Their letters were mainly progress reports laced with requests for more research funds. Will's replies were mostly notifications that checks had been deposited in their accounts.

For nearly four years, it appeared that the engineers were making out better than Will was. Jim wondered how long you kept on backing your cavemen before you got nervous. But Will kept on paying, and he kept on contributing to the Computing College of West Virginia. Then a new series of letters started.

Using the name Sentinel for the first time, Will applied for a research grant from the McVay Foundation for Humane Science to fund the moletronics program at the Computing College. He satisfied intricate not-for-profit tax code requirements with his CompColl WV connection.

Money started coming in. But despite claims that Sentinel would revolutionize medicine, for over a year it seemed small-time: Will would apply for a twenty-thousand-dollar grant; the grant officer would dole out five or ten thousand. When Will expressed disappointment, the grant officer would apologize, blaming "my lowly position on an enormous totem pole," and promise that one day busy "chiefs who oversee thousands of worthy projects" would take note of Will's.

Suddenly it happened. The foundation's chief grant officer, a woman named Val McVay, pressed Will for specifics about the sources of his software. Will dodged repeated requests, saying that while many engineers and scientists reported to him, "I'm just the man in the middle."

"Good science and hot engineering don't flourish in secret," she wrote. Will did not write back. A month later, Val

McVay's father, the head of the foundation, stepped in, "confident I can assuage any feelings of neglect."

Lloyd McVay apologized for Will's grant applications' "falling between two stools due to the inexperience of a young grant officer who failed to grasp the magnitude of Sentinel. And while my daughter is a brilliant engineer, she is not—shall we say—a man of the world." Perhaps Will would visit the foundation in New Jersey "for a discreet chat about Sentinel's commercial applications and the possibility of a glass of wine."

Will dodged that invitation and several others until McVay wrote, "Our attorneys inform me that the Internal Revenue Service casts a scrutinous eye upon not-for-profit laboratories like yours that fail to submit reports to not-for-profit granting foundations like ours. They counsel that you and I informally review our options regarding Sentinel's future."

"Jackpot!" Will had written to the engineer Singh.

Suddenly the numbers were mind-boggling. Will seemed on the verge of reaping hundreds of millions of dollars. But, like his daughter, McVay had pressed for more details about Will's laboratories and engineers. Their exchanges grew terse, the mood cool. Finally, McVay used the word *withholding*. With that the letters stopped abruptly. A year and three months ago. Right around the time that Will had disappeared from Jim's spinning class in the Bridgeport health club.

He checked on Will again. Still sleeping. He made his rounds on deck, started the engine to charge the batteries and freezers, had some soup, and sat down again at Will's desk.

The antique watch was beautiful. The lid opened on a face mysterious with dials. It even showed the phases of the moon. He wound it three turns and held it to his ear. A high-speed ticking, an amazingly rich sound for something so small. Turning it over and over in his hands, he noticed what appeared to be a second lid on the back side. Pressing here and there, he got it to pop open. An inscription was etched on polished gold: "For Billy Cole, who 'can cure' what ails."

Another Will.

Saddened by learning more than he had wanted to, Jim closed up Will's desk and put Will's shorts with the key back on their hook. Before shutting down his computer, he sent an e-mail.

Dear Shannon,
Try "Billy Cole."
I love you,
Jim

He awakened, groggily, with a vague sense of disquiet, a feeling he could not immediately define. But something was wrong. It was light outside. Six-thirty on his watch, the sixth morning under sail. Today, if the wind picked up, he hoped to clear Cape Palmas. When he last queried the GPS, the electronic navigator had indicated that the cape lay some sixty miles to the right. Sixty miles off the starboard bow.

Neither the wind nor the waves felt stronger than they had when he had crashed into deep sleep an hour earlier. Yet something was definitely wrong. He catapulted out of the hammock and scrambled up the companionway.

The boat was off course. The rising sun, perched hard and white on the horizon, was throwing daggers of heat from the left, blazing over the port side instead of behind him. The shift of light had awakened him. Or the change in wave action as the swells, which had been rolling from the left, were hitting the bow head-on. The boat had turned toward the south.

He went to the wheel to figure out why the auto-helm had gone wrong.

"Morning, sleepyhead."

20

JIM WHIRLED TO the voice behind him. And there on the cabin roof, leaning on the boom, was Will Spark, dressed in shorts and a T-shirt that the hot wind molded to a body as wasted as a scarecrow's.

"Jesus, Will. You scared the hell out of me. How'd you get up here?"

Will looked as if his flesh had been liposuctioned from his frame. His skin hung in wrinkled, empty folds and stretched tightly only where his bones poked it. It was a miracle that he was standing, much less adjusting the vang that held down the boom—releasing it, Jim noted, so that the sail bellied rounder.

Will's voice was thin, reedy from disuse. "They used to hang people who slept on watch."

"Are you okay?"

"Hungry. Shaky. Weak. My head's swimming. And I still can't catch my breath—feels like a collapsed lung—but pretty good otherwise. How about you?"

"You've been out for five days. I got a little water into you. I couldn't get you to eat."

"The IV helped; thanks. Made a mess of my arm, though. Look at these bruises."

The skin was black where Jim had made repeated attempts to insert the needle. "Well, I'm glad you're up," he said. "I was going to do another today and I wasn't looking forward to it."

"Neither was I. My arm feels like you were using it for fencing practice."

"How's the shoulder?"

Will's face clouded, and he gave up trying to sound casual. "I don't know. Something's going on in there that I don't like. Damned infection, or something."

"I couldn't get you to swallow the penicillin."

"Yeah, well, I'll be swallowing doubles now."

"Does it hurt?"

"More than it should. That's why I think it's infected. . . . Listen, now that you're finally awake, give me a hand shifting the jib car." He pointed at the pulley attached to a rail embedded in the deck; the angle of the sheet that controlled the jib could be adjusted by sliding it forward or aft. "It's too far forward."

"The sail's been pulling fine for three days," Jim protested, suddenly proprietary about the cut of *Hustle*'s jib.

"The car's too far forward for running downwind. Your jib's too flat."

"Yeah, well, that's because the auto-helm lost the course. When I bring her back on course she'll be fine." Jim turned to the helm. "And we'll want to tighten that vang again, too."

"Leave it," said Will. "She's on course."

"She is not. The course is west. She's veered south thirty degrees."

"West-southwest is the course."

"What do you mean?"

"She's on course."

"For where?"

"Buenos Aires."

"What!"

"Buenos Aires. Argentina."

"No. We're going to Florida. Soon as we round Cape Palmas, we're cutting up to the Cape Verde Islands Strait and across the North Atlantic to Florida."

"We are not 'rounding' Cape Palmas. We are bearing away from Cape Palmas, on a course two hundred and ten degrees west-southwest across the South Atlantic to Buenos Aires."

Dumbfounded, Jim asked, "Why?"

"Because it's my boat."

Jim stared a moment longer in disbelief. "No," he said finally. "Not good enough. Right now, for all practical purposes, this is *our* boat."

"I can see that playing captain has given you some delusions, young fellow."

"You got in trouble, which put me in trouble, too. This boat is our ticket out of Africa—away from that girl you shot—and this boat is going to Florida, where I'm getting off on safe American territory and flying home."

Will blinked. He looked surprised by Jim's sudden determination. And he looked, Jim noted with no little pride, like he believed him. Indeed, instead of arguing further, Will retorted in a grave voice, "If you make me sail to Florida, I'm a dead man."

"I don't care. Get this, Will. Get it straight: we're sailing to Florida. And this time, if anybody bashes anybody's head in with a winch handle while they're sleeping, it will be me killing a defenseless wounded sick old man. And throwing his fucking body overboard. And telling anyone who asks that you jumped off one night when I was sleeping."

"You have a short memory for the things I've done for you. Who pulled you out of the drink? I saved your life, Jim."

"I've got a much *longer* memory for the trouble you've got me into."

"Please, Jim. I am a dead man in Florida. I'm dead almost anywhere. But I've got friends in Buenos Aires."

"You had friends in Nigeria. Loved them."

"You don't understand. You just don't—"

"That's right. I don't understand. What could I understand? I have no facts. I don't know what's going on with you. All I know is I'm going home, on this boat, straight to Florida."

"Believe me, Jim. If I go to Florida, I'm dead."

"Spill it, Will. What the hell are you mixed up in?"

"You don't want to know."

"You know something," Jim retorted. "You're right. I don't want to know. I know all I have to know. I know I'm sailing to Florida."

He stepped onto the cabin roof and took Will's arm. It was frightening how frail he was. His bones were like sticks in his skin. "Come on, Will. Let me get you into bed."

Will pulled away feebly and Jim let go, afraid of injuring him if he held too tight. Will climbed, wincing, sucking air, down into the cockpit and unsteadily walked the several feet back to the helm. He stood behind the wheel, which was moving in the ghostly hand of the auto-helm, and braced himself with a grip on the wooden handrail that formed an arch over the compass. He squinted at Jim as if Jim were a distant obstruction, poorly lit, that the *Sailing Directions* had warned him to watch carefully and steer around.

"Do you remember what I told you about moletronics?"

"I remember a bunch of techno-bullshit I could have read in the *New York Times* or the *Economist*."

Will didn't blink. If he got the allusion to his carefully re-hearsed high-tech show, he didn't care. "What I didn't tell you about were my partners."

Jim almost asked, "Were their names Lloyd and Val Mc-Vay?" But he thought he had a better chance of keeping abreast, if not ahead, of Will's machinations if Will did not know that he had access to his computer files. "Partners? I don't want to know about your partners. I don't care about your partners. Come on, let's go below. Get some food in you and some water. A little soup?"

Will started to cough. He let go of the rail, muttered, "Wait a moment," then pressed his hand to his mouth to con-tain the cough. Jim felt his own body brace, imagining the spears of pain that a racking cough would send tearing through Will's wound. Dead pale already, the old man's face turned as white as the sails. He pointed feebly at Jim's water bottle.

Jim thrust it toward him. Will dropped it. Jim scooped it

off the cockpit sole, opened the nipple, and gently squirted some water between Will's lips. Will swallowed, moaned, and sagged to the cockpit bench, bent over like a half-empty laundry sack.

"Whew . . . Sorry. I can't breathe. . . . I'm trying to say—"

"Drink more water."

"Right. Thanks."

Jim watched Will fumble the bottle to his mouth. "Let me help you below. You've got to lie down in your bunk and sleep. And you have to eat something. I'll bring you some soup."

"In a minute. Just hang on a minute. . . . Look, I'll admit that I've been less than truthful with you, Jim."

"About little things like your name being Will Spark instead of Billy Cole?"

Will blinked. "Where'd you learn that?"

Jim had blurted more than he had intended to. Keep it simple. Keep it simple. He said, "I broke into your desk."

"You broke into—"

"I should have done it sooner. You would have."

Will nodded. "Okay. I understand. Don't worry about it."

"I found your watch? 'For Billy Cole'?"

"Oh, that." He shrugged. "It was not so much lying as just trying to keep it simple. Trust me, it doesn't mean anything."

"So what's your name?"

"Will Spark—do you recall Sentinel? My microprocessor?"

"Sentinel. Faster than a speeding bullet, years ahead of the competition. The one that's going to put all the chip factories out of business so they're going to kill you."

"Yes, it will put them out of business. But no, that's not who's going to kill me. You were right, of course. Legitimate businessmen aren't going to kill me. It's my business partners. My former partners. They want to kill me."

Jim sighed. "If I listen to this, will you promise you'll go below and rest?"

"Shut up and listen," Will shot back fiercely. "Listen!

There is a powerful foundation that believes I possess the prototype of a superminiature, ultrafast microprocessor."

"The McVay Foundation for Humane Science. I know. I read your file."

"They're the 'they.' What do you know about molecular diagnosis?"

"Only what I read in the *New York Times* and the *Economist*."

"Such speed on such a tiny scale—coupled with the Internet—offers a total revolution in medicine. A watchman of the body—which is why I named it Sentinel. Goddamned Sony already had Watchman. . . ."

He stared at Jim. Jim, intrigued by the Sony aside, gave up for the moment on getting Will back in his bunk. "How?"

"Sentinel offers medicine's Holy Grail. Diagnostic sensors small enough to sail the human bloodstream."

"I rented the video. *Fantastic Voyage.*"

"This is *real*! It's a diagnostician's wet dream. With Sentinel, a doctor—doctor, hell, a minimum-wage technician—can inject you with a molecular microprocessor that will cruise through your entire body and check it out for the earliest signs of anything wrong. Anything. The *first* cancer cell. The earliest chemical imbalance. The initial bulge of a stroke, the microscopic narrowing of an artery. Okay?"

"Okay," said Jim.

"Twice a year. Even once a month. It runs through you, reporting and cross-checking any problems against every data bank in the world via the Internet. Say you've got a parasite and there's one case of it in Africa—Sentinel's search engine makes the match. You've got an aneurysm forming in your brain—the software pinpoints exactly where. You've had a stroke—it shows what's got to be rewired. No problems? See you next month. Ten dollars, please. Okay?"

"Okay."

"I should have realized it. But I was so stupid—so anxious to swing a deal—that I didn't see it coming. . . .

"See what coming?" asked Jim.

"You know, greed will make even the smartest man stupid. It never occurred to me until it was too late that what the

McVays really wanted was to use my breakthrough to destroy the entire medical establishment: doctors, hospitals, HMOs, insurance companies."

"Why?"

"So they could build a new system and put themselves in the middle of it."

"But wasn't that your goal?"

"No. I wasn't thinking on such a cosmic scale. I just saw Sentinel as a major discovery that could make me very rich. Nor did it occur to me until after the several outfits I was underwriting had produced the various hardware and software components of a Sentinel prototype that my partners would have to kill me."

"Why?"

"I would be the one man who could blow their cover. They had to kill me to silence me."

"That doesn't make sense. You must have done something else."

Will stared at him.

Jim stared back. There was a pattern to Will's e-mails that had led to his exultant "Jackpot!"

"Would it be safe to say," he asked, "that the thing you were trying to get money for succeeded in a much bigger way than you thought it would? And maybe you switched from trying to rip them off in a small way to ripping them off in a big way?"

Will laughed.

"What's so funny?"

"Not funny. I'm very impressed. You've been listening." For a long moment he regarded Jim with genuine pleasure. Then he dropped his eyes. "You're right. Of course I did."

"What?" For the first time, Jim thought he was going to hear the truth.

"I kept Sentinel for myself. I'm going to bring it to market myself."

"You cheated your partners."

"Before they could cheat me—I would have been lucky to see one percent out of it."

"So you stole it."

"Call it what you will. I was walking dead, Jim. The Mc-Vays wrote the book on ruthless."

"*You* wrote the book on larcenous."

"I don't kill people."

"They're not killers, they're scientists."

"Where'd you get that idea?"

"You had the foundation's annual report in your files."

Will rolled his eyes at Jim's naïveté. "Lloyd McVay is ex-CIA. His old man got rich bribing congressmen. He got richer bribing senators and generals, not to mention tin-pot dictators all around the world. They made their fortunes selling weapons. You sell weapons by bribing the buyers and destroying your competitors."

"I read they were high-tech."

"High-tech *weapons*. They know the military-industrial complex inside and out. They *are* the military-industrial complex. Or were. They know where the money is and where the bodies are buried. And when they shifted into consumer technology they bribed their computers into half the schools in the nation."

"But now all they have is a nonprofit foundation."

Will turned red in the face. "It's a goddamned tax-dodge *front* for stealing new technology from gullible fools like me. Lloyd McVay is a poetry-quoting, Ivy League, white-shoe *thug*."

"You really don't like him."

"Not at all. He represents the worst of the unearned-privileged class."

"What about his daughter?"

"Val?" Will ran his hand through his hair. "Val's a somewhat different case. I sort of liked her, actually. She used to be a sailor—big time. Raced in the Southern Ocean. We talked boats at first. . . . Strange woman, pale as a vampire, smart as hell—Jesus, was she smart—smarter than the old man. I could never figure out how she could stand being under the thumb of that manipulative old bastard. . . . But Val's complex . . . full of contrasts—shy, arrogant, utterly sure of herself. And like all sailors ashore, you can sense that nagging in the back of her soul. Wondering."

"Wondering what?"

"Why aren't I out there, sailing under the Milky Way?"

"Did you make it with her?"

"That's not a gentleman's question, Jim."

"Forgive me if I don't apologize, sir. I was hoping in my crude, ill-mannered way that we might have a friend in that 'powerful foundation' that's trying to kill us."

Will answered him seriously. "I suspect that Val is as vicious as her father. The difference is that old Lloyd is vicious for the fun of it—the power trip; he likes to feel superior. Val knows she's superior. She would be vicious just to get the job done."

"A thuggette?" Jim asked with a smile.

"No joke, Jim. Those two took a very public shellacking in the Internet market. They lost money, they lost status, they lost the kind of New Economy power—the billions—that had vaulted them above everyone, even the government. They were slapped back down to the level of 'old money.' These days, 'old money' has to scramble like the rest of us to hold on to it. The McVays will do *anything* to claw their way back on top.

"Thanks to me they are homing in like cruise missiles on the biggest, richest prize in the world. Three *trillion* dollars a year. That's how much Americans and Europeans alone spend on health care.

"Lloyd and Val McVay will kill for the power of Sentinel. And the glory, too. Starting with the Nobel Prize for Medicine. They've hired the worse gangster scum you could imagine to do their dirty work. And the smartest. That's who's hunting me."

Will placed a trembling hand on *Hustle*'s helm. Jim let him steer. The old man was about to collapse and the few miles he might eke out of his fantasy course wouldn't matter.

21

SHANNON RILEY FOUND Billy Cole through the Connecticut State Interlibrary Nexis newspaper connection. But when the headline first leaped off the screen, Shannon got confused. It seemed like another World Wide Web wiggle where oblivious computers tossed out weird links to Yeats and William Tell.

"CanCure.com Medical Stock Fraud Will Spark Aggressive Prosecution" read the headline.

But she was searching for Billy Cole.

Then it hit her. Could this headline have given him a joke idea for a new name? Very funny. But when she read the article it was clear that he had needed one. Billy Cole's CanCure.com rip-off had taken Seattle investors for millions.

As Jim had known it would, the effort to steer the big sloop proved exhausting. Will soon slumped to the cockpit bench and let the auto-helm do the work. But he refused to go below. Jim brought him some soup and saltines, which he devoured hungrily.

That should put him to sleep, Jim figured, at which point he would return *Hustle* to her proper course. But Will started talking again. "I had to stall finishing Sentinel until I could get away from the McVays."

"If they're that ruthless and that smart, how'd you get away?"

"I got lucky." Will dipped his good shoulder in a weary shrug.

"Their hitter—the chief of security, a fixer named Andrew Nickels—was a really twisted hypochondriac. I got to know him pretty well—drinking together—and learned he was a total nutcase, afraid he'd catch germs by shaking hands, like Howard Hughes. With an extremely paranoid imagination. But a truly cruel bastard. He gives me a deadline to turn over Sentinel and he tells me to have another drink. And while we're drinking, he flips on a video he had made of one of his victims being tortured."

"Tortured?"

"With electricity. Hooked electrodes to this poor guy's sensitive parts. Top-quality video, crisp picture, professional sound. The guy was screaming for mercy. It went on forever. . . . Near the end, he was just begging to be killed."

"It could have been a snuff film they downloaded off the Web."

"I had reason to believe it was absolutely real."

"What reason?"

"The guy being tortured was one of my software engineers."

"What? One of your cavemen?"

"Somehow they'd got their hooks into him. Spirited him out of China. God knows how they pulled that off. Anyhow, the poor devil didn't know much—not enough to save him. . . . A very effective demonstration, Jim. That was going to happen to me next if I didn't finish Sentinel and hand it over. I was in a fix. I had no guarantee when or if we'd finish it."

Jim's attention shifted to the empty horizons and the sails. He eased the jib a hair. It stopped luffing. Will was still talking.

"How'd you get away?" Jim interrupted.

"Like I said—I got lucky. Andrew Nickels' Achilles' heel

was his hypochondria. Do you remember how Sentinel works?"

"You're going to inject microscopic minicomputers inside patients to examine their bodies and teach them French."

Will Spark was deaf to irony. He said, "I told Nickels that I spiked his malt whiskey when he wasn't looking and that hundred and hundreds of tiny Sentinel computers were streaming though his veins and gathering in his head."

"You're kidding." Jim shivered.

"Grisly thought, isn't it?"

"Gross."

"I told him that if anything happened to me that my people would activate the minicomputers to avenge me."

"How?"

"By cell phone signal. If they didn't get regular check-in calls from me, they could dial Nickels's brain from anywhere in the world."

Jim shivered again. "Then what?"

"I told him that when the phone rang the computers would be programmed to congregate in one part of his brain—the part that controls motor movement—clog his blood vessels, and give him a stroke that would leave him paralyzed forever."

Will looked up with a dry chuckle. "Know what the man did?"

"What?"

"He stuck his finger down his throat and threw up all over his shoes. Speaking of gross . . . Wipes his mouth with a silk handkerchief and tells me he's got the electric machine in the next room and he's going to hook me up right now—one tough, smart son of a bitch."

"What happened?"

"I told him he was too late. Throwing up wouldn't do him any good. The computers had already entered his bloodstream through his esophagus. Like champagne bubbles."

Will laughed again.

"Son of a bitch fell for it. I was home free. Pretty good

story off the cuff, staring down a gun barrel, don't you think?"

"So why are they still chasing you?"

Will sighed. "My luck ran out. Apparently it tipped the crazy loon over the edge. One day he started smashing his head against a wall, trying to get them out. Eventually, well, he died."

"If Andrew Nickels died, who's chasing you?"

"His nephew. Young Andy."

"Nephew? What for? Revenge?"

"No doubt. But the main reason is, he took up his uncle's fixer duties at the McVay Foundation and now *he's* leading the charge to recover the Sentinel prototype. Jim, anyone would look at this man and think, this is an animal. A brute in the deepest, most primitive, oldest sense of the word. A mindless destroyer. I made the deadly mistake of thinking that was all he was. He almost nailed me with your tracking device—what are you staring at?"

"You seem to be connected to a lot of dead people."

"I didn't go looking for this."

"I know how that feels," Jim said. "Neither did I." But suddenly he believed Will's story. The whole weird tale. What tipped it, he thought, was Will's offhand remark about not being able to call Sentinel Watchman. He seemed genuinely annoyed with Sony for taking the name for their mini TVs.

And then, before he could stop himself, he asked a question that he knew he shouldn't. Not if he truly wanted to get home to Shannon safe and sound and to manage a health club for her father.

"So where's the prototype?"

22

REFLECTING OFF THE sails, the harsh morning sun painted Will Spark's haggard face Kabuki white. But when he looked up from the wheel, his deep-set, dark eyes were lively with a speculative gleam. "Do you know how much they want Sentinel?"

"A key to a new kind of medicine? A lot. Where is it?"

"They want it so much that they drained every drop of Andrew Nickels's blood to scan it with electron microscopes."

"It wasn't inside the hypochondriac's brain?" Jim's heart was pounding. He wasn't fully sure why. But to own a piece of something so valuable was generating pure excitement and boundless dreams of possibility.

"When they got done sifting Andrew Nickels's blood, they dissected his brain, cell by cell. I'm told they prepared a thousand slides."

"No prototypes?"

"No."

"So where are they?"

Will smiled. "In a safe place."

His smile was ghastly. Only his lips moved, twisting parallel on a face worn by trauma, starvation, and dehydration.

Jim said, "You're asking me to sail to Buenos Aires instead of home. You're not telling me why."

"I just told you."

"You don't trust me."

"I don't trust anybody, Jim. I made a deal with the McVays on faith—look where it got me."

"Then it's no deal," Jim said firmly. "Don't forget, you tried to rip them off."

Again, the speculative gleam revived Will's eyes. "What do you want? A piece of it?"

"Well, what if I did?"

"Your shot at the big time?" Will asked mockingly.

"Why not? Like you said, everyone else has gotten rich. Why shouldn't I?"

"It's a pig in a poke," Will cautioned him. "Cashing in could get pretty dicey."

"How far is Buenos Aires?"

Will studied him carefully for a moment. Then he said, "Why don't we look it up?"

Jim got *Ocean Passages*. From their position off Cape Palmas on the southeastern tip of Liberia, the distance to the Argentine city situated at the thirty-fourth parallel south on Río de la Plata looked the better part of four thousand miles. A thousand more miles than Florida—not to mention that in Buenos Aires Jim would still be six thousand miles from home.

The GPS confirmed it when Will punched in Buenos Aires: 3,848 miles. He predicted that *Hustle* would average 150 miles a day. A thousand miles a week. A month if they were lucky and could maintain the pace. "Figure more like six weeks," said Will. "Seven, to be on the safe side."

"Do you think that you can last seven weeks?" Jim asked.

"I don't know," Will answered simply. "I certainly hope so."

"So where is the prototype?"

"Well, let me put it this way: where do you think I got the idea to spook the hypochondriac?"

Jim felt his face go loose and suddenly understood the meaning behind the word *gape*. He got what Will was saying right away, but he couldn't quite believe it. Then he laughed out loud, delighted. "*You.* They're in *your* head?"

Will returned a weak smile. "Better make sure I don't fall overboard."

Jim laughed again. "I'm going to tie you to the mast—wait a minute, Will. Is it safe? What about the cell phone call? Will you get a stroke?"

"No, no, no. It's safe. I made that up about the cell phone."

"How do you get them out?"

"A lab procedure."

"Where's the lab?"

"There was one in Rio, but Rio's out. I have another place I can go to in Argentina."

Jim studied him closely, peering at his bony skull and trying to focus his perception to extreme miniature so as to visualize the microscopic instruments flowing through the narrow capillaries that fed the brain. "What's it like?"

"What do you mean?"

"Having these things floating around in your head."

Will gave another of his good-shoulder shrugs. "We've all got things floating around in our heads."

Jim imagined them tumbling like a *Star Trek* version of meteors in space. Yet flowing freely, neither blocking the channels nor disturbing their fragile walls.

"Unbelievable," he said. "The perfect hiding place."

"It was."

"What do you mean, 'was'?"

"I'm afraid that Mr. Nickels and the McVays have figured it out, by now. They've guessed what's in my brain. That's why young nephew Nickels sent that little girl to cut my head off. Nickels, by the way, starred in that torture video. He operated the electricity and seemed to really enjoy himself."

In Kansas, in a cell in Leavenworth Penitentiary, Serge Rudolph lay awake listening to his fellow prisoners cough and wondering when he was going to truly believe that this was the rest of his life.

How the mighty "Golden Ears" had fallen—or, in his case, with all due modesty, the "Handmaiden of the Mighty"—from ingenious electronic spying for the National Security Agency to eavesdropping on cops, which had been a lucrative sideline until he got caught.

He felt the grinding vibrations of a heavy roller gate opening. Boot steps and leaping shadows announced guards marching down the corridor. It was late for them to stir from the bubble. They stopped outside his cell. Serge sat up fearfully.

"Rudolph!"

Above him in the dark he felt his cellie sag back in relief. Blindly, heart hammering, he reached down for his shoes.

His stomach clenched with the anticipation of violence as they led him through the roller gate, down a long, long corridor, through another roller, past the inch-thick windows of the prison library, and past a classroom painted yellow and blue like his kid's public school, with bright posters warning about AIDS and drugs.

They led him through four sets of gates and around two checkpoints where the correction officers had their heads down watching the security screens. This was looking worse and worse. They were taking him to a place where no one could say they'd seen him go or see what they did to him. They took him through a COs' locker room and past another ducked-heads checkpoint and out a solid door into a parking lot lit as bright as day. One of them spoke into a radio. The lights went out. A Humvee, as wide and flat as a suburban deck, clattered out of the dark.

"Get in."

There were three shaved-head special operations military types inside: a silent black and white pair in front, with the black guy driving, and one in back, who repeated, "In," as if he didn't want to have to say it again.

The COs shoved him hard.

It wasn't his first ride in a Humvee. His Mafia boss had

tooled around his upstate farm in a luxury version. This one was pretty basic. But unlike the Mafia boss's, this one had tags that got it through the prison gates like it was the warden's limo.

He waited a long time, until they were on the Interstate, before he asked, "Where are you taking me?"

"To a shower."

Fair enough. Anyone with the power to spring him from a federal penitentiary wouldn't go for the stink of the hellhole. Maybe things were looking up. Maybe someone needed his services, someone who could afford the best electronic surveillance on the planet. Had to be Feds, had to be the government. He had only one question and he would wait to ask the right person: how could he turn a temporary release into a permanent one?

But after a fast shave and shower in a HoJo's, where he changed into a gray jumpsuit with smart red piping that made him look like a bellman, a private jet flight to somewhere—which looked, in the only glance he got, like it could be Miami but could just as easily have been Phoenix or any other big, flat place speckled with streetlights and neon—and another Humvee ride, blindfolded, from the jet's stairs to a big house, he got a nasty awakening.

It was still dark, but Rudolph thought he smelled water on the steady breeze. This was the kind of house that had expensive views. But they walked him past the night-blackened windows into a windowless cellar that was set up like a war room. Rows of computer towers made the air stuffy.

A Sarnoff jumbo flat-panel showed a big nautical chart, but what riveted his immediate attention was the high-resolution display itself. When the Feds had locked him up, multi-ganged, magnified, diode-backlit LCD screens served by multiple-image processors were still on the drawing board. It was hard to imagine such a piece of hardware in private hands. Two pieces, he realized, as the image altered. This one was a repeater, networked to a master that was feeding it data from somewhere else—next door or across the country.

But the guy in gold chains and pointy croc boots who was staring at the chart was definitely not a public servant. Not a Fed, although judging by the build on him he had trained in Special Forces. Given the choice, Serge Rudolph thought grimly—which he most assuredly had not been—he would prefer Leavenworth. This was private. And if you made a mistake, there was no Constitution that said you couldn't be stomped to death.

The guy gave Serge a smile and thrust out his hand. A strangler's hand and a smile no sane man would trust. "I'm Andy. And you're Golden Ears—until you got caught. Wha'd you learn in jail, Golden Ears?"

"Don't get caught."

Andy roared with laughter. "You hear that," he shouted to the others. "Don't get caught."

Serge was liking this less and less. Andy laughed like a guy who'd been doing coke. Andy's people laughed like guys who wished they were elsewhere. Something big going down here had gone very wrong.

"Come here, Serge!"

Serge Rudolph followed him to the Sarnoff display. Andy pointed to a red X flashing off the bulge of Africa. "That's a sailboat. They have SSB and VHF radios, Inmarsat C satellite phone, and e-mail through the SSB and the sat phone. I want them to think that a boat sinking nearby needs their help."

"A bogus distress call." Rudolph nodded. Simple enough. Modern marine radios usually received on the distress channel even when off. Don't even think about the poor bastards who fall for the ruse.

"I don't want anybody else but them to hear that distress call."

Rudolph nodded a little less certainly. Doable.

"And I don't want anybody to hear their reply to the distress call."

Rudolph asked, "Can you platform communications nearby? Say within two hundred miles?"

"It's on its way."

Rudolph nodded. "In theory I can transmit a lower power

distress call only they will hear. In theory I can suppress their long-range transmissions. But their sat phone could be a problem. I can't necessarily suppress it like the radios."

"I'll have their satellite phone account terminated."

Rudolph was impressed. *That* was not easy.

"I don't like this 'in theory' talk," Andy said.

It was time, Serge feared, to try to explain the limitations of the real world. "There are variables I can't control: atmospherics, the quality of their equipment, the skill of their operator, and how close you position the communications platform. These variables mean I can't guarantee."

"But you must," said Andy.

Rudolph pretended to study the chart. The sailboat's known course was indicated by a red line. He traced it back to Nigeria. Ahead of the blinking X, several dotted lines continued, angling into the North and South Atlantic Oceans and out toward Florida, the Caribbean, Rio de Janeiro, Buenos Aires, the Cape Verde Islands, Spain, and the Azores. Very long—very hopeful—dotted lines. But some things never changed. NSA, FBI, Mafia, these guys: the bosses operated on assumptions not so easily made on the ground.

"What is the communications platform?"

"One of your old SIGINT trawlers."

Rudolph's eyes widened. A Signal Intelligence ship—its superstructure forested with high-gain antennas, radomes, and microwave dishes, its hull pocked with every sonar and extremely low frequency device known to science—was a floating electronic-warfare fortress.

He decided not to ask where Andy had acquired a ship packed with highly sensitive listening gear, top secret radar, and immensely powerful jammers. Though you had to wonder who he was working for.

Andy volunteered the information anyway, probably to indicate that Serge would have top-notch support, so any screwup would be his own fault. "She's steaming from Angola. The oil companies are drilling exploration wells in the deep-water blocks. We had her upgraded to monitor their progress."

Why not, thought Rudolph, who in his youth had once spent a year bobbing around the northern Pacific spying on Soviet rocket tests. If you could eavesdrop on the drilling, the geologists' underwater explosions, ship-to-ship traffic and reports back to headquarters, you'd know who'd struck oil early enough to make money out of it.

"A SIGINT ship," he admitted, "should improve the odds."

"So no more 'theory.'"

"But first you'll have to get within two hundred miles." Which meant, though he wouldn't be the one to say it, figuring out which of those dotted lines the boat would follow.

"We're working on that."

It's now or never, thought Serge, and he took the plunge. "I got to ask: what do I get out of this?"

Andy raised a big hand and someone gave him a sheaf of paper. He showed Rudolph the top sheet. Under its own letterhead, the U.S. Marshals Service confirmed that Serge Rudolph had died of a stroke while being transported to New York to testify in federal court; enclosed were hospital statements, autopsy report, and the death certificate.

"If the sailboat takes the bait, Leavenworth gets this and you get a new identity anywhere you want."

Rudolph was astonished. "That is more," he admitted, "than I had hoped for."

"Make sure it isn't more than you deserve: either way, Leavenworth gets the paperwork."

"What's that roaring sound?" the man on the phone asked Shannon.

His name was Charlie Post. He was recently out of prison. And she would not be talking to him if Jim hadn't floored her with a totally unexpected e-mail that he had changed course for Argentina in exchange for a piece of Will Spark's latest big deal.

"Sorry. I'm in a whirlpool."

"That must be a sight."

"My weight-lifter boyfriend likes it."

"Oh. Well, you can't blame a man for trying. You have a nice voice."

It was night. The club was closed. She had the whirlpool to herself—a tub of warm water swirling around like her brain. She loved that Jim had surprised the heck out of her. The daredevil in her said, Go for it! But it made the question "Who is Will Spark?" more important than ever.

Charlie Post had retired to a Daytona Beach trailer park after serving a sentence for stock fraud. Shannon had met him in an Internet chat room—Mooches Anonymous—frequented by victims of telemarketing rip-offs. This stockbroker seemed to be atoning for his crimes by letting his former victims flame him. He seemed lonely and had leaped at the chance to talk on the telephone.

"Will Spark?" Shannon asked. "Do you know him?"

"Never heard of him."

"I saw his name attached to CanCure.com."

"I didn't know anybody called Will Spark at CanCure."

"Maybe he was after your time?"

"No, I was there from the day we opened shop to the day the Feds kicked the door in."

"Did you know everyone there?"

"Sure. It was just six guys in a room. No Will Spark."

"Only six?"

"Six guys, six phones. And the boss. The guy who had set it up."

"Could any of them have ever changed their names?"

"All six, and the boss." Charlie Post laughed.

"Did you?"

"Naw. I was getting too old for that stuff."

She had to be sure Billy Cole and Will Spark were the same crook. "Was CanCure.com completely a scam?"

"What do you mean?"

"Was there a cure?"

"It wasn't about a cure. It was about *investing* in a cure. People are greedy. They want to get rich quick. We used the buzzwords, pushed the hot buttons. We gave them the chance to feel that it was their turn to get rich like everybody else. Which it was. For a while."

"In their dreams."

"Where do you think people live?"

"One more question."

"I got all night."

"Were any of them sailors?"

"Sure. The boss was a heck of a sailor. A regular yachtsman. Owned his own boat."

"Was his boat named *Hustle*?"

"No. It was called *Runner*." He laughed. "Didn't work. They caught him anyway. Funny thing, for a smart guy, he pulled a mighty slow getaway."

"And his name was Will, right?"

"No. His name was Billy. Billy Cole. A pisser, excuse my language. Hell of a guy."

"What happened to him?"

"Five years."

"You mean in prison?"

"Out in six months, I heard."

"Have you seen him?"

"Christ, no. I told you, I've gone straight."

"Did Billy go straight too?"

Charlie Post laughed again. "Billy Cole? Straight? If Billy ever died, they'd have to dig a crooked hole. Hell of a guy, though. He could make you feel good about selling your sister—"

"Could Billy Cole have changed his name to Will Spark?"

"What does Spark look like?"

"Sixty-something, white hair, and looks like a banker. He's in good shape."

"Billy Cole's older than that, I think. Can't say he was in good shape."

"Could he look like a banker?"

"Anytime he had to."

"And he is a sailor?"

"Long John Silver. Minus the parrot. Plus a leg."

"Well, thank you very much."

"That's it? Good-bye? We just got started."

"I really appreciate it. If you're ever up this way, come by and I'll be happy to comp you into the club."

"Terrific. Maybe I'll take you up on it. Try your whirlpool. Hey, if you run into Billy Cole, say hi."

"Is Billy Cole his real name?"

"It was when I knew him."

Shannon found a Seattle magazine with a photo of Billy Cole in handcuffs. She wondered if she had made a mistake. The elderly mastermind of the CanCure fraud looked frail and much older than the vigorous Will Spark Jim had described. If anything, he looked a little like the blurry picture of the old man on Will Spark's health club membership card. She compared the two photographs carefully, until she realized what he had done. It was neat trick. He wore eyeglasses and looked down from the camera. In the full-body shot in the newspaper he had lowered his arms to shrink his shoulders. The overall impression was of a bent old man peering uncertainly through his glasses.

The newspaper quoted the prosecutor's lamenting the mild sentence—millions of dollars had been stolen and little of the money was returned to the bilked investors. But his case had been weak. The only codefendant who turned state's evidence had been shredded by the defense lawyers. While Billy Cole, in testimony one reporter described as "dazzling," had hammered home the fact—in a "quavering" voice—that the charges, which he vigorously denied, were for *investor* fraud, not patient fraud.

"No one invested their money hoping for their own cure; they were hoping to make a killing."

In the end, the jury returned minor convictions on a technicality. Billy Cole was released soon after with time off for good behavior, time served, and consideration of his age and poor health. Upon his release, a reporter who had obviously grown to like Billy quoted him as saying that disappointed investors were a hazard that investment bankers had to live with, just as people in Seattle had to live with constant rain. Claiming he was tired of both, he boarded a sailboat and headed into Puget Sound, bound, he claimed, "For a faraway sunny beach where I hope to live out my days trading seashells."

* * *

Hustle crossed the equator on a dark night. There was supposed to be some ceremony, Jim recalled reading. Some custom of the sea where sailors who had "crossed the line" initiated those who hadn't. But Will was fast asleep, zonked out on penicillin and morphine, so he sat alone in the cockpit, holding the GPS in his hand, watching it tick the long, lingering tenths of miles like the world's slowest video game.

The South Atlantic spread to the ends of the earth. The boat was doing six knots. Seven miles an hour? A brisk walk? Which made the vast sea measureless. Three thousand four hundred miles to go. He thought of writing Shannon. E-mail offered a striking illusion of closeness. Virtual proximity? Not tonight. Not when distance felt so real.

He wandered below to look at the chart. His penciled line from GPS fix to GPS fix pointed southwest into emptiness— a hyphen-sized fleck of lead for each day's run. He inspected the line through Will's magnifying glass. The boat was a dot lost in a dot.

He switched on the depth finder. It read no bottom. Out of range. He found the nearest depth reading on the chart— 3,861 meters of water under the hull. Three miles deep.

Still thinking that crossing the equator deserved some ceremony, he found *Moby-Dick* on Will's bookshelf and thumbed through it looking for what Melville said about crossing the equator. He couldn't find it anywhere, but he did stumble over the phrase "unshored, harborless immensities," which aptly described what lay ahead. And he learned that the whalers called the grounds off the mouth of the Río de la Plata "the plate," which gave his goal, 3,400 miles ahead, a name to savor.

We are not lost, he thought. We are only hiding.

He missed green salads. He missed the smell of laundry driers on a suburban street. He missed Shannon's cat, a wild one she had tamed. But most of all he missed Shannon. Missed her big laugh. Missed the hand she would slip into his. Missed her in bed. He went looking for his wallet to find her picture.

The depth-finder alarm dinged urgently.

Jim rushed to the monitor, his heart leaping.

Fifty meters. He ran up on deck. Land? This was the middle of nowhere and of course there was no land. He returned to the screen. No bottom. Then, as he watched in puzzlement, sixty meters, fifty, forty . . .

Will called. The alarm had awakened him.

A school of fish, he explained to Jim. Or a whale. Or even, he added with a smile, a giant squid, on a placid voyage under theirs.

"Sailing," said Will, walking shakily into the galley, "doesn't have to be the most expensive way to be uncomfortable."

He was holding counter edges and hand grips with his right hand, favoring the left. "How do you feel?" Jim asked. Something about him looked better. His cheeks were pink and smooth.

"You shaved."

"Of course I shaved. How many times do I have to remind you that cleanliness, intelligent food shopping, careful stowage, kitchen skills, and a decent bottle of wine are requisites for a talent for civilization."

"I see you're feeling much better."

"Not quite up to the bottle of wine."

"Hungry?"

"I want a shower, first."

"The water maker's on the fritz again."

"Hose me down on the foredeck."

Jim helped him up on deck and into a harness, then walked him forward. He gave Will a saltwater bath with the fire hose, then turned it on himself.

Drying off in the cockpit, before the salt stuck to his skin, Will said, "I would kill for French toast and black coffee. And then I think it's high time we give *Hustle* a spring cleaning. We'll start with the galley. It's looking a little grungy."

With Will directing, Jim mixed dried eggs and long life ultrapasteurized milk. Then he hacked thick chunks of bread from their last frozen loaf. They thawed swiftly in the heavy heat. He glanced at Will, and the instant he started to speak Jim chorused, "Now here's the secret of French toast."

"Okay, wise guy. You know the secret?"

"Tell me the secret."

"Patience. Most people don't wait for the bread to be thoroughly soaked."

Will tried to help clean the galley, but he quickly tired. Jim said, "Why don't you check your e-mail? You haven't in a while."

When he glanced over Will's shoulder, he saw that the screen was a crazy quilt of numbers and symbols.

"What's with the squiggles? Secret formula for Sentinel?"

"It's encrypted. I told you the McVays can intercept e-mail. If they interpret this all they get is our e-mail addresses—which tells them zip—and a code they can't crack before doomsday."

Will leaned forward suddenly, shielding the computer's keyboard with his body, and typed in a command. When he straightened up, Jim saw that the laptop was displaying an ordinary e-mail.

"What did you do?"

"Told the computer to decode the e-mail."

"How?"

Will shrugged. "My people installed a chip and a program."

Jim saw the greeting: "My very good friend."

"Who's that?"

"One of my cavemen. Wants to know why he isn't rich yet."

Okay, Jim. Here's who I think your friend is:

Jim read Shannon's e-mail over and over. He didn't want Will to be a crook. And he sure as hell didn't want

Sentinel to be a fraud. He wanted a piece of something that was real. Something that would make him and give him a place in the world. The trouble was, Shannon's last lines read:

> Will Spark/Billy Cole landed in jail because he suckered people into investing money in so-called high-tech medical research that was nothing more than a scam. I'm sorry, darling, but your shipmate is a con man.

He started to type back, "You have no absolute proof that Will and this Billy Cole are the same . . ." He stopped, reopened the incoming-mail window, and stared hard at Shannon's letter. Of course she did—much more than just the letter with a common name Jim had given her, or the inscription on Will's watch.

Runner. Will's last boat, previous to *Hustle.* He flipped open *Ocean Passages.* The names of three boats were written inside the cover: *Cordelia. Runner. Hustle.* Jim looked into Will's cabin. The old man looked asleep, but he opened his eyes. Then he removed his headset and said, "You have to hear this."

He pulled the wire and music poured from his cabin speakers. "Mel Torme."

"My mother listened to him. My father couldn't stand him, but he was an old hippie, so what did he know?"

"Hey, grow up. Cut your father a little slack."

"He called me 'man.' As in, 'You had to be there, man.' Demonstrations, free love—like he'd won World War II or something. Talked and talked and talked like you, Will. On and on."

"And you listened?"

"It got to be a habit."

"Then listen to the piano. George Shearing. Do you hear what he's doing? Not a single note on the melody. Mel's carrying the melody, Shearing's playing *between* the notes. It's so beautiful."

"Will. We have to talk."

"Jim, there's so much to love. . . ." He closed his eyes.

"And so goddamned much to envy. So much you wish you could do. Wish you could have done."

"Is that why you're a crook?"

"Crook? What are you talking about?"

"Billy Cole? CanCure.com?"

Will turned off the music.

23

SHANNON CHECKED YOU out on the Internet. She found the trial and that you went to jail."

"Clever Shannon. What else did she tell you?"

"You didn't go to Yale."

"Never said I did."

"But you wear Yale shorts."

Will gave him a look. "They came back in the laundry. They fit. I kept them."

Jim shot back, "No, you bought 'em or stole 'em. You wanted to look like something you weren't."

"So?"

"It's dishonest," Jim yelled, and when that word seemed to echo too thinly to matter, he yelled louder, *"It's a lie!"*

"It's a world of labels, Jim. When people think you're Ivy League, they treat you better than a kid from the wrong side of the tracks."

"Is that how you got into the Larchmont Yacht Club? By claiming you went to Yale?"

"Oh man, you are on a tear. Do you really want to know how I got into the Larchmont Yacht Club? I hung out there since I was eleven. You want to know how? I needed work. I got my first job painting boat bottoms. I kept my ears open and learned how to act. Pretty soon I realized that the ritzy high-class sailing world was actually quite open to newcomers. All you needed was money. Or skills. Anyway, one day this rich old guy was short crew on his Soling. We won the race."

"Will? I was a lit major, remember? I read *The Great Gatsby*."

"I was more like a slow-motion Gatsby," Will replied. "It took time. But instead of bagging groceries to help my family make ends meet I was spending my weekends with the swells. And their daughters."

"Is it true?"

"Is what true?"

"Did you go to jail?"

"Most people my age have a past."

"You don't deny it?"

"I don't deny I was indicted, arrested, tried, and convicted. Why should I? You already know those 'facts.'"

"Do you deny being a crook?"

"I denied it at the trial. The jury didn't believe me."

"Are you saying you were innocent? Why'd you run if you were innocent?" Be innocent, Jim thought. Please just explain this. I don't care about your names. Just convince me that Shannon's wrong. Tell me you're not a crook. . . . Tell me that Sentinel is real.

"Run? In a sailboat?" Will sighed elaborately.

"That's what the papers said. The FBI caught you in San Francisco."

"Everybody laughed."

"It's a pretty slow way to run."

"They never caught me in that sense of *catching up*. But they were waiting at the dock when I sailed into 'Frisco. The special agents were busting a gut laughing. I fled the Federal Bureau of Investigation in a sailboat. How quaint. How foolish. How comically stupid."

"Were you surprised they were waiting for you?"

"Well, I'll tell you something, Jim—don't repeat this—

I'll deny it if you do: the Feds had their laugh. I had mine last."

"What do you mean?"

"There was money involved. A considerable amount of cash."

"So you *were* guilty."

Will ignored that, saying only, "I've always believed that one should tithe one's paper profits. Ten percent a month added up rather nicely."

"You hid the money you stole."

"I deep-sixed the money I cashed in."

"What—"

"Doesn't anybody read anymore? 'Deep six' refers to the bottom of the sea. The deepest fathom. It means to throw overboard."

"I *know* what deep six means. I don't know why you threw the money overboard."

"In shallow water. I weighted the waterproof container so it would sink and stay put. I marked the spot with the GPS. Then, when I got out of prison, I dove for it.

"After I recovered the money, I bought a new boat. Boats are good. If you have a boat, people assume you're rich. Keep that in mind, Jim. Here, I'll tell you about a trick that never fails. Say you make landfall where you don't know a soul, aren't connected. Do you want to spend your first night in some ratty motel? Hell, no.

"So instead, you drop anchor off the richest house you see. Row ashore—no motor; oars are classier, suggesting you've been brought up properly—and ask permission to anchor for the night. You don't *need* permission—they don't own the water—but it's polite. Nine times out of ten, they'll ask you in for drinks. Once you're in for drinks, dinner follows naturally. And what kind of host would let a charming sailor row home in the dark? You're good for a week, longer if the husband's away."

"Who's going to have the last laugh this time?"

"Me," Will shot back. "Just like last time. And you, if you continue to play your cards right."

Jim shook his head. "You don't even apologize?"

"I don't owe you or anybody else. I paid my 'debt' to society."

"So why is the boat 'invisible'? Why did you need a getaway boat?"

"What are you talking about?"

"The carbon fiber mast?"

"No, for Christ's sake. Carbon fiber's lighter than aluminum. With a high rig like *Hustle*'s it's a hell of a lot less weight swinging around the top of the mast. The reduced radar signature is a bonus."

Jim realized that he did not believe Will and for some reason that fact tore his heart. He was silent for a while. Then he said, "You fed me coffee and doughnuts my first night at sea. You made me as sick as a dog. Deliberately. Why'd you do that to me?"

Will hung his head. "I'm sorry. I was running for my life, Jim. I was half hoping you wouldn't catch up. When you did, I just had to put you out of my way until I sailed us out of there. I am very, very sorry I did that to you. I know now you would have worked your ass off to help me in any way you could."

Jim flinched from what he could only call Will's charm assault. "Can I ask you something?"

"Go ahead."

"Why'd you have to be a crook?"

Will looked at him. "What is your problem, Jim? You're taking my past mistakes personally. You didn't even know me then. Why are you making it personal? You are the most exasperating kid."

"Wasn't sailing enough, goddammit?"

"Why are you so upset!"

"I'm not upset. I'm merely asking."

"You're clenching your fists."

"I look at what you do—the way you and the boat are one, and how you can fix anything and read the water and feel the wind and know so much—and I think, If I could be that good at something, I'd be completely satisfied."

"Jesus H. Christ. You're making me into a role model."

"I'm just trying to—"

"I told you, I've been messing around in boats since I was a kid. Sailing's like breathing. And breathing, young fellow, while vital, is not satisfying. Nor does it pay the bills."

Jim blundered out of the cabin, ran up the companionway, and stood in the cockpit turning around and around in confused circles. From below he heard Will's music start again, then cut off abruptly as he plugged in his headset.

He had to go below to answer Shannon's e-mail. But instead, he jumped out of the cockpit and hurried along the narrow side deck to the bow, where he gripped the thick forestay and leaned out over the water. Then he hurried back to the stern and leaned over the bubbling wake. He felt trapped on the boat: trapped with Will, trapped with himself and his disappointment.

He walked forward again, and on sudden impulse began to haul himself up the jackstay, climbing one-armed pull-up by one-armed pull-up to the top spreader fifty feet above the deck. He stood on it, breathing hard, his arms burning with lactic acid.

Jesus, he was out of shape. His pecs and biceps were shrinking. He was so busy running the boat that he was neglecting his workouts. He had to do more curls and winch the spinner up and push his body.

"Again," he said to himself. "Here and now. Do it!" He went down in slow reverse, arm-drop to arm-drop, his body growing stronger as his muscles heated, then immediately climbed again. Standing on the spreader he looked out at the sea. A gust heeled the boat. His perch leaned far out over the water. Suddenly, he could see past the foresail.

"Jesus Christ!"

A huge ship lay dead ahead—waiting for them.

24

THE SHIP WAS a dirty red and built slab-sided and square as a factory. Containers stacked high from bow to stern made it look even bigger than it was. And closer, Jim realized, as his adrenaline-speared panic threatened to paralyze him. It was three miles off, he guessed. No, closer in the haze. Another two miles he'd have run smack into it. It had a single funnel, painted blue and white. A blue and white ensign flew from its telemetry mast. Russian merchantman colors, Will had drilled into him.

Hustle was sailing straight at the Russian, close hauled on a starboard tack, mainsail and fully unfurled jib pulling six and a half knots from the southwest monsoon.

"What am I doing?"

He descended the wire as fast as he could, burning his hands, and hit the deck running. There was no point in dousing the sails: even if the Russians had posted a blind lookout they'd have seen him by now. His fastest move was to fall off the wind and flee south on a broad reach. He steered off the wind, let out both main and jib sheets, and started the diesel. The engine gave him another knot.

The ship had a lifeboat hanging from the big house in the

stern. He focused hard with the binoculars and saw the propeller. Motor driven. If they lowered that boat, he was dead.

"Hey," Will called through his cockpit port. "What's with the engine?"

"There's a ship."

"What kind?"

"Russian."

He heard the fear in his own voice and thought, I'm as paranoid as he is now.

Will climbed the companionway, slowly and painfully. His pale face was sleep-wrinkled. He reached for Jim's binoculars, braced his elbows on the cabin roof, and studied the freighter.

"A goddamned Russian—why isn't he moving? Did he spot us?"

"I don't see how he could miss us. I wonder why he isn't chasing us."

"Probably stopped for repairs."

"I just hope he doesn't send that lifeboat after us."

"So do I," said Will. "So do I." He descended painfully down the companionway and when he struggled back up, he was holding the little silver derringer.

"I doubt that will stop them," said Jim.

Will weighed the gun in his hand. "It's not for them. It's for me."

"You're going to kill yourself?"

"I'll leave you the second bullet."

Slowly, the three miles increased to four. At five, the monsoon haze softened the boxy silhouette. At six, they were alone on the sea.

"Back on course?"

"Let's give him a few more miles."

"Good idea," said Jim. "God, that was close. What if we ran into him at night?"

Will asked, "How long before you changed course?"

"What do you mean?"

"How long did the Russian see you before you saw him?"

"I'm—I'm not sure. Why?"

"Long enough to determine our course?"

"I—"

"Long enough to see we're heading for the River Plate?"

"I don't know. Maybe we better not go to Buenos Aires."

"I'm running out of places, son. I've got to go there. Jesus, what a lousy break."

Dear Shannon,

I got your letter and I confronted Will. Will Spark and that Billy Cole are definitely the same guy. But even though Will is the con man you say he is, I don't believe that he's dangerous in the sense of being violent or anything. Maybe I wouldn't buy stock from him. But I'm not afraid to turn my back on him either.

Jim studied what he had written. Wasn't he, in fact, "buying stock"? Hoping for a piece of the microprocessor in payment for helping Will sail to Argentina?

Shannon wasn't fooled, either.

Dear Jim,

But you *are* buying "stock" from him. You're "investing" your safety by helping Will sail to Argentina, for which you're hoping to be paid a piece of his so-called microprocessor. You're risking your life sailing that far with a sick man. You're risking your life by making a bargain with the devil. You're buying stock with your life. And the worst thing is you're buying stock from a con man. How can you be so sure that Will Spark will keep his side of the bargain? There may not be any stock. There may not be a microprocessor. What makes you think that Sentinel isn't as phony as CanCure.com?

That was, of course, the big question ever since Shannon had first called Will a con man. Hoping against hope, Jim had to know the truth. So he waited until Will's defenses were low to pop the question.

Right after they saw the Russian, Will's fever had bounced to 103. He'd been too wasted to eat. Jim rigged another saline drip and sat on the edge of Will's bunk as the old man lay with his eyes closed. He had come to realize that Will had the ability to put himself in a state somewhere between waking and sleep, like meditation—a word Jim hated, as he associated it unhappily with his mother's self-improvement mania.

It was as if Will could transport himself into a healing state where his body took the opportunity to repair damage. Jim was reminded of a time when Shannon's cat won an awful fight with some animal and had slept for days, healing, just as Will was now. For a second so intense that he had to drive the thoughts from his mind, he missed Shannon and home so deeply that it hurt.

"So, Will. Can I ask you something?"

"Shoot," he whispered, his eyes still beneath lids so thin that they molded the orbs like a coat of paint.

"Is the microprocessor any better than CanCure.com?"

"What do you mean?"

"Is Sentinel real? Or is it just another scam?"

Will was quiet. After a while Jim feared that he had slipped from a meditative state into a deep sleep. As he started to leave him, the old man spoke, eyes still closed.

"Jim, I spent my whole life trying to hit a home run. Other men my age have built something solid, accumulating achievements until they've got something they can bank on, something they can point to and say, This is me. But I was always swinging for the fences. Fouling out, striking out, starting from scratch every day. But now it's my turn. Sentinel is my home run."

He opened his eyes and smiled at Jim, and the expression on his face was suddenly so hopeful that Jim didn't have the heart to ask again whether it was just another scam. But when he looked away, Will knew what was in his mind.

"Is Sentinel real?" Will said. "Why don't you ask Lloyd McVay? Or Val McVay? Or Andy Nickels. They think Sentinel's real enough to kill for it."

25

WHAT IS THAT horse doing?" asked Admiral Rugoff.

The McVays' private dining room overlooked pastureland that was turning green with spring. The Russian had called an hour ago and invited himself to lunch, which could only mean he had something good on Will Spark. Avuncular-sounding on the telephone, he was a harder man in person, and it took no great leap of the imagination to picture him, more than a decade ago, as a flag officer of the second most powerful navy in the world.

"That is a Tennessee walking horse," explained Lloyd McVay. "Their smooth gait allowed southern planters to tour their vast plantations."

"A horse bred specifically for American aristocrats?"

"Not quite," Val corrected him. "Walking horses were developed for the nouveau riche. King Cotton created many a wealthy man who hadn't been brought up to ride."

The admiral laughed. "I have always said that the strength of your nation lies in its contradictions."

Impatience flaring in his daughter's coal-fire eyes prompted Lloyd McVay to refill Rugoff's glass and ask, "To what do we owe the pleasure of your presence in our remote corner of New Jersey, Admiral?"

"Coincidence," said Rugoff. "I happened to be doing business in Port Elizabeth, when one of my captains reported that he had sighted a yacht that fit your profile in the South Atlantic."

"*Sighted?* Why didn't he seize it?"

"His ship had broken down. He was dead in the water, making repairs."

"Well, couldn't he have sent a boat after it? They carry lifeboats, don't they?"

The old admiral looked at him curiously and McVay realized that his nerves were showing. He glanced at Val. She was waiting, as still as an ice sculpture. "I mean—"

"They carry a lifeboat. If their ship is sinking and the crew is sufficiently sober and the davits haven't frozen with rust from inattention to maintenance, they might be able to launch in half an hour. At which point, if they are very lucky, the motor will start. If they are not very lucky, not only will their motor not start, but their lifeboat will sink because they forgot to screw down the bilge plug—pursuit was not an option."

"Did they happen to notice which way the sailboat was headed?"

"It changed course when it sighted my ship and bore away to the south. But before they changed course they were headed south by southwest. Their exact compass course was two hundred and twenty degrees, magnetic, and the boat was making five and a half knots, under full sail."

McVay shook his head. "Wouldn't you say that that's suspiciously precise? Sounds to me like they're trying to make up for their failure to seize the yacht?"

"The freighter's captain served under me in the old days," Admiral Rugoff replied evenly. "He may have lost the stomach to whip a crew into shape, but he has not forgotten his seamanship."

"Well, what does that all mean? Where are they headed?"

"Two hundred and twenty degrees, magnetic, would put them on course for Río de la Plata. They could be headed for Montevideo or Buenos Aires."

"And you're reasonably sure it fit the profile?"

"Would you like to see a photograph?"

"You're joking?"

"I don't joke about my foreign friends who deposit large sums of cash in my London bank." The admiral slipped a liver-spotted hand into his lizard-skin attaché and left it there until Val McVay said, "We have the account number."

"Thank you. The captain, having stopped drinking recently, has taken up photography as a hobby. And he purchased a very long lens, duty-free, somewhere. Of course, the radio fax isn't so precise."

The fax copy was overly exposed, and the yacht was just disappearing into the mist. But the tall mast and the businesslike sliver of the cabin roof matched the photos from Hong Kong. And the sailboat *had* changed course when it sighted the ship.

He passed it to Val, who nodded at once.

"Under a magnifying glass, you can see the wooden helm," Admiral Rugoff said. "It's him, all right. Bound for the River Plate. You got a lucky break, my friends. You'll find him in Buenos Aires or Montevideo."

Two nights after he dodged the Russian ship, Jim lost the wind. The southwest monsoon had grown weaker by the hour and quite suddenly it was gone. *Hustle* wallowed on a confused sea for half the night, sails banging in the dark. Jim braced for another bout of seasickness. And then, just as suddenly as the monsoon had died, the southeast trade wind filled the sails.

He put the boat back on course, trimmed to a port reach, and lay down to rest. He woke to a changed ocean—a crisp blue sea different from any he had seen.

From Barbados on the eastern edge of the Caribbean Sea, across the Atlantic to the Saint Paul's Rocks, on to Africa, into the Gulf of Guinea and out again, he had sailed only tropical waters, where a hot pearly sky often hovered like a lid on a pot and the horizons bunched close in the thick air.

Now, well into the South Atlantic, crossing the eighth parallel a hundred miles east of Ascension Island, Jim noticed that the sky was sharper and brighter and bigger than on the clearest day in the tropics. The vistas lengthened. The horizons seemed more distant yet more distinct—dark blue sky and darker sea in sharp divide. It looked as if infinity loomed near.

The southeast trade wind bore a hint of far-off cold. Jim rummaged around for the sweatshirt he had packed in Connecticut and found it smelling damp and moldy. He hung it from the boom to air. When he checked on Will, the old man was huddled under a sheet. Jim draped his bony back with a blanket he found among the winter things kept in cedar drawers under the bunk. Will muttered gratitude.

"Who's Cordi?" asked Jim.

"What?"

"You said, 'Thanks, Cordi.'"

Will opened his eyes. They were red from fever, swollen, and flickering with confusion. "I thought I was somewhere. . . . Oh, my head is spinning and spinning and spinning."

"How's the shoulder?"

"Tender as hell . . . Where are we?"

"Eight degrees south, thirteen west," said Jim. He watched anxiously as Will tried to fix latitude and longitude on the chart he carried in his head. The fever and the massive doses of antibiotics he was ingesting were scrambling his mind. His condition had been vacillating between good days and bad. Today was beginning to look like a bad one. But Will surprised him.

"Make sure you don't run into Ascension Island."

"Good. Feeling better?"

"The Brits lease out an air base there. They, or their American tenants, might take offense."

"Maybe *we* should go there, Will. If they have a base they'll have a hospital."

"Can't do that."

"Why not? I doubt they'll attack you on a British island."

Will shook his head. "I wouldn't put it past the bastards, but that's not it."

"So why not? Let's do it. We could be there by tomorrow morning."

Will was shaking his head.

"Why not?"

"I had a bit of a mix-up in London several years ago. An equities situation. Purely a misunderstanding—but there were charges and I thought it best to leave British territory."

"By 'equities situation' you mean a stock swindle?"

"Absolutely not. Water over the dam as far as I'm concerned. But Johnny Law has a long memory. And John Bull a long reach."

Annoyed, Jim backed out of the cabin. The crisp new light pouring through the ports revealed the little scratches, bangs, and dings in the once-pristine woodwork that spoke of too many months at sea. By the time they reached Argentina, *Hustle* would be long due for a visit to a shipyard.

"I'll make us some breakfast. Will you eat?"

"I better. I feel like hell."

"And while I'm doing that, maybe you could write me a list of countries where you're not being chased by the cops or the robbers."

"Very funny."

"It shouldn't take long."

Will surprised him by nodding. "There's truth in that, son. Truth in that."

The southeast trades grew stronger. Steadying up, they gave *Hustle* her first two-hundred-mile run, averaging more than eight knots for the next twenty-four hours. Jim spent nearly all that time on deck, fine-tuning the sails and basking in the pleasure of the speed and the sheer beauty of the blue, blue ocean and the black and starry night. Around the time of the false dawn, he fell into a deep sleep on the cockpit bench, cocooned in a hooded windbreaker. He was ripped awake by a loud and steely *bang*.

His first thought was that something had broken. He swung his bare feet to the deck in a panic, his mind shuffling groggy hopes that when he located the parted line or the slipped fitting or the torn sail that Will would be in a condition to diagnose the problem and show him how to fix it before a crisis turned into a disaster.

He saw, silhouetted against the pale sky, a halyard swinging from the masthead, angling down through the main hatch. He heard the busy click-click-click of winch and then, to his disbelief, one of the Schwinn spinners came banging and smashing up the companionway. It was swinging with the boat's motion, gouging wood and fiberglass.

"Belay that!" yelled Will, and now Jim saw him at the mast, a ghostly shadow in the half-light, madly cranking the winch halyard.

"What are you doing?"

"Belay that!"

Jim rushed to obey.

"Not with your hands. You'll lose a mitt. Wrap a line on it!"

Jim scrambled, grabbing a loose sheet end and flipping the line around the wildly swinging bike.

"Cleat it."

He threw a turn around the nearest cleat and tied it off so that the heavy bike was immobilized at the side of the hatch. "What the hell—"

"Spinning class!"

Jim headed forward along the narrow deck beside the cabin, then onto the cabin roof and face-to-face with Will Spark. In the shadowy half-light Will wore a stiff, twisted expression. His eyes seemed to glow, lit from within, unfocused and confused. And when he tried to speak, the words sprayed like water from a broken faucet.

Gently but firmly Jim removed Will's hands from the winch, made sure the halyard wouldn't slip, then gripped his shoulders. Will cried out, flinching with pain.

"Sorry. Sorry. Okay, let's just go back—"

"You're not putting me below."

"I just want to help you lie down, Will."

"You're not locking me up. No one's locking me up." His body stiffened and he brought up his fists.

"Will."

"No one's sending me below."

"No. Not below. I just need your help in the cockpit."

"What's wrong?"

"We got a problem with the . . ." He tried to think of a boat problem—the auto-helm was slipping lately as the gears wore. "The auto-helm. You gotta help me with the auto-helm."

Will said, "You new kids, you're so dependent on high-tech."

"That's right, Will. I need your help. Come on back and give me a hand. . . ."

They began inching their way back between the cabin roof and the safety lines. Suddenly, Will grabbed Jim's arm with a clawlike hand. "Jim, what's wrong with me?"

"You're okay."

"No, I'm losing it. I'm losing my mind."

"You'll be better in the morning."

"Jim?"

"What?"

"Promise me something."

"What?"

"This is really important. If I die—"

"You're not going to die. Jesus, you better not. I'd be fucked."

"If I die, you have to promise me that you will deliver my body to Buenos Aires."

"You're not going to die. Come on back to the cockpit before we fall overboard."

"Promise!"

"Okay, I promise."

"The doctor. You have to take me to the doctor."

"What doctor?"

"The one who's going to remove this thing from my head."

Suddenly, Will wasn't sounding so crazy anymore. "What's the doctor's name?"

"Her name is Angela Heinman Ruiz. Dr. Angela Heinman Ruiz. Her address is in my book. Promise."

"I promise. Now, let's go. Let's just swing past here—careful of the winch—and down into the cockpit."

"Hey, where the hell did that come from? What are you bringing the spinning bike up for in the middle of the night? Are you crazy?"

Jim looked at him. The brightening eastern sky revealed a face that was returning to the planet. He said, "I just got this impulse, Will. I was feeling stiff. I thought I'd spin it out."

"Yeah, well, next time, wake me and I'll give you a hand. You belted the hell out of the boat. Look at these gouges. Next time you call me, okay?"

"You bet, Will."

"Do you remember the doctor's name?"

"Dr. Angela Heinman Ruiz."

"She's part English, part German. Married a *porteño*—that's a Buenos Airesian—lovely woman. Used to be a real looker—prefers Rio—has a practice there, too. Plastic surgeon. Her husband was a shrink. They had a hell of a business going."

Just to determine to what extent Will was once again making it up as he went along, Jim asked, "Why does she prefer Rio?"

"Buenos Aires is like a second-rate European city—very white, Italian-Spanish, no blacks, no Indians. Too many intellectuals who're afraid they're in the wrong hemisphere."

Jim found himself in touch with Dr. Ruiz sooner than he had expected. It started with an e-mail message to Will, which was encrypted like the messages from his cavemen. He wondered when Will had e-mailed the woman. Apparently, the sick old man drifted around the boat, as silent as a ghost, while Jim was up on deck or sleeping. He carried the laptop into Will's cabin and left him alone for a moment while Will entered the decode command.

Dear One,

It sounds like you're in an awful fix and of course I'll help. But I most emphatically do not recommend an "operation" at sea unless you have no other option for treatment—meaning, can you get to a hospital? Neither a "lancing," to use another of your quaintly old-fashioned terms, performed by your young man nor, God help us, one you perform on yourself could fall remotely within the definition of a medical procedure. That said, I've reviewed everything you wrote me.

The knife surely penetrated the pleural cavity, causing the pneumothorax that collapsed the lung. As you are no longer experiencing shortness of breath, apparently your collapsed lung has self-corrected as I hoped it might. But, yes, your wound is almost certainly infected. Yes, draining the abscess now, rather than later, is paramount. I'm particularly concerned that the abscess might break and travel down the path of the knife into your lung. So, despite my many reservations, I am prepared to assist from this great distance.

Love,
Angela

YOUNG MAN, READ THIS VERY CAREFULLY.

Your goal is to incise and drain an abscess. Once you have enlarged the opening of the wound, you will use your gloved finger to break up the loculation—little pockets of pus—into a unicameral single cavity pocket of pus, which you will push out through the larger hole you are making. . . .

His stomach churning, Jim read it three times. Will, propped up on pillows, watched with a faint smile.

> *"My good gal loves me,*
> *Everybody knows,*
> *'Cause she paid a hundred cash dollars.*
> *Just to buy my suit of clothes."*

"I presume I'm the young man," said Jim.

"Are you up to it?"

"I've taken a whole mess of first-aid courses. CPR and all that."

"That's why I hired you. Next best thing to sailing with a doctor."

"Not quite. I've never cut anybody open."

"No problem," said Will. "I'm open already. Little Margaret really had a way with a shiv."

"What do we do about the pain?"

"I swallow morphine. You shoot the area around it with Marcane."

"You have *Marcane*?"

"Of course I have Marcane. This is a blue-water boat. I can't call an ambulance three thousand miles from the middle of nowhere."

Jim was still trying to get his mind around a picture of his cutting Will's flesh. "Yeah, well, just in case it's not enough, maybe I better strap you down somehow so you can't start thrashing around in the middle of it."

"Not necessary. We'll localize me until I'm numb as a piece of wood. I won't feel a thing. Hell, I'd do it myself, except my chin would get in the way." He winked, but even though they were discussing cutting him open as casually as they might plan a change of sails or a repair of the autohelm, he looked as scared as Jim did.

Angela had advised them to do it outside, not in the cabin.

The light is better outdoors. Salt-swept decks are rather more sterile than an interior space inhabited by two males. And as the procedure will turn messy—not to mention the odor of an anaerobic infection—it's much simpler to hose down the cockpit afterward, wouldn't you think?

"Thoughtful of her," Will grunted.

"She sounds like a funny woman. 'Inhabited by two males' makes us sound like orangutans." The fact was, Will was as strict as hell about cleanliness; the cabin was immaculate.

"Any suggestions about how to control the bleeding?"

Jim was rereading anxiously. Her instructions were as specific and matter-of-fact as the *Sailing Directions*, and made the unlikely seem slightly more possible. "She says that controlling the bleeding is going to be a bitch. I'm supposed to pack it with Iodoform gauze. Do we have enough?"

"Tons."

"I should press on anything that bleeds and hold it for a

while. Do we have a retractor? I might need it to hold the incision open while I poke around inside."

"Yes."

"She says I should use my fingers."

"I presume she means while wearing a glove."

"Oh, cool! She says, 'Your eyes are in your fingers.' And look at this."

Will peered at the printout and read aloud, " 'In medical school my professors said, "Watch one, do one, teach one." You will have to skip the first and it's unlikely you'll be called upon for the third.' That should put you at ease."

"Listen, can't we get her on the radio? We could rig up a headset so she could guide me."

"There's no privacy on the radio. Anyone can listen in. They'll know we're here. They'll know everything."

"Who's going to find us in the middle of nowhere?"

"How about that Russian you almost ran into? There're ships everywhere. Or some goddamned do-gooder will come sailing up to lend a hand and we'll end up 'rescued' on the six o'clock news and Andy Nickels will find us. No radio."

"It's your life."

Will gestured toward the open sky gleaming through the hatch. "Shall we?"

"I gotta sharpen my pocket knife."

"Very funny."

Will's medical kit contained scalpels, numerous replacement blades in sterile packaging, and a surgical prep kit. Jim laid them out in Will's stainless-steel baking pan, along with absorbent twelve-by-twelve cotton sponges, the self-retaining retractor—which looked like a bent kitchen spatula with a handgrip—and several disposable preloaded Marcane syringes.

This was step by step, he told himself, like planning the crossing by reading *Ocean Passages*. That is, until he read Angela's warning: having never done this before, he would not know what to feel for.

"I'm going to wash. You better start popping morphine."

"I already have."

"Do some more. My hands are shaking."

"That's exactly why I'm not popping any more. One of us needs a clear head."

"I'll wash my hands."

"Didn't she say to wear sterile gloves?"

"I'm still going to wash my hands first. Come on, Captain. Let's do it."

26

A SHARK WAS pacing the boat like a malevolent shadow. Will saw it when they came up on deck and all the banter fell out of his voice. "Oh, that is a lousy omen."

It was swimming twenty feet behind the stern, dorsal and tail slicing the wake. Will watched it gloomily as its head churned the surface and it appeared to rise from the water for a closer look at the cockpit.

For a moment, Jim couldn't take his eyes off the animal. But with a pan full of surgical tools in one hand and Will's shrunken arm in the other, a shark was the least of his worries.

"It's just a shark."

"It's a blood omen."

"Okay. I'm going to lay you right across the back here so I kneel on the bench."

"Jim, listen to me."

"Hey, if you don't want to do it, that's fine with me. Don't let me talk you into this."

"It's not that."

"Yeah, well, the only reason I'm willing to try this is because I'm the only one who can. But it was your idea, and if you want to change your mind, feel free."

"If I die . . ."

"You're not going to die," said Jim. What the hell else could he say to the man?

"Listen!" Will turned harshly toward him and for a moment he was the old Will, strong and healthy, singing along with Fountains of Wayne as he pumped away on the spinning bike like a young jock. "If I die . . . take my body to Buenos Aires. Bring it to Angela."

"Will, you're not going to die. But if you did, we're at least three weeks from Argentina and you would be a very smelly corpse."

Jim heard his voice slide into high personal-trainer mode, taking charge of the client's body by taking charge of his mind so the client didn't lose focus by dwelling on pain and defeat.

"Lie down. If you want to do this, let's do it."

"Put my body in the freezer."

"The freezer isn't big enough."

"Then put my head in the freezer."

"Will, are you asking me to cut off your head?"

"Put it in the freezer and take it to Angela."

"I don't think I could do that."

"Use the serrated Global bread knife. Did you know that the Japanese laminate leaves of steel for the Global in the same way they made samurai swords?"

It was not possible for Jim to put his own hand on the knife in a mental picture of someone cutting off Will's head. "No way, Will."

"If you want what's floating around in my head you bloody well will do it."

Will showed Jim how to use the prep sponge. Then he stretched out on his back across the deck behind the cockpit, glanced fearfully at the shark, and closed his eyes.

Jim slapped the sealed container the way Will had demonstrated, causing Betadine and alcohol to combine, and tore it open. There was no way on God's earth or the whole damned ocean that he would cut Will's head off if he died.

But as he scrubbed the skin around the raw, red gash in Will's left breast with the brown disinfectant mix he found it just as impossible to imagine picking up the scalpel to slit his living flesh.

Sticking him with the Marcane syringe was hard enough. Will jumped at the first prick, then bit his lips and braced himself as Jim pierced the tender skin again and again, squeezing the local painkiller from the hypodermic in the same way he recalled the dentist's spreading it around his gums. It took effect immediately, and when Jim shot him again, with a second syringe just to be on the safe side, Will didn't even notice.

Still, he emptied the syringe, stalling while he tried to get ready to do what had to be done next. It was the first close look at the wound that Will had allowed him, and it dispelled his last doubts about the intentions of Margaret in the white dress. When the blade slid between Will's second and third ribs only dumb luck had prevented it from ripping through his heart or severing the big arteries rising out of it.

What the hell was the second rib called? His many training courses had included some basic anatomy. Very basic. The second *sternal rib*. Sternals were true ribs, as opposed to the lower false ribs and the floating ribs.

He was fleeing the moment.

He forced his eyes back to Will's collarbone. Will's *clavicle*. But bones were remote, safely invisible. Dr. Angela had referred to *tissue*. But this was about flesh. Cutting into flesh, exposing rotten flesh, lancing—incising—pus-poisoned flesh. Flesh was real—there was nothing remote or detached about flesh. Unless you forced yourself to remember that flesh was made of muscle—the improvement of which, training, firming, and sculpting, put meat on the fitness instructor's table.

Jim picked up the scalpel, poised it over the red gash, and tried to concentrate on cutting the skin on either end of the red gash by remembering the names of the muscles he had studied in anatomy. Margaret's knife had plunged into Will's pec. *Pectoralis major.* The depth the knife had pierced indicated that it had gone through the *pectoralis minor* as well, depositing bacteria on every single layer that it penetrated. Angela had written that the way the blade initially resisted being pulled out suggested that it had been pinched or caught by a rib.

"I'm really starting to float out on the morphine," Will whispered. "I don't feel a thing."

"How about this?" It was now or never. Jim held the scalpel like a pencil. The angle was wrong. He shifted it in his hand and guided it with his index finger.

"Jesus!" Will gasped.

Jim jumped back. Blood was oozing from a half-inch slit that lengthened the knife wound. Blood as bright red as the sky was blue and the clouds white.

"Do it!" said Will. "It didn't hurt. I can't feel it. It just surprised me." He took a deep breath, let it out, and relaxed his entire body. "Go," he whispered. "I just remembered something I heard somewhere: the incision heals from the sides, not from the ends. It doesn't matter how long you make it."

"My surgeon told me that's one of those old truisms that's not true."

"Yeah, well, it used to be true. Come on, Jim, do it!"

Jim cut into the flesh. Blood welled, red blood, sharp red in the sea's light. He mopped with the cotton sponges, which instantly soaked wet red. He cut again, lengthening the incision and working deeper. About a half inch in, he started to feel detached, far from the rhythmically rolling boat, the clean wind, and the blood; but closer too, close to the blade and the job he was trying to do. He cut tissue and mopped, trying to see what was going on inside, under the sheath of the man.

Something dark and grayish appeared, swollen, bulging, like a miniature shark swimming in the ocean of Will's flesh. Jim couldn't see it clearly through the welling blood and he wondered whether he had exposed an artery. Would his next stroke send Will's lifeblood geysering into his face? But no, there was no pulse to it, no sense of rushing life. It was dark and repellent, and he sensed as much as guessed that this was the infection that had been dogging Will for weeks.

Jim probed it tentatively.

There was pressure under its surface. He wondered if it was within the muscle cover. What the hell was the muscle sheath called? The *fascia layer*. He mopped a wet, red blot, then pushed his finger in and poked.

Gray pus oozed. An overwhelming stench filled his nostrils. He turned his face to the trade wind, which whipped it away. Then he forced himself to shove his finger in again. . . . Irrigate the incision, Angela had written. If there was any pure water left in a polluted world, their boat was sailing on it, thousands of miles from poisoning shores. Jim dipped the bucket they used to swab the decks, scooped it back by its rope, and sluiced the contents into the gaping incision.

Will shouted, "That's cold."

Jim sluiced the wound again and again. The salt slowed the bleeding. He took a long hard look at his handiwork. There was stuff still in there. He probed and squeezed repeatedly around the incision. He paused to wash it with seawater and did it again.

Something gleamed. Jim leaned closer, focused the halogen penlight, and saw to his astonishment a small piece of metal winking from the depths of the wound. He ran below, found a forceps in the medical locker, wiped it with Betadine, sluiced blood from the wound, and probed for the metal. He felt it scrape on the forceps, gripped it, and withdrew it. The tip of Margaret's fish knife must have broken off. It was half an inch long and heavy enough to *clink* when he dropped it in the pan. God only knew what bugs had been on it.

Jim irrigated the wound with seawater again, then poked around some more. When at last he felt no more pockets and saw no more pus, he packed the incision with the iodine-treated pads and pressed on them until the bleeding stopped.

After all the cutting and all the blood, he was surprised by how small the incision actually was. In his mind it stretched for twelve inches: in fact, it was barely three.

"How do you feel, Will?"

"Stoned."

Jim cradled Will in his arms and carried him as carefully as he could to his cabin; he laid the old man on his bunk and covered him with a sheet. Then Jim checked the packing and climbed back on deck, where he cleared up the mess, cleaned and put away the instruments, and finally sank exhausted to the cockpit seat, where he zoned himself into a restful, mindless state by staring at the sea and the fleeting shadows cast by the scattered clouds.

Jim felt proud at first. Will's soaring energy and the strength to complain bitterly about how much his shoulder hurt and how clumsily Jim had "butchered" him seemed to be proof that the operation was a success. He had not regained all his strength.

When they crossed the twentieth parallel and began to lose the southeast trade wind to a jumble of fitful breezes that demanded course changes and sail adjustments, Will couldn't crank a winch, much less wrestle the sheets as they changed from tack to tack. Instead he steered, manipulating the wheel with one hand and his knee, to hold *Hustle* into the wind while Jim made the sail changes.

And for a while, Will started eating again, resurrecting roasts and long-frozen stews from the freezer for meals whose heat and rich flavor were welcome as they neared the thirtieth parallel and the wind grew cooler and stronger. *Hustle* responded with bursts of speed, though their daily miles fell as the constant wind shifts reduced any chance of consistency. At night after the sun went down, Jim took to wearing a windbreaker on deck and sleeping in a sweatshirt.

After a week, Jim asked if Will was ready for him to stitch the wound. But Will wouldn't let him look at it, and he put Jim off repeatedly, claiming that it was still draining. It was around that time that Will got on Jim's case about maintenance.

"You've got to keep on top of it, Jim. Regular rounds, daily, checking lines, blocks, sheets, chafing, winches. I'll show you how to tear down the starboard sheet winch this morning, so you can get the crud out of it and grease the bearings."

Jim held the tools. Will enumerated the steps. After lunch, he said, "I want you to run up the mast and grease the halyard sheaves." He gave Jim a tool belt and a clip-on VHF radio and showed him how to rig the bosun's chair, a harness seat, which they shackled to a halyard so Will could crank Jim up. But with only one usable hand he didn't have the strength to lift Jim's weight with the smallish mast winch.

"That's okay. I can climb the stay."

"I know you can, Tarzan, but it's safer in the harness."

Will led the halyard back to one of the huge sheet winches and cranked Jim slowly skyward. From the mast-head, they communicated by the VHF, with Will talking him through the inspection and lubrication of the blocks. When Jim described them as "pulleys," Will corrected him. "*Blocks.* As in blockhead."

Next morning, Jim was wrapping fresh tape around a sharp fitting to keep the sail from snagging or chafing on the starboard shroud when Will came up early, carefully setting his own mug on the cockpit sole before he hiked himself one-armed through the hatch.

Jim said, "Good morning."

Will nodded a remote good morning and took a long look to the southwest, the source of the cool, stiff wind that had sprung up at dawn. "Damn."

"What's wrong?"

"As any fool could plainly see, we've got a full gale bearing down on us."

Jim had steered around two small squalls since he came on deck, easily managing to avoid the disturbances. "It doesn't look that bad."

"Have you looked at the barometer lately?"

With censure looming darker than the approaching weather he had failed to read, Jim hurried below. The atmospheric pressure had dropped sharply. He went back up on deck, full of apologies. He was embarrassed but also irritated by Will's superior attitude.

"Couldn't you feel it?" asked Will. "I feel it on my skin."

"My skin isn't as fine-tuned."

"Then until it gets fine-tuned, please remember to read the goddamn barometer. That's what it's there for. It could save your life."

Thoroughly annoyed now, Jim said, "Since when are you afraid of a little blow?"

"Since I can't sail the boat alone."

Silence spread between the two men. Finally, Will spoke. "Why don't you take another reef in the main. And furl the jib. And hank the storm sail onto the jackstay just to be on the safe side. Can you find it?"

"Yes."

"I'll drive. Reef the main first."

By the time Jim got the sails in order, the squalls were bunching closer together, squeezing the routes between them into narrow alleys. Soon there was no place to steer around them. They hit the boat one after another, sweeping the decks with hard rain.

The gusts smacking into the sails and heeling the boat made for heavy work at a helm controlled by one hand and a knee. Jim took over. Will stood at his shoulder, offering suggestions that sounded very much like orders. The wind rose, as he had predicted, to thirty knots. It moaned through the rigging and scattered whitecaps. Soon the sea was streaked with windblown foam.

"She's steering like a dream!"

"She wouldn't be if you'd left the jib up."

The gale was short-lived, dropping by afternoon, as the wind veered east and north again. Jim rerigged the sails and auto-helm for the change, went below, caught a short nap, and woke to a bad odor. Will was at the stove.

"If that's lunch it smells like hell."

"The smell means we're running low on gas. Want to switch tanks? There's one more under the port cockpit bench."

Over the soup he had heated, he said, "Let's pull the drums off the winches. I'll show you how to lubricate the roller bearings."

"We already serviced the winches."

"I did—you watched. This time you're going to do it."

Under the gleaming barrel of the starboard sheet winch, they found caked and blackened grease. Will cleaned it himself, with solvent. Then he showed Jim how to repack the bearings. "Not too much grease. You'll gum it all up."

He reassembled the winch, showed Jim where to dissolve the sea salt that had caked up on the pawls, and sprayed them with light oil. Then he pointed at the port sheet winch.

"Your turn."

They made the rounds of all the winches. Jim finished reassembling the halyard winch as dark was falling. The wind was picking up again, veering south, and *Hustle* was throwing cold spray that hissed across the foredeck and the cabin roof. Jim was looking forward to drying off below and eating something warm.

"Okay, let's service the auto-helm."

"It's getting dark," Jim protested.

Will disengaged the automatic steering, locked the rudder so the boat would hold her approximate course, and began pulling parts from the auto-helm, which he passed back to Jim.

"You'll find half the day is dark. You can fix the refrigerator in daylight. You can substitute winches if one freezes until daylight. But there are certain jobs that won't wait— like things to do with the steering—so it's kind of helpful to know your way around in the dark."

"Will?"

"Hand me that—"

"Wait a minute. Just wait a minute. You've been testy and sarcastic, which is not your way. And you're riding me hard. I have a feeling either something is bothering you or you're trying to tell me something. Why don't you just say it?"

"I'm not trying to *tell* you something. I'm trying to *teach* you something."

"Which is?"

"I'm trying to teach you to take care of yourself and the boat."

"Why all of a sudden?"

Will looked away. "I should have started months ago."

"But you didn't. And now all of a sudden you're putting me through a crash course."

"You're in need of one. You're in the middle of a serious ocean. You're not quite a novice anymore, but you're no pro, not even a high amateur."

"Will, are you all right?"

Jim waited for a reassuring answer. By some completely unspoken agreement, they had not discussed his shoulder since the "operation." Will had continued to refuse stitches and had turned very private. Jim had respected that, for whatever reason, the state of Will's health was an off-limits topic. Or, he had to admit, maybe he was afraid to ask, and maybe Will was afraid to voice his fears out loud.

"Are you all right?" he asked again.

"I'm not sure," Will answered.

"I thought you were getting better."

"I think I ought to talk to my doctor."

Will meant actual voice-talk, not e-mail, which indicated to Jim how seriously concerned the old man was, because he had said repeatedly how he feared that the McVays might track him by phone or radio signals.

Will couldn't get a connection with the satellite phone. "I'm getting a recording—no longer in service."

"Did you forget to pay?"

"It's billed to a card. . . . Bloody awful time for a screwup." He switched on the long-range, single-sideband radio and tried to hail a ship-to-shore radio-telephone station.

"Most of them are either shut down or reduced because of sat phones," he muttered to a worried Jim, who stood beside him at the nav station, gripping an overhead rail as the boat rolled and wondering whether a new infection had invaded Will's wound or if he had screwed up and not eliminated all of the first one. "They used to track your signal with movable antenne, but with sat phones—and cell phones inshore—that's all going by the boards."

Will had no luck raising the South American communications centers to the west, so he tried South Africa, twenty-seven hundred miles to the east. But the Cape Town station did not respond either. He took a last ditch stab at Portishead, England, on the chance that if the atmospherics were right, a skip signal might carry the six thousand miles to the North Atlantic station. "It all depends on the atmospherics, but the Portishead operators are top-notch. If anybody can hear me it'll be them."

"Portishead, Portishead, Portishead, this is *Hustle,* Yankee-Niner-Yankee-Romeo-Romeo-Lima. Do you read me, Portishead?"

He tried repeatedly, fine-tuning and switching channels, but raised no response from Portishead. Finally, he tossed down the headset and switched off the radio. "Maybe tomorrow."

Two days later he still hadn't made radio contact with the single sideband. No high-seas station responded in the west. Nothing east. He took another long shot at Portishead, England.

"Maybe this time—"

Static roared suddenly.

"What the hell is that? Sounds like they're next door."

Whistles and clicks crackled from the speakers.

"What *is* that?"

"Distress channel." Will fiddled with the knobs. A voice—shrill with fear—leaped out of the speakers. *"Mayday. Mayday. Mayday."*

Will leaned intently into the radio and flicked the transmit switch.

"I read your Mayday. Speak your vessel and position."

"Mayday, Mayday, Mayday."

Over his shoulder Will said, "Remember this, Jim. If you ever have to transmit a distress call always, always, always report your position first. That's the one thing you have got to get through if they're ever going to find you." He lifted the microphone to his lips again. "I'm reading your Mayday loud and clear at 2182 kHz. What is your position?"

"Mayday."

"For Christ's sake." Then he said to Jim. "They're probably scared silly."

"Maybe they can't hear you."

"I read your Mayday. Report your position."

"This is the motor yacht *Pegasus*. Call sign India-Five-Juliet-Tango-Echo. We are taking on water. One man and two women aboard. Two children."

"What is your position, *Pegasus*?"

"Twenty-six degrees, 30 minutes, 14 seconds south; 30 degrees, 28 minutes, 32 seconds west."

Will looked at Jim.

Jim pointed at their own pencil track on the chart. "They're close."

Will measured the distance with his calipers. "Twelve hours. *Pegasus,* I copy 26, 30, 14 south; 30, 28, 32 west."

"Roger that. We're sinking. Please come."

Jim said, "Tell them we'll help."

"Where are you?" shrilled the panicky voice.

"On our way," said Will.

"What is your position?"

"We'll be there in twelve hours," said Will. "Out."

He switched off the radio and entered *Pegasus*'s transmission in *Hustle*'s log. Then he marked the sinking vessel's position on the chart, glanced at the GPS for *Hustle*'s exact position, marked it, and drew a line between the two vessels. Then he looked up at Jim. "There's our course."

"They're lucky we're near," said Jim.

"Extremely," said Will. He drummed his fingers on the chart for a moment. "Unbelievably lucky." He checked the wind direction and said, "All right, let's get some more sail up. We can make it on a broad reach if this wind holds."

The rescue course took them a little north of west.

Hustle flew on the south wind, which continued freshening, pouring hard over the port side just aft of the beam. Jim concentrated on the helm—with Will coaching him to nurse more speed out of the sloop. But before long, Will sat down on the bench. His helpful recommendations came fewer and less frequently until he sank into a deep and lasting silence.

Even a cursory glance at the frail figure at Jim's elbow showed a man running on his last reserves. Fatigue had gouged deep lines in his cheeks. Jim had the eeriest feeling that the infection was like a volcano, smoldering in Will's being, building inexorably toward an eruption.

"Will, I'm okay up here for a while if you want to catch a little sleep."

The old man stood shakily and shambled toward the hatch. "I'll check the radio again. . . . Maybe shut my eyes for a couple of minutes."

Jim sailed alone for the next two hours using every trick he had learned on his own and every trick Will had taught him to eke another half knot from the wind. When he finally engaged the auto-helm he was so tired that he knew that it would outsail him in his weary state and that the boat would make faster time in its mechanical hand.

Belowdecks, he found Will asleep at the nav station, slumped over the chart table, the radio mike under his hand. Jim stretched out on the pilot berth and closed his eyes and listened to the water racing past the hull.

Then he got an idea. Other rescuers steaming to the distress call would speak to each other on the VHF. He got up, reached around Will, switched on the VHF, and listened to static.

"What are you doing?" asked Will, blinking awake.

"Checking for VHF traffic."

"I've been listening. Nothing. No one's talking, no one's coming but us."

"Wait a minute. Shouldn't we pass it on? Call for more help?"

Will shook his head. He seemed not to like what he was saying, even as he was trying to convince himself he was doing the right thing. "Plenty of ships will have caught the distress call. Commercial vessels monitor the emergency frequencies 'round the clock. We're heading their way, but I'm hoping some steamer will beat us to them. A container ship can easily do three hundred or four hundred miles in the time we do one hundred. We can check in an hour. . . . Still . . . in case they didn't . . . You're right, Jim. I've got to relay it. Dammit. Should have done it hours ago."

Will transmitted on the distress channel, "Mayday relay. Mayday relay. Mayday relay. Motor yacht *Pegasus*. India-

Five-Juliet-Tango-Echo reports sinking 26 degrees, 30 minutes, 14 seconds south; 30 degrees, 28 minutes, 32 seconds west."

He repeated the relay twice.

An operator on Ascension Island responded in a London Cockney accent. "Thank you for the Mayday relay. What is your ship and your position, please?"

Will shut the radio off.

"What did you do that for?" Jim asked.

"Same reason I didn't tell *Pegasus* our position."

"Why?"

"I don't like this."

"What do you mean?"

"Something's off."

"Off?"

"It could be a setup. I think they're gunning for us."

"They? You mean the McVays?"

"Could be."

"Yeah, but if they're not, then there are five people, including a couple of kids . . ."

"We relayed the distress call. And we'll keep heading that way and listen. See who responds. See what they find. See if it's really a sinking boat or some hired guns waiting for you and me."

"Well, you said there's an air base at Ascension Island. They'll launch search planes."

"I'm sure they will—if that was really Ascension Island."

"What do you mean 'if'? You just heard them."

"I heard a London accent on an island leased to Americans."

"Maybe we're getting a little too paranoid?"

Will answered slowly, as if explaining long division to a student reared on calculators. "What if the McVays and Andy Nickels arranged for someone nearby to broadcast a phony distress call."

"Nearby? How do they know where 'nearby' is?"

"Simple. They plot our likely route from the point you let that bloody freighter spot us. Knowing our course, the weather, and a general idea of the boat's sailing qualities, they could plot us pretty close to where we are right now. Then it's a simple matter to wait along that track and transmit a low-power distress signal on 2182 kHz—"

"Come on," Jim snorted in disbelief. "And hope we have our radio on? And hope no one else is so near they hear?"

"They would have heard me trying to get through the last three days. So they wait there until whoever else might overhear in this very empty area steams past, and when we blunder along they snatch us and sink our boat."

"Except we relayed the distress call to Ascension Island."

Will shook his head. "Did we? I'm willing to believe that people who earned billions supplying the United States government with mil-spec electronics and spy satellites possess radios and electronic countermeasures that are sophisticated enough to block our miserable little hundred-fifty-watt SSB signal. *And* answer back pretending that they are Ascension Island."

"Maybe," said Jim. "But—"

"You are such an innocent!" Will roared at him, a roar that ended in a racking cough. "Think, Jim. Think. They're playing to win. And they hold all the cards."

"But what are we going to do? If those are real people drowning, and we're the only ones who are near, we're their only hope."

"I know that!" Will shot back. "That's why we're still sailing their way. But the problem is, if I'm right, if it's the McVays, then they're going to have absolutely top-notch radar good enough to pick up a speck of steel, like our winches or even the wire stays."

"They didn't have it on their ship when they tracked my heart-rate monitor."

"Maybe it wasn't their ship. Maybe it was borrowed. Maybe they didn't have time to set up. They've had plenty of time since Nigeria. But once they spot us, there is no way we can outrun them. So yes, those people are drowning if they're real. But if they're not . . . if they're a ruse . . . if they don't exist . . ."

"How close can we get before their radar might spot us?"

Will shrugged. "Radar generally operates line-of-sight.

Thirty miles. But there's over-the-horizon radar that could boost it to forty, fifty miles. What are we making, eight knots?"

"Eight and a half."

Will patted the teak table. *"Hustle,"* he murmured, "you're a flier. . . ." Then he took the compass and drew a circle on the chart. "There's *Pegasus* in the middle." He drew an *X.* "Here we are on the edge." He drew a triangle to represent *Hustle.* Then he drew a second circle. "Here's their radar range. We have from here to here. . . ." With the brass calipers he measured the distance between the two circles. "Twenty-five miles. Once we cross this line, they might see us. We've got three hours to decide who's who."

Jim said, "I'll catch some sleep. But leave the radios on. Both of them. In case."

Jim slept fitfully, yanked awake by sporadic bursts of static shattering the soft, empty hiss of the midocean radio spectrum. Suddenly he heard a man speaking clearly in English. He jumped to the radio. Will was there ahead of him. They listened intently. No connection. By a trick of atmospherics, a radio operator was transmitting from a freighter in the Caribbean, four thousand miles away.

Shortly before the deadline when they would enter the dangerous inner circle, Jim went up on deck and scanned the afternoon sky, hoping to see a rescue plane. But the sky was as empty as the sea. And the horizons, which stretched many miles distant in the clear, bright sunlight, remained deserted.

Will came on deck, pulling himself one-handed up the companionway, clearly distressed. "Not a peep. Not from *Pegasus.* Not from any rescue ships. If only there were some way to make contact with ships in the area without tipping off our position. If it's them, they can track our radio signals."

"Sat phone?"

"Still not working."

"Maybe you're right. *Pegasus* should have kept sending distress signals. Wouldn't they?"

"Unless their radio died. Or they already sank—it's astonishing how quickly a boat will go down sometimes. What's killing me is, what if they're real people in a raft? Wait a minute, wait a minute, wait a minute. E-mail! Jim, hop below. Send an e-mail with their last position."

"The sat phone isn't working."

"E-mail on the SSB. Flash a quicky before they can jam it."

"Who are you going to send it to?"

"Rafi."

One of his "cavemen."

"Rafi Sikim. Software guy."

"What are your cavemen going to do for you?"

"Give me a hand getting below. I'll show you."

Jim half carried him down the companionway and eased him into the nav station, where Will sat at his laptop a moment, trying to catch his breath. Then he wrote *Pegasus*'s call sign and last position and a note to his Indian engineer telling him to alert the Argentine, Brazilian, South African, and American navies and coast guards.

Jim, reading over his shoulder, asked, "How's he going to do that?"

"Rafi could hack his way into purgatory if he believed it existed. This report will be on twenty different admirals' desks in half an hour. If those people are real, there'll be aircraft bumping noses over them. If it's the McVays, they're going to set a new world's record for high-speed skedaddling."

Jim stared at Will in open admiration. "You are one resourceful old—"

"Not old. Just sick."

"Then I suggest we stay right here and get rescued, too. You should be in intensive care."

"No."

That night, as they resumed their southwesterly course toward Río de la Plata, the radios were alive with ship-to-ship and ship-to-shore in several languages. Will, cackling triumphantly, said, "The navies are on restricted frequencies, but there are four commercial ships heading that way, too. Someone will find them if they are real."

Three days passed. But no raft was found and no boat reported lost. Jim reflected soberly on the fact that a naturally devious man like Will was better equipped than he to survive. Left to his own devices, Jim would have charged to the rescue and ended up sailing blithely, innocently, naively, and fatally into a trap.

27

ANDY NICKELS SAID, "One way or another Shannon Riley will lead us to Jim Leighton, and Jim Leighton will lead us to Will Spark."

"I am enormously pleased to hear that," said Lloyd McVay. "As there are more than a million Uruguayans in Montevideo and fully *twelve million* Argentines in Buenos Aires. Give or take countless slum dwellers in the *villas miseria.*"

"We are very strong on the ground in BA," Nickels assured him. "And Montevideo. Army, cops, judges—anybody who can get the job done, they're ours."

"Embassies?"

"Both. But I'd rather use our own."

"Quite."

"What do you mean, 'one way or another'?" asked Val McVay.

"As you know, ma'am, we're watching the girl in Connecticut twenty-four-seven. One of several things will happen. They will talk on the telephone when the boat lands. I've got people on the phones for when he tells her where he is." He glanced at Lloyd McVay and added with unconcealed sarcasm, "Or Ms. McVay might still get lucky with that e-mail address she turned up."

Val ignored the jibe, saying only, "What if Shannon goes to him? They've been separated for three months now."

"Yes," said her father. "They might meet where Will Spark lands the boat."

"In which case," said Andy, "we will follow Shannon to Jim."

"What if neither of those things happens?" asked Val.

"We can always take her hostage."

"Kidnap her?"

"Do you have a problem with that?" He glanced at Lloyd McVay, who was gazing out the window at a horse.

"I have a huge problem with that," Val shot back. "A million things can go wrong and then where are we? Your people are sitting in a Connecticut jail with a federal prosecutor telling them, 'The line forms *here* for those who get immunity for naming their employer.'"

Andy Nickels waited until Lloyd McVay faced him and answered, "I've got cutouts. No way it'll come back to us."

Lloyd McVay said, "Cutouts often put me in mind of Watergate, the Contras, and Iran. 'What tangled webs we weave . . .'"

Val said, "My father's right. Get real, Andy. Just follow her. It can't be too hard to follow a girl in a wheelchair."

"Whatever you say, ma'am. You're the boss."

After Nickels left, her father asked, "Do you find our hunter attractive?"

"It occurs to me," Val answered, "that hunters cannot be the brutes portrayed in the common imagination. They've got to be highly sensitive. If they're not sensitive to their surroundings and their prey, they'd never catch anything."

"So you find him attractive?"

"Why do you ask?" She was listening with half an ear when his question came out of left field and she paid it the minor attention it deserved. Her mind was on Will Spark. They had a strange affinity. Could she use that to find him?

"I ask because we'll be seeing quite a bit of Andy before this is over."

She was thinking about how she and Will Spark had shared, independently, a similar concept of the Internet as an active, omnipresent communication system, so much more than just a gigantic, passive file. The general thought was hardly unique to them; nor was their realization that it would make knowledge an active force. But their refinements of common knowledge had led straight to the brilliance of Sentinel. While others were predicting that refrigerators would order fresh milk from the grocery store, their stroke of genius was in choosing to use it to transform medicine.

"I said, we'll be seeing a lot of Andy."

"I heard you. But Mother always told me, 'Don't dip your pen in the company ink.' "

"Your mother was a prude."

"I didn't have the opportunity to know her as well as you," she replied icily. "But I don't like thinking of her that way."

"You weren't married to her."

"You were an excellent parent, Dad. For the kind of kid I was. But I'd like to think she would have been too, if you'd let her."

"If I had let her, you would be ordinary."

"I would never be ordinary."

"What does the doctor say?" Will called from his bunk. He had slept round the clock and Jim had rigged the last IV to keep him hydrated. His fever had risen; he was in great pain and profoundly weak.

"I couldn't get through."

"Well, did you—"

"Angela's e-mail account seems to be shut. And when I finally got the high-seas operator to put me through, her answering machine said she was away for a week."

"What's my temperature?"

"One hundred three."

Jim couldn't meet Will's desperate eye. They had tried every antibiotic in the well-stocked medicine locker—penicillin, erythromycin, Cipro. But the infection just wouldn't go away. They were out of options. Will knew it. His face hardened into bitter lines.

It was way too late to try to sail back to Ascension Island. The Argentine capital was closer, but still a week away. They could try to contact a ship, if there were any nearby, but, as Angela had pointed out when Jim operated on Will, a freighter's sick bay wasn't likely to contain any more exotic antibiotics than Will carried.

"Shall we try to hail a ship?"

Will shook his head. "Aside from the risk of broadcasting our position to everybody with a set of ears on, even if we could rendezvous with a ship, what with the lousy seamanship on most ships and heavy seas there's a good chance I'd get killed in the transfer."

"So a ship doesn't improve your odds."

"So what are we saying?"

Jim shook his head.

"In other words, I'm dying."

"In other words, I'll get you to Buenos Aires as fast as I can."

Will cast a miserable look out the port. "If this wind holds. We're still in the variables."

"It's swinging west."

"Great. Then we'll butt heads with the westerlies."

"I'll do what I can."

To Jim's surprise, a warm smile softened Will's expression. "I know you will."

"I just wish I was a better sailor."

"Hey, listen, Jim. This whole mess is not your fault. You just had the bad luck to fall in with bad company. Don't start blaming yourself if I don't make it."

"You'll make it," Jim retorted automatically.

And Will shot back, "Absolutely."

But the next morning the wind failed them. It backed gently to the north and slowed. *Hustle* banged along in choppy seas, losing much of the time Jim had gained by driving her hard all night.

He had survived this much of the crossing thanks to Will's instructions, luck, reliable electronics, an excellent boat, and decent weather. Now, when speed was everything, the variables had turned contrary.

Hoping for another change for the better, Jim did his rounds. The spinnaker pole had worked half out of its chocks on the foredeck. It seemed that if something could break on the boat it would, if it could work loose it would, and if it could chafe it would. With his rounds completed and the wind still dropping, Jim went below, yawning, scrambled some freeze-dried eggs, and brought them to Will.

The old man was awake and staring moodily out the port. "That smells good."

The daylight fell on his face, which was pink with fever. Jim was shocked; the last time he had seen Will his skin was so dead white that he looked as if he had been bleached.

"You okay?"

"Head's spinning."

"Hungry?"

"Not really." Will took a tentative forkful. "You used olive oil. Very nice. I'll make a civilized man out of you yet—could I borrow your spare heart-rate monitor?"

"What for?"

He looked at Jim. His eyes glistened. "I just want to wear it. See how I'm doing."

"Sure."

Jim got it from his bag in the tiny forward cabin. "Still working." He helped Will strap the sensor around his chest. He had lost more weight. Like a fish skeleton, his ribs pressed against his flanks.

Will stared at the monitor for a while. Deeply concerned, Jim looked at the readout. The man's heart was racing as if he were climbing a hill.

Will asked, "Have you eaten?"

"In a minute."

"You have to eat."

"Can I bring you some juice?"

"Get your breakfast. I want to talk to you."

Jim scraped the pan, heated a fresh splash of oil, poured in the second batch of eggs, and scrambled them with slow swoops of the flexible spatula the way Will had taught him. Then he grabbed a fork and carried the pan to the door of Will's cabin.

"Get a plate, for Christ's sake. You look like a—"

"Jesus, you sound like my mother. I'm tired and I'm hungry and I don't feel like washing another plate when I'm done."

"There are two reasons to use a plate rather than stuff your face from a frying pan. One, order is good for the soul—particularly on a boat, where it is all too easy to turn into a slob with the kind of sloppy habits that can get you killed."

"Next time," said Jim. "What's up?"

"Two, if you eat from the pan, the pan will continue to cook the eggs and your excellently cooked breakfast will turn hard and dry."

Jim went back to the galley, used a spatula to transfer the eggs onto a plate, then returned to Will's cabin. Will watched him eat and waited until Jim was done to speak.

"I haven't been totally honest with you."

"I've heard this before."

"Well, you're going to hear it again. It's important. I may have misled you a little if I suggested that you were not in danger."

Jim yawned. "I better catch some sleep so I'm ready for the wind, if it ever comes back."

"You're not listening."

"Will, you could confess to me all day and at the end I'd know everything but the truth."

Will returned a beaten, weary look. "Humor me, please."

He sounded frightened. Jim turned his full attention to the old man.

"Do you remember that I asked you to take my body to Buenos Aeries if I die?"

"You're not going to die."

"If I die, take it to Angela. She knows what to do. There's a list of addresses in the drawer under the chart table. Angela's lab and a safe house in BA and some friends who can help."

"Considering our reception in Africa, I'm not sure I want to meet your friends."

"These are different."

"What if your friends can't or won't help me?"

"If something happens to Angela, bail out and head for the Falklands."

"The Falkland Islands?" The Falklands were a thousand miles from Buenos Aires. So far south that they were practically off the chart.

"There's a woman there, she can help you. Her farm is marked on my Falklands chart."

"And what if *this* friend can't help?"

"Run south, kid. Run deep south. Don't stop till you hit Antarctica."

Jim yawned, not believing they were having this conversation. "What happens in Antarctica?"

"There's a place for the CC Kid—"

"I am *not* the CC Kid. Not anymore. If I were, you'd be fucking dead already."

"Sorry. From now on we'll call you Cockpit Man. You should see it down there, Jim. The sun lights the icebergs from inside all pearly green—of course, there won't be a sun when you're there. Winter's coming. Dark as a coal mine."

"So what happens when they find me there? I go to the South Pole?"

"No one will find you there."

"Will, we're a thousand miles from anywhere and you look like hell and I'm so tired I can't see straight, much less deal with your fantasy. I'm going to sleep. Wake me if we sink."

"I've written my will."

"Will? What are you talking about?"

"It's in the nav station drawer. What it says is when I die you get everything."

"What are you talking about?"

"I am leaving you everything I own."

"You're making me your heir?" Tired as he was, Jim placed his plate at his feet and stood up straight. His mind was swarming with opposites. Will was jerking him around again. Will meant it. Will was rich. Will said he was broke. Will wasn't going to die. Will looked like he had died already.

Will said, "I see I have your attention at last."

"How can I be your heir?"

"I have no kids of my own and I'm sure as hell not leaving anything to my ex-wives."

"This feels a little strange."

"Don't get too excited. There's no real money to speak of. But you can have all my possessions and all my royalty rights—which includes Sentinel."

Good luck cashing that in, Jim thought. And then, as if from a distance, like thunder over the water, he heard Will say, "And *Hustle.*"

"You're giving me the boat?"

"I am *willing* you my yacht."

Jim looked forward, up the passage to the main cabin. Light was pouring in the ports, glowing on the varnished wood. Pretty to look at and a powerful machine. He could feel her pulse through the bulkhead. She was heeling just enough, shoving surely through the scrambled seas. There were times when he hated being stuck on her, but she was a fine and beautiful object.

No. It was too crazy. Besides, he couldn't afford to run her. He'd seen the bills in Will's desk: thousands a year just to keep her in trim; a rich man's toy.

As he had done so often in their conversations, Will read Jim's mind. "You could charter her out. They'll pay a premium for luxury. People go nuts for the workmanship. They want excellent food, first-class accommodations, a pleasant captain, and his beautiful first-mate-slash-wife."

"Sounds great, Will, but I can't. Shannon couldn't do it."

"Why the hell not?"

"She can't walk."

"What do you mean?"

"She's crippled, Will. She can't walk more than a few steps on crutches."

"You never said anything. . . ." He trailed off, his expression hurt. "Why didn't you tell me?"

"I didn't want to talk about it, Will."

"I thought we were friends."

"Well, we were. We are. We became friends. But you're also my boss and I didn't want to talk about it."

"But of all things not to talk about."

"The trip was the time to think about it, not talk." But he did have to ask himself the same question. "I did not want to admit to you that as much as I try to ignore the fact, Shannon's affliction is central to any future we might share."

"That poor kid. Poor both of you. Christ on a—You poor—"

"We're okay," Jim cut in. "It's not like she's paralyzed or anything. We have a sex life—a great sex life—had . . ."

"I'm really sorry, Jim. . . . What happened?"

"She got creamed in a ski accident. Multiple compound fractures, both legs, knees . . . you name it, it shattered."

"Where were you? Oh, I get it. You came *later*. You were the physical therapist."

"Something like that . . . They pinned what they could. She's got more titanium in her than an F-16, but . . . She's a very strong woman, but sometimes she's hanging by strength alone. So I don't see her doing yacht charters."

"Why don't you let Shannon decide what she can and can't do?"

"How could she even brace herself against the roll of the boat?" Jim retorted angrily.

"Decide together when *Hustle* is yours. If . . ."

"If what?"

"If you put my head in the freezer and deliver it to Angela."

"I told you, I can't do that."

"This is a dying man's last wish."

"You're not—"

"I am, Jim. I surely am. Today, tonight, tomorrow. I'm a goner. The infection is rampaging through me. It's burning me up. I'm sailing on fire like a dead Viking."

He lunged at Jim and grabbed his arm; there was desperate power in his clawlike grip. "Jim, you must help me undo what I started."

"What are you talking about?"

"The McVays are the last people on the planet who should have the power of my processor. Whatever you do, you must not let them get it."

"I promise you, Will. I'll do everything I can to keep it for myself."

"Promise you'll take my head to Angela."

"I promise. Now go to sleep."

What Val McVay found most maddening about Will Spark's e-mail encryption scheme—aside from the fact that she hadn't been able to crack any of the letters she had intercepted—was that the gibberish that covered her monitor made it appear as if her computer had crashed. It made Notes or Domino look like a crossword puzzle, and if you didn't attack it carefully, she had discovered the hard way, it bit back with a virus that took a week to eradicate. It wasn't possible that Will himself had devised it. It was the product, she was sure, of one of his talented Indian engineers.

As a scientist and an engineer, Val held a bred-in-the-bone belief that ever-expanding computing power meant that there was no such thing as an undecipherable code. Gang together enough McVay-Hyper workstations and write some hot cracking code and eventually you could decipher anything.

But even Val had to admit that if there was ever going to be an uncrackable, utterly secure secret communication, it would involve developing quantum cryptography coupled to a randomly keyed onetime code similar to the one Will Spark used in his e-mail correspondence with his Sentinel engineers and, just recently, Dr. Angela Heinman Ruiz of Rio de Janeiro.

Having failed to crack e-mails intercepted to and from Will's engineers, Val knew she hadn't a hope of reading the contents of the long messages he had exchanged with the South American doctor. A clue to his destination? Perhaps.

Cross-checking revealed that Dr. Ruiz was a plastic surgeon. But she had practiced microsurgery years ago, before she went for the money. And although the booming Brazilian economy kept her busy most of the time in Rio, she had a second practice in Buenos Aires. The problem was, Dr. Ruiz was currently in neither of her offices.

28

JIM WENT UP on deck and trimmed the main and the jib.
All he could do was try to make the boat go faster.

To hell with the McVays. They were Will's problem. His
problem was simpler, his goal clear: sail *Hustle* close
enough to Buenos Aires to radio a medevac helicopter. A
helicopter would save two days in the race to get Will into a
hospital. Sail the boat to Buenos Aires. Nurse Will along.
Helicopter to a hospital.

The wind was edging west, moving into their teeth,
which meant beating into it, sailing close hauled. Will had
shown him a trick of flying a third sail, an inner jib or staysail, from the jackstay, which angled between the foredeck
and a point two-thirds up the mast. In theory the boat would
go faster with a single big headsail, but *Hustle,* Will had
taught him, didn't always play by the rules.

If he could get the wind flowing just right through the
narrow slots between the two headsails and the main, she
might go faster. The sail was in the forepeak and the fore-
hatch was dogged down tight, so he had to go down the main
hatch again and head forward.

"What's up?" Will called.

"I'm going to try a staysail."

"Wear your harness."

He found the sail. It would be easier to take it up the forward hatch. But the bow was rising and falling and spray was flying heavily over the foredeck. A new sense that from now on he alone would run the boat made him cautious. What if he opened the hatch just as the bow dipped under a big sea? With good luck he'd only get the forepeak wet. With bad luck several tons of seawater would come blasting in. With really bad luck he'd be knocked down and injured so badly he couldn't sail.

Ludicrous. He was thinking like an old man.

Nonetheless, he dragged the bag through the main cabin and up the main hatch into the cockpit, donned his harness, clipped onto the jackline, and dragged the sail forward.

He pulled it out of the bag, sorted top from bottom—Will had marked the difficult-to-distinguish head and clew with indelible ink—and shackled the tack to a pad eye set in the deck at the foot of the jackstay. Then he hanked the sail onto the stay with snap hooks and shackled a halyard to its head. He bent two lines to the clew and led them through blocks and back to the cockpit. And with those sheets ready to control the sail, he winched it into the sky.

It slammed around in the wind, crackling and thundering, until he made his way back to the cockpit, where he took three wraps of a sheet around a portside winch and cranked until the Dacron sail was us taut as the main and the forward jib. He eased the main a hair and hauled the jib in two clicks of the winch, and when he finally looked at the knot meter it told him what his body already knew. He'd increased the boat's speed by almost half a knot.

With triumph came sudden hope and the powerful belief that if he just drove the boat hard and true he could keep Will alive until he had sailed him within helicopter range of Buenos Aires.

He fiddled with the auto-helm until he had it responding properly to the additional sail. Then he ducked below to feed Will and get some hot coffee. Will was sprawled on the couch in the main cabin. He thrust his arm toward Jim and pointed at his heart-rate monitor.

"I'll bet you've never seen numbers like these."

Jim looked. His own heart jumped. Will's pulse had fallen to forty beats a minute.

Jim said, "I'll radio Angela."

He switched on the single sideband. If he couldn't get Angela, he would broadcast a distress call on 2182. Some doctor somewhere would tell him what to do. Shoot Will full of Adrenalin or something.

Will laughed.

"What?" Jim turned from the radio. There was a finality in Will's tone, a firm sound of resolution, like a solid door swinging shut.

"I just had a wonderful revelation: when all is lost, there is nothing left to lose."

Jim leaned toward him.

"You'll love Buenos Aires, Jim. Most hospitable people you've ever met, half Italian, half Spanish, most of 'em speak English, and they'll give you the shirt off their back, only they've got an inferiority complex, so when they ask what you think of Buenos Aires just tell 'em you never saw a city like it. And don't ever talk about the Falklands War or the 'disappeared' the military killed during the dirty war against the left. Jim, don't forget our deal. Here's the serrated knife."

He extended the scalloped blade. Just as he did, an errant swell smacked *Hustle* on her port side, staggering the sloop. The knife fell from Will's hand and landed straight up on its rounded point, stuck squarely between two planks of the teak deck.

Will peered blearily at the quivering blade. "Amazing," he whispered. "What are the odds?" Swaying, he leaned forward and began to sing,

*"Standin' on the corner,
  I didn't mean no harm. . . . "*

Jim jumped to catch him, but he got tangled in the nav station and before he could swing his legs out from under the desk, Will tumbled to the deck.

Jim knelt and turned him over. His cheek was cut and his nose was bleeding, but he was struggling to pull something from his pocket. "This is for you."

"Let me help—"

"No big deal. Just my bosun's knife."

"Hang on to it," Jim said. "You'll need—"

"Wear it always. Keep it sharp. It could save your life sometime. See this key?"

"Yes." The key Jim had stolen—borrowed—stolen—to open Will's private desk.

"It opens the desk in the bulkhead. A bunch of stuff there you can look at. Keep anything you want—I know you rifled the desk—but there's a secret panel underneath that you missed. It opens when you release a little spring under the drawer. False bottom. Something in there you might enjoy when you grow up."

"Let me help you into bed."

"No. I'm outta here. It's all yours, Jim. Have fun with it. Just make sure you get my head to Buenos Aires." He closed his eyes. "Watch this, Jim." He raised his arm. The heart-rate monitor was recording a deadly thirty beats a minute. And as Jim watched in helpless fascination, the numbers spooled down to zero.

29

JIM PULLED THE knife out of the crack in the cabin floor and returned it to its rack. Then he picked up Will.

For the first time in his life he understood the phrase "a bag of bones." He carried Will into his cabin, laid him on his bunk, and pulled a sheet over him. Then he backed out of the cabin. The body barely indented the sheet.

> Dear Shannon,
> Will died at nine-twenty this morning at 33° 49' S, 40° 19' W. I feel so alone. I crossed two oceans with the man; already I miss his talking and talking and talking, teaching me stuff, telling me stuff, talk, talk, talk, constant talk, the sailing lessons, and tons of advice, most of which I didn't need or didn't want to hear. We sailed from Barbados to Nigeria and then back across the South Atlantic. Thousands of miles. I know he was a con man. I know he was a liar. And it looks like he was a thief, too. But he was fun to sail with and he was so full of hope. He made me want to be an optimist, like you.
> I'll write you more later. I have a ton of stuff I have to deal with, but I just had to tell you this first.
> I love you. I wish you were here with me.
> Jim

He entered Will's death in the log. He wrote the time he died, *Hustle*'s position, and his opinion that Will had died from an infection resulting from a knife wound suffered in Nigeria.

He stood in the main cabin for a while, just standing and turning, not knowing what to do next. Air. He needed air. He hurried up the companionway. The sea was empty and the sky sharp, with several bold white clouds. The wind was chilly, invigorating, like the first cool day of autumn.

It is autumn, he thought. Almost. Down here winter is summer, and summer is over. And there's a dead man below, whose head I'm supposed to cut off and put in the freezer. Thank God they were out of the tropics. The cool weather bought him a day or two to make up his mind.

He should read the will. Will's will. But he didn't want to yet. So instead he went below and unlocked the teak desk and found the release for the false bottom, which pivoted open, revealing a square drawer. Folded inside was a carry-on suit bag. He unzipped it, smelled cedar, and discovered a black tuxedo. The coat had satin lapels, the pants a satin stripe, and there were suspenders, a silk cummerbund, and a snowy white pleated shirt. Jim had worn a rented tux with a plaid cummerbund to his high school junior prom and a couple with colored jackets to friends' weddings. But Will's was midnight black. *When you grow up*. What was Will thinking? It would never fit him . . . though it might if he lost some more definition.

He put it back in the suit bag and closed the desk. Then he sat down at the nav station and opened the drawer. There was a business envelope with his name written on it in Will's fine, clear handwriting. The paper was heavy and textured, as was the single sheet folded inside. Jim took it up to the cockpit, sat on the windward side, and read. It began in the same clear hand:

I, William Spark, aka Billy Cole, aka Pendleton Rice, aka Randell Smythe, aka Mickey Creegan . . .

What a time Shannon would have tracking all those names on the Web. He'd bet it was Mickey Creegan who had moved up in the world by painting boat bottoms.

. . . being sound of mind and frail of body, write my last will and testament: If Jim Leighton, my good friend and loyal shipmate, delivers my body—or, failing that, my head—to Dr. Angela Heinman Ruiz in Buenos Aires, Argentina, I bequeath to him all my worldly possessions, including my yacht, *Hustle,* and royalty rights to all my patents.

Maybe if he covered Will's body with a blanket and wrapped his head in a towel. . . . Am I losing my mind? he thought.

Will's handwriting deteriorated, with crossouts and confusions of words not finished.

If Jim Leighton fails to hold up his end of this bargain, everything goes to Ms. Cordelia MacDonald, Borlum Farm, East Island, Falkland Islands, UK.

No surprise there. Perform, or you get nothing. Have I lost my way? Jim thought. But he wanted his piece of Sentinel.

Will had signed it "William Spark," and dated it, "Aboard the yacht *Hustle,* 32 degrees south, 40 west. (Voice copy on tape cassette and in voice mail of Dr. Angela Heinman Ruiz, Rio de Janeiro—just in case any of my ex-wives try to dispute this.)"

Finally, Will had scribbled a note on the bottom of the page:

JIM: JUST HANG ON TO MY HEAD. JUST PROMISE ME THAT, PLEASE. Keep it in the freezer, even if you can't find Angela, maybe you can get in touch with my—

Frantic scribbles tumbled off the bottom of the page and landed on the back.

—cavemen. . . . Do me this one favor, shipmate. And even if you screw up, and everything goes to Cordi, you can keep the boat. Cordi hates sailing—she gets even sicker at sea than you do, if that's possible—and she doesn't need the money. She's doing fine with a hydroponic farm. . . . Here, I'm signing it again to make this codicil legal.

He had signed all five names again.
Jim said, "Thank you, Will. Thanks for the out."
Will had scribbled some more, in lighter ink, in a scrawl so chaotic it was almost impossible to read:

You're in a win-win situation, kid. Do the right thing. Or as you loved to say to me: "A deal's a deal."

Jim said, "Do the right thing? Oh, give me a break." Will was manipulating him to the end. Even after the end. The right thing was to bury Will at sea in his wonderful tuxedo and sail home an honest man. But Will had backed him into a box, a double trap of greed and need. I want it all and I want to take care of Shannon, if she'll let me. All I have to do is butcher my former shipmate.

30

LIKE THE OPERATION, this postmortem decapitation would be less messy on deck. What if someone sees? Who would, in the middle of nowhere? A spy satellite looking down? Forget it. What was the big deal? Will was already dead.

He was on his own and no one would ever know—except for Angela, when he handed her Will's head.

He wrapped Will in the sheet and carried him up to the cockpit. "You wanted this," he said out loud. "And you're not alive. So what the hell?"

He got a towel and the serrated knife. The boat was heeling, leaning hard over as it beat into the wind, bound for Buenos Aires. He wrapped the towel around Will's head. Maybe there wouldn't be much blood, but who knew? He was feeling sick to his stomach.

He eased the mainsheet and both jib sheets. The sloop stopped straining and stood a little taller. He picked up Will's body and laid it across the afterdeck where he had "operated" on Will's wound. Operation successful, patient dead. He picked up the knife, glanced automatically at the sails, looked around the empty ocean, and glanced at the compass, which showed them heading due north.

"North?"

He leaned closer. The card spun until it pointed due east. He stepped back and it spun west. He was holding the knife. The steel was affecting the compass, throwing it off, confusing it, making it false. He looked at the gleaming, finely scalloped edge. A beautiful tool, Will had called it. A thousand years of Japanese war technology tamed for the kitchen.

Jim threw the knife high in the air and watched it spinning, gleaming, blinking in the sun. I am not false, he thought. I know what's right and I know what's wrong. Maybe someone else could do this. But not me.

The knife sliced without a splash into the sea. The compass swung southwest and stayed there, as steady as a rock.

It seemed foolish to waste an anchor.

But Jim couldn't just drop Will's body over the side and let it drift. Birds and sharks would worry it to pieces. So he went below, pulled one of the spinning bikes out of the locker Will had had constructed in the former front cabin, and muscled it up the companionway. Then he tied Will's arms and legs to it. Muttering a rest-in-peace prayer that didn't mean much to him but couldn't hurt, Jim squatted down on the deck, gathered Will and the heavy bike in his arms, and lifted them over the stern rail. He had the strangest feeling that Will's fantasies were dying with him.

He opened his arms.

With a concussive splash, Will and the spinning bike cannonballed a hole in the water. The hull wave rolled over it. Jim leaned out, pressing his legs against the stern rail, trying to distinguish the spot. But it was fast falling in the wake, and already the sea was the same.

Feeling numb and very empty, Jim went down to the nav station and wrote in the log, "Will Spark, buried at sea." He noted the time, the date, and *Hustle*'s position on the GPS and signed his name.

Had Sentinel just gone overboard? Was it really *in* Will's head—or only in his imagination? Or was it still bits and pieces of hardware and software in the hands of widely scattered "cavemen"? Will's stories were starting to run together in Jim's head, fading, dissolving. Sentinel, McVays, Nickels— a blur, a sea of words.

It struck him that he knew he was going to have to get used to life without Will's dreams. Maybe there *was* a way to keep the boat. . . . Or should he simply go back to being what he had been before they met?

The one thing Jim knew for sure was that the only way to get through the rest of this day was to concentrate on form. He surprised himself with his first bold move, writing in big block letters: COURSE CHANGE—HOME.

If Will's enemies wanted what was in his head they could keep on chasing him. Jim was going home. If the McVays asked him, he would tell them that Will hadn't really died but had faked his own death, and that the last time he saw Will Spark the old man had gone ashore in Uruguay. At home, if they hassled him, he could dial 911.

The wind was still blowing from the west, the anemometer reading a steady fifteen knots. Donning his safety harness, Jim furled the small headsail and hanked on the big genoa jib.

"Start the engine first to hold the boat into the wind when you're changing sail alone," Will had cautioned.

"But I've seen you do it without the engine." To which Will would reply with elaborate patience, "When you've been sailing fifty years you can do it, too."

Jim cranked the diesel, powered into the wind, and raised the genny. Then he let her fall off until the wind was pushing from her port side. She flew northeast on a broad reach.

Ocean Passages of the World said that the best way home from latitude thirty-two degrees south, longitude forty-one degrees west was to head north to latitude 4°45' south, longitude 34° 35' west—a waypoint off Cabo Calcanar on the bulge of South America—then steer 3,460 miles northwest to New York.

But *Jimmy Cornell's World Cruising Routes* recommended that northbound sailboats bear farther east until they picked up the trade winds, then cross the equator at longitude thirty west and on to New York, via Bermuda or the Caribbean.

Jim didn't even know if he had enough food and water left to sail straight home. Maybe he should stop at some American island in the Caribbean. Or why not just pull into Rio de Janeiro? He had an open airplane ticket.

No, he wanted to keep the boat. And if in the long term he couldn't keep it, he was at least determined to sail it home. Besides, Rio, Bermuda, and the Caribbean all presented the same obstacle: how to prove to foreign immigration or port customs that he owned the boat.

Where is this "Will Spark" listed on her documents, señor? a customs agent was sure to ask. He's dead. He gave me his boat. Here's his will. . . . How interesting. . . . Buried at sea, you say?

Then Jim started to get really paranoid. What if I arrive home alone—sail all the way to Connecticut and pull into the Larchmont Yacht Club—how do I prove I didn't throw him overboard to keep the boat? An autopsy would confirm how he died. But no body, no autopsy.

He had entered Will's death in the log, a legal document, and recorded that Will had died from an infection resulting from a knife wound suffered in Nigeria. Prove that! Then he had a brainstorm. He rushed below, printed the e-mails Will and Angela had exchanged, and slipped them into the log. They confirmed Will's infection.

With that score settled, Jim went up on deck.

He had no appetite, nor was he tired. He had only a desire to make the boat go faster, so he worked her through the rest of the afternoon and into the evening, tweaking the sails and learning new tricks with the helm. For the first time since he'd fled Africa on the gritty Harmattan wind, he saw the sun go down in spectacular color. Will had told him that would happen when they drew near enough to a continent for land dust to redden the gray-yellow midocean sunsets.

He knew that he should go below to inventory his supplies to see whether he could sail straight through. But he hated to leave the cockpit. So he kept driving her, through the evening and into the night. Just at the point where he was blind-tired and thought he absolutely had to go below, he snapped on his harness and made one more round of the decks.

Moonlight suddenly broke through a heap of swift-moving cumulus clouds, which were splashed dark and light as they galloped across the moon, smothering it, uncovering it, and enveloping it again. Will used to call it a *"Treasure Island* sky." And then, when he least expected it, Jim's eyes grew warm and he began to cry.

BOOK IV

Villa Miseria

31

JIM SLEPT IN the cockpit, waking hourly to shorten sail. At dawn it was blowing thirty knots. The seas were streaked with foam and salt crusted his hair. He was flying a scrap of jib and had taken two reefs in the main and *Hustle*'s knot meter was still jumping between eight and nine. Screaming, Will would call it. A vote of confidence from the weather: go home.

He cooked some breakfast and wrote to Shannon again.

Dear Shannon,

I've been thinking about Will. With all his delusions and illusions, this was probably the right way to go—dying at sea. Out here, he was no con man. When sailing the boat, he was a champion—always sure of himself, always focused, always in "the zone."

I'll write more later. I know we have lots to talk about. I hope to be back in seven or eight weeks. I wanted an adventure and I got one. I love you,

Jim

He sent it by the SSB radio and found two e-mails waiting. One was titled "MAILER-DAEMON: Returned mail, Host unknown." The other was from Shannon: "SEE YOU SOON!"

The MAILER-DAEMON read, "Name server: FACE-PLANTRILEYSPA.COM: host not found." Of all the damned times for a computer screwup. It was the letter he had written right after Will died. He opened "SEE YOU SOON!" wondering what she meant. A quick glance stopped him cold.

> Dear Jim,
> People have been asking questions about you—on the phone—and they're insinuating that you're involved in some kind of criminal activity. I'm sure that your friend Will is behind it—he must have tangled your name into one of his scams. Whatever, Daddy is really pissed—really pissed—and he's saying what kind of a guy is this to be joining the business. (If I were talking to him at the moment, which obviously I'm not, I would remind him that just because we've been e-mailing often doesn't mean that we're getting married or that you would even want to work for him if we did.) I would like to kill him. He's actually *ordered* me to stop writing you until you come home and explain yourself. F him and the horse. . . . Which is why we're not talking. And Mom says that he says he'll fire me if I disobey him. (Do you detect Mom's hand in this? I do.) Fire *me?* We'd be out of business in a week.

Jim doubted that. Shannon's mother didn't want to work for RileySpa anymore, but if she had to step back in she was a brilliant manager and RileySpa would forge on without a hiccup. At which point Shannon would have to look for work in the real world. With a real-world salary, real-world benefits, and real-world inconvenience.

> But when I heard that, I was like, It's every woman for herself. So I wrote myself a ten-thousand-dollar check on the company credit card and bought a ticket to Buenos Aires.

"No!"

> I'll be waiting for you at the Plaza Hotel on the Plaza San Martín, which sounds really cool—and unbelievably expensive, so I withdrew another five thousand on Daddy's card. They said

anyone can tell you how to get there——it's right in the middle of the city. (It's a Marriott, so I'm sure they speak some English.) I reserved my plane ticket with my own card so Daddy can't find me. Ditto the hotel. If only I had time to sell his house out from under him!!! And his big fat SUV. I'm leaving tomorrow morning. You must be pretty close to Buenos Aires by now, so with any luck I will see you in just a few days. So until then, olé——or whatever they say in Argentina. And by the way, don't tell Will. God knows what he's gotten you into, or the kind of people he'll know in Buenos Aires. So just "jump ship" and meet me at the Plaza Hotel.

PS: I closed both my e-mail accounts in case my mother pulls a full-court-press snoop in the computer.

I hope you're not mad I'm coming. At first, I thought we would wait until you got home to sort things out, but the situation is different now, thanks to Will. I feel I got you into this mess and I want to help get you out.

Jim pushed from his mind an image of Shannon struggling down a mile-long airport corridor. They'd have wheelchairs. And she was very resourceful. And people liked her, so they would help her. Still, he had trouble breathing. *Who the hell was asking questions?*

Was it someone investigating one of Will's scams? Or the McVays? Nickels? Shannon might be right, but if she wasn't . . . And if they were asking questions at the club, then they already knew about Shannon and him. What would happen when she left Westport? Would they follow her?

The broad reach on which Jim had been sailing home——booming along on a strong breeze from behind——become a close-hauled battle when he turned the boat around. *Hustle* seemed to go faster, with the wind whipping over the deck and salt spray in his face, but she wasn't. Worse, he had to tack, approaching Río de la Plata obliquely, angling to the south, then to the north, and back again and again and again——angle, angle, angle, with his bow never pointed directly at Buenos Aires.

32

A GUY IN a baseball jacket and backward cap was following her. She had first noticed his beat-up Toyota when she left her mother and father's the night before. The Toyota stood out like a sore thumb in their neighborhood. It might have been driven by somebody's maid, but not by a guy in a baseball jacket and backward cap.

This morning, he and the old car fit right in across the street from her low-rent condo, and she wouldn't have paid him much mind if she hadn't seen him the night before—and if she wasn't a little jumpy about getting to the airport without her parents' finding out until she was safely off the plane in Buenos Aires.

So now she was letting this guy think she didn't know he was following her. A private detective, she guessed, working for one of Will Spark's victims. Maybe an undercover cop looking for Will. Whatever, there was no way she would let him follow her to Kennedy Airport. She decided to make him bored. Then make him nervous. Then make him crazy.

She headed toward the club. The regular route would lull him, make him feel as if he knew where she was going. It was early, but traffic was getting heavy on I-95. It would be hard to see her low-slung 740 among the big trucks and the boxy

SUVs. She sped up and swung into the passing lane. That would make him nervous. The Toyota followed, pulling up close to keep her in sight. Shannon shifted to the middle lane, passed a Lincoln Navigator in the passing lane, and tucked in front of the bulky SUV, leaving no room for the Toyota. The guy actually pulled alongside of her, pretending not to glance over. When he did, she gave him a little wave. That would make him very nervous. She smiled. Let him think she was just waving because she thought he was cute. Ahead was a median crossover. The guy locked his eyes on it.

That made her a little uncomfortable.

He'd been following her for weeks, she realized. You saw me pull that one-eighty with Daddy in the car. He was bracing to shove between her and the Navigator. Okaaaay. She passed the crossover and the guy practically smiled with relief.

She squeezed the brake lever with her left hand. The Navigator's tires screamed and it would have hit her if she hadn't swung onto the shoulder and across forty feet of grass.

She hit the southbound passing lane right in front of a Lexus and swiveled her twist-grip accelerator as hard as she could. Horns shrilled. People screamed at their windshields. Like anybody could hear them at seventy miles an hour.

Buenos Aires, here I come. Except first, when she got to the airport, she had to find a parking space close enough to drag herself and her bags to the shuttle bus. It would get better once she checked in. They'd have wheelchairs.

" 'She's not going anywhere,' " Val McVay mimicked Andy Nickels.

"She pulled a cute one."

" 'She's a cripple.' "

"We'll find her."

"She's *handicapped*. Our best link to Will Spark *cannot walk* and you let her disappear."

"She's a great driver."

"I can't believe you've done this."

"Nor can I," said Lloyd McVay.

"This is a temporary setback," Andy replied coolly.

"Damage control is in gear. I've got people fanning out over Buenos Aires—Will Spark's destination—"

"Assumed," Val McVay reminded him. "Assumed destination."

"A city of twelve million people, for the love of God," said her father.

"They are on course for the River Plate."

"Assumed," Val repeated. "The fact is, Dr. Angela Heinman Ruiz was last seen in Rio de Janeiro."

"We're watching her apartment in Buenos Aires."

"We do not *know* that Will Spark is headed there."

"He and the doctor exchanged long e-mails."

Val went on as if Andy had not spoken. "As we have not been able to decipher *what* Will Spark has written to Dr. Ruiz. For all we know, he's arranging to alter his features with plastic surgery so he'll be even harder to find. She *is* a plastic surgeon."

"She's also a microsurgeon. Which is exactly the kind of doctor that Spark would go to to get those goddamned things out of his head."

"Look at the data, for goodness' sake. She published her last paper on microsurgery ten years ago. As for Shannon, we know only that Shannon canceled her 'public' RileySpa e-mail account, but we don't know whether she and Jim Leighton are communicating under other screen names. Do we?"

Nickels turned to Lloyd McVay and played his trump card. "I put the ex-resident on the payroll."

Lloyd McVay banged a big hand on his bony knee. "Well done, Andy! A-plus!"

"The 'ex-resident'?" demanded Val. She felt the ground suddenly slipping out from under her. "What does that mean?"

Nickels explained that the former Central Intelligence Agency station chief in Buenos Aires—for many years the United States' chief spy in Latin America—had been hired to enlist the city's famously corruptible *policía federal* to watch the airports and tourist hotels for an American girl in a wheelchair.

"But by now—if she even went there—she has already passed through the airport."

"She has to sleep somewhere. Plus, we've put the word out on the streets."

"What word?"

"We've put a bounty on them."

"Alive!" warned Lloyd.

"Of course, sir."

Val McVay was not impressed. "If they're there, they're not on the streets. They're on a boat. BA is a sailing town. There are a hundred marinas on the Río de la Plata, fifty yacht clubs, and thousands of private moorings."

"The second they make contact with the girl, we've got them."

Val typed in a macro that locked her computer tighter than Will Spark's onetime code and stood up. "I'm going down there."

"That is not necessary," said Andy.

"Oh, really?"

Andy turned to her father. "Mr. McVay. This is not a scene for the generals. This is down and dirty. BA is one tough town. I'm dealing with scum. The bosses should stay home."

Lloyd McVay shook his head no emphatically. "You're forgetting your Shakespeare, Andy. We'll be pulling many strings in Buenos Aires, calling in a lot of favors.

> *"The presence of a king engenders love*
> *Among his subjects and his loyal friends."*

"But sir, either she'll screw things up for me—"

"Something you've managed quite well on your own," said Val.

"—or she'll get hurt."

Lloyd McVay's face hardened. "The bard also wrote,

> *"I see no reason why a king of years*
> *Should be protected like a child."*

"Go! Both of you. Retrieve Sentinel from that thieving son of a bitch!"

33

THE RÍO DE La Plata sluiced the muddy runoff of half a continent into the South Atlantic Ocean, and when Jim saw the blue water under *Hustle*'s speeding hull turn gray-green, he was still 120 miles from Buenos Aires. It was the closest he had been to Shannon in three months and he practically wanted to climb the mast for an early look at her.

Concerned that the McVays were the ones who'd been asking questions, and terrified that they might have followed her, he wished she were safely home in Connecticut. But he was deeply touched that she would come all this way to help him out of "this mess." Touched, and hopeful. Had she changed her mind? Was she reconsidering marrying him? Or was it just her sense of duty? And what, he wondered, would she make of him? Would she notice a "new Jim," changed by all that had happened and all he had learned to do? The big answers to these big questions lay only 120 miles away. Though at sea he would be just one day away from seeing her, entering "the Plate" posed any number of difficulties that could drag it out to three.

The *Sailing Directions* warned bluntly of sudden lethal changes in the weather, particularly the ferocious squalls that thundered off Argentina's pampa, an immense, flat plain that spread hundreds of miles inland. He watched for the distant roll of dark cumulonimbus clouds that might herald a *pampero*—though the books warned that the killer squalls could strike without warning from clear skies, too. Conditions were ripe for one, with a warm humid wind blowing from the north and the barometer indicating a gradual drop in pressure.

While the estuary was as broad as an inland sea, more than 60 miles wide and 120 long, much of it was shallow. With traffic funneled into the dredged channels, Jim soon found himself in busy waters, with many ships around him.

Will had warned him about the difficult transition from the relative simplicity of blue-water navigation to inshore piloting. He had likened offshore navigation to the first shot in pool—bang the rack with the cue ball, hope for the best, and repair the damage later. Piloting inshore was like calling pockets for each and every ball. You had to know where you were at every moment, which demanded skills Jim didn't possess. He had never come close to mastering Will's sextant and hadn't done much better with the math required to use the almanac.

Thank God for Will's "push here, stupid" electronics. The GPS, the knot meter, the depth finder, and the radar showed him where he was on the chart, how fast *Hustle* was moving, whether there was enough water under her keel, and warned when he was about to run into something. He was good to go, as long as none of those instruments stopped working.

"They forgot to lock the gates of heaven."

"Are you talking to me?"

"An angel escaped."

"I said," Shannon repeated, "Are you talking to me?"

This was what the guidebooks called *piropo,* the Argentine male's poetic pickup line. He had come over from a nearby table, where he had been drinking maté—the local tea they drank from a gourd—with another young guy and an older, silver-haired man in a blue blazer.

The guidebooks had not prepared her for how handsome *porteños* were; even though the poetry got pretty corny, it would have been hard not to smile back. Of course if a woman happened to have her own agenda—and happened to be sitting alone in a tight blouse in the lobby of her hotel—it was like taking candy from a baby.

She let him do all the work. "You're American?" he exclaimed. "I would never have guessed."

"I'm speaking English with an American accent."

"I have traveled throughout America and have never saw a woman so beautiful in your entire country."

"Thank you. But I'm waiting for my boyfriend."

"Not yet engaged?"

"Not yet."

"Then I still have a chance."

Shannon laughed. "Not a chance in the world."

"My name is Carlos. May I show you Buenos Aires?"

"No thanks." She indicated her forearm crutches leaning against her chair in the lobby of the Plaza Hotel. A turnoff if ever there was one: with its cracked and broken sidewalks and free-for-all high-speed traffic, Buenos Aires was no city for wheelchairs. "I really can't get around too easily."

The *porteño* didn't blink and his smile actually got bigger. "No matter. My cousin Ramón has a car. A convertible." Carlos gestured long and low. "We will drive you everywhere. And between us help you walk."

He was so cute. He had a big strong nose and the most unbelievably thick curly black hair. Dark eyes. And that to-die-for smile. Shannon flashed him one back. "Could we drive to the harbor?"

"Beautiful angel, we would drive you to Tierra del Fuego, if you asked."

He shot a thumbs-up across the lobby. Cousin Ramón shook hands good-bye with the silver-haired man and hurried over. He was even cuter, and he greeted Shannon with what seemed to be the standard welcome: "*Buenos días.* So how do you like Buenos Aires?"

"*Una masa,*" said Shannon, which she had learned meant "awesome."

"This glorious angel says that she's waiting for a man who is not yet engaged to marry her. The fool."

Ramón gripped his heart. "It would be a crime—" He searched for a word and lapsed into Spanish. Carlos translated. "Ramón says it would be a crime against the entire United Nations for such a beautiful woman to marry anyone but an Argentine."

Jim got worried when he started seeing islands where the chart showed no islands. He studied them nervously through the binoculars, fearing that he would run aground in shoal water.

After being up all night, watching out for ships and spotting channel markers on the radar, he was losing focus. Had he strayed into the shallows? Should he veer northeast? Or should he turn around and retrace his course? The GPS put him right in the channel, without an island on the chart. Trust it? Keep going? Will always said, "Don't do anything until you know what's going on. Know the score."

Jim climbed the mast to the first spreader and in the rising light of morning saw that the "islands" were clumps of trees dotting a land as flat as the ocean. The trees shaded ranch houses and vast, prosperous-looking barns.

He was getting flaky. He drove out of the channel and, watching the depth finder carefully, ran a mile toward the distant shore, then dropped anchor, lay down on the cockpit bench, and fell asleep. Twenty minutes, he told himself.

He awakened, clearheaded, in twenty minutes. It occurred to him that Will's enemies were expecting him to arrive in Buenos Aires by boat. Why not dump the boat now and catch a bus or a train or even hitchhike. He'd get there faster and slip in the back door while they were watching the waterfront.

Jim found out where he was on the chart and reviewed the *Sailing Directions.* The bay of San Clemente looked like a good possibility. He prepared the anchor and sailed southeast, away from Buenos Aires, on a course that paralleled the shoreline. When it curved to form the bay, he looked for other sailboats to moor among. A marina with floating docks and a clubhouse with a yellow veranda was home to a cluster of boats, but he wanted a more private landing where he wouldn't have to get into passports and customs. Here and there single boats were moored at the foot of large estates where lawns flowed from mansions down to the water's edge.

With his eyes glued to the depth finder, he steered for the biggest estate, which had a huge two-masted schooner tied to its dock. A boat that size had to draw much more water than *Hustle*. And such an estate looked ready-made for Will's rowing-ashore scam.

He dropped anchor a hundred yards off, furled the sails, inflated the dinghy and tied it alongside. Then he quickly scrubbed his face, shaved, and combed his tangled hair. His face looked gaunt in the mirror. His torso was still pretty ripped, but he'd lost a ton of bulk in his arms and chest.

He put on the clean polo shirt and jeans he had originally packed for the flight home from Rio. Then he filled his backpack, shut the hatches, and rowed to the dock. *Hustle* seemed to stand high on the gentle swell, perched like a bird, her fuel and water tanks nearly empty, her stores consumed. With a strange feeling that he would never see his "inheritance" again, he turned the dinghy around to back into the dock.

So far, this beat landing in Nigeria. There were no teens with machetes, although the sad-faced middle-aged man hurrying down the lawn did have a gun on his hip.

"Buenos días," he called. His crisp blue shirt and starched khakis reminded Jim of retired-military clients he had, an impression heightened by stiff posture and a direct gaze.

"Good morning, sir. I don't speak Spanish."

"Yankee! Good morning."

"My name is Jim Leighton."

"Captain Rodolpho Faveros, navy of Argentina, retired. *Buenos días.*"

Of all the dumb luck: a naval officer who'll probably call

immigration. "Would it be all right if I anchored off your home?"

"Where are you from, Mr. Leighton?"

"I've just come in from Nigeria. I have to meet my girlfriend in Buenos Aires."

"And before Nigeria?"

"I live in Connecticut."

Captain Faveros brightened. "I know it well. I visited the naval school in Groton."

"I live in Bridgeport. You would have driven through on your way from New York."

"Well, actually, I landed in a submarine. Heave a line. I'll tie you up."

The Argentine caught the dinghy's painter, double-flipped an expert clove hitch around a piling, and extended a hand to Jim. "Steady!"

The dock felt like it was rolling. Faveros grabbed his arm.

"This always happens to me," said Jim. "I have the worst inner ear. And when I get back on the boat I'm seasick again."

"The walk to the house will restore your land legs. Though I can't promise you won't be seasick when you get back on your boat."

"Would it be all right if I left the boat while I go to Buenos Aires?"

"It will be safe here. We have our 'pirates,' but they won't fool with the navy." Steadying Jim, Faveros steered him up the lawn. Jim found the colors of grass and flower gardens to be almost painfully intense after so many weeks of sea blues and grays.

Faveros's mansion had a tower on one end, topped with a radar dish and weather instruments.

"A gift from my wife when I retired," Faveros explained with a self-deprecating smile. "My 'bridge' as it were: radios, radar, weather fax, and even a small helm. Rather good fun. I'll show it to you . . . have you had lunch? Perhaps my wife . . ." Faveros's voice trailed off and the sad expression darkened his face again. They were nearing the house. Jim saw a woman watching through the windows. She drifted away like a ghost.

"I ate, thanks," said Jim. "I've got to get to Buenos Aires as soon as possible. Is there a bus? Or a train?"

"Ah." Faveros, apparently relieved that Jim could not stay for lunch but still required hospitality, said, "I'll drive you to the train."

"I hope it's not too far."

"It is nothing."

It turned out to be forty miles, but Faveros wouldn't hear of Jim's hiring a taxi. In the car, a new Audi station wagon, he started talking, and the words were soon gushing as if he had been rehearsing them for days in his head. "If only things were better at home, you would have lunch and dinner and a bed. But my wife—we've had a tragedy. Our son has left. He's searching to find his so-called real parents—he's adopted. But I am his father 'really.' As is my wife his 'real' mother. His biological mother is almost certainly dead. This is not uncommon."

Jim, who was dazzled by the speed of the car and the bright colors of the land, nodded politely, trying to follow Faveros.

"What is 'not uncommon'?"

"During the Proceso—you know, of course, about Argentina's *Guerra Sucia? Desaparecidos?* The so-called dirty war? The disappeared?"

"I'm afraid I don't know much about it." Whatever you do, Will had cautioned, avoid discussing the last twenty years, particularly the "dirty war" and the "disappeared."

"The juntas, military governments, tried to reorganize the nation. Argentina had many, many terrible problems: inflation, labor unrest, protesters, subversives, and terrorists. In the course of restoring order, many left-wing radicals were killed. They were called the Disappeared, because they were taken away in secret. . . . Prisoners were thrown from airplanes. Into the sea—*Desaparecidos.* . . . It happened. We can't change that. No one was blameless."

Not even the victims? Jim wondered. He knew he was staring but couldn't stop himself.

"The church herself has asked for forgiveness," Faveros said staunchly. He looked at Jim. What reply did he demand to his cold-blooded account of bloody history? Jim sat still and silent. To speak or to move would appear to condone.

Faveros gesticulated with his left hand while he shifted gears with his right and steadied the wheel with his knees. "It was a desperate time," he explained. "And desperate times breed desperate measures. . . . Sometimes the *desaparecidos* left children behind. Orphans. Those children were adopted. Orphans who had nowhere to go were taken in by childless couples. . . . Our child was adopted. My son. Twenty-five years ago. Now he wants his 'real' mother. We gave him everything. My wife's family is wealthy. He was raised like a prince. His mother is surely dead. In the sea."

Jim looked at him and was thunderstruck at the transformation. A second ago Faveros had been a monster. Now he was a sad little man, a heartbroken parent.

Faveros looked across the steering wheel at Jim. "Is nothing simple, young man? Or is it simply that every act has a consequence?" He gave a desolate shrug.

"So now we spend our days waiting for him to come to his senses. My wife is his mother. She's gone back into therapy. And so have I." He tried to smile. "Psychoanalysis, the Argentine vice. Sigmund Freud is the patron saint of Buenos Aires. . . . We would give our son anything. But all he wants is his so-called real mother. And she is surely dead."

Tears trickled from his eyes and ran down his cheeks. Then, to Jim's horror, his entire face seemed to crumple. He wept violently, heaving tears, gulping for air. The car skidded. Crying uncontrollably, Faveros slammed on the brakes and stopped in the middle of the road.

"I'm sorry," Jim said, trying to comfort him. "I know—I know what you're going through."

"You can't possibly know. No one who hasn't been here could."

"I've been here," said Jim, surprising himself and wishing instantly that he could take the words back.

"What? What do you mean?" Faveros demanded. "What do you mean, '*here*'? You were not *here*."

"On the other side," said Jim. "On your child's side."

"What are you saying? Oh! You mean you were adopted."

It would be so easy to answer yes. Faveros was calming down and would soon resume driving Jim to the train. Let him think Jim was adopted, if it made him feel better. But the intensity of being on land, the relief of having brought the boat in safely, and the sorrow of Will's death were suddenly overwhelming. Jim felt his eyes burn with emotion.

"No, I wasn't adopted." He couldn't say it.

"You were either adopted or not, young man. Which was it?"

Will made me his heir, Jim thought. He taught me stuff. Will was like a father. Suddenly he was on the verge of blurting out a secret he had never told anyone in the world, except Shannon.

"My mother 'confessed' to me once." He fell silent, swallowed hard. Will, he thought. Will *acted* like a father. Like a real father.

Faveros was watching him closely.

"She was very disappointed. My mother. Her life hadn't worked out as she had hoped. She was always searching . . . anything to make things better. Health food. Meditation. Vitamins. Gurus. . . . Do you know what est was? Did you have it here?"

"It was here. There were some who found it an effective shortcut examination of their soul and/or psyche."

"My mother had done it—before I was born. She told me that my real father—my biological father—was a trainer she'd met on an est retreat. A he-man rugged outdoors type. The exact opposite of my father . . . the man I thought was my father."

"How old were you—when she told you?"

"Fourteen."

"*Qué macana!* That is terrible. She obliterated your adolescence."

"I don't know if it was quite that bad."

"Do you have phobias?"

Jim shook his head. Part of him was thinking, Why am I telling Faveros this? He's not even listening. Another part, the part on the verge of tears, couldn't stop talking. "The thing was, I didn't know what to do with it."

"If you hadn't sailed in single-handed from Africa, I would have predicted that you would detest anything that evoked your mother's outdoorsman lover. Ah! Perhaps you are trying to emulate him. Transference."

"I had this secret. I knew what my mother had done to my father—the man I always thought was my father—but I couldn't tell him. So I didn't do anything about it."

Captain Faveros sat up straight and looked Jim directly in the eye. "That was not your job, young man."

"What do you mean?"

"It was not for you to tell, to betray your mother's confidence—misdirected and irresponsible as it was."

"She did worse than betray him. She tricked him into raising a kid who wasn't his."

"Your father had eyes. He should have seen what was going on." Faveros's nostrils flared with indignation. "What sort of man would let his wife go off alone on a 'retreat.' He should have done something about it—he should have confronted her! Ha! Listen to me talking." He laughed bitterly. "The 'father' expert. I couldn't even give my wife a child."

"I'm not talking about simple cheating on her husband, I'm talking about my *father*, for Christ's sake."

"Which one?"

"What?"

"The father who raised you? Or the father who doesn't know you exist?"

Jim stared, silenced. Neither one, he thought. The feeling of tears passed, and he felt as light as air. I got lucky, he thought. Will Spark made me his heir. For a moment, I had myself a *real* father.

Faveros smiled back at him, then took out a handkerchief and mopped his cheeks. "I warned you earlier about Argentina, young man. You have made an excellent landfall if you wish to be analyzed."

He helped Jim buy a ticket at the train station and took him into a smoky café, where he bought Jim maté, a hot, bitter drink in a gourd. They shared it from a straw with a silver mouthpiece. When the train came, Faveros clapped Jim on the back as if he were an old friend, gripped his hand hard, and promised that his boat would be safe.

"What would you like to see today, Shannon?"

"The harbor."

"We saw the harbor yesterday," said Ramón.

She had learned there was no swimming in the River Plate. The water was too dirty. But there were soccer fields along the waterfront and yacht clubs to the north of the city. South of the city, the shore was heavily industrial, with factories and warehouses and docks and shipping canals. So she kept looking in the north.

The Argentine Yacht Club stood at the entrance to North Harbor. They parked their big old Lincoln convertible by the lighthouse. The car burned gas like crazy but they wouldn't let her buy any. They called it *nafta* and it cost a fortune. Finally, today, they had allowed her to pay for lunch—but only because it was Carlos's birthday.

"I think he'll come today."

The cousins shared a look.

"Perhaps," Carlos said gently, "he is delayed."

"Or had bad winds," said Ramón.

As Val McVay paced the floating docks on her third visit to the Argentine Yacht Club, scanning the basin yet again, her racing eye was drawn repeatedly to a giant black catamaran moored in a shallow, silted corner of the basin. Two knife-thin hulls straddled the water in a wide stance that promised it could carry an awesome spread of sail. The hundred-foot-long hulls and rigging were as black as night, except for the red letters that spelled out her name: *JoyStick*. It intrigued her for some reason she couldn't quite explain. Surely she wasn't getting a yen to sail again.

The wind, she noticed, was veering to the northeast. Yesterday it had been so clear that Buenos Aires's high-rises seemed carved out of the sky and she had seen the Uruguay coast all the way across the Plata. Today the air was thickening and she sensed an ominous change in the weather.

"Val!" An old friend smiled down at her from a several-million-dollar high-tech ketch.

"Watson!" She hugged the charter captain, a handsome, sea-worn Brazilian who could talk all night in nine languages. "What are you doing here?"

Watson indicated the ketch, the biggest yacht in the basin. "Leaving for the Med, soon as that bloody front passes. Do you have a boat?"

After having too many shipmates ask whether she or her father would like to finance a radical new boat, Val had taken to pretending she wasn't related to Lloyd McVay of McVay Microwaves, McVay Computers, McVay Internet, and the McVay Foundation: She was just one of the paid crew.

"Just looking around."

"See that Swan 76?"

"Beautiful."

"She's all provisioned for the Med, when her captain breaks his leg. The owners'll pay good. Nice people, gorgeous boat. Charters booked all summer in Greece. Brilliant cook. And the mate's from Anguilla. What more could you ask for?"

Val's restless gaze settled on the Swan. It was a very beautiful boat. And she was stunned by the sudden desire to simply sail away. Maybe it was seeing Watson with his sleepy smile. Forget about goals— forget about Sentinel. Just meld into the sea. Catch up on her reading. Eat good food. Let the mate do the work. And when the wind honked have a little fun putting a thoroughbred through her paces.

How many years had passed since she had last allowed herself to drift—years of never letting go, except occasionally in bed with a carefully vetted man? She heard her own voice speaking from a distance, as if she were standing up on the seawall and calling down to the handsome Watson.

"Have you seen a sloop called *Hustle*? Fifty-foot. Center cockpit. Tall rig."

Watson shook his head. "I got your e-mail. Never saw the boat. Do you have a thing for the owner?"

"Hong Kong–registered?" Why did her voice sound muffled. *Stop this!* "Brand-new teak decks?"

"No," he said. "Take the Swan—we could hook up in Rio."

"Watson!"

"What, dear?"

"Oh, God. . . ." This is unprogrammed nonsense, she thought.

She saw a flash of gold hair far away on the Dresena Norte seawall. A girl who looked like Shannon Riley, sitting up on the back of a convertible, laughing with two men.

"Do you have binoculars?"

Watson ran up his gangway, but before he returned with the glasses, the threesome had driven off. How many beautiful young blondes were there in Buenos Aires? At least a million. She was getting nowhere.

Watson was purring. "If you meet me in Rio, I bet we hook up again in Antigua."

"Watson! For goodness' sake, I'm not eighteen anymore." She kissed his weathered cheek. A beautiful man. If a woman had time for a penniless thousand-dollar-a-week captain. She took one last look around.

"What's that *JoyStick*?"

Watson explained that the catamaran—formerly named *Dot.Com*—had been gearing up for an around-the-world race when her owner went bankrupt. "I thought they changed her name to *Dot.Gone*. But they went with *JoyStick*."

"Is she as fast as she looks?"

"Cruise missile, downwind."

"But how does she point?"

"You would know better than I," said Watson. Val had skippered a cat for a maniacal owner bent on breaking speed records.

"Like a catamaran," she answered, which was not a compliment. "Why all black?"

"The owner believed that black sails pull more wind."

"Where did he get that idea?"

"He was a businessman." Watson shrugged. "But I hear she's a serious machine—they say faster even than old *PlayStation.* Were you thinking of 'persuading' someone to buy her for you?"

"No, Watson, I'm thinking of buying her for myself."

The Brazilian laughed. "And I'll buy mine. We'll be yacht owners! And hire each other. I'll crew yours. You'll crew mine. You bring me breakfast in bed. I bring you bed for breakfast."

A taxi stopped on the seawall. Andy Nickels got out, scoping the marina like a hungry wolverine. "Gotta go," said Val. "Happy voyage, Watson." She kissed his cheeks and the Brazilian surprised her by holding her very tightly.

"Take the Swan."

"I'm booked."

Watson knew something was off. "It's a better berth."

To Jim's ears attuned to wind and water, Buenos Aires was a thunderstorm of noise. And even though the cars were old, and the buildings were in disrepair, and the trees were browning in the dry southern autumn, to his eyes the colors seemed as bright as fire. He climbed out of a black-and-yellow taxi a few blocks down a wide boulevard from Shannon's hotel so he could check it out and avoid blundering into Will's enemies.

He was pretending to browse at a newsstand—while he surreptitiously studied the entrance to the Plaza Hotel—when he suddenly realized that every newspaper had a picture of the same middle-aged woman on the front page. He didn't have to read Spanish to understand the name in the picture caption: Dr. Angela Heinman Ruiz. Headlines screaming *"Muerte"*—death. *Desaparecidos:* the grim word he had learned from Captain Faveros.

He bought an English-language paper called the *Herald,* sank to one of the park benches, and read in disbelief that Dr. Angela Heinman Ruiz had fallen from her high-rise terrace while attempting to escape kidnappers. The *Herald* speculated that the prominent plastic surgeon—whose husband had been one of the "disappeared" murdered twenty years ago by the junta—had mistaken a simple ransom kidnapping for a political one and had panicked and jumped from her balcony.

"Dear one," Angela had called Will, and it had sounded so intimate. Jim couldn't buy that her death was a coincidence. It had to be the McVays, trying to get to Will.

He walked as fast as he could to the Plaza Hotel.

Shannon's laugh filled the lobby as he entered. He whirled toward the unmistakable sound with an overwhelming sense of relief that he wasn't too late.

He saw the flash of her hair. She was at the bar, surrounded by guys, waving her empty Coke glass for a refill. Jim's heart jumped. Propped up on a bar stool, she had looked for an instant like she was standing on her own two feet.

Shannon sensed his rush. She stared blankly, then broke into a big smile. "Omigod! Jim."

She threw her arms around him.

Jim lifted her off the stool, felt the familiar strong grip of her arms, and drank the perfect fit of her lips.

She pulled back. "Let me look at you. Oh, Jim. You look so thin. You're so dark. You're so handsome. You're beautiful."

The men burst into applause and started pounding Jim on the back and kissing Shannon's cheeks. *"Churro,"* one told Shannon.

"What's *churro*?" she asked.

"How you say? Good-looking."

"I told you."

"What do you think of Buenos Aires?" several asked Jim.

He leaned in close to whisper in Shannon's ear, "We've got to get out of here. It's not safe."

"No one knows we're here."

"Yes, they do. Please, we've got to split—now."

"Did Will—"

"Will is dead."

That stopped her. "Oh, Jim, you poor thing."

"So is a friend of his that he was supposed to meet here—oh, shit."

"What?"

"Over there, by the front door. Those suits are watching us."

Shannon said, "They're hotel security."

"How do you know?"

"They're in the lobby all the time. It's okay."

Is this what it had been like for Will when I wouldn't believe him? Jim wondered.

Shannon saw how troubled he was. "Let's go to our room. Bye, guys. We're going to go—"

"You must dine with us."

"Later, Carlos. Talk to you later."

Jim looked across the lobby again. The two suits in the doorway had vanished. He had to get Shannon upstairs and call for a cab to the airport. He scooped her into his arms. She grabbed her forearm crutches. "Tenth floor."

"I'm sorry about Will," she said in the elevator. "I know you liked him."

"A lot. Sometimes."

"You've changed. You're different."

"Who are those guys?"

"Carlos and Ramón? Sweet boys. They drove me to the harbor every day to look for you."

"How'd you hook up?"

"Here. In the lobby—are you jealous?"

"I would be, if I wasn't scared. Didn't it strike you as a little convenient that they just drove you around?"

"Why would a handsome Argentine pick up a cripple?"

"No. Why would two of them stick to you like glue until I got here?"

"You really think I'm stupid."

"Shannon, for Christ's sake—"

"Listen to me. When I checked into the hotel I went to the workout room. I made friends with a trainer—a girl. She helped me go shopping for clothes—I came with nothing, because they were following me."

"Who?"

"I got away from them. Before I went to the airport."

"Who?"

"I thought it was the police or detectives—something to do with Will Spark. I didn't know he had died. Anyhow, when I got here, I went shopping with that girl and we had maté—it's this local tea . . ."

"I had some."

"And I asked her about these boys I saw every afternoon in the lobby. She told me they were cousins who often stopped for coffee with their father and uncle. Okay?"

"All right. I guess they were safe."

"I knew what I'd got you into and I wanted to be absolutely sure it was safe. I kept my eyes open. No one followed me. No one is watching me. Are you sure we have to leave?"

"Will got me into bigger trouble than we thought. We're getting on a plane home."

"Help me pack." She pulled a brand-new travel bag from under the bed and struggled to the closet. "Call the concierge for our plane tickets and we're outta here. Use my card."

The concierge put him on hold. "How have I changed?"

"You're more direct."

"Can you stand it?"

"I think so."

"I'm so happy to see you."

"Still?"

"Oh God, more than ever. Shannon, I—"

There was a knock at the door.

"Who is it?" Shannon called.

"Room service. *Amigos* send champagne."

"Those boys are so generous. They can't afford champagne."

Jim put down the phone. Through the peephole he saw a waiter with a bottle in an ice bucket. "It's champagne, all right. I wouldn't mind a glass in the taxi." He opened the door. Shannon said, "Wait! It's a hundred and fifty a bottle—no way they—"

The waiter was already coming through the door, launching a soccer kick at Jim's groin.

34

SHANNON'S WARNING ALMOST saved Jim's balls. He was already stepping backward. The kick brushed him with fiery pain, and as it peaked he was able to slip a hand under the guy's heel and keep lifting. As his foot traveled higher than his head, the waiter landed hard on his back in a shower of ice cubes and water.

The hotel security men Jim had seen in the lobby sprang in from either side of the door. The first stepped on the bottle, lost his footing, and fell on the waiter. The second vaulted over both and attacked Jim with a blizzard of kicks and punches.

The man was big in the shoulders and devilishly fast, with a long reach and long legs. He landed a shoe to Jim's stomach, and two punches to his head. Jim fell back. In the instant when he tried to put himself between the others and Shannon, he caught a second kick to his torso.

Jim fell back again, still moving to cover Shannon. He felt wonderfully clear. The kicks were bouncing off muscle. The months of learning how to survive at sea had tempered his workout strength, boosted his reaction time, and focused his eye. Quick and sure, he could read the man's face, see that he was closing in for the kill, and anticipate how to beat the more experienced fighter in a wholly unexpected way.

Jim lowered his forearms, which had deflected most of the punches, and when the guy stepped boldly closer, he wrapped him in his arms and squeezed with all his might. The man screamed. Jim felt something snap—ribs, he thought, maybe spine. The body went limp, the voice silent.

Shannon screamed, "Jim."

The other security man jumped off the floor like a jack-in-the-box. Jim threw the man he had bear-hugged and the two went down in a heap, just as the waiter rose on one knee, yanking a gun from his cummerbund. Jim dove at him, frantically trying to grab the waiter's hand before he got the gun out. The waiter's wrist was wet and he slipped free, jerking the gun in a wide arc around the ceiling, at Shannon, past her, into Jim's face.

Jim seized his wrist with both hands and bent it back, trying to break it to make him drop the gun. The waiter's arm was like cooked spaghetti. It wouldn't break. It just kept bending and bending and bending until suddenly the gun fired with a dull, quiet thud.

"Jim!"

"I'm . . ." He rose slowly, shakily, and stared at the waiter, who was sinking to the carpet. "I'm okay. It hit him. It didn't hit me. I'm okay. Are you?"

"Oh my God, Jim. Look at this." The waiter lay gasping for air. The man Jim had bear-hugged was sprawled like a bent paper clip.

"Where's the other one?"

"He ran. Look out—"

The bent paper clip was straightening, pulling something black from his jacket. Jim flattened him with the champagne bottle. The man's hand convulsed. A black wallet flipped open as it fell.

Shannon rolled across the bed and snatched up the telephone. "I'll call the police."

A gold-and-black badge shone in the light that spilled from the hall. Jim kicked the ice bucket out of the way and closed the door.

"No. Don't call."

"We have to call the police."

"They *are* the police."

"Will warned me."

Jim was breathing hard, taking the steps two at a time down a utility stairwell. Shannon, as light as a feather on the tenth floor, was getting heavy. "He told me the people who want Sentinel are connected all over the world. I guess he wasn't exaggerating."

Shannon was clutching her backpack, her forearm crutches, and the *Lonely Planet Guide to Buenos Aires;* it listed the U.S. consulate in the Palermo barrio, about five miles to hell and gone across the huge city. The guide cautioned that embassies weren't much help if you were in trouble with the local cops. But it seemed to be their only chance to tell their story to officials who wouldn't slap them around, shoot them, or hand them over to the McVays.

"Why didn't they just arrest us? Why try to trick us?"

"Because they're freelancing. It wasn't official. Until one of them got shot. Now it's goddamned official."

One flight below the lobby floor he found a corridor reeking of garbage that opened onto a loading dock. The cooks and maids who were taking cigarette breaks watched them curiously.

Sirens sounded in the distance. Jim and Shannon exchanged a look. Fire? Cops? Who knew?

"There's a taxi." Shannon waved it down as Jim hurried them to the street. He got Shannon in one door, then ran around to the other side and hopped in. The driver seemed to understand, "U.S. consulate. Palermo. *Por favor.*"

He drove like a madman through the evening traffic. Jim tried to follow along the *Lonely Planet* map as they crossed the Retiro barrio, skirted a dark shantytown, and plunged through the Recoleta. He got confused in the Palermo barrio and suddenly they were there, the driver slowing in a traffic jam caused by a dozen police cars blocking the front of the U.S. consulate.

"Oh, shit."

Shannon was quick. "We said, *British* consulate. U.K. Not U.S. *U.K.*"

The driver shrugged and turned away.

"Now what?" she asked.

"We'll get out there, and hail another cab."

"Then where?"

"I don't know." If the cops were looking for them at the consulate they'd be watching the airports, too.

Shannon said, "There's a ferry to Uruguay."

"Then what?"

They rode in frightened silence.

At last Shannon asked, "Where's the boat?"

Jim glanced at the driver. God knew if he spoke English. He leaned in close to whisper in her ear, and despite his growing terror, he thought she smelled lovely.

"About a hundred miles downriver. I came in by train."

"They'll be at the station."

"We'll rent a car." The boat was low on diesel, but the north wind was still blowing and they could sail out of the Río de la Plata and into the open Atlantic in half a day and be gone on the limitless sea. Low on diesel, low on water, low on food, but gone.

They changed cabs outside the British consulate and told the driver to take them back toward Retiro, where the guide-book said the rental agencies were clustered. Police cars were screaming all over the place. Every traffic cop seemed to stare at the taxi. The driver had an all-talk program blaring on the radio. News? He kept watching them in the mirror. He spoke enough English to ask Shannon, "How you break leg?"

"Acting."

"*Como este* 'acting'?"

"Stop the car," said Jim.

"*No. Retiro.*"

"Stop."

The guy mumbled, *"No entiendo,"* and kept going, eyes darting, clearly looking for a cop. Jim closed his hand on the driver's shoulder, found the radial nerve, and sent a twinge traveling down the man's arm into his fingers. The driver pulled over. Shannon paid. They got out on a wide café-lined boulevard beside a park and waited until a raging chorus of horns forced the taxi to move.

"He's going straight to the cops."

Eight lanes of traffic roared, the speeding cars and trucks spewing exhaust fumes as thick as cigarette smoke in a sports bar. Crowds of people hurried along the narrow sidewalk, shouting conversations over the thunder of a big jet roaring in the sky. Jim oriented himself by it. Jorge Newbery, the domestic airport, was on the river.

He wanted to wait until the cab had disappeared in the dense traffic. People were watching from the cafés. He reached for Shannon to pick her up again. She stopped him. "We're too conspicuous. Let me use the crutches."

"It's too slow."

Balancing herself on one crutch, she struggled into her backpack. "I'll get myself to the third café. Go the other way and find another cab." She hobbled off.

It beat standing there waiting for the cops.

When he looked back, he saw that Shannon had stopped to buy something from a street vendor: a hat to cover her blond hair. Because the city was so dense with cars and pedestrians, within a hundred yards he was out of sight of anyone who had seen them get out of the cab together.

He was looking for another cab, when down the gentle hill of the park he saw bicycles gliding past statues and a Ferris wheel. He hurried down the littered grass slope to a newly paved bicycle path. A signpost indicated that it led back to the city center at Retiro. The third rider he called to spoke English. The nearby Velodrome had a rental kiosk, she told him. And there he got lucky.

Shannon was sitting at an outside table, watching the road for taxis, so Jim saw her first. The exhaustion on her face tore at his heart. She had covered nearly two hundred yards on the crutches, a brutal haul. But her face lighted with relief when she saw him pedaling toward her, and she gave him such a big smile that for a second he could believe that they were just lovers on vacation.

"You genius. A bicycle built for two."

He helped her onto the front seat, got her feet on the pedals, and strapped her crutches alongside her backpack. Then, with a running start, he pedaled onto a red crushed-brick walk that led to the *bisisenda*.

The flat path was easy going for a couple of miles, though Jim was soon sweating in the humid heat. "I'm thinking our best bet might be to ride straight through out of the city to the next town and to try to catch the train there."

"How far?"

"I don't know. Twenty miles. Piece of cake on these flats. Maybe we should ride right to the boat. The bike's got a light. I could do it."

"That sign says FIN BISISENDA. I think that means the end."

Jim stood up on the pedals to see farther. "No, there's a big fancy building up ahead. Some kind of museum. If we run out of bike path we can get on the road."

He pedaled past the FIN BISISENDA sign, down a slight incline, and under some massive brick arches that supported a railroad track. A commuter train was rumbling overhead. When he emerged from the arches, the bike path petered out and they were quite suddenly out of the green park and on a narrow, rutted dirt road that entered a neighborhood of low brick houses.

Ahead and off to the right he could see modern high-rises poking above the houses. But the road zigzagged and the houses, which stood cheek to jowl, began to squeeze it hard.

"Wait a minute. What the hell is this?"

Shannon said, "Wow. It's like we're not in Europe anymore."

She was right, Jim realized. Until this moment, as Will had predicted, Buenos Aires had felt like a European city, exclusively white, with nary a black or an Indian. Here, the people staring at them exhibited none of the lively gestures of the ebullient *porteños* and looked totally different from anyone they'd seen so far—smaller, darker, and dressed in rags.

Jim steered around a pile of garbage and dodged a heap of scrap wood studded with nails. Around a sharp bend he found the way partially blocked by burning garbage. He pedaled around the smoke and wove a path through people pushing rusted shopping carts.

"Jim, I think we should get out of here."

He took the next turn, to the right, which should have brought them back to the center city. But the street grew narrower still and the houses had turned to shacks made of corrugated metal and scrap lumber.

The bike was too long to turn around. Another bend brought them to a halt on a lane of cardboard and flapping plastic. A trench down the middle of the lane overflowed with sewage. Jim stepped off the bike and walked it, looking for a turnoff.

A child in ripped jeans and a dirty T-shirt darted from a slot between two plastic-covered crates. He shook a torn paper cup in Jim's face.

"I have change," said Shannon. "They want money—hey!" she shouted as another child—as tiny as a six-year-old—tugged at her backpack. "Let go!"

Jim pushed the kid away. The child was so skinny that he felt his palm brush bone. In an instant they were surrounded by ragged children who were reaching for their packs and grabbing at their pockets.

The children were so silent that Jim and Shannon could hear the distant whine of another train. Jim saw a flash of steel, then felt something sting his thigh. When he looked down he saw that they'd slashed right through his pocket. A walnut-sized fist emerged from the cloth, stuffed with money.

They were grabbing the bike, dragging it with Shannon still on the seat. He shoved through the swarm of arms and pulled her off. The bike slid away and vanished. Jim backed against a wall, gripping Shannon in the crook of his left arm and fending off the silent, swarming children with his right.

A ten-year-old grabbed one of Shannon's crutches. Without them she was helpless, and Jim felt her erupt into a torrent of frightened muscle. She thrust the other crutch like a cue stick and the kid let go and fell back, holding his eye.

He saw steel flash again—a box cutter. He struck first and

was appalled to see an eighty-pound child go flying. Two more took its place. Jim whipped off his backpack. "Give them your stuff."

Before the hand could close on his pack, the children scattered, melting away into holes and slots and over low walls. Six teenagers, as silent as the children, stood staring at Jim and Shannon. Five held knives. The sixth had a pistol: he gestured with it for them to follow.

The group moved around them and Jim had no choice but to swing Shannon into his arms and walk with them through the maze of narrow streets and muddy lanes that stank of sewage. Shannon whispered, "What is happening?"

"I don't know."

They stopped in front of a brick house with a second story made of wood. The leader knocked and the door opened instantly. He gestured again with the gun. Jim had to turn sideways to fit through the narrow door with Shannon. It closed behind. A match flared, and an oil lamp was lit.

They went through a series of rooms and narrow doorways, up some steps and down again, descending finally into a dank cellar—a low-ceilinged room crowded with children. In the glare of several oil lamps, they saw a broad, squat man sitting at a plank table.

Jim felt Shannon shudder. The man's face was grotesquely scarred. Burns had seared his flesh and left patches of hair on shiny skin. He had no eyebrows, and, Jim realized with a twisting stomach, no ears. His legs appeared to be curled under him. One arm was a withered claw. The other, gracefully muscled, with a fine, long hand, seemed to be the final remnant of a once strong and handsome man.

His milky left eye was blind. The other flicked from Shannon to Jim and back to Shannon's crutches. Then he crossed his heart with his good hand, smacked the table, and announced with a childlike glee: "Word of an Englishman! You found them."

35

WELCOME, SHANNON. WELCOME, Jim. Thank you, Mother Mary." He snapped his fingers. "Tell Eduardo we have them." Two boys hurried out. The children—a dozen or more—crowded closer.

"Who," asked Shannon, "is Eduardo?"

"Eduardo, pretty woman, is my negotiator. My agent. He will help set the price."

"Of what?" asked Jim.

"Of the famous Jim and Shannon everyone is looking for."

"You're going to turn us in to the police?"

"*Policía?* No, my muscled friend. The *policía* beat us and shoot us. They do not pay us."

"Who?"

"Put your pretty woman down, muscle man. Your arms must be tired. We'll bring her a chair. It is hard to stand on crutches, is it not?" He pointed at his useless legs.

They brought a cracked plastic kitchen chair and Jim lowered Shannon onto it as the mutilated man watched. She and Jim exchanged looks of fear and confusion. He was racking his brain, wondering if they could buy their way out of this with the gold Krugerrands in his pack, or those still on the boat, when Shannon broke the silence.

"Your English is excellent. Where did you learn it?"

"I was born Brazilian. When Portuguese is your native language, you are wise to learn new tongues." He looked down at his shriveled body. "My nurse spoke English—a nun. She taught me how to read, too. Which, you know, comes in handy when you are 'recuperating.' Here in BA, of course, there is much English, so mine has been exercised. I am called Stallone, by the way—my 'surf tag.' May I ask what happened to your legs?"

Jim felt Shannon stiffen. He laid his hand on her shoulder and she grabbed it. Throwing the word *cripple* around like a hard-won badge could never erase her loss. She had told him only once the horror story of her accident and made him swear they would never speak of it again.

"I asked, what happened to your legs?"

"An accident," she answered at last. "And yours?"

"An accident."

Shannon and Stallone stared at each other for what seemed to Jim a very long time. Then Shannon said, "Skiing."

"Surfing," said Stallone.

Shannon looked at him, clearly surprised.

Stallone broke another silence with a loud laugh. "You're asking yourself how does a man get roasted to a crisp in the ocean. *Train* surfing. Do you know about train surfing?"

Shannon shook her head.

"*Surfistas* ride on the train's roof, dance in the wind. It feels wonderful, especially when you are going home to hell. In Rio we had shantytowns that make this one look like your Plaza Hotel. Where you shot the cops—for which, in a better world, you would be rewarded, if this were only a better world."

"Who is paying you for us?"

"There are problems with train surfing. Falling off is one problem. The train runs over you. Or you land on your head at a hundred kilometers per hour. The other problem is electrocution. The electric cable that powers the locomotive is just above the roof. Four thousand volts. You start to fall, you grab the cable. You can't help it."

He flashed white, even teeth, which, like his beautiful arm and hand, had survived intact. "'Shocking,' they say. But they never say how the electricity burns you. It burned the fat right out of my legs and this arm. This one—the funny one."

Shannon said, "My father is a very wealthy man. He will pay you for us."

Stallone shook his head. "Sadly, your father is not nearly so wealthy as the people Eduardo is dealing with. Nor is your father here, while these people have gone to the trouble of coming all the way to Buenos Aires. All week they've been asking for you. All over BA. They tell the police, the mafia, the gangs of the *villas miserias:* whoever finds the pretty blond girl who can't walk, whoever finds her muscle man—name your price. Jim and Shannon are a very popular couple."

"Double your money," Jim said. "It's me they want. Not her. Sell Shannon to her father. Sell me to the—"

"No," said Shannon.

Stallone said, "Be quiet, pretty woman. Your muscle man has a good idea."

"Just get her away before they come," urged Jim. "They're only using her to get to me."

"I won't leave you."

Stallone started stroking his twisted hand with his good one. "You will leave him if I say so."

"Then please don't say so."

Stallone laughed. He shook his head, clearly intrigued by Jim's suggestion. His eyes glittered as Shannon said to Jim, "Please don't leave me."

"You'll be okay."

"Not without you."

Stallone jabbed his finger at Shannon's crutches. "Tell me, how did skiing do that to you?"

Jim started to speak in her defense, but Shannon's hand bit into his and he listened in fear and wonder, thrilled by her spirit. She challenged their captor.

"I did something as stupid as you did."

Stallone's twisted body seemed to swell up. Blood suffused the skin on his head. He gripped the table and Jim thought he was going to throw it at her. He rubbed his face and shouted, "What did you do?"

"I sneaked onto the ski mountain at night. When it was closed . . . I climbed in from the next mountain—with skins on my skis."

Stallone nodded, though it was doubtful he had ever seen skis, much less climbing skins. "You didn't pay?"

"Not a peso. It was free."

"And you *felt* free."

"All alone racing down the mountain."

"In the dark?"

"The snow glowed blue."

"Enough to see?"

"I thought I could see."

"Fast?"

"Fast as a train."

"The air was good?"

"The air was beautiful. Clean and cold. Stinging cold. Pure as ice."

"You feel yourself start to fall."

"No. I don't fall."

"You skid into a tree."

"I don't skid."

"You fall from a cliff."

"I *jump* from a cliff."

Stallone flashed another smile. "You crash."

"I soar like a bird."

"You crash to the ground."

"I *float* to the ground. My knees bend to take the shock; they cushion the landing and I make a magnificent turn through a blue-glowing curve. . . ."

"Then?"

"There, in front of me, is a snow cat."

"What is a snow cat?"

"A tractor they drive up and down the mountain to groom the snow trails."

"No lights? No warning?"

"It had broken down. It was a dark, silent mound of steel. I couldn't stop. No one could have—that was my last thought. No one could stop. Not even me."

Stallone stared at Shannon and a deep silence descended on the room. Finally, he whispered, "I know. I know. I knew I was reaching for the cable. I couldn't stop myself. I was afraid to fall."

He looked sharply around the cramped, dim room, stared into the faces of his gang. Children and teenagers gazed back impassively and Jim could not figure out whether they understood English. Stallone shrugged. "Who cares who knows? I went soft. I was finished."

"How did you end up here?"

Stallone shrugged. "What do these people want from you?" he asked Jim.

"Something I don't have."

"They'll expect a better answer than that."

"I don't have it."

"They will 'ask' until you give it to them. Or die. Her, too."

He cocked his ear to a sound Jim couldn't hear. Those who had gone out earlier had returned with those who would be doing the asking. Two Americans by the look of them, soldiers or cops, the leader not that tall but plenty wide, with arms and a chest that said he could bench-press four hundred. Andy Nickels?

His backup was taller, but just as wide, with a swimmer's chest and shoulders. Buzz cuts, smooth-shaven hard-planed faces. Definitely military types. Special Forces or SEALs.

"Where's Will Spark?"

Jim squeezed Shannon's hand lightly with his fingers, warning her not to speak, praying that they wouldn't notice that he was trying to beam a million-volt thought into Shannon's brain: *Don't tell them Will is dead. If they think we have Sentinel they will torture us to death to get it.*

They had one hope. The McVays would chase Will, believing him to still be alive. But that demanded a Will Spark answer. Details, details, details. Smoke and mirrors. And a thousand "facts."

"Last I saw he was headed east."

"Where?"

"Ten miles off Montevideo."

"Where were you?"

"I was on the ferry to Buenos Aires. We had already said good-bye. I went out on deck and suddenly I saw his boat. Close enough to wave. He was really tramping, a broad port reach on that north wind. Good point of sail for that boat."

"What ferry?"

"Will didn't want to come into Buenos Aires. So he dropped me at Montevideo, in Uruguay, on the other side of the Río de la Plata, and I caught the boat. What is all this about?"

"How long did Will Spark stay in Montevideo?"

Jim built his answer from the truth—after three months at sea, the boat was low on everything. "Will bought diesel. I helped him fill the water tanks. He picked up a sack of rice and coffee, a couple of cases of ultrapasteurized juice and milk, and a heap of frozen food, and he was out of there."

"No one saw him in Montevideo."

"What do you mean?"

"No one saw him there."

"So?"

"So you're not telling me the truth."

"It's a big port. I don't know where you were looking, but we were there. He dropped me right at the ferry. The main dock, for God's sake."

"Where is he headed?"

"I told you. East."

"For where?"

"I don't know. What the hell is this about?"

"Why didn't he tell you where he was headed?"

"He claimed somebody was chasing him and that it would be better if I didn't know. I'm beginning to believe him."

Andy Nickels turned a sudden cold eye on Shannon. "Is that true?"

"Absolutely."

"Honey, you don't want us to catch you lying."

"Fuck you. How dare you threaten us? What are you, some kind of mafia?"

Was this the one who had bungled kidnapping Angela? Jim wondered. Or had they hired locals? Or bought cops to do it?

"You're lying. If Will Spark had sailed east like you say our people would have stopped him."

"It's a big river," said Jim. "A hundred miles wide. You'd need a lot of people on a hell of a lot of boats to spot one little sailboat."

"We have both." He turned to Stallone, who was hunched at his table, eyes flickering back and forth as if he were watching a tennis match. "All right. We'll take them."

"Take us?" yelled Shannon. "What do you mean, 'take us'?"

Stallone said, "He doesn't mean take. He means *buy*."

36

STALLONE SAID, "SHOW me the money."

"Greg!"

Greg opened his windbreaker, pulled out an orange and blue FedEx mailer, and tossed it on Stallone's table. Stallone moved back as if fearing it would explode. "Open it."

Every child in the room eyed hungrily the switchblade that Greg flicked open to slash the envelope.

"Empty it."

Greg dumped the contents on the table. "Dollars," said Andy Nickels. "Like you asked."

Stallone nodded at the banded stacks of twenty-dollar bills.

"My father will pay you more," said Shannon.

He turned to her and again his straight white teeth gleamed. "When you get home, ski lady, perhaps he'll write me a check."

He looked up at Nickels. "I accept this money as ransom for you and your friend. A guide will lead you safely out of my barrio."

"What?"

Greg and Andy Nickels exploded into motion. Crouching, reaching down, spreading apart, each whipped a pistol from an ankle holster.

Children scurried. A box cutter laid a deep, red track across the back of Greg's hand; his gun fell to the dirt floor.

Two razors brushed his throat, two his face.

"Tell them to stop," said Andy Nickels. Blood was pouring from his hand, too, but he still held his pistol leveled at Stallone. *"Now!"*

Stallone spoke to the children in Spanish, then said, "I instructed them to cut your balls off if you shoot me."

"Won't help you," Andy replied coolly. Blood was splashing on his shoes, but he held the gun rock steady and ignored the blades at his groin.

Stallone said, "Check out the ceiling." Nickels's eyes never moved. "Greg, what is it?"

Jim looked up and flinched. Children in the rafters were aiming short-barreled shotguns. Greg said, "They've got sawed-offs."

Shannon said, "Stop. They're children."

"Do you know who you're cheating?" Andy asked Stallone.

Stallone pounded his chest. "Here, I am king. Here, you are nobody."

"They're little kids," said Shannon. "You want us all dead?"

Nickels put down his pistol and squeezed his flowing cut with his fingers. Small hands fished his switchblade from its pocket, his money, his cell phone, his wallet, and another gun.

Raging, Andy turned on Stallone. "I'm warning you one last time. If you cheat us we will hunt you to the end of the earth."

Stallone shrugged. *"This* is the end of the earth. No one who enters leaves unless I say so—no cop, no gang, no Yankee foreigner."

Nickels turned to Jim. "Give me Will Spark. Name your price."

"I already told you, Will is sailing east. All we want to do is go home."

"We will help you go home. We'll protect you from the cops."

Jim looked at Shannon. "Do you believe that?"

Shannon said, "No."

Stallone laughed. Then he said to Nickels, "My little friends will show you out—the long way."

He brushed aside their stunned thanks. "Surfers and skiers hang together. Besides, I keep the money."

"You saved our lives."

"Temporarily. I am king of a very small land. Outside my *villa miseria,* I am just another scavenger. You are safe only as long as you stay in my garbage dump. If you're going to leave, you must leave immediately. Ahead of those two. How will you get home to America?"

"We have a boat."

Stallone smiled. "The boat that sailed east?"

Jim nodded.

"Excellent. A criminal mind behind that baby face. Where is your boat?"

"A little north of San Clemente."

Stallone shook his head mournfully. "San Clemente is very far from my kingdom."

"It's about a hundred miles down the coast."

"I know where it is. . . . Have you any money?"

"I have cash," said Shannon. Jim displayed his slashed pocket. "I lost mine."

"It happens," Stallone replied distractedly, pondering the problem.

"I have some gold Krugerrands in my pack."

"Gold is good. . . . There is a person in La Boca who drives a van to Mar del Plata. For gold he might take you. San Clemente is on the way. The party season is ending, but perhaps he has a shipment going tomorrow."

"What kind of shipment?" Shannon asked.

Jim said, "We don't want to know."

"Correct," said Stallone. "But first, somehow, I have to move you across the city to La Boca."

* * *

At dawn, thousands of garbage trucks began their daily shuttle between the city's residential and business neighborhoods and the shantytowns where they dumped their loads. One that trundled into Stallone's barrio full left still carrying a cardboard refrigerator box it had found on a prosperous street of fine old houses in the Recoleta barrio. Laid flat, hidden by the wooden sides of the truck from pedestrians and automobile drivers, it was visible only to the commuters peering down from the early trains streaming into Retiro.

The truck slowed at the bus station. Bolivian Indians loped alongside, throwing full garbage cans up to the catcher, who tossed them back empty. As they passed through the Retiro barrio, the refrigerator box was buried under office trash and restaurant waste. Filled to the brim, the truck groaned on, carrying its reeking load through San Nicolas, San Telmo, and finally into the old working-class barrio of La Boca, where it disappeared into the dark loading bay of a vast city hospital.

The Fiat van that pulled out of the hospital moments later raced through La Boca and crossed an iron bridge over the Riochuelo. It sped south on Route 2, the main highway to Mar del Plata, Buenos Aires's playground on the Atlantic Ocean. Twice it was stopped by police, who greeted the driver like an old acquaintance, took their regular bribe, and waved him on.

He told Jim and Shannon that he was a university student and only dealt *fadopa* to his friends. Later, a couple of hours out of Buenos Aires, while rolling along the edge of the pampas, he admitted that he'd been out of school for some years. The economy was bad and he held down two jobs in addition to these distribution runs.

The third stop was at the hands of the provincial police, who were not at all friendly. Still, *coimas* is *coimas,* the driver had assured Jim and Shannon, a bribe is a bribe. The notoriously greedy, corrupt, and brutal provincial police, he maintained, "aren't about to kill the goose that lays the golden egg, much less overturn the applecart by searching the goose's vehicle." His assurances offered little comfort to Jim and Shannon, who envisaged drug smuggling charges compounding their predicament.

Huddled under a blanket in the cargo bed, they listened fearfully to boots crunching gravel. The provincial police circled the van, banging on the sides, shouting. The driver sat quietly, humbly taking the abuse. At last they accepted his bribe and waved him on.

An hour later, Jim directed him to Captain Faveros's front gate. Shrubs, trees, and Faveros's mansion blocked the view of the Río de la Plata, but Jim could smell the sea on the stiff wind. It was hauling around to the east, which wasn't going to make getting out of the estuary any easier. But tired as he was from the long, crazy night, the wind sped his pulse. Just a few more feet, a few more minutes, and they'd be under sail.

The driver noted the ornate ironwork, the surveillance cameras, and the electrified fence. He whistled appreciatively. "*Cha masa. Mucho guita.* Rich man."

Jim waited for the van to go before he rang the bell. Captain Faveros came down the driveway in an open jeep.

"I see you were successful, my young friend. *Buenas tardes,* señorita."

Jim said, "Captain Faveros, this is my friend, Shannon Riley."

Faveros hesitated when he saw Shannon's crutches. But he bent low over her hand to kiss it. "Welcome, Señorita Riley. Come in, come in."

Jim felt an intense relief as the jeep rounded the first curve in the driveway and they were no longer visible from the road beyond the locked gate. He said, "Could you drive us right to your dock?"

"You must have lunch. My wife is much better today."

"Thank you, Captain. But we have to sail immediately."

"I would recommend you wait. The wind has shifted. There's a cold front approaching. You might encounter the *pampero*. Stay the night. Sail in the morning."

Jim saw little choice but to be up-front and hope that the retired officer was still in absolution mode. And that confession went both ways. "Captain Faveros, I have to tell you, the police are after us. We did absolutely nothing wrong, but the sooner we're out of here, the better for us. And you."

"Not to worry. I'll telephone my friend the district commander."

"It's the federals from Buenos Aires."

"I see."

"If we leave immediately, no one will know we were here."

Captain Faveros drove in silence toward the water but stopped the jeep before the dock was in view. Jim's heart jumped. There was a patch of empty water where he had anchored *Hustle*.

"Where's my boat?"

Faveros ignored his question. "You must realize, it would be my duty to report your presence."

"I swear to you we did nothing wrong."

"That would not be for me to judge, though I have no doubt that you are a good person." He drummed the steering wheel for a moment. "Both good people." Then, with a perplexed glance at Shannon, he spoke decisively: "What you tell me explains what I've been hearing on the marine radio channels this morning. They are looking for your boat."

"Who?"

"Once I heard the name of your boat, I switched on all my radio scanners—VHF, SSB, and a certain cellular telephone scanner that civilians and even retired officers are not supposed to possess. Interestingly, it is not the navy that is looking, nor the *policía*, but, shall we say, 'private interests.' Certain fishing boats—smugglers—even a customs cutter that I happen to know is crewed by thieves. It appears there's a sizable bounty."

Jim heard him through a roaring in his ears. Would the McVays ever give up?

"May I ask—without prejudice—did you steal your yacht?"

"No! Who's offering the bounty?"

"Those on the radio were circumspect, of course, but I've learned that there's a Taiwan freighter standing off the coast.

And several other Chinese ships have reported ETAs to Puerto Buenos Aires—more than one would expect ordinarily, though they could be explained by the harvest. . . . I took the liberty of taking your boat off the mooring."

"Where is she?"

"Right there." Faveros put the jeep in gear and drove to the dock. "Behind mine."

Then he saw her, squeezed between the dock and Faveros's huge schooner. Only *Hustle*'s mast would be visible from the water, bracketed confusingly by the schooner's. You would have to come within a hundred feet to distinguish the sloop from the bigger yacht.

"It is known who I am," Captain Faveros said. "No one would dare to come too close. You'll be safe till dark."

"Why?"

"Why what?"

"Why are you helping us?"

Captain Faveros tried to meet Jim's eyes but couldn't. He looked out at the Río de la Plata—oddly tan-colored as thickening high clouds obscured the sun—then down at his polished shoes. "I truly believe that I am not really a bad person. I know that I cannot undo my mistakes. Nor can I repress them. Perhaps if I can help you—and if you are truly innocent—God will return me to my son's heart."

Faveros was practically begging Jim to ask for more help, believing that the more he helped, the quicker he would atone. Even in retirement, the wealthy naval man seemed somewhat connected. Argentina may have become a democracy, but everyone feared that the military still had teeth— and the cops were corrupt. Could Faveros use his influence to get them onto a plane to New York?

Jim felt Shannon's gaze and he was struck by how totally responsible he would be for her safety, her life, once they set sail. Was she, too, wondering whether it was more dangerous to flee than to take their chances with the authorities?

"What do you think?" he asked Shannon.

"I can't believe you sailed all the way across the ocean on that."

Jim had always thought of *Hustle* as big—bigger than the Barbadian fishing boat, bigger than Margaret's outboard canoe. But now, huddled in the lee of Faveros's enormous yacht, Will's sloop looked quite small and insignificant.

What would happen if they were arrested? The first thing the cops would do was separate them. But if they took their chances on the boat it would be just the two of them—the "adventure" he was supposed to have alone, they would have together, an "adventure" that would define them one way or another.

"She's a solid boat," he said firmly. And Faveros chimed in, "I would imagine she is very forgiving."

"Very forgiving," said Jim, wondering what the naval veteran had picked up to guess that Jim was really still an amateur with little more than half a crossing under his belt—less than a week single-handed without Will's yakking in his ear.

"Actually," said Faveros, "I would imagine you could foul up—and persist at it for some time—before she betrayed you." He seemed to be rethinking atonement in light of the complications of harboring fugitives. In fact, he looked immensely relieved when Jim called to Shannon, "Shannon, let's get aboard." He seized Captain Faveros's hand and shook it. "Thank you for your help. We'll leave as soon as it's dark."

"If there is anything I can do?" Faveros asked politely.

Jim was eyeing the schooner's fat hull like a pirate. "Let me buy some diesel."

"Well, yes, of course. We can pump it over from my yacht."

There was a garden hose coiled neatly on the dock, for washing the decks. "And would it be possible to fill my water tanks?"

"Yes, of—excuse me." He touched the beeper on his belt, snapped a cell phone from the holster, and punched a reply. He listened, his expression darkening. *"Sí . . . sí . . . gracias."* He holstered the phone and turned angrily on Jim.

"The police have arrested a drug smuggler who claims to have dropped you at my gate. They're coming now."

Jim scooped Shannon off the dock and swung her over the safety lines and into the cockpit. The boat was trapped in the spiderweb of the schooner's mooring lines.

"Help me cast off," he said to Faveros.

Captain Faveros said, "Show me what's in your bags."

"No drugs."

"Show me!"

"Make it quick!" Jim whipped off his backpack and dumped the contents on the cockpit bench. Shannon did the same.

Faveros stepped aboard and rifled through their things. He seemed glad to find no drugs but was not apologetic.

"I had to know," he said. "I will not be played for a fool." Now he sprang into action. He jumped to the dock, untied his yacht's stern line, and, nimbly crossing both boats' safety lines, carried it across Jim's afterdeck and onto his.

Jim got his engine started and ran forward to untie his bowline. By the time he got back to the cockpit, Shannon had finished repacking their bags and stowed them out of the way.

Standing on the afterdeck of his schooner, Captain Faveros leaned his weight on a boat hook and poled off of Jim's hull, widening the slot in which *Hustle* had hidden. Jim engaged his propeller and backed out.

Faveros secured his stern line and climbed into his jeep. "I'll keep them at the gate," he called, "as long as I can. Bon voyage. Look out for the *pampero*."

37

WHAT'S A *PAMPERO*?" asked Shannon.

Jim was driving, looking over his shoulder, as the diesel engine roared its slow six knots. They were a mile from Faveros's dock already and still no cops. The view of the coast was broadening behind them. He could make out the town of San Clemente. Which boats in the town's fishing fleet were angling for the bounty? Did the cops have a boat? He picked up the binoculars and focused on a yellow vessel putting to sea.

"Hey, Captain. What's a *pampero*?"

"Local storm. Squalls come screaming off the pampas. Will said they're a real bitch. Humongous gusts and sheets of rain."

"Would it hide us?"

"If it doesn't kill us."

"While hiding us from the people who want to kill us."

Jim looked at her and they both laughed.

She looked as frightened as he did, and as worn down by the long, hard night, but she pointed happily at the band of water broadening between them and the shore. "Neat boat, Captain. Would you show me around?"

"I'll show you how to steer. It's hazing up. After another

mile, when they won't be able to see us from the beach, we'll get some sail up. Here, scoot around beside the wheel. . . ."

It was humbling to see how fast she got it. She did very little oversteering and in minutes was laying down a respectable wake. Jim jumped below and brought up the storm jib.

"What's that?"

"Storm jib. All this *pampero* talk is making me nervous. So's that sky."

To their left, west, was a tangled checkerboard of bright white clouds on a field of black.

"Wow. That's weird. It was blue a minute ago."

Ahead the sky was bright blue. To the right, the low coast of the inside of Cape San Antonio was almost invisible. Shannon looked back. "There's a yellow boat following us."

"Yeah, I've been watching him."

It was catching up, probably making a third again their speed. Already he could distinguish its round bluff bow and boxy cabin in back. When he got the storm sail hanked onto the jack stay and its sheets led back to the cockpit, the shore behind had disappeared in haze. He thought he could make out Punta Rasa lighthouse at the tip of Cape San Antonio. But the yellow boat was close enough for him to see that it had a stubby mast.

"Soon as we clear that lighthouse we can swing east into the ocean."

"You'd think," said Shannon, "that with the sky looking that way he would turn around and head home."

"If he was just going fishing."

"Maybe the sky looks worse than it is."

Jim went below, put on his slicker, and brought up one of Will Spark's for Shannon. "Did you ever fire a shotgun?"

"No. Did you?"

"No. Will had a sawed-off."

"The one he killed that woman with?"

"It's down below, if we need it."

"I don't know if I could shoot at somebody."

"I'm guessing it's easier if they're shooting at you."

Shannon faced west, where the sky was now more black than white. "Come on, *pampero*. Come on."

"Look!"

Ahead, crossing their bow, a pair of fishing boats similar to the one behind them were racing toward the lighthouse. "The *Sailing Directions* said there's an anchorage. They're running for it." He looked back. The yellow boat was still on their tail and still catching up.

Hustle was starting to roll in the brisker seas outside San Clemente Bay. Jim raised the storm sail and the boat settled down a little and picked up a knot when he sheeted in. He looked back. The yellow boat's bluff bow was throwing clouds of spray.

A mile or so ahead, on a line with the lighthouse, he could see whitecaps where the wind and the east setting waves were no longer blocked by Punta Rasa. He looked again at the western sky. A curtain of black descended to the estuary, and it seemed to be curling ahead of them, too.

"The boat's catching up," said Shannon. "Do you want to steer?"

"You're doing fine. I'm going to raise the main."

He raised it only high enough for a double reef. *Hustle* didn't move much faster, but when whatever was making that sky crashed into them it would be too late to reef. Now with both sails pulling, he took the wheel and nursed a little more speed out of her.

The yellow boat was heaving entire waves. They could hear it pounding, smashing the water with sullen booms. But it was still catching up and Jim realized with a start that less than two hundred yards separated the two boats. There was no one on deck, but he could see several forms through the wheelhouse glass. Yard by yard it drew near.

Suddenly the wind stopped.

Hustle staggered and for a second he thought she had struck a sandbar. But her sails hung slack and she lost two knots with only her engine to drive her through the thickening seas. Two men dressed in sea boots and slickers stepped out of the yellow boat's wheelhouse.

"Do you see any guns?"

"I can't see. Wait, what are they doing?"

They were twirling ropes, standing surefooted on their pitching deck, one moving toward the bow, the other toward the stern, glancing around to make sure their ropes didn't foul the cabin or the mast.

"Look out! They're throwing grappling hooks."

Jim spun the wheel. Always slow to respond when driven by her propeller, *Hustle* veered clumsily. The hooks lofted through the air. The forward one splashed into the sea. The other crashed on the deck, a foot from Shannon's hand, bounced wildly, banged against the backstay, clanged on the aftmost safety-line stanchion, and, miraculously failing to hook it, fell into the water.

The yellow boat could turn tighter than *Hustle*. As Jim changed course, it circled closer, as the fishermen, methodically coiling their lines, hauled in their hooks. In unison, they began twirling them again, while the yellow boat maneuvered.

The stern man threw. Jim slammed the wheel over and the hook splashed harmlessly behind him. Only then, as the second hook came flying across the water, did he realize they had set him up. It was too late to turn, too late to do anything but shove the wheel into Shannon's hands and run forward, pulling Will's bosun knife from his slicker.

The hook caught the bow pulpit. The yellow boat turned away. The rope jumped as tight as a steel bar, and *Hustle* lurched into a clumsy, wallowing turn, dragged behind the fishing boat. Jim thought the line would rip the pulpit right off the deck, but when he reached the hook he discovered that one of the barbs had fastened around the immensely strong forestay.

Jim braced his knees in the pulpit, opened Will's knife, and frantically sawed at the rope. *Hustle* buried her bow, and a full sea nearly knocked him overboard. The rope parted with a loud bang and knocked the knife out of his hand. Will's lanyard saved it, and he ran, untangling the lanyard from his legs, back to the cockpit.

Shannon was fighting the wheel, trying to turn away from the high yellow bow aimed at their stern. The diesel engine skipped a beat, coughed, and revved back to full power. The propeller bit into the water at the last second and *Hustle* shot free. The yellow boat pivoted into another tight turn and circled back, as both fishermen twirled their hooks again.

Hustle's engine quit. The grinding rumble ceased abruptly. Jim and Shannon looked at each other, horrified by the sudden deadly silence. "What?"

"I don't know." He pressed the starter switch. The engine ground but didn't start. "Maybe fuel."

"They're coming."

The yellow boat was so close that Jim could see the expressions on the suntanned faces of the fisherman twirling the grappling hooks: intense concentration, hope, and triumph fired their eyes. This was it. They were coming in like professionals, a well-oiled team doing their job. Instead of a huge tuna or a swordfish, they were going to hook a sailboat.

Jim could hear their hooks whistling as they cut the air, accelerating for the throw. Suddenly, their expressions changed from unbending purpose to abject terror.

Jim looked over his shoulder. The black sky was yards from his boat—pounding down like a cataract.

38

"HOLD ON," HE yelled to Shannon.

A tremendous gust slammed into the sails. Scant as they were, the sliver of storm sail and the severely reefed main dragged *Hustle* onto her side. The safety harnesses were still under the cockpit bench where Shannon was sitting. But when he reached for her he saw that she had fashioned a hand grip out of an idle line and secured it to an empty cleat.

Jim tried to steer into the wind. But a slab-fronted sea struck before *Hustle* could straighten up. It smashed her hull like a bulldozer. The impact reverberated through the decks and as seawater burst over his head, Jim thought, If she were made of wood she'd be splinters.

He felt the boat try to rise from the burden of the wave. A second gust held her down. Heeled steeply, she shed the water from her decks, leaped up, and ran before the wind. Jim caught a single glimpse of the yellow boat's black bottom and then it was gone and he was battling for their lives, fighting to control the pounding, crashing hull and trying to figure out where the wind was coming from and where they were going before they ran aground on Cape San Antonio.

It was so dark he had to turn on the binnacle light to read the compass. They were headed due east, pushed by a west wind, straight at the cape. Somehow the sails had ended up wing and wing, the storm sail over the starboard side, the main over the port. Lightning flared on breakers, two hundred yards dead ahead, foaming on an outer bar.

"Shannon! Grab this!" He handed her the mainsheet. "Haul it in when I tell you." He put the wheel hard over and held it as *Hustle* cut across a sea that looked like a brick wall. She swung north. "Now!" As the mainsail swept across the cabin, Shannon hauled in the slackening sheet. Jim took one hand off the wheel and secured the sheet by guiding it into the grip of the self-tailer atop the winch. "Hands out of the winch."

A lightning bolt struck the land a quarter mile away and illuminated the sandbar, which was exploding with surf beside the boat. Jim tried to coax her a little more to the west. A gust veering north banged the sails and *Hustle* slid closer to the bar. Another gust, from dead ahead, seemed to stop her in her tracks, as if she were giving up and waiting for the waves to throw her onto the bar. He could hear the surf thundering and could feel it through the hull and when the lightning flashed again, he could see, close enough to touch, the line of breaking seas grabbing at the boat like a long, white tentacle.

The wind wheeled. The sudden shriek in the rigging took him completely by surprise—a powerful blast from the northeast. The sails crashed around, and *Hustle* stampeded off on a starboard tack, racing away from the shallows.

Jim couldn't believe how close he had just come to losing her. In his mind's eye he could see white water breaking a boat-width away: *Hustle* was ten feet from impaling the bar with her keel; ten feet from falling on her side, seas battering her mast underwater, pounding the sails, smashing her down.

Shannon was huddled beside him, hanging onto her handloop like a bronco rider. He put his mouth to her ear to be heard over the shriek of the wind: "Are you okay?"

She turned to him, her eyes huge, and yelled in his ear, "This is so cool!"

* * *

They had gained only two hundred yards when the wind shifted again and *Hustle* starting slipping toward the bar. Then the rain, which the wind had blown in fitful, sizzling bursts, suddenly poured from the sky, a slanting torrent so heavy that it flattened the sea. Blinded, Jim switched on the work lights, but he still couldn't see the bow, much less the bar. Nor could he hear the surf thunder over the roar of the rain. All he could do was steer north by the compass and try to nurse her west, against the seas, away from the cape and its deadly shallows.

Shannon tapped his arm. "I see a light."

Jim looked where she pointed, off the starboard bow, hoping it marked the Cape San Antonio lighthouse. "I see it." It seemed awfully close. He edged to port, clawing west, but he couldn't see to veer away from the light. For nearly ten minutes he struggled, but it seemed to have a magnetic pull on him.

"Is it moving?" He looked at the compass. The boat was heading west. Due west. He had fallen off course by a full ninety degrees, not realizing that the storm gusts were shifting with him and that he was, in essence, sailing back to Buenos Aires.

The rain slackened and now he saw a hazy red light near the light he had been steering around. "It *is* moving."

Not a lighthouse but a ship. A slow-moving ship, plodding carefully through the storm, was working her way up the channel toward Buenos Aires. He had to find his position.

He started to switch on the autopilot, then remembered that with the diesel dead, he shouldn't waste battery power.

"Can you just hold this course a sec?"

Shannon moved behind the wheel and hauled herself to a standing position so she could read the compass. Jim ran below and checked their GPS fix against the chart. Returning to the cockpit, he took the wheel, steered behind the ship, turned east, and trimmed the sails for their new course.

"We're miles clear of the point."

"Nice going, Captain. I'm impressed."

Jim's spirits soared. It looked like they had made it. The wind was swinging south and the temperature was dropping, which indicated the end of the *pampero*. "Thanks. But she's a good boat and we caught a few breaks."

"She is a beautiful boat."

"Will gave her to me."

"You're kidding."

"In his will. Will's will. She's ours, if we want her."

"Wow. Well, we have plenty of time to think about it. Now what?"

"We'll clear the coast tonight. And haul ass home tomorrow."

"I'm starving."

"I can't leave the cockpit. Too many ships."

"I'll make something. Don't worry, I'll find my way around."

Jim showed her how to open the hatch and remove the washboards. Shannon lowered herself into the cabin. The last he saw she was locating light switches with the penlight she had found in Will's slicker.

Half an hour later, as the rain stopped, she tapped on the aft cabin port, popped it open to pass him a thermos of coffee, and dogged it shut before sea spray soaked Will's bed. Their bed, he realized, once they were safely at sea. The hot drink was a godsend, but thin. If they got out of this alive, he resolved to teach her how to make coffee Will's way.

After another half hour, Shannon pulled herself up through the hatch. She was wearing another slicker and Will's sea boots. Attaining the cockpit, she reached down and produced two insulated mugs of soup.

"It's wonderful to get dry. I borrowed some clothes from Will. Fabulous cashmere—cheers." They clinked mugs, the way they did at home. "Great kitchen. It's really beautiful down there."

But as Jim finished the soup, he realized that Shannon was troubled. "What's up?"

"I tried the radios. The short-range."

"The VHF."

"Whatever. I heard a lot of *'Hustle.'* They're still looking for us."

"Lots of luck; it's a big ocean."

"But you said we're out of fuel. And low on water. And I didn't see much food. Where can we go to get enough to sail home on?"

Jim was bone-weary. "I don't know. We'll figure it out in the morning."

"Sure. But I'm wondering . . . I looked at the chart. It's a long way to Rio de Janeiro. Maybe we could get on a plane there, but what if they're waiting? Or what if the Argentines ask the Brazilians to extradite us for shooting a cop? Fat chance we'll be able to explain we were defending ourselves from being kidnapped. I'd rather fight extradition from home with Daddy's lawyers."

"That's why we're going home."

"Except we don't have food and water and fuel to get home with."

"Tomorrow, soon as it's light, soon as I get a little sleep, I'll check out the engine. I'm sure we weren't that empty. Meantime, let's go easy on the electricity. She's got enormous batteries, but they won't last forever."

"All I'm saying is we need a plan."

"All I'm saying is I'm so tired I can't think. Let's just get through the night—put some miles between us and them—and we'll tackle a plan in the morning. Why don't you catch some sleep? I'll be okay up here."

"I'm staying with you."

"It's getting cold."

"Not if I can help it."

"One of us has to watch for ships."

"We'll take turns. You first."

It was a pitch-black night without a star in the sky. Squalls overtook them, kicking the sea up and drenching the decks with rain, but moving on quickly. After the last, the wind began to ease a little. When it ceased to gust and wheel and finally settled into a cold breeze from the west-south-west,

Jim unfurled a bit of jib. He thought of rigging the dodger—the canvas and clear plastic hood over the companionway that protected the cockpit from cold wind and spray—but decided against it until they were farther out of the shipping lanes; the dodger made it hard to see.

In another hour, with the sea conditions easing, Jim shook the second reef out of the main. *Hustle* responded with a gratifying eight knots. After the crazy scramble on land it felt wonderful to be in control of the boat again.

Twice, while Shannon slept, Jim slipped below and listened to the VHF and the SSB. Most of the long-range radio traffic involved ships reporting their ETAs to the Port of Buenos Aires. The short-range was between ships, tugs, and Río de la Plata pilots. Spanish, Chinese, and Russian sprinkled repeatedly with the name of their boat.

Returning to the cockpit, he covered Shannon with a heat-retaining, waterproof foil space blanket from one of the survival kits. Then, while monitoring the dark and the compass, he held her in his arms and tried to put himself in Andy Nickels's mind.

What if it was true that the McVay Foundation possessed the enormous state-within-the-state power that Will had claimed? If McVay wanted Sentinel enough to kill for it, wouldn't he use his power and money to divert ships to hunt Will Spark?

Andy Nickels knew his speed. All he had to do was draw a circle from the Río de la Plata determined by time and speed and hunt within it. When the circle got too big, he would cover their likely landfalls.

Which left him and Shannon with the problem of where in hell to replenish their supplies. The entire Argentine coast was out. The same sorts of cops and smugglers and slum dwellers were surely to be found in Rio. The same was true for most parts of the Caribbean. Who knew how many enemies were waiting in Florida? No wonder Will had fled to Hong Kong. How far was that? Two oceans, twelve thousand miles. Six thousand to Connecticut was daunting enough.

He dozed a little despite the danger of ships. Once when

he started awake from a spooky nightmare and stared wildly around, he felt Shannon's fingers on his brow. "Sleep," she whispered. "I can see."

They took turns through the night. At sunrise, she was curled beside him, her head on his lap. Her face looked free of care, secure in trust, sure that he would protect her. Her trust made him happy. It made him feel useful. Until he saw the salt-coated space blanket he had spread over her and suddenly remembered that Will had told him that the foil space blanket provided a strong radar signature—the perfect thing for a sailor lost in a life raft, the worst possible cover for one trying to flee. He pulled it off gently, folded it into a tight wad, and threw it below.

Shannon opened her eyes. She smiled at him, blinked in surprise at the sky, and sat up. Birds were wheeling and darting at the water. The sky was so clear that stars were still visible behind the boat. Foaming crests were tinged red by the dawn. "It is so beautiful."

" 'Red sky at morning, sailors take warning.' "

"It's still beautiful."

BOOK V

The
Ice Field

39

WE'RE GOING TO go south," he said.

"What's south?"

"The Falkland Islands."

"How far?"

"Eight hundred miles."

"Could we talk about this?"

"Well, sure, I mean . . . but what's to talk about?"

Shannon took his hand, opened it up, and traced the lines in his palm. "We've both been operating alone for the last three months. I think we have to sort of reboot—if we're going to be together."

Jim looked around and laughed.

"What's funny?"

"We're in the South Atlantic Ocean, seventy miles off the Argentine coast, heading for the Roaring Forties in a fifty-foot boat. We're about as together as two people can be."

"So there's no 'if'?"

"Wait, wait, wait. I didn't say that. All I'm saying is, if there wasn't an 'if' in the middle of Buenos Aires, why would there be an 'if' out here?"

"Don't take it for granted—that's one of the things that worries me about not being able to walk."

"What do you mean?"

"You think I can't run away."

"Have I once bugged you to marry me since you turned me down?"

"No."

"Have I done anything but be your friend?"

"No."

"Are you happy to see me again?"

"I'm thrilled. I told you. My heart flipped inside out when I saw you."

"So, why would you want to run away?"

"The point is that you think I can't. That allows you to behave as if I won't. Like announcing, 'We're going to go south.' That affects our relationship."

"Shannon, we have a very big decision to make. Could we decide on our course first? Before we discuss the relationship."

"Yes! Of course. It's been on my mind, is all. I've been thinking a lot about us. As I hope you have."

"I have."

"I don't want you to think that I'm the best you can do."

He was about to say that she was the best he *wanted* to do. But her face was closing down, like that of a fighter crouching to cover up, and he could hear his own voice getting louder. He was pushing hard in high "captain" mode—quick and precise, and utterly sure of himself—but demanding more than she was ready to give.

"Maybe," he admitted, "I might have felt that way sometimes in the past. I'm sure I don't now."

"Will you think about it?"

It had occurred to him in the nick of time that this was not an argument to win. "Yes," he said. "I will think about what you said."

Shannon brightened immediately. "So what's the scoop on the Falkland Islands?"

"Number one, being British territory, they're the nearest place the Argentine cops can't touch us.

"Two, the McVay Foundation might not have much clout there, either.

"Three, they're probably expecting us to go north, so they'll string their ships in that direction, figuring we're heading for home, via Rio and the Caribbean.

"Four, the Falklands are relatively close—a week or two with luck—and we need food, water, and fuel.

"Five, they might even let us get on a plane to London. We could fly home in a few days."

"And leave the boat?"

"We'll have to talk about the boat. . . . Six, Will has an old girlfriend there. If we go to her first, maybe she can help us with the officials."

"Why would she?"

"She's in his will."

"But if the McVays knew about Will's doctor, wouldn't they know about his Falkland partner in crime, too?"

"She wasn't that kind of partner. She dumped Will because he was a crook."

Shannon said, "Okay. Six good reasons. Any reasons not to—aside from the fact that the Falkland Islands are in the opposite direction of home?"

"Yes. One big reason. Very heavy seas."

"Too heavy for the boat?"

"The boat can handle it. The question is, can we?"

"You were great yesterday."

"Thanks. We did all right; but like I said, we got some breaks."

"Any more reasons not to?"

"How do you feel about it?"

Shannon stretched her arms and took a long look around. The sun was burnishing *Hustle*'s wet decks red and gold. "How do I feel? After the last two days I am so happy to still be alive. And I am so, so, *so* happy to be with you again. Right now, if you said, Let's sail to the North Pole, I'd say, Why not? How about you?"

"I'll be even happier when we're home safe."

"Grouch."

"Falklands?"

"Falklands."

"Okay, we're going to hang a ninety-degree right. We've

got the wind behind us, so we're going to let that mainsheet out and the jib sheet."

"Hey, I just realized, you changed the sails while I was sleeping."

"Shook a reef out of the main, doused the storm sail, and set a jib."

"Well, don't we sound nautical."

"Ready? . . . Here we go."

He eased the jib sheet and helped Shannon with the main, then turned the wheel until the compass needle pointed 190 degrees—just west of due south.

"The *Sailing Directions* recommend hugging the coast to avoid the current, but I'd rather fight the current than any ships they've got covering that angle—I'll show you on the chart. We'll figure out an exact course on the GPS, but one-ninety will do for now."

"I'm starving again."

"Let me have a look at the engine first."

"Bring me a morsel."

"Don't you feel at all seasick?"

"Not at all. Are you?"

"Just a little. I'm getting over it. It's just from being on land. I'll bring you a morsel."

He sounded the diesel tank with a stick Will kept for that purpose. "Yeah, we've still got some." He found the Cummins handbook on the wide shelf filled with the operating manuals and read up on the engine, starting with the troubleshooting chapter. Clogged fuel filters were a common cause of breakdown, the manual warned—as had Will—particularly if the tanks had been allowed to get too low at the same time that the boat was tossed around in heavy seas. Right on both counts.

The engine crouched in a mystery space behind the companionway. Will had shown him how to change the oil, so he at least knew how to get the cover off, where the tools were kept, and how to arrange the work lights that turned the tight space into a functional, if airless, repair shop. It stank of fuel and burnt oil and paint. He lay down, reached into the sloshing bilge, and with the help of the manual located the fuel filters, removed them, found them clogged with gunk, washed them in a can of diesel, and reinstalled them.

"You look green," said Shannon, when he hurried up to try to start the engine. "Are you seasick?"

"I just need some air."

"What happened to your hand?"

"Cut it." He breathed a few mouthfuls of clean air and hit the starter. The engine ground over, fired, and settled into its patient rumble.

"Hey, Mr. Goodwrench."

"We'll charge the batteries and there'll be some hot water if you want a shower."

"I would kill for clean hair."

Jim was studying a sobering weather fax at the nav station, when Shannon emerged from her shower in the forward head. She wore a towel like a turban on her head and a thick terry robe she had found in Will's hanging locker. He put down the weather report. "For three months," he said, "I missed the sound of women's voices. And the smell of a woman in the shower."

Shannon reached for the heavy-weather teak handholds that lined the cabin ceiling. Strong arms rippling, she moved toward him by swinging herself from handhold to handhold. "Look at me! I'm flying."

She made it look effortless, but traversing the twenty feet from the head to the nav station left her flushed and gasping for breath. "Whew. Beats crutches. What's that? Oh, the weather fax . . . oooh, those are depressions, aren't they?"

"Moving right across our path."

"From what I've read about the Roaring Forties, that's not a surprise. How much time before they hit us?"

"Tonight, tomorrow morning."

"Then we've got time."

"For what?"

"Why don't you take a shower? I'll meet you in bed."

*   *   *

Wrapped in a towel after his shower, Jim went shivering up on deck to check the sea. The horizons were clear of ships, the red-sky threat postponed, though the wind was getting colder and stirring spray from the tops of the waves. He took a third reef in the main just to be on the safe side and looked once more for ships. All alone. Still, he switched on the radar and set the collision alarm before he joined Shannon in the aft cabin.

Shannon was sitting up in the bed, still in her robe, her legs under the blanket. "It's been so long I feel like it's our first date."

"You wouldn't sleep with me on our first date."

"I would have if my parents hadn't been in the next room. I knew the second I saw you that things would get noisy."

Jim sat on the edge of the bed. She ran her hand across his chest. "God, you've really gotten thin."

"Don't look. I'm having trouble facing the mirror."

"No, I like it. It's just a different you. Not so bulked up . . . What about me? How do I look?"

"Delicious."

"You're probably so horny after three months you'd say a whale looked delicious."

"You look absolutely delicious. Your arms are prettier than ever."

"Amazon arms."

As her main power for moving around, they were beautifully sculpted. "Shapely, pretty Amazon arms," he said.

"That's all you notice?"

"I can't see a thing under that robe you're clutching like chain mail. But from the blouse you were wearing to entertain your Argentines, I gather you've been working on your pecs."

"Well, they're better than my legs."

"As your physical therapist, I'm better qualified to make that judgment. Please let me open your chain mail."

"No." She pushed his hand away.

"Have you been doing your exercises?"

"Yes."

"Prove it."

She looked away. They were joking and not joking. Jim wondered—as he had so often—whether their dance with reality would be even harder if he had known Shannon before the accident.

But he hadn't. The Shannon he knew first was the bedbound, weeping Shannon. He leaned close and brushed her ear with his lips and kissed her neck. "Come on," he whispered. "It's me."

Her parents had hired the hottest surgeons that money could buy. As they cobbled smashed bone back together, repeatedly inserting and removing pins and drains, they had left a lacework of scalpel tracks from Shannon's pelvis to her knees. But most of her scars were as thin as the fathom lines on the South Atlantic chart, most of the punctures shallower than raindrops.

"I swear they're fading."

"Am I too skinny?"

"No." Shannon's legs were undoubtedly much thinner than when she had skied, but they had not atrophied as they would have if she were paralyzed. She had lost less definition than a more heavily muscled man would have.

"Too fat?"

"No." Exercise and massages helped maintain a semblance of muscle tone.

"I'm getting either fat in the butt or skinny—I don't know which is worse."

"Skinny would be worse," said Jim.

"I guess I'm getting fat."

"Round," said Jim. "Pleasingly round."

" 'Pleasingly round'? That sounds as sexy as 'pleasingly plump.' "

"Sexily round. Beautifully round. Grabbably round."

Their dance continued. She pushed his hand away. "You're lying to make me happy."

"You make *me* happy. I have no reason to lie. And I am now going to grab you to make me even happier."

Shannon pushed him away again, but she was laughing. "Tell me about the women you met in Africa—other than the one Will shot."

"I wrote you. It was monk time. Just shut it down. It made things easier not to even think about it."

"That's fine at sea, alone with Will. What did you think when you saw his girlfriend?"

Jim smiled. "I thought, 'Shannon, Shannon, Shannon, I love Shannon, I don't even notice this African lady who happens to be built like a *Baywatch* babe on steroids and falling out of this tight white dress.'"

"You didn't notice her."

"Will, the bastard, says, 'Check out her sister.'"

"Did you?"

"No! I shut it down so tight I'm afraid I've lost all feeling forever."

"Then what is that thing bulging under your towel?"

"My bosun's knife."

"May I see it?"

"I only take it out on deck."

"Come here, let me hold you. . . . I loved your letters. At first I didn't—I mean, you said nothing: 'the wind blows, the water is blue,' thanks a lot. But then you told me stuff you were thinking and feeling and I really felt another kind of closeness to you. Do you know what I mean?"

"Shark attack."

"That was obviously hard to write. You didn't say much. It was all between the lines. But you're a guy, you can't help it. Macho—Mr. Muscles. I was really flattered and glad that you tried. You were talking to me, at last."

"I worried I was bitching and moaning too much. And I gotta tell you, it's hard to open up to somebody who's said, 'No thanks.' I didn't want to be a pest. And I didn't want to sound more miserable than I was or more pissed off."

"You told me what you were feeling. Like when you wrote about those poor people in the gas explosion. And how you felt when Will was sick . . . It was almost like meeting somebody new." She laughed. "It makes me feel kind of funny being in bed with you. Like there are two of you, the Jim I used to be with and my new e-mail Jim. Am I going to be cheating on my e-mail Jim when I sleep with the old you—what? Or am I going to be cheating on the old you when I sleep with my e-mail Jim—why are you laughing?"

"I'm not laughing. But, if you've ever had a threesome fantasy, now's your chance."

40

MIND THE CABLE, Senator."

Lloyd McVay led their visitor past an armed guard into a hastily assembled satellite receiver room in the cellar of the former brood barn. Technicians in gray jumpsuits were snaking fiber-optic cables from the rough-hewn ceiling beams. Cooling fans hummed, keyboards chattered, light danced on flat-panel displays.

"I call this our war room—betraying my years. Val calls it our CPU, asserting hers."

Val ignored his conspiratorial smile. Of all the moronic moments to waste time and energy showing off. . . . She was tired, her face as pale as snow, after the fourteen-hour flight home from Buenos Aires—most of it spent on the sat phone with the engineers setting up the receiver room.

"This is the nerve center for an experiment the foundation is underwriting. It amalgamates developments being worked on by a number of our grantees."

The inside guard shut the steel door firmly behind them.

"The exercise this morning is to monitor shipping in the sea-lanes between Antarctica, Africa's Cape of Good Hope, Australia's Cape Leeuwin, and South America's Cape Horn.

The object is to locate and track objects as small as a sail-boat."

"All these wires," remarked the senator. "It looks like campaign headquarters on election night."

McVay smiled down at the senator from his great height. "Smoke defiled the Industrial Revolution; cable defaces ours. At your last fund-raiser you cited Heber's hymn to emphasize your commitment to the environment,

> *"Though every prospect pleases,*
> *And only man is vile."*

"You gave me that quote, Lloyd."

"It was on the tip of your tongue," McVay replied with wholly false modesty. "I merely reminded you."

As chairman of the subcommittee that fine-tuned tax codes for nonprofit foundations, Senator Jeff Weiner was a treasured guest at McVay headquarters. Lloyd McVay was conducting the expected prelunch tour. He pointed out the jumbo Sarnoffs that were surrounded by a dozen smaller flat-screen monitors. Spiderwebs of cable connected them to a gang of Hyper-McVay workstations, which were linked by the fiber optics to tracking antennae on the roof.

"The satellites transmit visual, heat, and radar images. In the event of conflict, the system would pinpoint up-to-the-minute targets of opportunity." He shined his laser pointer at a Sarnoff. "Such as—"

Val pressed the remote control.

Up popped a chart of the Southern Ocean—the vast sea that circled the bottom of the planet between Antarctica and the southern tips of the continents.

Lloyd McVay indicated the widely scattered ship icons on the Sarnoff screen. "Such as these freighters that the system is tracking from the infrared signatures generated by their smokestacks and the radar images of wave patterns generated by propeller wash."

He's putting on a show for his own amusement, Val thought grimly, displaying our power for the hell of it. Missing the point, not concentrating on the goal. Blitzing Senator Weiner with minutiae. Just like Will Spark razzle-dazzled us. Her goal list was down to one item, repeated hourly: locate.

"We are sifting data streams of visible and infrared images compiled from extremely sensitive electro-optical high-resolution sensors and radar-imaging systems, aboard both low-earth-orbit and geosynchronous platforms."

" 'Platforms' sounds cosmic, Lloyd, but I can't help wondering why the Foundation for Humane Science is tapping data streams from spy satellites."

Lloyd glanced at Val. The senator was no fool, but, like other savvy politicians of their acquaintance, not half as clever as he thought he was. There were times, however, like this one, when her father wasn't that bright either.

"Some are Global Awareness specific," he told Senator Weiner, and Val watched with growing annoyance as her father failed to conceal the slyest of smiles. His red laser dot darted like a smirk from screen to screen. "DMSP, for instance: the Defense Meteorological Satellite Program. MASINT: Measurement and Signature Intelligence. IMINT; Image Intelligence.

"But in actual fact we draw as much or more data from the civilian Comprehensive Earth Monitoring and the Global Emergency Observation and Warning systems. With our defense satellite experience—don't forget, McVay Microwaves developed integrated phased-array antennae decades ago—we actively support these international humanitarian efforts to develop catastrophe prediction and manage disaster relief worldwide."

"Sounds like you're still pretty tight with the Defense Department to tap into—"

"For goodness' sake, Jeff, if the foundation can help buy two days' warning to evacuate ninety million people from low-lying lands threatened by a flood we will consider our job well done. . . . Now, in this exercise we're conducting a sea search for one particular boat. We chose these remote waters because with winter approaching there will be very few sailboats to complicate the experiment."

He pointed at a jumbo screen.

"We are storing the satellite data—downloading new data from every pass—with a view to building a model of the boat's characteristics."

"You think you can identify a fifty-foot yacht from a satellite?"

Lloyd McVay indicated another monitor. "This image is enhanced from an array of electro-optical and SAR radar data we received twelve hours ago. You're a sailor, Jeff. Look familiar?"

The senator frowned at the fuzzy top view of a sailboat. The hull was remarkably broad for its length, particularly from midships aft. "Could be a Vendée Globe racer. But the Globe isn't running right now."

"Good eyes, Senator. It's a French solo sailor attempting an around-the-world record."

"Dangerous time of year down there."

"No one ever said the French sailor wasn't bold."

Val switched it off.

Surprisingly, since she herself had created this system, she felt invaded. For the price he was paying to race there, the lone sailor deserved his privacy. She knew the reality that lay behind the detached and bloodless image: wintry night falling fast in the high latitudes; the ultralight racer bashing the tops of thirty-foot seas; the cold, wet, skipper constantly changing the sails for more speed, then ducking below to husband his strength where the din of the composite flat-bottom hull slamming the water was so loud he needed earplugs.

"Show me another."

Another fuzzy yacht materialized on the screen. This purported to be a top view; two dots were centered on the hull.

"That's a ketch or a schooner."

"Actually, a yawl."

"Come on, Lloyd. How can you be sure it's a yawl?"

"Val can explain. Tell him, Val."

If not quite civil, Val's answer was to the point. "Try to understand, Senator, you are looking at an 'impression' of a yacht 'seen' from various perspectives above the earth—a digital reconstruction of data acquired from numerous satellite passes."

Her father interrupted her with a chuckle: "In this case we also know it's a yawl because we are monitoring its radios."

"You can eavesdrop on them, too?"

Enough, Val decided. She said, "Sonia, can you lead the senator toward a deeper understanding of what we're doing here?"

The foundation's chief applications engineer rose from her workstation with a warm smile. Red piping on her form-fitted gray jumpsuit designated her high rank, and while she was uncommonly attractive, she was also age-appropriate—exhaustive investigation into Weiner's habits having bared no unseemly interest in the young. "Mind the cable, Senator."

Senator Weiner stepped under, careful not to stare at Sonia's breasts while under the patrician gaze of Lloyd McVay and his wintry daughter. In fact, the McVays had turned their attention to the Sarnoff the instant Sonia led him away.

Val clicked her remote and, while the computers churned, she said coldly, "You take more interest in the process than the goal."

"At my age you learn that process is life."

"I intend to reach my goals before I reach your age."

Up floated a computer-generated schematic of *Hustle*'s hull, sails, and rigging. Another click and the image panned from a side view to an overhead perspective, as if a camera were floating. Another altered the silhouette to indicate various sail configurations.

"Where did you get that model?" her father asked.

"Andy Nickels found the boatyard that did Will's refit."

"I wasn't aware that Andy was in Hong Kong."

"I left him in Buenos Aires. He did it by phone and fax."

"Why did you leave Andy in Buenos Aires?"

"I'll tell you in a minute. First, look at this."

She zoomed in on the southwestern quadrant of the South Atlantic Ocean, where a line zigzagged south from the Río de la Plata. Up came a modified cruising hull, rigged in cutter mode with a second headsail on the jackstay.

Lloyd McVay checked that the senator was engrossed in Sonia on the other side of the room and said quietly, "It matches. That's Will Spark."

In answer, Val clicked again. Data appeared in the lower-left corner. *Hustle? POS: 42° 21 S, 61° 17 W. SPEED: 5.4 knots. COURSE: 190.*

"South?" said her father. "He's headed south?"

"Straight at the Falkland Islands."

"But winter is setting in down there."

"He's got six hundred miles still to go, but it could be that he intends to provision in Stanley."

Val imagined the conditions on Will Spark's boat butting into the Falkland Current: a slow passage, but fairly comfortable, still many miles from the brutal Southern Ocean, and with three people to share watches so everyone gets some sleep; Will in the comfortable owner's stateroom aft; the couple bunking in a small forward cabin or crashing singly on the pilot berths, conditions not being that conducive to sex; of course gear would be breaking down after two crossings; and, unless they provisioned in Argentina, they were probably running out of food.

Her father studied the chart. "Why is he so far east? He should hug the coast to avoid the current."

"He's avoiding our ships."

The technician responsible for the military feed hurried to them with a phone. "The Pentagon, Mr. McVay. Some colonel with a poker up"—a flash of genteel fire in Lloyd McVay's eye stopped him cold—"bent out of shape."

Lloyd McVay took the phone. "Yes, Colonel, may I suggest you patch me through to General Huchthausen. . . . I mean right now, Colonel. He's at his farm, we spoke not thirty minutes ago. . . . Peter! . . . Yes, yes, I heard, security. Peter, when you think about it, how am I to stay on top of your problems if the best you can send me are interrupted data streams? . . . Frankly, this has cost us time and money, and if it were up to me, that colonel would retire on half pay to a Florida trailer park . . ."

An MBA hurried up with an open dossier. "Give my regards to Samantha. Still hoping she'll send that book proposal. . . . Not to worry about the 'writing.' We have a man who takes care of that." He passed the phone to the MBA, checked again that Senator Weiner was distracted, and said to Val, "Who do you think is on the boat?"

"What do you mean?"

"Who is on the boat?"

"Will Spark. And I presume that Jim and Shannon joined up with him."

"But you don't know for sure."

"Andy was told that a sailboat outran a fishing boat, which had gone out for the reward."

"So Andy told me on the sat phone. Did they actually *see* the old man?"

"I believe that the fishing boat sank in the *pampero*."

"Andy told me that, too. Though he didn't explain how Spark's sailboat survived."

"It was more up to the job. . . . Dad, I made a command decision—wait, we're about to receive the next live images."

Val began clicking. Nothing changed on the monitors. "Standing by for the new data stream."

Her father crossed his arms and waited. The computer continued mindlessly panning the model, giving the false illusion that old information was new. Images of images, Val reminded herself. She tapped some more. "Clouds. Dammit. We lost half the day's stream except for the radar and it's not enough on its own."

"Twelve hours since anything new?"

Val gestured at the bleak stats on the weather monitor. The low-orbit infrared scanners that measured the temperature of cloud tops showed thickening overcast that stretched from the fortieth parallel south to the Falklands.

Her father said, "Twelve hours. They could have sunk to the bottom of the sea, for goodness' sake. Where are you going?"

"Tierra del Fuego."

"What for?" Her father loped after her, clearly caught off balance, a rare and deeply satisfying sight.

"The Argentine air force has granted permission to land

the Hawker at their Río Grande base. Andy and his men are picking me up in a boat I bought in Buenos Aires."

"Don't be ridiculous."

Val McVay fixed her father with a cold eye and then, in a move more mocking than tender, straightened his bow tie. "What is ridiculous about tracking Will Spark by satellite and recapturing Sentinel with a faster boat?"

"Well, look here, Val. I mean, for goodness' sake, the Tierra del Fuego Río Grande base is a thousand miles from Buenos Aires. You'd best stay here until we positively ID Spark's yacht."

"It's all set up, Dad. Sonia will handle the tech side. All you have to do is relay their position."

"Dammit, it will take Andy a week to sail there."

"I bought a rocket ship. They tied up an hour ago."

41

SLOW BOAT TO China," Jim said to Shannon.

The knot meter read eight, a respectable speed close-hauled in the southwest wind. But the GPS told a different story. Over the bottom, they were barely making five knots against the powerful Falkland Current.

"Peaceful boat to China." Stretched out on the cockpit bench, her head on Jim's lap, Shannon was watching an albatross. Most of those she had seen soared in enormous slow circles around the boat—five or ten minutes to a pass. But this huge bird was floating over the boat on motionless wings, a few feet above the mast. Only its head moved as it occasionally surveyed its domain. Otherwise it held itself so utterly still that it appeared to be suspended from the low, dark nimbostratus clouds that had blown in from the west at noon and now extended from horizon to horizon like a broad-brimmed hat.

Peaceful it was. With Shannon to share watches, Jim had finally caught up with his sleep, napping in Will's hammock by the companionway. The weather fax showed no big depressions for a while. They had crossed the forty-third parallel. And Shannon was taking to the boat like she was born on it, poking into every nook and cranny, reading the manuals, and happily looting Will's winter wardrobe.

"No stars tonight, Captain?"

"Rain. *Mucho* rain." He could see it marching ponderously out of the west. It would reach them around dark, and by the look of the low, uniform cloud, it would probably pour all night. Fine with him. Steady rain beat by a long shot the squalls that had knocked them around the first two days out of Río de la Plata.

"Then let's eat in—Jim, the albatross winked at me."

"He's Argentine. What do you expect?"

"I'm going to name him Carlos. Hey, where are you going?"

"I'm going to get a clean sail and see if we can catch some rainwater."

"I'll get the tools."

With Jim's help she had rigged a line from a clamp on the backstay that she used to swing herself from the back of the cockpit to the companionway. There she fastened the line for when she came up and lowered herself down into the cabin. Handhold to handhold, she flew to the tool chests and fished out some shackles and twine while she caught her breath. She stuffed them in a canvas bag, slung it over her shoulder, paused at the nav station drawer that held wooden hull plugs and various keys, took the key to open the water tank intakes, and got back to the cockpit ahead of Jim.

"At last!"

Alone in the war room, Lloyd McVay exulted out loud.

It had been two days since Will Spark's yacht had disappeared under cloud too thick for the space-borne sensors. Suddenly, the monitors were finally springing to life, suffused with color, as new data streamed in like fresh blood.

"There we are!" He reached for a phone. "Sonia!"

Where the schematic of Will Spark's yacht had been tumbling about the monitor was sudden evidence of a new data stream. *Hustle? POS: 45 ° 18' S, 61 ° 11' W. SPEED: 5.0 knots. COURSE: 191.*

Sonia hurried in, hair askew, rubbing the sleep from her eyes. "What happened?" McVay demanded. "There's still cloud."

Sonia spent a full five minutes studying the displays. Finally, she nodded her head with the satisfaction of an engineer who had added to her knowledge. As one of Val's protégés she projected the same irritatingly cocksure confidence.

"First, Mr. McVay, if you read the data you can see that the cloud has thinned by eighty percent. Second, you see the temperature. Air temperature has been dropping as they sail south. It's getting cold. You see these ships—here, here, here, and here?" Each ship icon she activated with her laser pointer spewed position, speed, course, and identification. A Taiwanese bulk carrier, two British, and a Russian—one of Admiral Rugoff's, a twenty-thousand-ton container ship *WorldSpan Czar Peter.*

"We 'see' them by high-resolution infrared because they are steamships. Their smokestacks expel sufficient heat to penetrate the thinning cloud."

"I know that. But there is no smokestack on a sailboat. Even if they run their engine to charge their batteries and their refrigeration, the engine exhaust sits near the waterline, washed by the seas, thus creating a minor, intermittent heat source. What happened?"

"It's getting cold. I would postulate that they have a heater venting through the top of the boat. As their speed and course and likely position match the boat we've been tracking, it is almost certainly them. They're holding their course for the Falkland Islands."

"Fire?" Lloyd McVay peered intently at the monitor. "We see the heat of their fire?"

"Yes, Mr. McVay. From their heater. Burning diesel or bottled gas. I don't know much about boats."

"One recalls Melville."

"Yes, Mr. McVay."

" 'The try-works.' The whale rendered in *Pequod*'s fiery furnaces!" Lloyd McVay rubbed his hands together:

"The burning ship drove on as if remorselessly commissioned to some vengeful deed."

"Yes, Mr. McVay."

McVay stared her down and said, "The last time one of Val's protégés attempted to patronize me, the woman found it impossible to land another job in our industry."

He went to the privacy of his own office to call Val on the encrypted satellite phone. When she didn't pick up, he left Will Spark's course and position in her voice mail.

"Obviously, they unshipped their heating stove, which burns diesel fuel and vents through a stack in the cabin roof. And just so you know, it appears that Admiral Rugoff has a freighter headed for Stanley Harbor. If you're not quick off the mark, he'll catch Spark first—in which case we will have to pay him an obscene amount of money. So, be 'Winged Mercury,' Val, not 'some tardy cripple,' or Rugoff's fee will be assessed from *your* account."

42

"HELLO, STOVE. GOD bless you," said Shannon, swinging down through the hatch to the bottom step of the companionway, where she sat to remove her dripping foul-weather jacket. "Oh, it's so cozy down here. It is *awful* up there—what's this? Tea with honey! I love you, I love you, I love you."

Shannon had found the owner's manual before they even knew they had a stove. As the wind grew colder they'd gone hunting. They discovered that Will had shipped the chimney and stowed it behind the same mahogany panels he had installed to hide the heating unit when it wasn't needed in the tropics.

She took the mug and drank deep. "It's *gorgeous* up there."

"I thought you said it was awful."

"Well, it's cold and wet, but the rain stopped and it's so beautiful. The waves are like giant whales."

Jim went back up with her. The wind was rising: time for another reef in the main.

"Stars!" A pale sprinkle marked the Southern Cross, the first stars they'd seen in four days. The cloud scrim was finally breaking up. The barometer was rising. The wind was backing a little south of west and picking up, while the current they'd been butting into was definitely easing.

Jim saw eight knots on the knot meter, and the GPS showed they were keeping most of it, traveling over the bottom at nearly seven and a half. At this rate they would clear the last hundred miles by midday tomorrow, and be off Stanley Harbor the following morning.

He was not prepared for Shannon's reaction.

"What's wrong?"

"I don't want it to end."

"Don't you think we should get home safe, as soon as we can?"

"Yeah, but I don't want to."

"Well, we need food and diesel."

"We're okay on water."

With four days of steady downpour to develop rain-catching skills, they had filled *Hustle*'s tanks to the brim, along with dozens of empty plastic bottles.

"We've got two months of emergency rice. And a ton of beans."

"We'll get tired of rice and beans."

"But we won't starve."

"We could freeze if we run out of diesel."

"I sounded the tank while you were sleeping. We've got about five gallons left."

"We won't get very far on five gallons."

"But if we just use the engine to charge the batteries, the heater doesn't burn much. And we don't have to run it all the time. And if we sail somewhere warm, we won't even need that."

"Why don't we wait and see what we find in the Falklands? Maybe we'll find plenty of food and fuel. Then we can talk about maybe sailing home. If you really want to. Or maybe we can just fly home and come back in the future."

"That will never happen. That's the kind of thing people talk about but don't do. Besides, what would we do with the boat? Just leave it?"

"Store her in a yard?"

"That sounds expensive."

"Maybe we could anchor her at Will's friend's place."

"Not to mention ten-thousand-mile airplane tickets back and forth. Money that could go into maintaining her instead of abandoning her."

"You're talking about her like she's your cat."

Shannon turned away and wrapped her arms around herself. "She has a soul. Maybe you don't feel it, but I do."

If Jim had any doubts about the real subject of their talk, he got it later, belowdecks, when he saw Shannon seize the ceiling handholds, swing off the bed, and launch herself smoothly out of the cabin, along the corridor, and up the companionway.

He lay there, reading descriptions of the approach to Stanley Harbor in the *Sailing Directions* and worrying about the inherent fragility of this rich man's toy they were sailing in: all the hundreds of parts that the sea seemed to take pleasure in wearing down. Just this afternoon the little foot pump that supplied seawater to the galley sink had stopped working. Maintaining the boat would be like getting nickel-and-dimed to death trying to keep an old car going—a hundred old cars. . . . What if he replaced the saltwater foot pump with the freshwater foot pump? Or—better yet, much better—installed one of the extra valves in Will's plumbing box to act as a shunt between the two? Then they could use one pump to pump either fresh or salt.

Shannon rapped on the cockpit port. Jim opened it a crack but caught a faceful of spray anyhow. "What's up?"

"The cat would love this, you know."

It was not a moment, he decided, to talk sense. "Maybe Nancy could FedEx her."

Nancy was cat-sitting, but Jim had forgotten that, when determined, Shannon lost all sense of irony. "You're right! FedEx or UPS. I read somewhere that one of them does cats."

"I'm going to close this before the bed gets wet."

While mulling over ways to keep the boat, Jim began to get a bad feeling about sailing into Stanley Harbor. There'd be too many officials in the capital. But what were their options? He went to Will's desk, and opened his old logs for *Runner* and the yacht he had named *Cordelia*. It was ten years since Will had sailed in from Plymouth, England. Would the approach to Cordi's home on West Falkland Island be the same? Kelp beds might have gotten bigger or smaller. On the plus side, the minefields sown during the Falklands War would be cleared by now, or at least marked.

Will had recorded the courses so meticulously you could probably go in at night with the GPS if you absolutely had to. By day, if the weather wasn't too hairy, it was a precise road map off the ocean, into a bay Will had dubbed Cordi's Bay, and "Cordi's Cove" within. Will had noted landmarks— a very tall rock at the entrance, an abandoned jetty half-submerged by breaking seas—even a range mark into the inner anchorage, where he lined up a white house with the peak of a rocky hill behind it.

He found Will's chart. His ten-year-old course was penciled on it. Ten years. Did Cordi even live there anymore? On the other hand, with Will's notes and chart, this would be a lot easier and safer than trying to land anywhere else in the rock-bound islands.

What if they got caught? According to the *Sailing Directions* a military commissioner maintained security in the British Crown Colony, as well as defense, obviously a holdover from the war. On the other hand, the two main islands and hundreds of smaller ones had an eight-hundred-mile coastline and a landmass the size of Connecticut, but fewer than three thousand people farming sheep, processing wool, and fishing for squid. An excellent place to get lost. Who would even notice a single sailboat? He took final heart in a *Sailing Directions* note that the legal system was based on English common law. So getting lined up against a wall to be shot wasn't going to happen.

He brewed some tea and brought it up to Shannon in the cockpit. She greeted him with a big smile. The wind was blowing hard and *Hustle* was starting to labor even with three reefs in the main and the jib rolled into a sliver.

"I've been thinking," he said.

"So have I," she said. "I've been thinking about Stallone. Can you imagine being so completely destroyed and still making a life?"

"Some life. He's living in a garbage dump."

"But he's made a life. Those children—it's awful the way they live, but he's made some kind of a home for them. And given them more of a family than I'll bet any of them ever had. I mean, he could still be festering in some slum hospital. Instead he's a kind of daddy to a whole village."

"Well, 'Daddy' saved our asses. That's for damned sure. Listen, I've been thinking, too."

"What?"

"Umm . . ." He looked around. The light was fading already, though it was only three in the afternoon. "Maybe we better raise the storm sail. Let's head up and crank in the jib."

They reduced sail. Jim clipped on and went forward to raise the storm sail. When he got back to the cockpit, Shannon said, "What?"

"We could have problems in Stanley."

"What kind of problems?"

"Your passport was stamped in Argentina, so I can't say we sailed in from Nigeria or Barbados. Barbados is my last stamp. In. I never even got one going out. So if we try to clear customs we could have paperwork hassles, and they could lead to where-is-Will-Spark hassles."

"They'll figure it out. I mean, you didn't kill him. He died."

"I've got the log and Angela's e-mails and his will. Of course, with Angela dead, her corroboration isn't worth squat. But yeah, they'd figure it out eventually. Problem is, when they do, they might seize the boat."

"Why?"

"I told you. Will said he was wanted for fraud in the UK. The Falklands are part of the UK."

"We didn't think of that."

"I was too worried about the McVays and food and diesel and all."

"So what are you thinking?"

"What if instead of going to Stanley, we just 'popped in' on this Cordi friend of Will's? Show her Will's will—she gets everything but the boat, whatever that is. Maybe she could sell us food and diesel and we could just get the hell out of here and head north. She's way down on the southwest coast of West Falkland Island. Stanley's to hell and gone a hundred miles away on the northeast side of East Falkland."

Night was nearly fifteen hours long this far south. Jim thought that they could mask most of their approach in darkness, timing their arrival so as to navigate the dangerous coastal waters in the light of dawn.

"I've got Will's charts and his sailing notes from his old log. The forecast is heavy cloud and fog. Maybe we could just slip in 'under the radar.' We'd have a short day there, loading up, and slip out just before dark."

"Slip out on the boat?" Shannon asked.

"Well, yeah, that's what I'm saying."

"Stay on the boat?"

"Isn't that what you wanted?"

"I would love that so much."

When the depth finder, which had been registering three and four hundred meters, suddenly clocked in at 180, the shallower water told them they were within sixty miles from the north coast of the Falklands. The first sign of civilization, however, was a surprise. Instead of the low, rocky islands dotted with white sheep and surrounded by fishing boats that they had been expecting, their first sight—while still thirty miles out—was of a multistory oil-drilling platform looming out of the fog.

"Looks like the Niger Delta all over again . . . well, not quite." The wind, the deepening cold, and the drifting fog belied the memory.

When Jim saw that the rig was on a barge, he gave it a wide berth, remembering Will's warning that where there was a tow there were tugboats. He switched on the radar and there they were, two tugs a half mile ahead of the platform barge.

Ten miles on, slow-moving targets began to speckle the radar monitor. They passed close to one, just as darkness was falling, and saw a large deep-sea fishing vessel with a high flaring bow and net-hauling machinery astern. Shannon eyeballed the nets with the night binoculars. "Those aren't fish—oh, squirmy things. Squid! Oh, calamari. Calamari. I would kill for calamari."

Jim had the VHF radio on. But when the squid boat hailed them, he didn't reply, slipping into the fog, hoping that busy fisherman had better things to do than report uncommunicative sailboats to the military commissioner a hundred miles away in Stanley. "It's not like they're still in a shooting war," he called to Shannon, who was below, watching the radar.

"Another big target," she called back. "Not a barge. It's moving too fast. Fifteen miles to the west." Thirty minutes later, she called, "Do you see anything? He's passing behind us. Five miles."

"Too hazy." Jim looked back anyway, piercing the gloom. He had a faint sense of something large and boxy. The binoculars revealed a darker spot that might be a container ship. Then it was gone as the night rolled in in earnest.

The wind, which had been blowing at near thirty knots since morning, increased to forty and settled steady out of the west, piling up an enormous swell. They sailed south across the swell, on a broad reach with the main fully reefed and the storm sail for a jib, and skirted the west coast of West Falkland Island.

Dawn showed them closer to the shore than they had thought. The cool numbers on the GPS that they had followed all night, and the reassuring eighty-meter readings on the depth finder, did not prepare them for the sight of the heavy seas pummeling steep cliffs.

"Are we too close?"

Spray was shooting a hundred feet in the air, and when an errant back draft blew salty clouds of it over the boat, Jim said, "We're not sticking around to find out."

He headed up into the west wind. Close-hauled, shoved by the swells and gripped by currents he hadn't noticed in the dark, *Hustle* seemed caught by the opposing forces. She clawed off and fell back, clawed off again and fell back again. Jim continued hand steering, coaxing the boat. Shannon was trying to match the coast to the chart. "I think we're supposed to be on the other side of that point."

"Goddamned Will was always saying, 'Never get caught on a lee shore. Never get caught on a lee shore.'"

"From what I've read, this is a lee shore."

The point was marked by a stony bluff barely visible a mile ahead. Jim marked its bearing on the compass and watched tensely for an indication of movement either way. "What's that in the water?" asked Shannon. "Oh, it's kelp."

Jim felt a chill. Kelp, warned the *Sailing Directions*, usually marked shallow water. But the depth finder said they were still okay. He tried to steer away from it, fearing the thick leaves of seaweed would slow them down.

"It's floating free," said Shannon. "It's not a bed. It's a piece that broke loose."

The first clue that the boat was making way was the sight of the rocky ridges of a string of hills behind the cliffs. The boat was moving off. Further out they glimpsed brown-green moors.

"What are those white dots?"

"Sheep."

Still close-hauled, holding *Hustle* as near to the wind as she would allow, Jim sailed off for nearly an hour before he felt safe to try to swing around the point. He had just turned back onto the broad reach and was planning the steps he had to take to jibe between the headlands that sheltered Cordi's Bay, when he heard a deep ripping noise approaching from the west.

"Is that thunder?"

"I don't know. It sounds—"

With a sudden shrieking crash, an enormous dark-colored jet fighter plane screamed overhead, skimmed the cliffs, and thundered east. They waited for it to swoop around for a second look. Jim couldn't meet Shannon's eyes. If the military plane spotted them they would have no choice but to radio who they were and try to clear customs.

A minute stretched to two and slowly to three before Jim said, "He must have been doing five hundred miles an hour. Maybe he didn't see us."

The sky was murky and the sea was spattered with white-caps—foaming crests as big as the boat. After five more minutes they decided that the pilot had missed them. "Okay. Is that the point?"

Shannon consulted the GPS and the chart. Jim raked the coast with the binoculars and checked the depth finder. He snapped on his harness, went forward, and readied the anchor. Back in the cockpit, he started the engine. Shannon spread Will's notes on her lap. "Let's do it."

The entrance between the cliffs was a third of a mile wide. All but dead center, however, was blocked by thick kelp beds. They lined up and swung nearly north, the sails banging around in a hard jibe. Jim felt the seas start to shove her off course. Then *Hustle* accelerated. He engaged the propeller for more push and drove a final hard, fast quarter mile down the center of the channel into a bay surrounded by a low, rocky coast.

The swell eased and the wind dropped.

"Straight across on two seventy."

He sheeted in the main and storm sails and powered into the wind, steering for the abandoned jetty Will had noted. They could smell wood smoke, sharp and sweet on the salty breeze.

"There's the tall rock."

"And there's her house."

A single-story whitewashed stone cottage with a slate roof slid into view. Smoke was curling from the chimney. There were long glass structures on either side, greenhouses that flanked the old stone house like gossamer wings. "Will said she's a hydroponic farmer."

When the peak of the rocky hill appeared to be behind the stone house, Jim motored into Cordi's Cove and steered for a sturdy dock that projected from the rocky beach twenty yards into the flat water.

The dock was an unexpected boon and he quickly ducked belowdecks for their mooring lines.

"Someone's coming," said Shannon. She waved.

A white-haired woman was running from the house, pulling on a windbreaker, calling "Billy!"

43

THE OLD WOMAN caught the line Jim tossed and took a wrap around a piling while he backed *Hustle* against the dock and jumped onto it with the stern line.

"Where is Billy Cole?"

"Are you Ms. MacDonald? Cordi MacDonald?" Jim asked.

"Yes."

"I'm sorry. Billy was—injured. . . . He died three weeks ago."

"Oh, my lord."

She looked like she was going to faint. "I think . . . I ought to sit down."

Jim grabbed her arm and seated her on one of the thick piles that held the dock. Shannon dragged herself closer, took Cordi's weathered hand in hers, and gently stroked it. Cordi sat blinking.

"Would you like something?" Shannon asked her. "Can we make you some tea?"

Cordi focused on the young woman gazing up at her. "Oh, my lord. Where are my manners? Come inside. I'll make the tea."

"Are you sure you're all right?"

"Fine, fine, fine. Bit of a shock is all. Comes to all of us someday. . . . It's just when I saw the boat, I thought—do come in. Do you need a hand, young lady?"

"I don't want it."

"It could be worth a lot someday."

"I don't want anything that Billy Cole left because anything he left he likely stole."

Jim said, "Obviously, you knew him better than I did, but I had the impression that this Sentinel was actually legitimate. The patents and royalties could be worth something—though God knows where it is or how it works."

"That's Billy in a nutshell." Cordi folded the will and handed it back to Jim. "It's very good of you to bring this to me. But I don't want it. Thank you very much. Was he in terrible pain?"

"Sometimes. It was hard to tell. He was good at covering."

"A past master."

While making tea and laying out sandwiches in her comfortable kitchen, Cordi kept glancing out the window. "I would get the boat off the dock sooner rather than later. We've got a blow coming in."

"I'm curious," said Jim. "How did you know this was Will's boat? I mean, Billy's."

"He sent me a snap when he bought her in Hong Kong. Told me all about the refit. I think he was angling for an invitation."

"You stayed close?" asked Shannon.

Cordi turned to her with a smile. "I loved him. Loved him with all my heart, loved his enthusiasms, loved his charm. But Billy's greatest enthusiasm was pulling the wool over people's eyes. With all his talents, he would prefer a dishonest penny to an honest pound. That was bad enough. But when he got older, he grew greedy. He wanted too much. And he didn't care how he got it. I loved him. But my charming rogue became a grasping scoundrel, which was not a pretty sight. . . ." She stared out the window for a while. Then she turned to Shannon and addressed her alone, as if only another woman could really understand. "One of the things I've enjoyed about getting 'of an age' was finally knowing when to say no and mean it—excuse me."

A radio was crackling.

She opened a cabinet and donned a headset. "Cordi, here. Who's that? . . . Thank you, Willard. My regards to Jenny . . . Out."

She closed the cabinet and turned to Shannon. "Dear, did you report in to Stanley?"

"No. We sailed right in."

"It seems that British Security has put out an alert about your boat."

Jim stood up. "Why?"

"Apparently an RAF pilot tried to raise you and got no reply."

"We left the radio off."

"Well, you're going to have to do something about it. I know you're not Arg saboteurs. But there are rockets going up all over. The Royal Navy frigate is two hundred fifty miles southeast searching for a French sailor. But the fisheries inspectors will be on the lookout. And the RAF. And anyone with a radio, which is everyone."

Jim and Shannon looked at each other. Jim said, "Maybe we should report in. Take our chances."

Shannon shook her head and explained to Cordi, "Billy got into some kind of trouble in England. We're afraid that even though he left the boat to Jim, the UK authorities might seize it."

Cordi said, "I cannot tell you the memories you're dredging up. It's like he never died."

"Could you ask someone in Stanley if there are any Taiwanese or Russian ships in the harbor?"

"Whatever for?"

"Will—Billy—had some dealings and they are—"

"Say no more. I can imagine any number of Billy scenarios provoking hordes of Chinese and Russians."

Cordi radioed her friend Dora. She switched on the speakers so Jim and Shannon could listen in. Dora reported that a Russian WorldSpan line container ship called *Czar Peter* had anchored south of Navy Point. But it had steamed away three hours ago.

"They just don't give up," said Jim.

"They're leaving," said Shannon.

Cordi's friend said, "But if it's Russians you're wanting, the paper says there are *nine* Russian squid boats fishing Falkland waters at the moment—ruddy great factory ships—and we wonder why the squid stocks are plummeting?"

"They're certainly not going to chase us dragging nets," Shannon said to Jim.

Dora said, "A *humongous* racing yacht put in this morning. I can see it from here. Ruddy great thing. Black as the devil's frown. It's a catamaran, Cordi. It looks like two Viking ships in close formation come to pillage us."

"Racing yachts we don't have to worry about." Jim looked at Shannon. "What do you say?"

"Odd time of year to race," said Cordi.

Dora agreed. "That lunatic Frog is bad enough—one expects no less of the French—but Americans, racing in the winter! With a woman no less! It's our lads who'll have to go out when they get in trouble."

"Dora, do you see any Taiwanese ships in the harbor?"

"In my opinion it is absolutely irresponsible to sail the Southern Ocean in the winter. How many Falklanders will risk their lives to . . ."

Cordi rolled her eyes at Jim and Shannon and, with the microphone off, said, "Dora loves a righteous stance."

Jim asked, "Did she say Americans?"

Dora's voice was still rising. "It's not as if they're honest workingmen—bunch of toffs with too much brass."

"What's the boat called?" asked Jim.

"Does it have a name, Dora?"

"JoyStick," came the reply. "Rather a rude name, but what do you expect?"

Jim shrugged. What name was he expecting? McVay Foundation Chase Boat? Didn't hurt to ask. Whatever, it was on the other side of the islands, a hundred miles away.

"What do you say?" Shannon said. "Let's just go—Cordi, could we possibly buy some food from you?"

Cordi laughed. "I'm a farmer. And no farmer ever turned down cash. I've got tatties, leeks, onions, turnips, yams, and Brussels sprouts from my garden—all of which should keep well on the boat. Hold on!—Dora, I *have* to go. I'll call you tonight. . . . My God, that woman never stops. She is a natural-born gossip and has a view of the harbor from her kitchen window. A deadly combination."

"What are tatties?" asked Shannon.

"Potatoes. And I've got lashings of tinned meat and fish—I've just provisioned for the winter. Plenty of tea—no coffee, if that's your cuppa—sugar, more McVities than my ever expanding bottom deserves. Not to worry, I can get more. Oh, and I could probably scare up a sack of rice. And lashings of pasta."

"Is there any place we could buy diesel fuel?"

"Not from me. I'm waiting on the tanker—I'm down to fumes. But I've a fishing friend. You can raft up with him and pump it into your tanks."

"What about the alert? Won't he report us?"

"Shouldn't think so. You don't look like Arg saboteurs. Would you like my spare Calor gas tank? For cooking. I'll take your empty."

They loaded the boat quickly; Jim wheelbarrowed bags and boxes of food from Cordi's pantry to the dock, and Shannon stowed it below. Cordi sailed out into the bay with them to rendezvous with her friend's boat. "I'll wager Billy told you I get seasick."

"That's right."

"He was terrified I would demand to run off sailing with him. Insisted I'd be seasick. Refused to take me even for a day sail. He had me half believing it. What a splendid boat this is! *Hustle?* You really must change the name—except I imagine that's bad luck."

Cordi's friend Peter Reid met them in the sheltered water just inside the kelp-guarded mouth of the bay. The young fisherman had a hand-cranked pump. Jim took turns with him, transferring seventy gallons from the big fishing boat into *Hustle*'s tanks.

Shannon called from below, where she was showing Cordi around, "We'll think of you warmly, Peter, every time we light the heater."

Peter, like Cordi, agreed to payment in half-ounce gold Krugerrands. And like Cordi, he kept a wary eye on the sky. "We've got a blow coming. Best clear off," he told Jim quietly, making sure "the ladies" didn't hear. "Get far offshore. Immediately."

"I want to head north."

"Not on your life. You'll end up on the rocks."

"I came down the coast last night."

Peter paused in his pumping to say, dryly, "I wouldn't press my luck twice."

"You really don't think there's time to sail north?"

The young Falklander spoke kindly, but firmly, as if to a child wandering in traffic. "If it were me, I would sail south for deep water—past the two-hundred-meter line—then run east before the wind. Only don't go too far south or you'll find yourself on the bloody Burdwood Bank."

The Burdwood Bank was marked clearly on the chart, a two-hundred-mile-long, sixty-mile-wide patch less than a hundred meters deep. It didn't take an old salt or an islander to picture the effect of storm-driven Cape Horn seas rolling over its shallow waters. But Peter cautioned anyway, "It will not be pretty."

Jim had never seen anything like the seas piled up by the low-pressure systems sweeping in from Cape Horn. The first, which struck with darkness falling when they were only ten miles south of West Falkland, had been a wake-up call, a blunt warning of what to expect from the west. But round two, roaring in less than six hours later in the dark of the night, convinced him that in the nearly four months and six thousand miles he had sailed since he first joined *Hustle* off Barbados, sailing to Africa and back across to South America, he had never really seen the sea at work.

They had just crossed the two-hundred-meter line into deep water. *Hustle,* reaching with only her storm sail set, was making three and four knots. In another hour, when they were well clear of the Falklands' shelf, Jim planned to run east. But the second storm obliterated the luxury of choosing when to alter course. The boat was going east whether he liked it or not, steamrollered sideways by the waves or running with them, take his pick. Then something started banging up at the bow, shaking the hull, and he made the mistake of switching on the work lights to see what was wrong.

Hustle was at that instant perched on the crest of a wave and the powerful work lights gave Jim a frightening view of swiftly moving mountains of white water. They couldn't be taller than the mast, he told himself, but they looked as if they were. Taller than the boat, and moving twice as fast.

The crest whipped out from under *Hustle* and as it raced ahead, the sloop descended into a deep trough. It was a long ride down, but suddenly they were at the bottom of the pit, rolling wildly. The down-pointing work lights shot nearly horizontal for an instant and in their shuddering beams Jim glimpsed the next wave. If he allowed himself to watch it come, he would freeze.

He clipped his harness to the jackline and sprinted forward, hunting for the cause of the banging. The whisker pole, the light aluminum spar Will had last used to pole out a headsail when they were cruising downwind in the trades, had broken loose from its deck mounts. Held at one end by a safety tether, it had fallen over and was being dragged alongside the hull. Jim reached for it, hauled it aboard, and was just finishing tying it down then he sensed an ominous rush.

The wave had caught up. A white slab of water was erupting behind the boat, taller than a truck. He threw his arms around the mast, held on with all his strength, and prayed the wave wouldn't tear him loose and rip him into the sea. But *Hustle* climbed it. She attained the crest, surfed ahead for an exhilarating rush, then started sliding down the back as the wave raced on.

He saw that there was order out here when the wind was steady and the water deep; the seas were advancing as implacably as an army marched, but they marched in harmony, and he could deal with a predictable pattern. So too, he discovered, could the auto-helm.

Will had shown him a trick while they were running in big trade-wind seas off Ascension Island that were nowhere the size of these, but the principle might hold. He set the auto-helm to take the waves at a slight angle to the stern. The big rollers overtook the boat, gave her a boost, and raced on. Assured that *Hustle*, briefly unattended, would climb their breasts, surf their tops, and descend their backs, he opened the hatch while crossing quiet water between them and jumped below.

"It is *wild* out there."

Shannon was wedged into the port pilot berth. She waved one of Will's widemouthed plastic thermoses. "Hot canned stew. Not as bad as the label sounds."

Jim looked at the knot meter while he stepped out of his boots. Riding the wave tops, *Hustle* was hitting nine knots. He hung his wet gear by the companionway and crawled in beside her.

Shannon gave him a spoon and unscrewed the lid. "I just checked the GPS. You put us right down the slot between the Falklands and Burdwood Bank."

"Let's hope we can stay in it. Oh, this is delicious. Did you have some?"

"Plenty."

"Wait till you see these seas. You won't believe them."

"What was that banging?"

He told her and finished eating, then slept in her arms for ten minutes. "Okay, I'm outta here."

"Don't forget your harness."

"Yes, Mother."

When he popped his head out of the hatch he caught a faceful of snow. But the boat was on course, surfing along the tops of the waves, falling behind as they sped on, slowing in the troughs where the high seas hampered the wind, rocketing up again, and surfing ahead. He checked that the storm sail was secure and made sure that nothing else had broken loose. Rest when you can, Will had taught him, so he went below.

They ran with the storm the full length of the Falklands' south coast, covering a hundred miles by dawn and forty more by noon. The wind had backed north in the night and driven them much closer to the Burdwood Bank shallows than Jim had intended. The depth finder still read a reassuring thousand meters of deep water under the keel, however, and the wind was veering west again.

But it was veering fitfully, battering them with crosswinds. And it blew harder. *Hustle* responded with surges of ten and twelve knots on the crests. Even deep in the troughs she was sprinting seven and eight. His fear of being blown onto the shallows gave way to the immediate concern of maintaining control.

"We're starting to go too fast."

"She feels funny," Shannon agreed. "Like she's going to suddenly spin out—except everyone I've read warns don't go slow in a following sea."

Another crosswind struck her.

"We're heeling too hard. The rudder's losing its grip." He went out to douse the storm sail, an operation that looked like it would be a real bear because the wind had filled it as tight as sheet metal. There was no way he wanted to turn the boat around to ease the pressure on the sail. By the time he got it down he'd be wallowing helplessly in front of waves that reared as high as the first spreader.

Should he motor around? But *Hustle* was a pig under power. Even Will couldn't make her dance for him with only the engine. Jim looked back, deep down into the next trough, and lost his taste for trying it with the motor.

Should he let the sheets fly and try to muscle the sail down? It wasn't that big, not much bigger than a cloth for a dining room table—but it was built of a heavyweight Dacron/Kevlar mix. Flapping in fifty knots of wind, the loose sail would pack an awful punch.

He had to do something. Quickly. The boat felt as skittish as a rubber dinghy. If she broached—suddenly turned sideways to the rollers—a breaking sea would bury her.

Jim started the engine and watched carefully as they ran along in the trough, rehearsing a safe turn through the peaks and valleys. A shaggy comber overtook them. He had a bad feeling that he was about to make an amateur's fatal error.

Hustle soared up the comber and hovered along its top. Jim looked back at the next trough.

The afternoon light was strong. The sky was blueing through wind-tattered clouds. Piercing the shredded scrim that remained, a thin, wintery sun lit miles and miles of desolation. Somewhere in their wake lay the Falkland Islands. Far to the south was Antarctica. Ahead, where a dimness in the east presaged the end of the short day, the ocean stretched across the planet, empty all the way to South Africa. But as *Hustle* lingered high on the crest of the comber and Jim looked back into seas roaring out of the west, he was amazed to see another boat.

44

JOYSTICK'S STEERING STATIONS were set aft on each hull, behind nacelles that sheltered the knot counters and wind instruments and the hatchways to the narrow spaces below. Val McVay was steering from the port station, constantly moving her head to keep one eye on the following seas, the other on the sixteen-story mast.

She and Greg and Pete and Joe were sharing tricks at the helm, an hour on and three off to keep their concentration. It was focus or die. The sea was an obstacle course of ever-moving hills and valleys. Wind shifts north and back to west were kicking up confusing cross seas. Abysses erupted in jagged peaks. Peaks dissolved suddenly into abysses.

The hydraulic assists required to steer the monster at twenty knots through heavy seas absorbed some of the underwater forces that battered the massive rudders. But even through her gloves Val could feel the helm vibrating like a tuning fork.

Still and all, *JoyStick* felt remarkably stable—an ocean straddler with the light, sure stance of a water spider. Steady, Val McVay corrected herself. The huge twin-hull sailboat felt *steady*—flat-riding and fairly smooth—but it was not *stable,* as several hairy near broaches in the night had demonstrated.

Her sixty-foot beam prevented her from heeling steeply under sail. But she had pitched forward twice since they'd gone screaming out of Tierra del Fuego, simultaneously burying her knife-thin bows under tons of seawater while flinging her rudders uselessly in the air.

So far Val had been able to maneuver out of the nose-dives, despite the long years since she had sailed competitively. Racing cats were much bigger now. *JoyStick*'s 110-foot length made her more seaworthy than the eighty-footers she had raced. But it was only a matter of time before the cat stuffed a bow while one of the guys was at the helm. And with the exception of their team leader, Greg, the former SEALs were good sailors, but they had little experience on cats. So Val had had no choice but to slow the monster down by heading upwind on the crests to take the wind and waves on the diagonal.

Andy Nickels complained about the slower speed. She took him below and showed him the escape hatch.

"What the hell is this?"

"An escape hatch."

"In the bottom of the boat?"

"So you can climb back in when the boat flips upside down."

"How do you right it?"

"With a crane." That shut Andy up for a while.

Val gave her crew high marks for keeping busy. When they weren't sailing the boat, they were fixing something, and when they weren't fixing something, they were cleaning their weapons. In between watches and chores, they slept like wolves digesting their last kill.

This was especially important because they were shorthanded. Ideally she'd race *JoyStick* with a crew of eight or ten. They were five, if she counted Andy, who was no sailor. But Will Spark was shorthanded, too. Nor was this race destined to last long. The satellites were homing in on him. And her boat could sail three times as fast as his.

Andy Nickels had risen somewhat in her estimation, despite his irritating habit of questioning her orders. For one thing, he was toughing out seasickness better than anyone she had ever sailed with. Enduring it was never a case of mind over matter but rather separating mind from matter— mind over discomfort. And he had quickly learned to puke downwind.

"Drink water," she reminded him. "You'll dehydrate."

He plunged below and returned with a bottle, his face green, his eyes like ice. Remote, yet aware—a born leader— the former Ranger kept a close watch on his men but displayed no interest in the boat other than as a means to catching Will Spark.

Whereas Greg was in his element—a born seaman. At daybreak, he had climbed the mast, which was raked like a black-diamond ski slope, and was scoping the sea from the top spreader, 150 feet above the deck.

Greg's "boys," the mountainous Pete and Joe, followed orders to the letter and concentrated on learning their tasks. Out here, success and survival were dependent on an ability to function at a professional level despite the cold and wet, which was precisely what the navy had trained them to do.

They were fearless. Thirty-foot rogue waves were met with grunts of "Whoa" and "Cool!" and the sudden burying of a bow with "Awesome."

Heart-stopping was more accurate, Val thought. *JoyStick* had been designed to withstand the stresses of Southern Ocean racing. But the engineer in her said that *Concorde* had been designed to withstand the stresses of supersonic flight only to crash and burn on a blown tire. *JoyStick*'s Achilles' heel was in her bows—too short and narrow, they lacked buoyancy.

Ten minutes before Val's watch was up, Pete emerged from the starboard nacelle, sixty feet away, and crossed the springy net that connected the hulls, bouncing like a moon-walking astronaut.

"We reduced sail again," she told him. "We'll take in more if she goes any faster. Just keep watching her nose. The cross seas are getting hairy."

She surrendered the wheel in stages, letting him get used

to it, and showed him the course and their position relative to a computer-projected fix on *Hustle*.

From high atop the mast, Greg spoke in Val's radio headset. "Can you bear right five degrees, ma'am? I think I see something."

Jim would never have seen the boat behind them at such a distance if it weren't black—the one color that stood out in the swirls of gray cloud and white water.

It was up on a wave top like his and for a long moment the two craft were the tallest objects on the rolling sea. It was about a dozen crests back—at five hundred feet between the waves, nearly a mile—and it caught the midday light as emphatically as if an uncharted rock had suddenly reared glistening from the depths.

Hustle slipped off the back of the roller and descended to the bottom of the trough, where the entire view was circumscribed by the swells.

"A ruddy great black thing," Cordi's friend had called the racing yacht in Stanley.

It could not possibly be chasing them. It was probably a squid fishing boat. Or a freighter running before the storm, waiting for the wind to subside before swinging north to Stanley. Or a tanker bound east for South Africa.

The next crest lifted *Hustle* until the sea again spread before him. The tall, spiky silhouette looked closer. He tried to count the crests that sprawled between them and found it a task as difficult as counting airliner seat backs to the emergency exit. They bunched in the distance, but it looked like eleven rollers separated the two craft.

When *Hustle* climbed to the top of the next sea, the boat behind had vanished. Deep in a trough, Jim realized, further back, or closer. From the next sea, he saw it again, only ten crests back. The tall, spiky, triangular silhouette it cut from the sky said it was no freighter, no tanker, no fishing vessel. Whatever the fast craft was, it was under sail, flying on the wind.

Jim forgot about dousing the storm sail. This was no time

to slow the boat but to speed her up. He was struggling to raise the main when Shannon came scrambling through the hatch and shut it behind her.

"More sail?"

"Look. Ten crests back. You'll see in a sec."

He raised the mainsail to the third reef. When he looked back across the swirling troughs and cascading swells the sharp point of the other vessel's mast poked the sky. It thrust higher, growing swiftly taller and wider as the black boat vaulted up a crest. Quite suddenly, the black sliver of its sail dominated the horizon.

"Wow. Where did that come from?"

"I don't know. It was just suddenly there."

"Is that the racer Cordi's friend saw?"

"I don't know. Can you count how many crests back he is?"

"Looks like . . . seven, eight . . . nine."

"He's gaining on us."

"What's that yellow thing up on top?"

"I can't tell."

"Some kind of a . . . lump."

"It's not a sail."

"Radar?"

"Too big."

Clipped onto the jackline, Jim worked his way back past the hatch. When the boat was in a trough somewhat out of the worst of the wind, he loosened the mainsheet and the sail filled with a bang. He passed Shannon the binoculars just as a roller caught up and lifted them.

"Jim, it's a person. There's a guy up on top with some kind of telescope."

Jim was busy trying to steer the boat out of a spin that threatened to throw her broadside to the sea. When he got her under control he sneaked a quick look over his shoulder, hardly believing that any man could be high up in the rigging in this wind. Virtually on top of the rig, his head nearly at mast height.

Shannon said, "It's too big of a coincidence. He's got to be looking for us."

* * *

"They're raising another sail," Greg reported from the mast-head.

JoyStick sprang to the top of a crest. The sea spread before Val, a vast gray corduroy of evenly spaced rollers. The sun pierced the thinning cloud, sharpening the scene as if an invisible hand had adjusted the contrast on a monitor. Val swept the water ahead with her binoculars.

Andy Nickels spoke into his radio. Joe, who had come up when Greg first spotted them, moon-walked to the mast with a high-power rifle slung over his back.

"Seven seas ahead," Greg said in her headset.

And there they were, half a mile in front, the white boat wallowing as it slid clumsily down the backside of an advancing sea.

Will was flying a storm jib on the inner stay. Val watched with some alarm as the main rose jerkily up the mast, from a triple-reef position to a double—far more sail than conditions warranted.

She said to Andy Nickels, "Better get somebody into a wet suit."

"What for?"

"They're carrying too much sail. If they broach—"

"The wind isn't that bad."

"It doesn't *feel* that bad. But we're on a hundred-and-ten-foot catamaran doing twenty knots: believe me, the apparent wind is nowhere near equal the real wind. They are on a fifty-foot monohull. If they broach or suffer a knockdown we've got to pull Will Spark out of the water."

Pete's barely perceptible nod confirmed the accuracy of Val's statement. But still Andy argued. "The water's forty degrees. He'll freeze to death in three minutes."

"Then prepare *now* to get him out in *two*—he's probably got Sentinel on his person. But if he's left the prototype on the boat we've got to find out where before it sinks—Pete, let me have the helm."

Andy said, "Okay. I'll suit up. You need the guys for the

boat. Pete, give me a hand." Pete followed him across the net to help him pull on the neoprene suit.

Val concentrated on keeping the catamaran under control. It had not occurred to her until this moment that she might frighten Will into accidentally sinking himself. What was the expression? "The fog of war." She had just learned that it meant the murk of all the things you forgot to plan for.

Joe was climbing the mast. The SEALs had rehearsed this repeatedly on the way out of Tierra del Fuego. He found his foothold on the first spreader and clipped his tether around the thick carbon-fiber spar. Then he leaned back in his harness like a telephone linesman to establish a steady shooting position.

Now she had two men up the mast, which left only her and Pete and Andy Nickels to drive the boat. With luck the wind would hold steady and nothing would break. But at twenty knots in heavy seas there were dozens of what-ifs waiting to happen and she hated leaving anything to chance. Opting for luck was her father's way, not hers. "Greg," she ordered. "Joe can see them now. I need you on deck."

"Yes, ma'am." And down he plummeted, riding the steep backstay in a fifteen-story free fall, which he controlled with a Rube Goldberg block-and-brake rappelling system he had fashioned during the voyage from Buenos Aires.

"Dead ahead," Joe radioed from the first spreader. "Five hundred yards."

Accustomed to driving a boat where eight knots was fast and ten screaming, Jim was shocked by the black boat's speed. In the time it took to shake out the third reef in the mainsail, it halved the distance between them and was suddenly close—little more than a quarter mile behind.

Startling, too, was its size. The thing was enormous, immensely tall. Its spire of sail and mast scraped the sky like a black steeple. And it looked very wide, wider than *Hustle* was long. Slicing through a crest in a cloud of spray, carving a flat course through the pummeling seas, it moved more like a ship than a sailboat.

Jim looked at his knot meter. Eight knots as a following sea kicked *Hustle* in the stern, ten as she surfed its crest. Then it raced on and she slowed with a sickening lurch, descending out of the wind. Eight knots, seven, six. Five and four across the trough, then a gradual acceleration as the next sea finally picked her up. The wind, fitful in the troughs, blew hard across the crest and she surged ahead.

He saw immediately that the black boat had crossed two troughs. "She's twice as fast," he said to Shannon. Shannon was studying it with the binoculars. "Two hulls. It's that catamaran Cordi's friend saw. No wonder she's fast. . . . There's a guy standing on the first spreader and four in the back. . . . I think the guy on the spreader has a gun—Jim, get down! It's them. He's aiming it."

Pushing off from the cockpit coaming with her arms, she threw herself at Jim. They sprawled to the narrow deck between the benches. A high-power bullet whipped past the mast with a sharp *crack* that made them both flinch.

The wind banged into *Hustle*'s mainsail and an errant cross sea smacked the side of her bow. The combined force overrode the auto-helm, and the boat headed up—turning into the wind—bared her hull to the following sea, and plunged back into the trough.

Jim lunged for the helm. Shannon dragged him back with both arms around his waist. "Keep your head down!"

"We'll broach! I gotta steer."

A second murderous *crack* drove them both to the deck. The sea reared, so high it blocked the light. A wind gust crashed into the mainsail. Knowing what was coming and helpless to stop it, Jim grabbed Shannon and held her tightly as the boat fell on its side.

The icy sea broke over them, flooding the cockpit and smashing them into the safety lines. "Hold on, hold on, she'll come up!" Jim yelled.

Shannon screamed. Jim yelled, "She'll come up. She has to." But the rolling sea filled the mainsail, which was already in the water, and held the boat flat like a pinned wrestler.

* * *

"Tell him to stop shooting," said Val.

Andy Nickels spoke into his radio mike. "Another shot across the bow. Make believers of 'em."

"I said no! You'll panic them. They're overpowered already."

"We'll debate tactics later," Andy said coldly. "Right now, you're on my ground and we're taking them my way."

"Lost 'em," Joe radioed.

"What do you mean, 'lost'?"

"They fell behind a wave. They disappeared. I can't see 'em. They're gone."

"They can't be gone," Andy Nickels yelled in his mike. "They're only two hundred yards ahead. Look for them."

JoyStick chose that moment to rocket to the top of a high crest. At the helm, Val could see for miles. She felt her stomach clench with the unfamiliar circumstance of being taken by surprise. From *JoyStick*'s bows to the dark horizon, the jagged, blistered sea was empty.

45

WE'RE GOING TO die right here and now, thought Jim. The sea must have smashed a hatch and *Hustle* was filling with water. Why else would she lay on her side like this? Thousands of pounds of lead in her keel should have whipped her upright.

Instead, she lay flat, her mast, storm jib, and mainsail submerged. Then, with a loud, wet, whooshing sound audible over the wind and breaking waves, the sails tried to spill their load of water

"Here we go, here we go. Hold on, Shannon."

Jim grabbed the helm as *Hustle* sprang upright. The wind was still screaming over the side. She was still beam to the sea and in danger of broaching again.

"Look!" cried Shannon.

The black boat had passed them. On a track less than a hundred yards away, it was racing east, running with the wind at an incredible speed, leaving them in its wake.

"They couldn't see us when we got knocked down."

"They'll see us now."

And indeed, before the catamaran had raced a half mile, the crew must have spotted them, because she suddenly changed course, turning left, peeling away to the north. A raked mast stepped way back on the hulls made her look all business, like a lion about to sprint.

"Where are they going?"

"It's a catamaran," said Shannon. "They can't sail as close to the wind as we can."

"At that speed they don't have to."

The catamaran was playing chess with the wind. Racing north a couple of miles on a broad port reach, it would spin around and come flying back at them on a broad starboard reach—at twenty or thirty knots, while *Hustle* plodded along at eight.

"What are we going to do?" asked Shannon.

Jim looked around frantically. The knockdown had been a blessing in disguise. But it was the only gift they'd get, and they'd better not waste it. Always see what's going on before you make a move, Will had said. Know the score.

The seas were rolling from the west. The wind had shifted again, angling to the south, and was booming out of the southwest. Whatever refuge the Falkland Islands might offer was far too many miles to the west-northwest. The only good news he could see was night moving in from the east. And the only direction in which he could go that the catamaran couldn't sail directly was south. But the Burdwood Bank lay south.

Jim watched the black boat charging along a trough, skimming the edge of a roller. She was going to whip around any minute. But suddenly she fell further off and raced downwind. "Where's he going now?"

Shannon had it in the binoculars. "They have a problem. I saw the left-hand bow go underwater—oh, wow, look! They're spinning out!" At their distance it was hard to tell precisely what had happened, but something had caused the big catamaran to suddenly wheel around and head upwind and stop. Its huge sail shimmered wildly.

Shannon said, "I read that sometimes they nose-dive into a surprise wave. Jim, what can we do?"

The catamaran recovered quickly, filling her sails. The mast was unbelievably tall. Judging by the gunman astride the first spreader Jim guessed two hundred feet. Any second now it was going to turn and come after them. He looked east at the night, their only friend.

"They're turning," said Shannon.

Jim started the engine.

The black boat grew large in the northwest. "He's doing forty knots."

But running at an angle across the seas was making the catamaran roll violently as the crests lifted first the starboard hull, then dropped it, while simultaneously thrusting up against the port hull. Now it was less shiplike than sailboat-like, heeling sharply, spilling the wind as the huge mast whipped across a broad arc.

"How many crew?" he asked Shannon.

"I see five."

"They must have their hands full."

When it was a mile behind and closing fast, Shannon said, "He's not aiming the gun yet."

"Get down." He dragged her off the bench onto the floor of the cockpit. Scalp prickling, Jim poked his head up to judge the distance. "Okay, get ready. We're going to do a one-eighty to starboard." He reached up to the engine controls without exposing his head, engaged the propeller, and shoved the throttle to full power.

Hustle was already surfing a crest at ten knots, so the prop cavitated, spinning uselessly in a pocket of air. When Jim looked up again, the black boat was only two hundred yards behind, its bows rising like a pair of knives. He waited until the last second, then hauled himself up on the helm, turning it as he climbed to his feet.

Hustle swung sharply to starboard, right in the path of the black catamaran. He saw immediately that he had cut it too close. The cat was nearer than he had realized, right on top of them.

He thought he heard the man on the mast yell. Jim had misjudged its speed. The twin hulls bracketed the slow-moving sailboat. Jim could see between them—under the massive connecting beam that would shear *Hustle*'s mast like a scythe.

He felt the propeller bite tentatively. The sloop swung

through the wind. The sails shifted from port to starboard and she accelerated across the path of the catamaran, which sheered to port, off the wind. It was so close that as it swung away, the starboard bow brushed *Hustle*'s stern. Jim braced for a hull-splintering crash. But a hull wave shoved them roughly aside as the huge cat roared past.

"Jim, look out!"

A diver in a wet suit, bristling with weapons, strode in long bouncing leaps across the net between the two hulls. Using the springy material like a trampoline, he launched himself over the side and into *Hustle*'s cockpit.

46

A HIGH-TOP ADIDAS came flying at Jim's face. He blocked it with both hands and the diver soared over him, crashed onto the cabin roof, and fell against the sail. His face mask was ripped off in the fall, and Jim saw that it was Andy Nickels, whom they'd last seen in Stallone's *villa miseria*. He jumped to tackle him, but his tether was clipped to a pad eye in the cockpit. That was all the time that Nickels needed to regain his feet and draw a bayonet.

"Where the fuck's the old man?"

"Left!" yelled Jim. Shannon turned the helm hard left. *Hustle* heeled sharply to port into the wind. Nickels kept his balance by grabbing the flapping sail. *Hustle* completed her tack. The wind smacked into the sail and the boom whipped across the cabin and swept Andy Nickels into the sea.

Jim looked again at the east. Was it any darker? The black boat was two miles behind them, circling as they tried to pick up the fallen man.

Shannon had dragged herself onto the cabin roof and forward to the mast, where she leaned, watching with binoculars. "They got him. They're hoisting him up with a halyard.

I hope that bastard freezes to death. Oh, God, here they come again."

"Okay," Jim said. "We're going south, as close to the wind as we can."

"That'll put us on the Burdwood Bank."

"Any second, I'm hoping." The depth finder read eleven hundred meters, but ahead, several miles on the rim of the darkness, he could see wildly broken seas. They were almost on the bank.

"Why?"

"Shallow water. It's too rough for them to make speed. We'll sail as close as we can and keep dodging them till dark. All we have to do is get away from them in the dark. It's a big ocean. By daylight tomorrow we'll be a hundred miles from here. They'll never find us."

Jim had expected sea conditions on the Burdwood Bank similar to the gale-blown Barbados waters his first night aboard *Hustle*. He expected to be bounced around. He even expected to be seasick. But he had not expected that he and Shannon would be thrown around the cabin like Ping-Pong balls. Nor had he expected to hear *Hustle*'s bulkheads resound with loud cracks and her hull groan with every bone-jarring fall from a steep wave. For the first time, he saw water streaming in where the mast pierced the cabin roof and through the frames of the window lights.

Bruised, cold, hungry, and exhausted, he and Shannon struggled to hold the boat close to the wind while driving her across the bank. It was only sixty miles on the chart, but at three knots it was a long, brutal night and an equally grim day. After they had each suffered painful falls, Shannon got the idea to wear their life jackets in the cabin, inflated to cushion their bodies. Neither dared to step on deck without a harness.

As night gathered in the east again, the crashing and banging had still not ceased. They went up on deck together while Jim made the rounds, securing things for the night.

"At least," said Shannon, "we got rid of them. I was so afraid we'd wake up and find them right behind us."

In the last rays of the setting sun Jim could see a black bruise that covered her left cheek where she'd been thrown against a cabinet while trying to open a can of stew.

"There can't be much more of this," he said.

"Is that a promise?"

They huddled below, listening for disaster. A sharp hissing noise drew Jim up on deck, but it was only hail, which left the decks slick and dangerous until the salt spray melted the glaze. Sometime after midnight the water grew deeper, the fierce chop began to level out, and the pounding slowly eased. They slept at last, wedged together in the port-side pilot berth. By dawn, *Hustle* was plowing a somewhat smoother course through a chain of snow squalls, climbing and descending long, deep Southern Ocean swells, propelled by fifteen knots of cold wind.

Between snow squalls, Jim went up on deck to make his rounds. The cockpit was a spiderweb of tangled sheets. He untangled and coiled them. A winch handle had gone overboard. He brought up the spare from below.

Up on the foredeck he discovered that the spinnaker pole, too, had gone by the boards, sometime in the night. The massive spar had been plucked from its cradle like a strand of linguine.

They had no spare. But on the upside, he had no intention of flying a spinnaker in the Southern Ocean. He double-secured the lighter whisker pole and headed back to the cockpit, pausing to remove the canvas cover they had lashed around the stovepipe. Through the vent he smelled coffee brewing and he was heading with a grateful smile to the companionway when he saw silhouetted between two squalls in the east a tall, black spike.

47

WITHOUT PAUSING TO think, Jim did what Will had done when he first spotted the ship off the Saint Paul's Rocks. He leaped to the mast, let fly the halyards, and dropped the mainsail on the cabin and the storm on the fore-deck. Quickly gathering the reefed main before it could fall over the side, he secured it with sail ties, then did the same for the small storm sail.

Shannon opened the hatch. "What is going on?"

"They're back."

"Oh, shit!" She popped up a moment later with the binoculars. Jim started the engine and put the boat back on course, tight into the wind. Did they have an engine on the catamaran? They must. How big? How fast? Who knew?

"Do they see us?" he asked Shannon.

"I can't tell."

Jim turned a desperate circle, looking for some advantage. Back on the Burdwood Bank? No, they'd get beaten to death. Besides, somehow the thing had found them. It must have sailed all the way around the shallows, racing downwind east, then beating into the south wind, and now reaching west, making up time on its better point of sail. How far, how long? How in hell had they found them? Was it just back luck?

"It's closer," said Shannon. "Maybe they see us."

"It's a long way to see a white boat," said Jim. But he couldn't meet Shannon's eyes, knowing they were both thinking about the lookout atop the fifteen-story mast.

The cold wind turned suddenly colder. A sharp gust bit at his face. Another whined through the rigging. Then an icy crosswind pressed hard on the bare mast. The source, they saw, was a new line of snow squalls roaming out of the west. Dark and dense, bunched like a herd of woolly black mastodons, they threatened another round of violent winds and chaotic seas.

He looked at Shannon. She shook her head in resigned disbelief. "Do it," she said.

He altered course, swinging southwest to intercept the darkest snow squall.

Before *Hustle* had closed within a mile, snow was swirling around her. Jim looked back and watched the black spire dissolve into a soft white horizon. By the time it had disappeared from sight, *Hustle* was pitching on short, steep seas. He ran forward on the slippery deck to raise the storm jib to steady her for the coming battle.

A fierce gust nearly blew him off the cabin roof. Crawling on his hands and knees, he felt his way back to the cockpit, where he shut down the engine. Shannon was already at the helm, attempting to steer a safe path through suddenly leaping seas. Jim removed his glove to brush the crust of snow from her eyelashes.

They pounded through the squall for half an hour. When the wind slackened and the snow thinned, they immediately changed course to hide in another. By nightfall they had lost count of how many squalls they had fought. The wind steadied up when the last squall passed and veered hard out of the west. The barometer was dropping. Cape Horn rollers were getting taller. Jim and Shannon shaped a course close-hauled into the west. Then they strapped themselves into the pilot berth, grateful to have escaped the black boat and too tired to care about the weather.

* * *

Jim woke up thirsty, hungry, and tired. Something had jarred him out of sleep. It was dark out, and it sounded like a gale blowing up outside. Then he heard a sharp *thump* against the hull. He pulled on his foul-weather gear and harness and went up on deck.

It was pitch-black. The wind was cold, the seas felt fairly even. Then he heard another thump and saw something gleam dully in the wake. He shined the handheld spotlight on it but couldn't make it out, and then shot the beam around the boat. Chunks of ice were floating in the water.

He played the light on the water ahead of the boat. It reflected off a piece of ice as big as a car. He took the helm and steered around it. For a while he saw nothing, but he was afraid to return to sleep knowing that they might run into another piece.

Thus he was still at the wheel, dozing intermittently, when dawn broke, casting a reluctant gray glow on a sullen sea. He took a long, careful look for more ice, then ducked below to make some coffee.

"You poor thing," said Shannon. "You look exhausted."

"I had to look out for ice. I'll just get some coffee."

"Lie down," she said. "I'll watch for a while."

He collapsed into the pilot berth and closed his eyes. After what could have been hours or only seconds later, Shannon called urgently and he sat up with his heart pounding, trying to figure out where he was. The wind was blowing harder. The boat was flying.

"What? What?"

"They're coming up behind us."

Will's fine sloop could sail closer to the wind. The catamaran angled away to cut them off. They found a cloud bank, which led to a blinding rain squall. Once again, *Hustle* sailed them out of danger. But even though they could maneuver in directions the catamaran couldn't go and found shelter in squalls and fog, the cat had an uncanny, terrifying genius for finding them again.

Night after night, they were sure they had escaped in the desolate waters; morning after morning, the spiky black silhouette cut the horizon. Sometimes it looked like a distant skyscraper, as if a city lay across the water, sometimes like an offshore oil rig, sometimes like a spear.

"We're like a mouse hiding in our little mouse hole of head wind," Jim despaired.

"But how is the cat circling?" asked Shannon. "How can they always know where we are?"

"It's not like when Will threw my monitor overboard. They don't have any tracking device on our boat."

"Radar?"

"According to Will they'd have to have an immensely powerful radar—like on a navy ship. No way they could generate enough electricity on a sailboat. Besides, they never find us at night. It's something else, like satellites. Will said the McVays were big in military electronics."

"So what do we do?"

"I don't know. Try to outsail them."

"But where?"

They pored over the chart. They could go anywhere in the world from the Southern Ocean—Atlantic, Pacific, Indian. If they could survive it. The easier routes were downwind, downwind all the way to Australia.

"We can't go downwind, they'll catch up in a flash."

"The wind is west. The only thing west is Cape Horn."

"If we could somehow get around the Horn, we could sail to Hawaii." They looked at each other, then checked *Ocean Passages* to see how many thousands of miles. Four thousand three hundred to Papeete in the South Pacific and another twenty-five hundred north to Hawaii.

"Seven thousand miles?"

Shannon said, "It's warm in Hawaii."

Too numb to consider long-range consequences, and terrified that when next the black catamaran suddenly appeared, it would pop up too close for them to escape, they decided to cut and run for the Pacific Ocean.

Head winds hurled them back.

Jim searched the sail locker in the wildly bouncing forepeak and came out sick to his stomach, dragging a small, stiff Kevlar jib. It took him two hours to hank it on the forestay and attach the sheets. But it was worth the effort. The hard, flat sail took a better bite of the head wind. With it and the reefed-down main, *Hustle* began inching ahead.

"She's heeling too much," said Jim, but he was too tired to leave the helm.

Shannon heated potato and leek soup. She lost half the mug when a cross sea buried the bow, staggering the boat just as she crawled through the hatch. But even three warm swallows were restorative and Jim went forward, while Shannon steered, to take another reef in the main so *Hustle* would sail faster.

It was a brief victory. Night was closing in again, another respite from the black catamaran, but with the dark the wind blew harder. The seas rose, and the sloop was repeatedly pounded back.

It was three hundred miles to Cape Horn. They made fifty miles in two days. The radio finally dragged in a fresh weather report. The fax page was splattered with low-pressure systems. Northerly winds were predicted to rise to forty knots.

Jim looked at the instruments. The wind had already shifted due north and was blowing forty-five. When the note it hummed in the rigging turned sharper, he checked again. The wind was rising to fifty knots, riling cross seas. And now it seemed that every other wave smashed the sloop back two yards for every yard it gained.

Still they fought the boat west through the dawn and into midday. Jim felt like a robot, a mindless machine that would run as programmed until it broke. But the immensely strong Kevlar jib broke first, ripping the steel ring out of its clew, which probably saved their lives. Because, cold, sleep-deprived, and exhausted, they finally admitted that they could not even reach Cape Horn, much less round it.

They bore off to the northeast. But no sooner had *Hustle* settled onto the marginally easier course than they saw the black steeple spike the horizon.

They retreated in the only direction left to them. South. South again, south into the violent seas of the Drake Passage, south into deepening cold. They stuffed every scrap of warm clothing they could find on the boat under their foul-weather gear, and they were still cold. A mouthful of hot food was a rare luxury, a night's sleep an ancient memory, respite from the ceaseless, violent motion a fantasy.

Val McVay taught the boys to sleep with their feet forward in their bunks. *JoyStick* had been stuffing her bows regularly since they crossed the sixtieth parallel and if they slept head forward they would crack their skulls into the bulkhead when the sudden deaccelerations brought her from twenty knots to a dead stop.

They were driving the cat deep into the Drake Passage, guided—sporadically—by satellite data relayed by Lloyd McVay. Communications were not conducted seamlessly in the high latitudes as they shifted between low-orbit and polar platforms.

JoyStick was pounded by the heavy seas. Gear was breaking down and Val had blown out two sails. Her crew fared better. Despite the misery, none seemed even close to beaten down by the cold and wet and the brutal wind.

Lloyd McVay sat-phoned with an update—yet another course change. He relayed some more grim weather data and had a quotation ready for the sound of the wind battering the phone in her hand.

" 'Such groans of roaring wind and rain, I never remember to have heard.' "

No surprise: he was throwing *Lear* at her. The young "king of years" was proving a wayward daughter. The rudders tugged hard. A deep trough yawned and *JoyStick* was suddenly bent on hurling herself into it.

"I can't talk now, Dad. Talk to Andy." She handed off the phone and gripped the helm.

"Yes, sir, Mr. McVay."

"Dammit, Andy, put my daughter on the phone."

"She's steering, sir."

"You steer, put her on the phone."

"I can't, sir. It's too wild. She's the only one who can drive in this wind. Greg tried earlier. Almost killed us."

"You tell her for me, this is getting out of hand. Go on, tell her right this minute."

Andy held the phone to the wind and said to Val, "You father says to tell you this is getting out of hand."

Val's dark eyes flicked once from the seas. "Deal with it."

Andy said, "Hey, I can't blow him off."

She wrenched the helm to fling the cat through a soft spot in a dangerous crest, then glanced at Greg, who was poised at the mainsheet.

"Can you answer him?" she asked.

Greg saw a fierce challenge in her gaze and maybe an offer, maybe not. Whatever, he was thoroughly convinced that the A team was right here on this rocket ship and that nothing that happened anywhere else mattered at all.

He snatched the phone from Andy Nickels, said, "Val says everything is under control, Mr. McVay," and keyed End.

Andy's expression told Greg that from now on he had better watch his back. But before either man could speak there came a cry from the first spreader high above the deck. Joe was yelling, "I see them! I see them. Two miles off the starboard beam."

The worst possible position. South of the boat. In the eye of the wind.

Val threw the cat to the northeast, intending to race downwind several miles and then come about and attack on a broad reach. The wind had been boxing the compass all day and the seas were confused, so she was busy trying to keep *JoyStick* under control. When she finally got a moment to steal a look, she stared hard.

"Give me the glasses." Bracing the helm with her body, she peered through the binoculars. Then, unable to mask her disappointment, Val steered back onto the course the satellite data suggested.

Andy said, "Hey, where are you going?"

"It's an iceberg."

"It is not."

"It's an iceberg."

"Check it out. It's only a couple of miles."

"Icebergs are brilliant so they seem nearer. It looks like two miles, but it is at least ten miles away."

Greg switched on the radar. "Ten miles, on the nose."

Up on the spreader, Joe focused and refocused his binoculars, still not certain.

The slab-sized tower of ice loomed as tall as a twenty-story hotel. Waves thundered against it, flinging spray on the boat. They were so close they could see rocks embedded in its blue-green side and feel internal explosions as huge chucks of ice broke loose and thumped into the sea.

All the while it was drifting down on them, riding a current that set opposite the wind, and Jim was busy with the throttle and helm, trying to hold *Hustle* off while sticking close enough to hide.

"They're turning east," said Shannon.

"Are you sure?"

Hustle edged around the iceberg, sheltering from view as the black boat faded over the horizon. Like a rodeo clown, Jim thought, keeping the barrel between him and the bull. It was their third close call in three days.

"Every time the sky clears," Shannon said, "can they see us from a satellite?"

There was heavy cloud in the south. Jim headed south.

48

LOW, SLANTED SUNLIGHT lit a rugged mountain range where the wind had scoured the snow from the rock. Icebergs and islands deep in snow marched on the rim of the sea. An undulating field of pack ice was reaching out from the coast, moving with the wind. Had they escaped the black catamaran at last, only to be trapped at the bottom of the world?

Jim looked over his shoulder. *Hustle* was plodding warily under staysail and reefed main somewhere off the Antarctic Peninsula--a finger of the polar continent that pointed across the Drake Passage toward South America.

It was a disorienting, ever-shifting world of float ice, drifting packs, towering bergs and pressure ridges thrust up like Gothic castles. At the moment, the sky was crystal clear, the sea oddly calm. But the wind was rising as it seemed to whenever the Antarctic sky cleared. The barometer was falling. And the weather fax showed a blizzard pounding up from the South Pole.

He didn't believe that they had escaped. In his bones he felt that the McVays were still searching. It was as if he had developed an internal radar that sensed the catamaran. Twice it had saved them, given them a jump on the pursuit. But now, two grim weeks and a thousand miles south of Cordi's snug farmhouse in the Falkland Islands, *Hustle* was running out of ocean.

They had no business being here. *Hustle*'s fiberglass hull was no match for the rock-hard chunks of floating ice. Suddenly they were in the thick of it, the wind-driven ice reaching for the boat like tentacles. Drift pieces as big as Hondas floated low on the surface, forcing him and Shannon to stay up on deck, on constant lookout. They were called growlers—according to Will's "bible" Bowditch, which devoted eight pages to ice in the sea—for the growling noise they made bobbing up and down in the water. Some were transparent, some were green, some as black as the boat chasing them. Bowditch said that you could spot them with radar if the sea was smooth. But Will's warnings about radar were fresh in Jim's mind, and he was afraid the McVays would home in on the signal.

"The sailing couple I read about called ice 'moving rocks,' " said Shannon.

"What couple?"

"I told you. They wrote that wonderful book about how they spent the whole winter in Antarctica on a boat."

"This isn't a book," Jim said more sharply than he had intended. "I mean—this is real. This is happening *now*. To us."

"They were real people," said Shannon.

"The GPS says we're on the west side of the Antarctic Peninsula. I guess that's those mountains. But I've got no chart, so I don't know where the hell we really are. Or where to go next."

He took his eyes from the water for a moment to look at Shannon. Huddled in her windbreaker, with her watch cap pulled down over her brow and Will's scarf over her nose, all she revealed of her face were her eyes. Jim saw them suddenly, unexpectedly, and wholly uncharacteristically fill with tears.

"What's wrong? What did I say?"

"They were real," she sobbed. "And it seemed to me they loved each other."

"I'm sorry. I'm really sorry. I'm just so tired."

"I'm so cold."

"I'm sorry." He put his arm around her and looked over his shoulder again. A gust shook the sails. The wind was swinging due south and it felt suddenly twenty degrees colder.

"I better take another look."

He climbed the mast. Sure enough, the sea was getting smooth. The last time that had happened they found themselves downwind of drifting pack ice, running for their lives before it closed around them. There was a kind of creepy yellow light in the southwestern sky. Just like last time.

"Ice!" he called down to Shannon. "We're outta here!"

Shannon jibed about and headed up the coast.

He started down the mast but paused partway. Something was changing. His tired brain wouldn't compute. He was back in the cockpit with Shannon before he realized that the mountains were disappearing from view. The dark rock looked soft. Snow. The blizzard—screaming in ahead of schedule. How were they supposed to dodge the ice pack, much less floating ice, in blinding snow?

He made a sound in his chest, part despairing grunt, part light-headed laughter. What the hell could happen next?

"What?" asked Shannon.

"Will said to keep running even after Antarctica."

"Where?"

"I don't know. The South Pole. Jesus, what a mess."

"But what did he mean?" Shannon asked. "It doesn't sound like him to just say that."

And suddenly Jim realized why Will wanted him to flee.

"Oh my God. We're running for him."

"What do you mean?"

"Will is using us."

"He's dead."

"But we're not running to save ourselves. He wanted me to keep Sentinel out of Lloyd McVay's hands—"

"That's what he said he wanted."

"No, no, no. He set us up to draw the McVays *away* from Sentinel. It isn't on the boat."

"Of course it isn't. It's in Will's head. At the bottom of the ocean, with the spinning bike."

"It's at the bottom of the ocean, all right. But not in Will's head. Will *said* it was in his head. Or he *hinted* it was in his head and I believed him, I fell for it. . . . The whole story was a setup to draw the McVays away from the real thing all along. He conned them. He conned me. He conned everybody with that tall tale about the microprocessor in his bloodstream. The Nickelses and the McVays fell for it. And I fell for it. Oh my God. I've finally figured him out."

"You're tired, Jim. You're not making sense."

"Yes I am! Will conned me into continuing the wild-goose chase. . . . I've finally figured him out. I finally understand him. Remember what Cordi said? He changed. For the first time, he wanted money too much. He changed."

"She said that Will turned greedy as he got older. 'My charming rogue became a grasping scoundrel. . . . ' "

"He told me that for the first time in his life he had a shot at hitting a home run. That's what he called it. A home run. For the first time Will Spark wanted the prize more than he wanted to play the game."

"What are you saying?"

"Will Spark was so desperate for one last big win—his home run—that he kept the microprocessor for himself. He hoped to escape the McVays and still cash in. But when I spotted their ship at the equator he panicked. So he 'deep-sixed' it along with my heart-rate monitor. Do you know what 'deep-six' means?"

"Throw overboard. So?"

"Just like he deep-sixed the money he hid from the FBI."

"Are you saying Will threw Sentinel overboard in the middle of the ocean?"

"Yes! I was so distracted worrying about my heart-rate monitor, I didn't register at the time that Will threw *two* things overboard. My monitor in a plastic bag and a second item—a waterproof container holding the microprocessor. Something heavy. That's what splashed."

"What splash?"

"I heard a splash. I didn't think about it then, but the plas-

tic bag wouldn't splash. He threw the microprocessor overboard at the same time—I'll show you—take the helm."

Jim dove below and checked Will's entry in *Hustle*'s log
for the day they spotted the ship hunting for them near the
Saint Paul's Rocks and checked the chart. Sure enough, Will
had noted the sighting of the ferry. He had determined their
exact position by GPS.

Jim returned to the cockpit in a daze. Snow was flurrying
around the boat, which was picking up speed as the gusts
grew stronger.

"What?" asked Shannon.

"He meant to go back."

"Where?"

"Back to where he threw it overboard. I just looked at the
chart. All you have to do is punch in the coordinates and follow the GPS back to that spot. Just like when the FBI caught
him. He deep-sixed his money and dove for it when he got
out of jail."

"But the ocean must be miles deep."

"That's what I thought, but it's actually less than a mile
deep where he dropped it. There's a kind of shelf that the
Saint Paul's Rocks are on. His home run is waiting there. I'll
bet you anything that right until the second he died he
thought he would still somehow manage to sail back there."

"And then what? Scuba dive a mile deep? No way, Jim.
Impossible."

"Yeah . . . impossible. No one could scuba dive a mile
deep. So he must have had another plan—some way to make
Sentinel float to the surface."

"How would he activate it?"

Jim looked to the north as if his eye would magically leap
a thousand miles from the square-edged polar ice castles to
the hot pearly sky and undulating contours of the equatorial
ocean. What he saw instead was the black catamaran looming out of the wind-driven snow.

49

IF JIM WERE anywhere else on the planet, he would head south, pinching tight to the wind, and disappear into the snow before the cat maneuvered into a downwind position. But south was the one direction in which he could no longer go, unless he wanted to crash into the ice pack and run ashore over the floes, like a latter-day Eliza, leaping open water and climbing pressure ridges with Shannon in his arms. But "ashore" was no promised land, only a deep freeze where they wouldn't survive a single night.

The huge cat was racing east to west on a broad reach. Zigzagging. He studied it with the binoculars, puzzled. It must be doing thirty knots, he thought, trailing spray and mist as it hurled port and starboard in lightning swift crash turns.

"Ice dead ahead!" Shannon cried.

Jim dodged the submerged floe. "Good eyes." It was smaller than a washing machine and almost transparent. That's why they were zigzagging. They were dodging ice, too. With a man on the mast to spot.

He put the helm hard over.

"Where are you going?" Shannon sounded more resigned than afraid, he thought.

"Either they'll crash into a hunk of ice and sink. Or we'll lose ourselves in the snow."

"They won't sink," she said. "Catamaran hulls are full of watertight compartments."

Crack!

A high-powered slug smacked past the mast.

"Down! Get down!"

Crack! The second shot passed the backstay.

Down he went, flat on his face on the cockpit sole, his ears ringing. He never even heard the third shot, but it passed so close it felt like he had been kicked in the head. Shannon screamed, "Jim," and threw herself over him.

"I'm okay, I'm okay—just knocked me off my feet." He raised his head for a quick look. The cat had come about and was reaching west, clawing closer to the wind to intercept them, while the gunman on its mast was pinning them down so they couldn't sail *Hustle*. Flat on the cockpit sole, he was out of tricks and done running.

Shannon said, "Promise me you won't do anything stupid when they come aboard. There's five of them and one of you."

Jim said, "Can you get below?"

"I'm staying here with you."

"No, listen to me. Will's shotgun is in the aft cabin in one of the bunk drawers. Pass it to me through this port."

Shannon was shaking her head. Jim said, "Will used to say at moments like this, 'When all is lost there's nothing to lose.' I promise I won't do anything stupid."

Shannon dragged herself to the hatch.

"Keep your head down."

She removed the washboards, slid the hatch open, and slithered down the companionway. Jim took another look. The cat was nearer, starkly visible through the snow. He jogged the wheel, altering course again to intercept. Ice banged along the hull. He popped his head up to see if any big pieces were floating in their path.

Crack! This shot skimmed the cabin roof. He threw himself flat, his heart pounding. They were still pinning him down so he couldn't sail the boat. Perfect.

"Jim!" Shannon opened the port in the side of the cockpit and started to pass Will's sawed-off shotgun through it. Jim took the stubby stock.

"Stay away from the barrel."

They worked it through the narrow opening. "Okay, close the hatch."

"Here." Her gloved hand reached through with three cartridges. "Do you know how to use this?"

"I shot clay pigeons in Boy Scouts."

He had to remove a glove to load the weapon. His fingers went stiff in the cold. Ice crunched against the hull.

He took a quick look through the binoculars. The catamaran had closed within two hundred yards. Andy Nickels was braced on the first spreader with a rifle. Another man was on the bow spotting ice. A hundred feet aft, two were manning the sheets for the jib and main, while the fifth worked an enormous stainless-steel helm. They made tempting targets in their yellow foul-weather suits. But the shotgun had a very short range. Besides, he didn't have a prayer of winning a gunfight with heavily armed professionals.

He raised his head for another look, still hoping that the snow would turn so thick that they would lose sight of *Hustle*. It was thicker, but not that thick, and through its swirling scrim he could see the catamaran looming large. A gust hit its sails hard and it surged ahead. The same gust knocked *Hustle* half over. It brought more snow with it but still not enough to hide them.

Jim looked again, concentrating on the foot of the big cat's mast. It was dead ahead and he stared hard, trying to distinguish through the blowing snow on which side of the mast her halyards ran.

"Son of a *bitch*."

The halyards that held up the mainsail and the jib were led down inside of the catamaran's mast and emerged just above a cluster of winches on the port side of the hollow spar. But *Hustle* was angling toward her starboard side. Jim grabbed a spoke and yanked the helm. He had to get across her bows.

An instant after he turned, the cat turned, too, swinging to starboard, sails thundering as she headed up to slip behind the wind so he couldn't escape.

"Thank you," Jim whispered.

But they were so close now that in another second the rifleman on the spreader could look down over *Hustle*'s sail and shoot him where he lay on the floor of the cockpit. It was now or never. Jim rose on one knee and took aim at the halyard winches clustered at the base of *JoyStick*'s mast.

The shotgun's report was a deafening *boom*. The recoil staggered him. Quickly, he jammed another shell into the breech and fired again. But the boats were moving apart and already the catamaran was out of shotgun range.

As the boats moved farther apart, Andy Nickels, who was standing high on *JoyStick*'s first spreader, saw Jim grab the wheel to steer around a bulldozer-size growler. He raised his weapon and took careful aim.

50

ANDY NICKELS BEGAN to squeeze the trigger, intending to take out the shotgun by shattering Jim Leighton's shoulder with a high-powered slug. Stop shotgun, stop resistance, start questions.

Focused intently on what was even for him a difficult shot between two boats in wild motion, he shifted into firing-range mode. Tuning out the distractions of wind, snow, and biting cold, he even ignored the high-pitched shriek of a broken halyard wire flying up its channel inside *JoyStick*'s mast. Only when a shadow passed over his face did animal instinct force him to look up. Like the wing of a giant albatross, fifteen stories of black mainsail tumbled down the mast and enveloped him in thundering, wind-struck folds.

Before the shotgun stopped echoing from the ice-rimmed coast, Val saw chaos erupt: Murphy's Law in spades. Everything that could go wrong went wrong at once. The mainsail fell, billowing like a parachute, blocking her view of the water ahead. A sixty-knot gust filled the jib at the same instant and with no mainsail to balance the foresail, the wind

slewed the cat into a ninety-degree skid and sent it off at
high speed.

She was sailing blind at twenty-five knots when the port
bow struck ice—a low, massively heavy growler. *JoyStick*
bucked. The deck slammed under her feet and Val felt herself go flying. Her braided nylon harness tether jerked her up
short. Something snapped with a loud bang. And suddenly
she saw gray water coming at her face.

Next thing she knew she was under water so cold that the
exposed skin on her face felt like it was burning. Her buoyant dry suit floated her to the surface just as the shallow-
draft *JoyStick* skidded over another growler and flew away.

Val watched in utter disbelief. The huge catamaran careened, as out of control as an unexamined life, and vanished into the blizzard. She was alone, with the snow falling
darkly, the sea growling against the advancing pack ice. Her
mind churned. Observation vied with incredulity, but there
was nothing to prevent it from spiraling into the bleakest despair.

A thunderous wind scythed across the sea. It parted the
snow like a theater curtain and she glimpsed, far away, the
big catamaran still racing for the horizon.

It suddenly reared up on its starboard hull and teetered
there for a long moment, its mast nearly parallel to the water.
Val could not see whether it had struck another growler or
fell prey to a wind gust. But it teetered further, dipped its
mast in the water, and turned upside down.

The snow descended like a dark blanket and she was
alone again, floating up to her chin in five-degree seawater,
fully aware that her HPX Ocean Drysuit would keep her
alive for two hours. Viewed logically, this was not an accept-
able option. She could imagine times in a life when two
hours might be viewed as a great gift. But not two hours of
self-incrimination.

Sentinel was lost. No. *She* had lost Sentinel. How could
she have been so stupid as to go sailing? *She* who knew that
the quintessence of computer science was to dominate
events from the distance. It was unimaginable that she had
succumbed to a romantic hands-on impulse at the precise

moment when her firm hand was required at the foundation. It was unacceptable.

Water transmitted cold thirty times faster than air. She grabbed the zip puller, tore open the front of the suit and stretched the latex neck seal. The wave that poured in was cold enough to stop her heart.

The buoyant suit still trapped enough air to hold her head out of the water. But within moments of embracing the intense cold, she wanted to sleep. She resisted only briefly, then closed her eyes in a dreamy delirium, recognizing the peaceful symptoms of an Antarctic death. Here's a quote for you, Dad: "To sleep, perchance to die."

Asleep, adrift—but her heart kept thudding, pounding her ribs like she had just pedaled a six-minute sprint on the Air-Dyne. An acid thought percolated through her brain: the payoff for her workouts would be a healthy body's longer death.

She willed herself to accept sleep. There was a shrieking in her ears so loud it hurt. She wanted to die in peace. Something was shaking her by the dry suit, something powerful, and she thought of a sea leopard. Shackleton's men had encountered one on the ice—a gigantic, voracious penguin-eating seal too big and arrogant to fear humans. The theory was they thought humans were penguins.

Like a killer whale, it actually lifted her out of the water. Killer whales played with their prey, tossing live seals to each other like lacrosse balls. It was a part of teaching their young to hunt. Val supposed they enjoyed themselves.

Adrift, asleep, her busy mind tucked around some final thoughts, like a cat settling into a corner. Her peace was disturbed by the purposeful click, click, click of a yacht winch. She felt as heavy as a rock. Suddenly there was a hard deck under her and Shannon Riley was shrieking in her ear, "Wake up! Wake up! Wake up!"

A man was shouting, "Let's get her below. I gotta steer. If that pack ice gets around us, we're dead."

Val's last conscious thought was that she hoped the pack ice crushed them, hoped that they were dead. Later, she became aware that she was in shelter, out of the wind and snow. She heard Jim Leighton struggling up on deck. A sail was flogging violently. The bow was plunging. Ice was banging against the hull. Shannon was slapping her face and screaming for her to wake up.

Val said, "Tell him he has to sail faster than the ice. Tell him bare poles won't do. He needs speed and steerage. Tell him to fly a storm sail and a Yankee jib."

Jim was at the helm. But even with the work lights glaring down from the spreaders, Shannon could barely see him through the snow.

"How's your patient?" he yelled over the wind.

"Babbling."

"Can you take the wheel? I want to go down and get the Yankee jib. It'll clear the seas breaking over the bow."

Shannon clipped onto a pad eye and dragged herself upright behind the helm. She took his arm. "Jim, I'm not stupid. If it was one of the men I would have left him in the water. She's just one small woman. We can handle her."

He went below. Shannon had removed the bulky dry suit from the woman they had winched out of the sea and strapped her into the leeward pilot berth. She lay dead to the world, eyes shut, barely breathing. Her skin was paper white. Pale as a vampire, in Will's words.

He went up into the forepeak and found the high-cut Yankee jib. *Hustle* slammed into a piece of ice. It sounded like an explosion in the cramped space. The fiberglass bulged inward. He held his breath, expecting seawater to follow. The dent was a foot wide, but the hull held.

For the moment.

He dragged the sail through the cabin. The woman opened her eyes and tried to sit up. "Where is Will Spark?" she whispered.

"Dead."

"He can't be."

"He died last month in the South Atlantic."

"That's not possible. Why didn't you—"

"Tell your killers in Buenos Aires? We hoped that your killers would chase Will and leave us alone."

"Where is Sentinel?"

She had huge dark eyes, but they weren't focusing. Jim looked deep into them and said, "Sentinel is where it always was: in Will Spark's head."

Her eyes flickered toward the dry suit heaped on the cabin floor.

Jim hauled the Yankee jib up to the cockpit.

"You know who we rescued? That's Val McVay."

"You're kidding—what's that?"

"It's her gun. I found it in her dry suit." Jim showed Shannon the compact pistol and tossed it over the side. "We caught ourselves a shark."

As he hanked the Yankee jib onto the forestay, he could hear the ice pack closing in. Grinding ice and surging water made a sound deeper than the wind as the pack undulated on the steepening swell.

Back in the cockpit, he began to despair. The grinding, surging noise was coming from both sides now, a sustained groan that meant the lead they were in was narrowing. Then the full force of the blizzard hit with a scream.

Hustle leaped ahead as if she had been kicked. Jim forced himself to his feet. "We've already got one dent in the bow," he told Shannon. "If we hit anything else at this speed, we're dead. I'll go up on the foredeck and show you where to steer."

The wind was holding the narrow lead open in the ice field. The danger was the massive chunks left floating. He stood in the bow pulpit with a spotlight, his legs braced against the stainless-steel frame, and guided Shannon with arm signals.

Somewhere ahead was the Drake Passage. It had taken them six brutal days to cross the six hundred miles of Southern Ocean that channeled between the Antarctic Peninsula and Cape Horn. He could not conceive of a worse stretch of water in the world. It made the Burdwood Bank a pleasant memory. But right now—if *Hustle* could only reach it—the Drake Passage would resemble heaven.

Jim was so tired he was hallucinating. He saw a human face watching from a growler, which was floating just below the waves. Will Spark smiling up at him. "Wake up, cockpit man. "You're not out of this yet."

Jim rubbed his own face, blinked, slapped his cheeks. Ice, dead ahead, a flat floe twenty feet wide. He signaled frantically for Shannon to steer to port. *Hustle* swung around it. When they were back on course, Jim glanced over his shoulder. Shannon had both hands on the helm and was watching for his next signal. Will Spark stood close beside her.

"She's your home run, Jim," the old man called in his "me-hearties" voice. "A lass for a pirate's wife!"

Jim turned his attention to the dangers ahead. It took him a while to realize that the sky had grown marginally lighter in the northeast. The snow blew harder than ever. But he saw no more floating ice and *Hustle* was battering through a vicious cross sea whipped up by the south-blowing blizzard and a westering swell.

All of which Jim hoped meant that they were nearing the edge of the Drake Passage. Out of one misery and into another. He unclipped from the pulpit and clipped onto the jackline to head back to relieve Shannon at the helm.

He saw two Shannons in the cockpit. Ice crusted his eyelashes. They looked like they were dancing.

He moved closer, feeling his way over the slick deck. God, he was going nuts. Two Shannons, still dancing. Locked in each other's arms, the Shannons lurched out of the cockpit and fell against the safety lines.

"Jim! Help me."

"Jesus."

He scrambled aft, slipping and sliding. Shannon was down on her back. Val McVay was climbing on top of her. Jim grabbed her and tried to pull her off. "Let go, Shannon. I've got her."

"Hold her! She's trying to jump overboard."

"Let me go!" Val shouted. "You have no right to interfere. Let me go!"

"Val!" Shannon screamed. "Tell Jim what you told me."

Val stopped struggling, then turned to Jim and repeated, "You have no right to interfere. I know what I'm doing and why." She looked utterly sure or utterly crazy. He didn't know which, until she exploded into action, fighting to get to the rail.

Shannon said, "Sorry, hon," and belted her in the jaw with all her considerable strength. Val McVay went limp in Jim's arms.

"Help me get her below. I'll tie her up. Can you handle the boat alone?"

"For a while. Get some sleep; I'll need relief. What did she tell you?"

"More babbling. Like she's in school or something. Something about not getting an A-plus. Whatever the heck that's supposed to mean. She's pretty traumatized from all that time in the cold water. . . . I am so tired I'm going to die. I just need to sleep half an hour. Then I'll relieve you."

Three days later, halfway across the Drake Passage, the wind dropped and the sea smoothed and they cooked their first hot meal. Shannon brought Jim's to him in the cockpit.

"Did she eat?"

"I got her to drink some water."

"We have a nut on board."

"No, she'll get better. She's just doing a lot of thinking."

"Did she talk?" For three days the woman had not spoken a word.

"She thanked us for saving her life. . . . *I've* been doing a lot of thinking, too. . . ."

"About what?"

"I have a question. If Will Spark threw Sentinel overboard, why did he insist you put his head in the freezer?"

51

IF WILL KNEW that Sentinel was sitting on the bottom of the ocean waiting to be salvaged, there was no point in putting his head in the freezer. But if you did put his head in the freezer, what's the one thing you would really, really hang on to and protect."

"The freezer!"

"Yes!"

"Why?"

"He must have hidden a device to signal the microprocessor to surface in the freezer."

"See if you can get Val to come here. I'll look for it."

Jim left the ELF underwater radio transmitter hidden where he found it, beside the freezer's compressor. It was bigger than a brick and weighed as much, as it consisted mostly of a powerful battery, which Will had hard-wired through the freezer to keep it charged.

Jim entered into the GPS the exact location from the log where Will threw the heart-rate monitor and the microprocessor overboard. Then he consulted *Ocean Passages* and *Jimmy Cornell* and worked out a course to set *Hustle* to-

...rd that point off Saint Paul's Rocks 3,540 miles to the orth.

They told Val that they were sailing to Florida. The Saint Paul's Rocks were a logical waypoint. Her only comment was that they would arrive in the Caribbean in time for the hurricane season. She made it clear that she couldn't care less if a hurricane blew the boat onto a reef.

Val proved a placid shipmate. She made no attempts to communicate with the outside world. She stood her watches faithfully, and her racing sailor skills paid off in startling boat speeds. While off watch she worked hard, cleaning and maintaining the battered sloop. When the GPS failed, she repaired it with a soldering iron. At the same time, she coached Jim and Shannon on how to use the sextant and the *Nautical Almanac*, remarking that it "boggled the mind" that Jim had sailed so far without learning to navigate without electronics.

Otherwise, she was solitary. Never intrusive, she appeared to have shut down emotionally. She slept long hours in the forward cabin. Her only complaint was the cold, which lasted well north of Buenos Aires; her only request was that they keep the stove burning for warmth.

Shannon, with her gift for taming solitary souls, befriended Val. Jim didn't trust her, though clearly the two women seemed to be becoming shipmates.

"Why don't you ask her how she tracked us for two weeks?"

"I did. They had some kind of high-tech military radar that her company had developed. She said it was so powerful it could pick up our engine when *Hustle* climbed up a wave."

"On a sailboat? Where'd they get the juice for such a unit? Will said they really eat electricity."

Sometime later Shannon reported back that the radar unit had been developed for foot soldiers and consumed very little power.

* * *

"Do you think she's beautiful?" Shannon asked one night when they were alone in the cockpit.

"Not my type."

"I think she's really beautiful."

"I'm a blond hair, blue eyes, bulked-up pecs man myself."

"It is not necessary to say things like that to make me feel secure."

"I'm saying that because I love you and the way you look. . . . Yes, Val is beautiful. In a strange way. Probably interesting as all hell in bed."

"In a strange way?"

They laughed quietly.

Jim said, "If she brings all that intensity into the sack, wow. . . . If I weren't in love with you I might try to hit on her. But I am in love with you, so it's not going to happen."

"She's rich."

"You're rich. Or your father is—though he's probably cut you off by now."

"No *probably* about it. If I'm not home it's going to be out of sight, out of mind. But I was never 'rich' like her. Not even close. We were talking a little. She's unbelievably rich. Power money. It's like they own their own country."

"By my standards, you're both rich." He winked at her. "But you're the best I can do."

"What?"

"You heard me. That thing you said to me off the Río de la Plata? The best I can do? You are the best any man could do."

"You're just saying that because—"

"Because I'm in love with you. You are the absolute best I can do."

"Why?"

"Why?" He took her hands in his. "Shannon, if I could tell you why I love you, it probably wouldn't be love. It would be like a job description."

"You could try."

"Before I met you I don't think being so far away on the boat would have bothered me the way it did. I was never an adventurer—like you—but if I had been far away I wouldn't have cared because I wouldn't have missed anyone. But this was a kind of torture—all I know is I get excited to see you when you come up on watch. I like the world with you in it. Everything is fun—hey, relax, I'm not going to bug you to marry me. The only woman I'll ever marry is going to be a volunteer."

"What if we find Sentinel?"

"I think we should split fifty-fifty. You do what you want. I'll do what I want. Maybe someday we can do it together."

Shannon sat quietly digesting that. Then she gave him a teasing punch on the arm. "Hey, Muscles, what's the first thing you'll buy when you're rich?"

"A refit for poor *Hustle*. Her sails are stretched. Val was showing me where the stays are corroding. And I found three soft spots that the ice bashed in her bow. The hull's delaminating. . . ." He squeezed her knee. "What will you buy first?"

"I don't know. Maybe a new spinnaker pole."

BOOK VI

The
Home Run

52

WITH THE THREE of them sharing watches and Val helping Jim and Shannon hone their skills, *Hustle* made a fast passage to the equator. Despite encountering uncooperative winds in the Variables, the broad belt of light and variable winds that they had to traverse before they picked up the powerful southeast trades, they covered the distance in less than a month—averaging a very respectable 165 miles a day, a little under seven knots.

Jim and Shannon had pushed the boat very hard on their last several watches, their excitement growing as they neared the spot where Will had deep-sixed Sentinel. As it turned out, it was on Jim's watch that they turned *Hustle* into the wind and backed her jib to heave to over the exact spot.

It was nearing noon. The sky was heavy, the water opaque. The heat would have been oppressive were it not for a light breeze and the fact that they still carried an Antarctic chill in their bones. Jim rigged the stainless-steel dive ladder off the stern and was about to lower it into the water when Val came up the companionway.

She was tugging on the long-sleeve shirt she always wore in the sun. Like Jim and Shannon, she was wearing sunglasses and sunblock and had a long-billed crew cap on her head. She glanced at the backed jib. Then she took the binoculars from their rack on the binnacle and focused on the western horizon.

"What do you see?" Jim asked.

Val handed him the binoculars. Jim exchanged a puzzled look with Shannon and raised the glasses. His hands started trembling. There was a hard spot on the horizon and very soon it grew soft, white edges.

"What is it, Jim?" asked Shannon.

"A very fast ship, coming this way."

Shannon's face fell. "Val?"

"What, Shannon?"

"Did you betray us?"

"Only by omission," said Val.

"What omission?"

"I omitted to tell you that I designed a system to track this boat with satellite data. At first I didn't give a damn whether my father continued using it or not, as you well know. But then it became obvious that Will had not taken Sentinel to his watery grave."

"How?"

"Most coincidences can be explained by the data. You two were beelining for the Saint Paul's Rocks like your lives depended on it—very near where Will got away from me last winter."

"Val, we saved your *life*."

"Did you expect me to say, 'Oh, by the way, my father is tracking your course. Be on the lookout if you are attempting to retrieve what was stolen from us'?"

"We saved your life twice," said Jim. "We should have let you drown yourself."

"I thank you for the opportunity to reflect on my future. In return, I promise to continue putting my life to important use."

"But we connected. I thought we were friends."

"Shannon!" Val said sharply. "I'm a hermit. I've always been a hermit. I live in my mind. I don't *mingle*. I don't *connect*. I excel."

Shannon looked as stunned as Jim felt. They had led the

McVays straight to their goal. There was no way their sailboat could outrun the high-speed ship, which was soaring on skirts of spray and approaching so swiftly that it was like watching an airplane land. As its features grew clear Jim realized that it was not a true ship but a seagoing ferry, bigger than the Montevideo ferries he'd seen in the Río de la Plata.

It swooped in a tight bank. The thunder of its engines ceased. The ship came to a stop a hundred yards off and drifted down on *Hustle*. Seamen rigged ladders down the hull. Armed men appeared on the stern deck in diving gear. A steward in kitchen whites struggled through the door with two big buckets.

"Who's the tall guy in the bow tie?" asked Jim.

"That is my father, Lloyd McVay."

Jim focused the glasses on the "poetry-quoting thug" who had hunted him across three oceans. Minus his gunmen, Lloyd McVay looked almost quaint in his bow tie and lightweight suit, like an older Westport gentleman boarding the midmorning train to New York for a set of squash at the club. With his bowed head and rounded back and shoulders, he appeared to apologize for his height. But his was the stance of a stork poised to impale. And the binoculars told Jim that the aloof expression on his face was also a lie. McVay was gripping the railing so hard that his powerful hands were corded with strain.

Jim shifted the glasses and got another shock. "Your Rottweiler Nickels got rescued, too. Something happened to his face."

Jim handed Val the glasses. Shannon, he noticed, had recovered. She looked mad enough to throw Val overboard. Not that it would make a difference. The big-time threat was on the ferry.

Val's jaw tightened. But all she said was, "It looks like Andy lost his nose to frostbite."

"He's lucky to be alive—just like you."

Luckier than you think, Val thought. He's had a month to worm his way into my father's good graces. She was going to have serious problems with the two of them if her father had come to believe that Andy filled his uncle's shoes.

Her father called down at the sailboat, concealing emotion as always. Was he happy to find his only child was still alive? Or disappointed that his demanding daughter was still vying for his crown?

"Is that you, Val? My goodness, I feared when you lost your boat you lost your life."

"I hope you didn't grieve too deeply."

"You put me through hell, as it were. The uncertainty was devastating. But I took comfort in my hymnal and never lost hope:

> *"And while the lamp holds out to burn*
> *The vilest sinner may return."*

In other words, he would never forgive her for blowing him off in the middle of the search and striking out on her own.

"It appears you also took comfort in my tracking system."

His answer confirmed her fears. "Andy is due much of the credit. He did some judicious digging and discovered that our old friend Will had an alias. In an earlier incarnation, he stashed ill-gotten gains on the sea bottom. Course projections for this boat led Andy and me to draw the obvious conclusion. Young man," he called to Jim. "Will Spark took what was ours. I want what's ours now."

"We don't have it."

"You have stopped Will Spark's boat at a position that is *precisely* where he escaped from me last February."

"So?"

"So if you don't have Sentinel, you had bloody well better have a way to retrieve it."

"It was in Will's head when I buried him at sea."

McVay gestured. Seamen scrambled down rope ladders, caught mooring lines, and secured *Hustle* fore and aft. Andy Nickels descended to the foredeck and steadied the ladder for the older McVay, who loped back to the cockpit with a sailor's easy gait.

Lloyd McVay leaned down and brushed his daughter's cheek with his thin lips. "High marks for survival, at least."

To Jim he said, "Suspecting that you would perpetuate Will's lies, Andy brought what used to be quaintly called a truth serum."

"What?"

McVay looked at Shannon. "It will be administered to the young lady."

Val exploded, "Dad, for goodness' sake, what are you gassing on about? It's on the boat somewhere. Search for it!"

"For all we know, it's booby-trapped. Andy!"

Andy Nickels signaled his men on the ferry. They started flinging meat into the water.

Lloyd McVay said, "Will Spark must have left behind some sort of floatation signal instrument. An extremely low frequency transmitter of a type used to communicate with submarines, I would imagine. Wouldn't you, Val?"

"ELF," said Val.

Before Jim saw the first shark, he knew he was beaten.

McVay said, "If you hand it to me in less than sixty seconds, Jim, Andy will not throw young Shannon overboard."

"It's behind the freezer, next to the compressor. And it's not booby-trapped, for Christ's sake."

"Go with him, Andy."

Nickels went down the companionway first and watched closely while Jim knelt to get the ELF transmitter. "You asshole. You really thought you'd get away from us on a fucking sailboat?"

Jim stood up and handed him the transmitter. "Love your nose job."

Andy Nickels threw a hard jab at his face. Jim slipped some of the stinging blow and landed a left that smashed the former Ranger into the bulkhead. As they squared off, Lloyd McVay called down, "Andy, we don't have all day."

"Right here, Mr. McVay."

"Bring up the bloody thing."

The ELF transmitter had a telescoping antenna with a cup-like protuberance at the end. They lowered it into the water and turned the instrument on. It beeped at ten-second intervals to indicate it was working.

"How long, Val?" asked McVay.

Val was already calculating the time for the signal to reach the microprocessor in the mile-deep water, how air bladders would fill in stages so as not to explode, and a rate of ascent.

"Ten minutes, I would guess."

At the end of ten minutes, all that was visible in the bloodied water was a pair of blue-tipped sharks. At twelve minutes, Lloyd McVay said, "Val, your data are suspect."

"There!" shouted Andy.

Fluorescent orange dye spread on the surface, twenty feet from the sailboat. In its midst was an orange balloon.

"Get it!" ordered Lloyd McVay.

"Dive!" yelled Andy.

The divers hesitated. Two sharks were circling. In that moment of confusion, Jim Leighton saw a chance to turn the tables. But it required mustering the courage to dive into the water.

It was a chance to keep the prototype out of the McVays' hands. But more important, it was his only chance to save Shannon. The gunmen lining the rails left no doubt that the instant Lloyd McVay had Sentinel aboard the big ferry the order would be given for all engines full ahead to smash *Hustle* and her witnesses under the sea.

Jim stepped over the lifelines and lowered himself smoothly into the water before anyone noticed. Careful not to splash, he swam a swift, quiet breaststroke toward the floating canister. He heard Shannon call, "Jim!"

A dorsal fin cut the surface. Fear sucked the breath from his lungs. He tucked up his legs and hugged his body with his arms, trying to make a smaller target.

A ten-foot blue-tip shark smacked into him, rasping his skin with its rough hide. Fighting panic, Jim slammed his elbow as hard as he could into its flank. He sensed another rush. He dove underwater, tucked into another ball, and kicked it full in the nose. His running shoe snagged on a tooth. Both sharks veered away and circled warily. Jim resumed his smooth swim into the orange stain.

He plucked from the water a shiny canister, the size of a beer can.

"Good lad," called Lloyd McVay. "Now just bring it right here."

Treading water, Jim ripped away the float bladder and the dye marker and held the canister over his head. It was heavy, made of stainless steel.

"No!" shouted both McVays.

"Guns overboard!" Jim yelled. "Or I dump it."

Lloyd and Val McVay couldn't take their eyes off the shiny canister. "Name your price!" Lloyd McVay called.

"It won't float. Guns overboard!" A fin circling closer began cutting toward him. Jim instinctively reached to block it with the canister.

"A million dollars!" shouted Lloyd McVay.

"*Ten* million dollars," shouted Val. "Get out of the water."

"Jim!" Shannon pleaded. "Get back on the boat."

"Guns overboard."

"Do it!" yelled Lloyd McVay. "Weapons over the side. Now. No holdouts."

Assault rifles and pistols rained into the water.

"All of them!" yelled Jim.

A sawed-off shotgun splashed near him. Trying to keep track of the sharks, Jim scissor-kicked toward *Hustle*.

"Help him," snapped Val and Andy Nickels reached out to pull Jim aboard.

"Get away!" shouted Jim. "Back off. Back off. Shannon, the dive ladder."

"Help her!" cried McVay.

"Get away from her."

Shannon crawled out of the cockpit and across the stern deck and shoved the dive ladder into the water.

Jim climbed partway up, inches ahead of another blue tip, and stood on the bottom rung as the rising and falling stern plunged his legs in and out of the sea.

"Here's the deal. Everyone off your boat and into our

boat. We'll trade. As soon as we can figure out how to run yours, I'll throw you the canister."

Red with anger, Lloyd McVay ordered his crew to abandon ship.

"Make 'em all stay up on the bow," Jim yelled.

"Wait," Val said to her father.

"Shut up," he told her. "On the foredeck, all of you!"

Jim watched six men clamber down to *Hustle*'s foredeck. He had no way of knowing whether they were the entire crew. They'd deal with that when they got aboard. The important thing was to put more space between them.

He climbed another rung on the dive ladder and looked around, gauging his next move.

The huge ferry loomed to his left, rubbing *Hustle*'s port side as the two vessels moved on the swell. The six men were crowding the bow, ahead of the mast, fifty feet from where he was holding the canister over the water. Shannon was crouched beside him on the stern deck. Val was twenty feet straight ahead on the cabin roof. Andy Nickels and Lloyd McVay were standing near her on the starboard side deck, eyes flickering between the canister and the shark-roiled water at their feet.

"Okay, Shannon." He touched her arm and she returned a level, I'm-all-right gaze. "You first. Can you pull yourself up that ladder?"

Shannon grasped the rope they'd hung from the backstay, hauled herself to her feet, and swung across the cockpit toward the nearest ladder dangling from the ferry. As she did, a swell tilted the boat, causing her to swing wide. Andy Nickels was on her in a flash, encircling her waist with one arm and dragging her to the lifelines.

"Pool party's over, asshole. If it sinks, she sinks. Give Mr. McVay the canister."

Jim felt himself die inside. So close. So close. They wouldn't kill Shannon now. They would kill her later. But he had to deal with now. Will, the great optimist, had laughed on his deathbed.

"Catch!"

He lobbed the canister in the direction of Nickels and McVay, along the side of the boat.

"Catch that, Andy!" Lloyd McVay shouted.

Nickels released Shannon, vaulted the lifelines, and lunged, bobbling the canister on the stumps of frostbitten fingers. As it bounced free, he tumbled toward the water, caught himself on the lifelines, and hung half over the side. The much taller McVay, as long and graceful as a shore bird, reached farther. Stepping over the lifelines, his shoes planted on the gunnel, one hand grasping the lifeline.

The canister containing Will Spark's microprocessor danced on the tips of his fingers. As it bounced away, he lunged farther, let go of the lifeline, and with a cry of triumph closed his hand.

Teetering on one foot, he reached back and hooked a finger of his other hand around the safety lines again. Directly under him, Andy Nickels screamed in terror as a shark smacked the hull beside him. Desperately swinging his legs out of the water, Nickels kicked the lifeline from Lloyd McVay's grasp.

McVay looked down in sudden amazement, as if noticing the churning water for the first time. He froze, suddenly rigid with fear. Sentinel slipped away from him and splashed into the sea.

"Val!" he shouted as he grasped for her hand, his eyes riveted on the sharks.

Val McVay did not hesitate. She had a split second to weigh her future without Sentinel. The Sentinel concept was still viable. But developing it would demand single-minded effort and unquestioned control of the McVay Foundation for Humane Science.

"You're forgetting your Shakespeare, Dad."

"Help me!"

"It's serpent-tooth time."

53

THE FAST FERRY had vanished over the horizon with Val and Andy and their crew. But only after the sharks had finally gone did Jim and Shannon speak, and then, only in stunned whispers.

"Why didn't they kill us?" Shannon asked.

"Val's not a killer."

"Or we weren't a threat."

"Or there were too many witnesses."

The sails were slatting. Jim let the boat fall off the wind and filled the jib. Then he sheeted in and locked the helm. It felt good to do something with his hands.

"From where I was watching, she could have saved her father."

Jim shrugged. "He might have pulled her under. . . . Will used to say to me, 'People do what they have to do. It's the real world, Jim.' He was talking about poor people, but the warning was clear: look out for the needy ones. Then he'd laugh at me like I was totally naive."

Shannon was looking at him strangely. "Didn't that bother you?"

"Why should it? I was naive. Or sentimental, which is

worse. Almost thirty years old but still dumb as a post. I had a lot to learn. He had a lot to teach."

"You really admired him."

"Shannon, we've been through this. You know I liked him."

"But did you admire him?"

"I liked him, warts and all."

"I think you should sit down."

"Why?"

"Sit down."

He sat beside her on the cockpit bench. "I'm sitting."

"There was never time to talk about this. And then when we finally did have time, Val was around. Maybe I used her as an excuse. But I didn't know what to do with it."

"With what?"

"I don't know what it means. But I have to tell you. When I first telephoned the Larchmont Yacht Club hoping to learn about Will, they hung up on me. Then after you found out about Billy Cole and we went through the whole Billy Cole thing, I was really worried.

"So I drove over there. Pulled right up to the front door of this gorgeous old building and hobbled in. 'Here comes the cripple with the brave smile.' They were very nice to me. I said I was looking for my grandfather, Will Spark. 'Mr. Spark is not here, blah-blah-blah. Simply ages since we've seen him.' His boat was gone. Somebody heard he was on another boat in Barbados. Anyhow, I kept smiling around until a nice old guy asked if I wanted lunch."

"Don't tell me you hooked up with a rich old man."

"Listen to me! I said, 'Sure, thanks.' So we're having lunch and a glass of wine: 'Oh, here comes an old friend of Will's'—'Hullo, Bunky. Meet Will Spark's granddaughter'—blah-blah-blah. Bunky and I start talking. When the first old guy shuffles off to pee and we're alone, he goes, 'Will never had a granddaughter.' "

"You were caught."

"Egg all over my face. Except I got this brainstorm. I said, 'Billy Cole had a granddaughter.' "

"Bunky laughed. 'Billy didn't either. And don't tell me it was Mick Creegan.'"

"Mick Creegan! That's the first Will! I think it was his real name."

"It was. Bunky knew Will way back when. They had always stayed in touch. I don't think he was another con man. I think he just happened to like Will."

"What did he tell you about him?"

Shannon reached for Jim's hand. "Jobs he'd had. All the things he learned how to do. Names. Some of the scams. He knew he'd been to jail."

"I always wondered, was he really in the Marines?"

"Oh, yes." Shannon began to stroke his hand in both of hers. "He did a bunch of stuff."

"Like what? What are you trying to tell me?"

"He'd been a teacher. He taught Outward Bound. And sailing. And survival courses." She kept rubbing his hand. "Back in the seventies, he was an est trainer."

"What?"

"He led est retreats. In California. In the mountains."

A hundred thoughts scattered. A thousand fell in place.

Shannon said, "I sat there. My head was spinning. Could it be a coincidence?"

"Has to be."

"Could your mother have—"

"I don't know. I mean, I—Jesus, I don't know *what* my mother . . . 'The dark at the top of the stairs' . . . Did the old guy, Bunky, know? About—about me?"

"No."

"Is that why Will gave me the boat?"

"He gave you the boat because you were ready for the boat," Shannon said firmly.

"He made me his heir."

"In my opinion the boat was a gift—a reward—from a teacher to his prize student."

"But if he was more, if he was—" Jim couldn't speak the word. "Why wouldn't Will tell me?"

"I thought a lot about that. Maybe he was ashamed of himself."

"He could have told me."

"Jim, I think he tracked you down. He joined the Bridge-port club to take your classes. . . . He checked you out. . . ." Shannon touched Jim's cheek. "And liked what he saw . . ."

Jim took her hand and pressed her fingers to a smile that opened his face wider than Shannon had ever seen. Sentinel was lost on the bottom of the ocean. They were low on food and water, far from any shore. They were broke. The boat needed work. The hurricane season had begun. And all was right with the world.

"He took me sailing."

If you liked
BURIED AT SEA,
you'll love ***SEA HUNTER***
by Paul Garrison,
the stunning new sea thriller, available in
hardcover from William Morrow.
For a sneak preview, turn the page!

1

DAVID HOPE KNELT to empty the urn that the crematorium had FedEx-ed to Tortola. He had sailed south all night and through the morning, racing down the backside of the Leeward Islands, fleeing a ghost that stuck closer than the wind. When he stopped his boat, at last, deep inside the Caribbean, St. Croix lay sixty miles in his wake, South America five hundred ahead, and the vast, blue sea spanned barren horizons.

Famous ashes-scattering disasters leapt to mind, gruesome, comic, twisted. The deceased who stuck to the airplane's fresh paint. Weeping mourners fleeing a change in the breeze. Before he'd quit the newspaper business, he'd written about a man who had arranged to have his ashes poured into his ex-wife's central air conditioning.

Hope had found a letter taped to the urn. "Barbara's dying wish," her parents claimed. She wanted her ashes spread on the ocean.

That was a lie.

She had loved the sea, all right. Loved it as fiercely as only an ignorant romantic could love. Loved it enough to die for it. But to express a dying wish, you had to be able to think. And Hope, who had persisted in telephoning the doc-

monitoring her coma, knew the truth. Barbara Carey had
ot voiced a waking thought in the long year since she
smashed her beautiful head on a semisubmersible offshore
oil rig that she had vowed to stop from "raping"—her furi-
ous word—the Gulf of Mexico.

A brave and magnificent woman. One in a million.

Her parents could have hired one of the professional services that scattered ashes for a fee. But it appeared that they
were still looking for someone to blame. Hard to blame
them. For they knew one immutable fact. Barbara's merry
band of eco-crusaders would never have set foot on the floating oil rig without the help of a blue-water sailor who had
the sense to know they were truly risking their lives.

Who better to bury her?

So Hope had sailed her ashes far from any shore and confirmed with binoculars and radar that they were alone. They
sat for a while in the shade of the bimini top. Finally he
asked, "Ready?" and carried her down the dive steps in the
back of the starboard hull and knelt on the grate.

Mindful of the wind, he submerged the urn in the clear
water and slowly unscrewed the top. The powdery ash was
sprinkled with larger bits that sank like pebbles. But the dust
that remained spread like a ghostly fog. He was wondering
whether he was supposed to keep the urn when her ashes enveloped his wrist.

He jerked his hand out of the water and dropped the urn,
which commenced a two-mile voyage to the bottom. The
low waves dispersed the fog. Heart pounding, stomach
churning, he rinsed off, repeatedly, until it occurred to him,
So what? They'd shared a hundred intimacies. Why not this?

Mission accomplished, he wiped his eyes on the long-
sleeved shirt he wore to protect his arms from the relentless
sun. He hadn't known her long, but she had grabbed hold of
him all out of proportion to time. A compelling and charis-
matic soul. And needy? asked a small dark voice. Though a

wiser one whispered the oldest adage of letting go, "Don speak ill of the dead."

When he calmed down, he was struck anew by the immensity of the ocean and how Barbara was quite suddenly and completely gone. Not a bad way to go. Though when his own time came, if he had a choice, he thought he would prefer an eternal version of the celebrated seasickness cure—a quiet spot under a tree.

He cranked out the roller-reefed main and jib, opening his sails to the northeast trade wind, and set the catamaran flying home to Tortola. A pair of scuba-diving couples arriving from New Jersey would be his last paying charter job before he sailed north for the summer. He had to clean up the boat and provision for a week of live-aboard reef exploring.

He was late, having procrastinated the burial—sailing much further south of the British Virgin Islands than he had to, then sitting around the cockpit for hours talking to her urn. So he pushed the cat hard, constantly tweaking the sails to extract the most power from the wind, adjusting, and readjusting, the depth of the dagger board that projected below the starboard hull to keep the swift, surface-skimming, twin-hull boat from sliding sideways.

Racing had the additional benefit of keeping too busy for memory and guilt and regret. It worked for a while. So well, at first, that he found himself thinking thoughts he had not allowed since the accident. I'm ready to meet somebody. Why not? He'd paid his dues. He had been alone—absolutely, celibately alone—with the possible exception of a drunken night with a New York lawyer at the end of Antigua Race Week. Now, at last, it felt all right to admit that he was lonely. It would be terrific to meet somebody who was looking, too. Maybe he would get lucky. He should put out the word to his friends: Hope was prepared to hope. He was savoring that thought, encouraged by a pretty sunset, when the helm jammed.

He reacted swiftly to stop the suddenly rudderless boat, winching in the main and jib sheets to steer her bows into the wind. Then he jumped belowdecks and found what he

ected: a loose rudder cable he had neglected to tighten
d jumped its quadrant. Crouching in a stifling hot steering
gear compartment, he worked the steering cable back into its
quadrant groove and repeated an oft-promised pledge to replace the entire steering system with hydraulics as soon as
he had the cash.

He was quickly under way again. But if David Hope had
entertained the belief that scattering Barbara Carey's ashes
would close a black chapter, he was mistaken. The darkness
that descended with the sun brought him the worst night
since the accident. Every time he closed his eyes to catch
five minutes of sleep in the cockpit, the nightmares struck,
familiar as a brutal jailer.

Again and again he started awake, already on his feet, gripping the helm, shaking head to toe, and astonished to discover *Oona* coursing over the open sea instead of weaving
through pools of blood and burning oil.

By dawn he felt half dead, his blue eyes red and stinging,
his heavy swimmer's shoulders knotted with tension, his
long, weathered face haggard. It was scored by two weary
lines that cut from his nose to jaw. As if he'd been branded
with a number eleven, he thought when he glimpsed his reflection in the mirror in the head. A sneak preview of how he
would look when he was old. Or in the grave. People who
usually assumed he was ten years younger than his forty-
eight would jump this morning to offer their seat on a bus.

He brewed some strong black coffee. It didn't help. He
riffled through his CDs. Cyrus Chestnut playing hymns on
the piano. He bumped through the tracks. "Onward Chris-
tian Soldiers" made him feel better. But not much. "The Old
Rugged Cross" helped, too. But not enough. Somehow, he
had to sleep. So he took a careful look around to make sure
that he and *Oona* were sailing alone. He set his internal
alarm for ten minutes, and the radar to sound if any vessel
came within three miles, then prayed—begged—for a
peaceful ten minutes, and closed his eyes.

Six minutes later, he saw an enormous dolphin leap ￼ the ocean. The animal rose straight up on its tail, stood ta. than seemed possible, and began to spin, burnished gold a. red by the morning sun.

Hope suspected another dream. He felt fast asleep and he was experiencing a dreamer's double perspective of a close-up and a long shot. Or was he dreaming a memory of waking for a moment and seeing the creature while he checked that the sea was clear of ships?

It had to be a dream. The dolphin was enormous—super-naturally large—as colossal as a killer whale.

But whatever the reality, at least the big, beautiful dol-phin wasn't a nightmare and for that gift he was grateful. Then something outside dream or memory made a noise. It banged against the starboard hull with a sharp, hollow *donk*. Not at all the sound he'd expect of a collision with a large mammal and Hope snapped awake to see what his boat had hit.

2

AT FIRST GLANCE, the fierce blue expanse of Caribbean Sea still spread flat and empty to every horizon. Nor had he slept through his internal alarm clock. It was still very early morning, the white-hot sun lancing under the bimini. What in hell had he hit?

He scrambled around the boat, looking for damage. They might have sideswiped a half-sunken container that had fallen off a ship. He jiggled the helm. Both rudders were intact. Had she struck the dagger board it would have spun her around like a top, not to mention bang the hell out of its truck, but that too thankfully had not happened. Then, as he started below to make sure that seawater was not gushing through a hole, something winked in his wake.

He grabbed his binoculars from their rack at the helm and focused on a cylindrical buoy painted fluorescent International Orange. It had a flasher, blinking twice a second, which at night would be seen for miles.

He turned *Oona* into the wind to stop her, sheeted in the flapping sails, and started her diesel engines. Inshore an orange buoy might mark a lobster pot, but not thirty miles south of Tortola, not in water a mile deep. It could have bro-

ken loose from a drift net, one of the commercial fi.
"death curtains" decimating sea life. If it marked a dope
ner's drop, he was outta here as fast the wind could take hi.

The gigantic dolphin was still leaping in his mind, sti.
spinning gold and red in the morning sun. His memory was
afire with the powerful image. But now he didn't know
whether he'd dreamed it, or had actually seen it earlier when
day first broke. Make it a dream, he thought, as he motored
Oona back to the orange buoy. It sure beat the nightmares;
he actually felt rested.

Maneuvering the catamaran alongside the floating cylinder took some doing. *Oona* was fast as lightning off the wind
when lightly laden, a real screamer on a broad reach, and a
remarkably steady platform even in heavy seas. But at close
quarters—his mono-hull friends were quick to laugh—a
twin-hull boat forty-five feet long and twenty-three feet wide
possessed sailing qualities similar to a garbage truck. Even
with her twin screws, she felt like a bicycle rolling too slowly
to control.

He saw that the buoy had a whip aerial and, as he worked
closer, that the flasher was ringed with cat's-eye reflectors.
When he finally could eyeball print through the binoculars,
he read the word AFT. It turned in the water, revealing USS
VERMONT (SSN-919).

"Jesus H."

It was a sub-sunk buoy, sent to the surface to broadcast a
distress call and mark the scene of the emergency. Somewhere under him a hundred sailors were trapped on a
stricken American nuclear submarine.

Hope ran to his radio. *The Sailing Directions* warned
against breaking a sub-sunk buoy's tether. No chance of a
tether in these depths. This one had broken loose and was
riding the current, clearly adrift. But for how long? Were
they still alive? Did anyone know?

Three steps led down into *Oona's* saloon, a wide, light
and airy cabin that bridged the hulls. He sat at his navigation
station and switched on the long-range Single Sideband.

"Mayday," he broadcast on the emergency channel.

day, Mayday, Mayday." He read his position from the
al Positioning System, repeated it three times, and gave
vessel's name and radio call sign.

Somewhere under him terror ruled. Decks pitched vertically and young men clung to their stations, fighting to regain control of their ship before deepening water pressure
caused the sea to rush in. Fighting to keep her from dragging
them all the way to the bottom, accelerating with every foot
she fell, until their struggle ended in an atom-shattering
crash into the ocean floor.

Hope switched on the depth finder he used ordinarily for
navigating scuba divers to remote reefs. If the men on the
sub heard the sonar "pinging" the depths, they would know
that help was on the way.

"Mayday, Mayday, Mayday. Sailing Vessel *Oona*, Victor-
Victor-Hotel-Oscar, reporting *USS Vermont* number SSN-
919 sub-sunk buoy at 64 degrees, 2 minutes, 13 seconds
west, 18 degrees, 1 minute, 4 seconds north."

SSN stood for "Submersible Ship Nuclear." And the ul-
tramodern *Vermont* was the newest of the new Virginia class.

Fascinated by ships in general, submarines in particular—and feeling special affection for the state of Vermont,
where his parents had taught him to ski—Hope had followed
accounts of its launch avidly. The *Vermont* observed the surface through fiber-optic cameras and sensors instead of
periscopes, utilized commercial off-the-shelf electronics to
stay cutting-edge on the cheap, and could fight both inshore
and on blue water.

A lean and hungry sub for lean and hungry times.

Hope repeated his position and radio call sign, reported
the buoy adrift, and asked anyone who picked up his signal
to relay it to the United States Navy. By now, if the buoy was
working, every satellite the Navy had in the sky would have
picked up the distress call. But if it wasn't working, he and
only he was on the scene, and so far no one had responded.

He stepped up to the cockpit, and locked the helm so the
boat would steer a circle. He could see the depth finder's
backlit LCD monitor from the helm as well as the nav sta-

tion. Under a boat icon, which represented *Oona*'s position, echoing returns were pictured in the form of black squares. He'd used it often enough to be able to distinguish coral and rocks from sunken wrecks, the wakes of passing boats, even a sand or mud bottom.

A single black square materialized at a depth of two hundred feet, directly below the *Oona* icon. It was much too small to be a submarine. He waited, scarcely breathing, for the image to grow into a bigger target. Instead, the single square moved to the edge of the screen. A large fish, probably a shark, it changed course and swam out of range.

Loath to accept that he was sailing over a graveyard, Hope stared at the blank screen. His second graveyard in twenty-four hours. This one about to swallow a hundred vital men, who seconds ago had probably no idea they were about to die. Feeling helpless and useless, Hope studied the sea. Sunny blue and utterly empty, there was nothing to see but some trade wind clouds marching tall and bright.

Could he *hear* the sub? He had a hydrophone he had bought secondhand for his whale-watching clients to listen to the clicks and whistles and creaking-door groans of whales and dolphins. Plugging its long cable into the stereo, he dropped the slim microphone, which was encased in waterproof polyurethane, over the back of the boat.

He heard a faint whistle. It faded, like a distant train, leaving nothing behind but an audio hiss. He turned up the sound. Only speaker hum broke the silence. In a way it was a good sign, he told himself. The last sound he wanted to hear was the thunder of the huge ship imploding in the depths.

Suddenly, a hundred feet ahead another buoy shot from the sea as if a seed had been squeezed from an orange. Then, behind him, an emergency flare rocketed out of the water, whooshed skyward, and exploded red. A smoke flare followed, gushing orange. They were letting loose everything they had.

Hope turned from the chaos that was erupting around the boat to the depth finder. Black squares massed under the boat icon, representing a big, stationary target 250 feet be-

w. The squares formed up in a long, thick shape that the monitor indicated was nearly four hundred feet long.

When it began rising at a steep angle, David Hope leapt to *Oona*'s helm.